PEACE

**Center Point
Large Print**

**This Large Print Book carries the
Seal of Approval of N.A.V.H.**

PEACE

JEFF NESBIT

CENTER POINT LARGE PRINT
THORNDIKE, MAINE

This Center Point Large Print edition is published
in the year 2012 by arrangement with Summerside Press.

The text of this Large Print edition is unabridged.
In other aspects, this book may
vary from the original edition.
Printed in the United States of America
on permanent paper.
Set in 16-point Times New Roman type.

ISBN: 978-1-61173-357-0

Library of Congress Cataloging-in-Publication Data

Nesbit, Jeffrey Asher.
Peace / Jeff Nesbit. — Large print ed.
p. cm. — (Center Point large print edition)
ISBN 978-1-61173-357-0 (library binding : alk. paper)
1. Nuclear crisis control—Fiction. 2. Peace—Fiction.
3. Israel—Fiction. 4. Large type books. I. Title.
PS3564.E73P43 2012
813'.54—dc23

2011051165

A FEW QUICK THANKS TO . . .

Ramona Tucker, a brilliant editor and friend who was there at both the creation and development of *PEACE* and this series;

Don Jacobson, a calm, shining light in the literary world, who saw the potential in this series;

Carlton Garborg, a true visionary who takes big risks for all the right reasons, and Jason Rovenstine, the talented, creative center of one of the most exciting new publishing ventures in the U.S.;

The poker group, now sixteen years strong, where some of the ideas for *PEACE* were first debated and formed; and

The members of my "relentless, positive storm" family, committed to making a difference across the planet like some of the archetypal characters in *PEACE*.

You are going to hear
of wars and rumors of wars.
See to it that you are not alarmed.
These things must take place,
but the end hasn't come yet,
because nation will rise up
in arms against nation,
and kingdom against kingdom.

JESUS, MATTHEW 24:6–7

Prologue

The large crowd gathered outside Bercy was restless. Most of them clutched tickets or checked their pockets every few minutes to make sure the tickets were, in fact, still there. The exhibition games at the Palais Omnisports de Paris-Bercy in the 12th arrondissement of Paris had sold out weeks ago.

Bercy seated, at most, fourteen thousand for an exhibition like this. The tickets were expensive, and the scalpers in the shadows and corners were pulling in huge sums.

But the young Asian boy standing off to the side in the replica Chicago Bulls jersey didn't care. All he knew was that he was here, with a ticket in hand, and he was about to watch the greatest basketball player who ever lived suit up and play against one of Europe's finest teams. Nothing else mattered. Not right now.

The headline, "Jordan Awaited like a King," was displayed boldly at the top of the sports daily *L'Equipe.* "Michael has captured Paris," said another paper. An overly exuberant, breathless

French sports columnist went even further: "Michael Jordan is in Paris. That's better than the Pope. It's God in person."

Not that anyone outside Bercy that day would dispute this. They were, in fact, here to see their god, Michael Jordan, play basketball.

For some of them, it would be the defining moment of their lives—the day they saw the great Jordan play at Bercy in Paris.

The Asian boy was, perhaps, one of those who would mark this moment forever in his mind. Virtually every corner of his bedroom was adorned with photos of NBA superstars. He had begged his father and handlers for the opportunity to see his hero play basketball. All he wanted was a chance to see Jordan play just once. He would never see the legend play in America. Paris might be his only chance.

In the end, he'd won his father and the others over. He could be very persuasive. He hated to lose at anything, and this quest was no different. He'd argued that it was just one wish before he had to leave to go to an exclusive boarding school in Switzerland. He could fly to Paris, watch the game, and then continue on to Switzerland, where he would start middle school.

What's more, he'd argued, he wasn't like his older brother, who'd forged a passport and sneaked out of the country to travel and had been caught drinking in bars. He was *asking* his father for permission to go to Paris to watch Jordan play. Framed in this way, it had been almost impossible for his father to say no.

They'd arrived in Paris just hours before the game started. The boy's handlers were careful to stay in the background. A simple black town car had pulled up to the curb at the airport to pick them up and take them to Bercy. Two other cars followed at a discreet distance.

Once at the famous indoor sports arena, the boy had simply stepped into the long line that had already formed outside. An older gentleman, who had been one of several caretakers for the boy since birth, stayed with him in line. Others, also with tickets to the event, took places in other parts of the line. Replicas of Jordan's Bulls jersey were selling for $80 American at several spots.

No one quite knew what to expect. Would the Chicago Bulls arrive one by one and enter the arena? Would they arrive in a big bus? Would they stop and talk to the legions of fans? Or would the organizers of the NBA exhibition take them around back, away from the throngs, so they could enter the stadium without having to stop?

The fans had nothing to fear, though. The brilliant, single-minded commissioner of the National Basketball Association in America who'd built his league into a worldwide marketing force wasn't about to let the arrival of the king of basketball in Paris go unnoticed.

The world press corps was roped off to one side of Bercy. They knew that the Bulls had flown over on the same 747 that had carried the Rolling Stones around the globe, and that they would arrive in plenty of time to meet with some of the fans and pose for pictures. This part was, in fact, more important than the actual game itself.

Somehow the word got to the fans outside the gates. Jordan and the Bulls were only a few minutes away. The fans started to press forward, anxious to get as close to the entrance and the world press corps as they could manage. The Asian boy was merely another face in the crowd, anxious to get as close as he possibly could to the entrance.

But the boy was in good hands. He simply didn't know it yet. A well-dressed, diminutive, older Korean gentleman talked calmly inside the arena doors with one of several officers from McDonald's, the American corporation that had sponsored the NBA exhibition here in Paris.

There was a small VIP room just inside the stadium, and the boy would be given a very brief audience with one of the Bulls players. Perhaps not Jordan, but with one of them, at least. It had all been arranged, well ahead of time.

The bus arrived. The boy caught a fleeting glimpse of Jordan as he stepped down from the bus and disappeared into the crowd. His heart leapt. He'd seen him! Michael Jordan, in the flesh.

The crowd pressed forward, eager to get inside.

His caretaker pulled the boy gently at the elbow. "Jong Un," he said quietly. The boy glanced at him and followed willingly. They made their way through the crowd and came to a small door nearby. Guards saw the badge carried by the caretaker and let the two of them in through the door. A dozen other VIPs were inside, all hoping they'd get a chance to see Michael.

One by one, each VIP was ushered into a small room inside the arena. The boy kept to himself. He spoke no French, and his English was still halting at best. He patiently waited his turn, content to follow along, to go where his care-takers and elders directed him.

His chance came at last, and he entered the room. The lights inside were hot and blinding but necessary for the high-end photos taken inside. The boy shielded his eyes as he entered and glanced around the room quickly. Was Jordan here, in this room?

No. He was in another room, with some other VIP. But Toni Kukoc was here. Once arguably the greatest player in all of Europe, Kukoc had made the trip over to Paris with Jordan. The boy was ecstatic. The press had lamented that two of Jordan's famous teammates, Scottie Pippen and Dennis Rodman, had decided not to make the trip. But Kukoc had made the trip. And he was here, in this place.

The boy's hands trembled as he stepped forward to greet the great Kukoc. He had a poster of Kukoc in his room at home. But it didn't compare to this moment, actually seeing the great Bulls player in the flesh.

"How are you?" Kukoc asked in his thick Croatian accent as the boy stepped into the glare of the bright lights.

The boy could only nod. Kukoc held out his hand. The boy shook it and nodded once, politely.

The official photographer snapped several pictures of the shy Korean boy in the presence of the great Toni Kukoc of the Chicago Bulls. It was a dream come true, a moment Jong Un would cherish forever. He was certain there would never come a moment in his life quite like this. Nothing, really, could ever compare.

And then the moment was over. Another VIP was ushered into the room, and the boy began to leave through another door.

Jong Un did not see the exchange that took place as he was leaving. Two of the boy's caretakers swept into the room quickly, talked to the McDonald's official off to one side, then waited. The McDonald's official moved to the photographer's side and explained the situation.

Like the tickets, this had also been prearranged. The photographer had known that someone would be making such a request—just not who it would be. He was mildly surprised that the request had been for the shy, young Asian boy.

He removed the roll of film he'd used to shoot the boy's pictures with Kukoc and handed it to the McDonald's official. Placing a fresh roll of film in his camera, he returned to work. He didn't ask who the kid was—he wasn't entirely sure he wanted to know. He was well paid for this gig, and asking questions sometimes got in the way of further opportunities like this.

The Korean men accepted the roll of film with polite nods and left the room quickly. They'd watched everything closely, just to make sure there had been no other cameras in the room. But they had nothing to worry about. It was a small room, and there had been only the one camera.

One of them hurried to the boy's side and whispered something quickly to his companion, who would be sitting with him during the basketball game. The older gentleman smiled broadly. It had all worked very well. They would have the picture of the boy standing with one of his heroes, Toni Kukoc of the world-famous Chicago Bulls, processed and available for his private apartment in an exclusive Swiss chalet within hours. The boy would be so very pleased.

And his father would be pleased as well—not only that the youngest of his three sons had seen the Bulls play, but that there would be just one picture of the boy with his hero, available only to private audiences in his bedroom and away from prying eyes.

There was only one picture of the boy anywhere in the free world—a schoolyard photo taken when he was eleven that had somehow managed to make its way out of North Korea.

His father knew that there was plenty of time for pictures. When the time came, many pictures of Pak Jong Un would be available. But not until then.

The shy, young Korean boy who had just entered his teens was little more than an enigma to the free world. But the world would learn of Pak Jong Un when he succeeded his father, Pak Jong Il, as Dear Leader of North Korea. They would learn of his heroics as the leader of his country's defense commission and of his many gifts of inspiration for the people.

But for now, he was just another fan of the king of Paris, Michael Jordan, and the Chicago Bulls, the greatest basketball team of all time. That was all that mattered.

01

TEHRAN, IRAN
PRESENT DAY

The car horn startled Majid Sanjani. Lost in thought as he walked to his next class at Tehran University, he didn't realize he'd drifted toward the center of the crowded street. Glancing over one shoulder, he stepped to the curb quickly and felt the hot engine exhaust as a black Mercedes sped past.

Majid peered inside the car briefly and saw five people—two in the front and three in the back. He was sure the person in the middle of the back seat, pinned between two large men, was his psych professor, his friend.

Without thinking, Majid pulled his cell phone from his pocket, held it up, and captured the speeding black car on video. He had the odd feeling that it might be the last time he would see his friend.

The two of them had talked for months—in private, away from prying eyes and curious ears— about the current government in Iran. They shared a common goal and philosophy, one that neither of them discussed much in public. They often drank coffee together until the early morning hours, just talking about the opposition movement and its leaders.

In his own way, Majid's psych professor was one of those leaders. He occasionally spoke in public forums about the government he considered illegitimate. He knew that placed him at great risk, but it was a risk he said he was willing to take.

Iran's hard-line leaders had managed to maintain control in most parts of the country—except on the college campuses. Student resistance to the government was very much alive, even if the opposition movement was a shadow of its former self throughout the rest of the country.

The conservative "principalist" clerics who'd once supported the overthrow of the Shah still regularly criticized the government, but it was the students who made the most noise and continued to organize protests.

Iran's theocracy had managed to quell mass street demonstrations, but it had been largely unable to stop widespread, spontaneous, raucous student protests. Majid's psych professor had organized many of the student protests at the university.

A chill swept through Majid. More than twenty student protests had taken place at a dozen college campuses in the last four months. Just in the past week, at Azad University, students had protested for two days. Some students had been expelled, and classes had been cancelled.

But this was different, out of place. Tehran University's campus had been quiet for many days. No one had organized a student protest in more than a month—not since the unannounced, surprise visit to Tehran University of Iran's president.

Majid grabbed the arm of another student as he walked by. "Did you see that?"

"What?" the student answered, clearly startled.

"The Mercedes. It looked like Revolutionary Guards inside, with one of my professors."

The other student took a step backwards and threw up a protesting hand. "I don't get involved in that," he said swiftly. "That's not something I—"

"I'm not asking you to get involved," Majid said angrily. "I just asked you if you've seen other professors being taken away. Have you seen Guards on the campus today?"

The student shrugged, shook his head, tucked his books tightly against his chest, and hurried off. He clearly wanted nothing to do with protests, Majid, or anything at all that might attract the Guards' attention.

Majid started to run. If something was happening, others at the student union would know. He sprinted the two blocks to the center of campus and burst through the doors.

A dozen of his friends were there already. Nearly everyone had a cell phone to one ear, even as they carried on loud conversations with others nearby.

Majid glanced around. Sure enough, there were two clerics at one end of the room, watching the growing group of students intently. The clerics had begun to arrive at Tehran University and other campuses that had been at the epicenter of the student protests in an effort to speak out against Western propaganda.

It hadn't worked. The students had very little use for the clerics and their anti-West language. They largely ignored them or, as they did now, viewed them with suspicion.

"Majid! Have you heard?" one of his friends yelled as he neared the group. They embraced quickly.

"No, brother," Majid said breathlessly. "What have you learned?"

"It is everywhere, on every campus," his friend said. He was carrying on a conversation on his own cell phone. He paused just long enough to talk to Majid.

"What is?" Majid asked.

"Arrests," his friend said darkly. "They have already picked up more than fifty professors on at least ten campuses, by our count."

"And here, on our campus?"

"At least six here, maybe more." His friend held his cell phone up to his opposite ear and listened intently. "They've arrested every one of the professors who've been involved at the Science and Technology school," he said at last. "Any professor who's ever been involved."

"Does anyone know where they're going?" Majid asked.

His friend sighed. "There's some speculation they're all being taken to a large holding cell at Evin."

Majid shuddered. Evin Prison was notorious. It now housed so many Iranian intellectual and student opposition leaders that some in the Green Movement had begun to call it Evin University—only partially in jest. Religious minorities, anti-government Iranian journalists, Christians the government didn't like, opposition leaders, and student protesters all mingled together at Evin.

"What of the opposition government leaders from the Green Movement?" Majid asked. "What of Reza Razavi?"

His friend shook his head. "No one's heard from Razavi. He hasn't shown up on mVillage or on any of our boards."

"So we don't know?"

"No, we don't."

Majid pulled his cell phone from his pocket. He typed in his password, called up mVillage, and started to comb through the various bulletin boards now capable of transmitting text messages and videos to the many connected followers of the Green Movement in Iran.

The worldwide mVillage network was based on the simple SMS and MMS text message capability of mobile devices, and it allowed one person to communicate with many through databases. It was the only real way that anyone could now communicate from within Iran. The government had closed off all traffic beyond mVillage.

The government controlled all other media—including radio, television, newspapers, and the Internet—but it could not control the flow of text messages without shutting down the country's entire cell phone network. And it was unwilling, at least for now, to take away people's mobile devices. Majid and the others in his network used mVillage to send videos out to the world that otherwise might never see the light of day.

His friend was right. Reports were circulating wildly about the arrests, which appeared to be taking place at every campus involved in the student protests. But there was no word of Razavi, who'd run unsuccessfully for the presidency of Iran and was at the center of charges against the current president for committing fraud to hold power.

The government had been careful not to arrest Razavi in the past year. The Revolutionary Guards had spoken out against him publicly and had called on the ruling Guardian Council to arrest him and try him for treasonous acts. But, so far, Razavi had been allowed to move about Tehran and the country freely.

"So why?" Majid asked the group.

Several others stopped talking on their own cell phones long enough to join in the conversation.

"There are reports that security is tight around the Guards' compounds," said one. "They've got roads shut down. No one can get near them."

"They've got Guards out in force near the government buildings too," said another.

"I heard they doubled security forces at Evin as well last night," someone else offered.

"But why?" Majid asked again.

"Something's going on, that's for sure," his friend said. "And they don't want anyone getting in their way or causing trouble right now."

"It seems crazy," Majid muttered. He checked the mVillage reports, but no one had offered any reasons for the mass arrests at the various locations. However, Majid knew it would only be a matter of time before reports and speculation would start to circulate. The government would denounce them, but it would not matter. Word would get out eventually.

"It *is* crazy," his friend said. "But the Guards do everything with a heavy hand. And who will stop them?"

Majid considered the clerics at the other end of the student union. Word had apparently gone out to them as well, because now a half dozen congregated at their end. Majid knew they would eventually make their way over to the knot of students, forcing them to disperse.

Majid decided not to hang around for the inevitable. He knew where Reza Razavi lived—just a few blocks from campus. Perhaps, if he was lucky, he could see something for himself that he could report to the mVillage network.

Majid had actually met the visionary leader of mVillage, Nash Lee, twice in the past year at international student leader conferences. Nash Lee was an unassuming, soft-spoken leader of the non-profit NGO that had made mass communication possible even in the middle of totalitarian regimes. Nash returned e-mails and occasionally weighed in on the mVillage network he'd created. Majid was impressed by that.

"I have to go," Majid said to his friend.

He waved to the group as he hurried out of the student union hall. Hustling around the corner, he looked quickly for his moped—affectionately called Sunny—that he always parked near the hall. An instant later, he was puttering at twenty-five miles an hour through the streets near Tehran University toward a side street his psych professor had once pointed out to him.

As he neared the street, Majid slowed down. The unmarked cars at one end had to be Guards. Without considering his own safety, Majid parked Sunny on another nearby side street and began to make his way behind the houses.

He slipped into the shadows behind a house

and moved forward cautiously. As he'd suspected, there were more black cars and Guards on the street in front of Reza Razavi's house.

Majid took the cell phone from his pocket and waited. He wondered what could possibly be triggering the events he was witnessing firsthand. The government was willing to go to great lengths to silence the opposition movement, but this reached another level—beyond anything he'd ever seen.

After the longest fifteen minutes of his life, he was rewarded. Four black Mercedes pulled up to the curb in front of Razavi's home. Majid held up his cell phone and began to capture video of the scene. Sure enough, Razavi had been arrested. They led him to his home, gave him instructions, then closed the door.

Majid had captured the entire scene on his cell. He searched frantically through his contact numbers for Nash Lee's personal mVillage address. He didn't want to risk dumping the MMS video message into the mVillage network anonymously. There wasn't time. Nash Lee would know what to do with the MMS message. He could bring it to the world's attention much quicker.

Majid attached the video of Razavi's arrest to an mVillage field, directed it to Nash Lee, and then typed in a short message:

Reza Razavi, the leader of Iran's opposition who should rightly be president, has been arrested by Iran's Revolutionary Guards Corps. This video is of Razavi being placed under house arrest by the Guards.

Majid pressed SEND and hoped the MMS message would reach its destination safely. He wondered again what could possibly compel the Guards to close the net so quickly and forcefully on Razavi and other opposition leaders.

Just then a blow struck the back of Majid's head. The pain was sudden, and vicious. Rough hands ripped the cell phone from his hand even as he tumbled to the ground.

He didn't black out immediately from the pain. He lay dazed for a few moments—just long enough to see two men in Guards' uniforms glance at the cell phone, then at him.

Even as Majid began to lose consciousness, he knew he'd soon be on his way to Evin Prison. He hoped his message had somehow gotten out to mVillage.

02

SHIRAZ, IRAN

The small drone wasn't impressive. It was dull gray, bore no markings, and had a blunt nose with a cloudy cover on top that partially masked its complex inner workings. The drone's smallish engine had been created to push it up a few thousand feet beyond the ordinary range of Iran's old, makeshift air-defense system, which had been pieced together with systems and parts from Russia, China, and North Korea.

The drone had only one mission, which it had performed dutifully for a little more than a year with no results whatsoever. Every evening, under the cover of darkness, its handlers launched it from a secure, little-known base at the western edge of Iraq. The drone made its way toward the heavens efficiently—engines whirring quietly as it climbed —then up and over Iran's countryside toward a destination near the University of Shiraz.

There were several other drones like this one— all experimental, all built in the past year and deployed in other parts of Iraq. Iran's air force knew of their existence and tracked them when they could. But Iran's leadership was convinced that they were harmless observers, of no consequence. They carried no weapons, and no surveillance system could be seen.

But in fact, the drones did have a surveillance system of sorts. They'd been engineered with a highly sophisticated system of infrared laser-light technology through a fledgling company launched by engineering students at Princeton University in the U.S. The company had created a suite of products around quantum cascade lasers that emit infrared light invisible to the human eye.

The American military defense research effort, among others, had given the company a grant to develop a very specific quantum cascade laser capability—one that could detect trace amounts of uranium hexafluoride through background noise at any given time. If tens of thousands of centrifuges were creating highly enriched uranium at a covert site underground and started to ramp up production of this HEU, it would create an early warning that Iran was beginning to develop enough for a nuclear weapon.

The company founded at Princeton had created its capability in a very short period of time. The drone making its way toward the lower earth atmosphere above Iran was equipped with that quantum cascade laser array and had the ability to sweep the air above a specific site that American satellites had under surveillance through a shared arrangement with Israel's defense forces.

Most of the intelligence experts thought Iran would cross over from a peaceful nuclear program to a weapons program at some point. What they hoped was that drones such as this—or human inspectors from the International Atomic Energy Agency who visited known nuclear sites in Iran on a regular basis—would see the telltale signs of an effort to create such highly enriched uranium early enough in the process to give diplomats at least a few months' time to do something about it.

The leadership in the U.S. believed it could work with Russia, China, and others in the event that such highly enriched uranium was ever detected. Even though Iran was bringing thousands of centrifuges online at a rapid pace, the many U.S. intelligence officials who had made a career of tracking Iran's nuclear activities knew that it would take months—not weeks—to enrich enough uranium for one bomb. And once that process started, the U.S. was very confident it could surround Iran with enough economic and diplomatic force to make sure the country backed down and stopped the enrichment.

But the little drone had no such illusions. It had a mission—one that had nothing to do with diplomacy or predictions. It swept the atmosphere for trace elements of uranium hexafluoride and dutifully recorded its findings—whatever they were. Its sensitivity was now in the parts per trillion, and it could detect almost anything in a mix of gases in the atmosphere.

In recent months, since the leadership changes in both Israel and the U.S., there had been disagreements about the drone's mission at the highest levels of both governments. The drones had begun their missions in the last year of the previous U.S. administration, in cooperation with the Israel Defense Forces (IDF). Now, with different administrations in both countries, much had changed—and the drone was at the heart of several contentious discussions about what could be done from Iraq.

For the time being, the drone carried out its mission. It would do so until the day arrived that it was either no longer needed or someone, somewhere, said it could no longer carry out its assigned duty high over Iran. The particular site this drone visited on a regular basis—next door to a highly secure missile plant run by the Revolutionary Guards near Shiraz—had shown no signs whatsoever of HEU activity during the entire time of its mission.

The U.S. felt it was a waste of time to monitor this particular site, which had once been involved in Iran's nascent nuclear program prior to 2003. But when Iran announced in 2003 that it was shutting down its nuclear program, this particular site near Shiraz had been closed. When Iran later announced that it was re-starting its nuclear power program—for peaceful purposes—this site near Shiraz did not come back online. Only sites at Bushehr, Natanz, Arak, and two others were active.

Israel, however, felt differently. It suspected Iran had created at least one or more massive, underground facilities with just one thing in mind—to house tens of thousands of centrifuges that could, in a matter of weeks, enrich enough uranium to create a nuclear weapon. How that weapon was delivered—and the warhead it carried—was another matter entirely.

So, at least for now, reports from this particular drone's mission were shared jointly with the IDF and the American military establishment. This particular drone's report had become monotonous in its lack of findings—so much so that the U.S. analyst assigned to monitor its reports on a regular basis had long ago begun to take them for granted.

Tonight, though, was different. The quantum cascade laser engineered into the drone swept the atmosphere—and hit something. The infrared light detected not only a few parts per billion of uranium hexafluoride—it detected amounts at something like one hundred times that level. This wasn't background noise. This was the telltale trace of a facility that, overnight, had gone into mass production. Nothing else would explain uranium hexafluoride at those levels. Unless it was an anomaly, something had clearly happened on the ground—or underground—at this site near

Shiraz. It was the telltale signature of a decision by Iran's leaders to sprint to the nuclear finish line.

When the report of the drone's mission came across the desk of the IDF analyst assigned to it, he stared at it for almost a minute. It was merely a computer printout, with numbers and graphs. But it didn't take a genius to understand what it meant. At those levels, someone had just started a massive effort to enrich uranium. There could be no doubt. It was, quite clearly, a smoking gun.

The IDF officer composed himself, then delivered his report to his superior officer. Step by step, the findings from the little drone's mission made its way up the chain of command. Eventually, it landed on the desk of the chief deputy at the Mossad, a retired IDF general who'd been put in place a few months ago by the leadership in Israel.

It was time for him to make the call he'd always hoped to avoid. But numbers and findings such as this could only mean one thing: Iran had made its decision and had set its covert enrichment process in motion in a very large way. The deputy head of the Mossad—a man whose name was publicly identified by just one initial—pulled the telephone number for the White House from his electronic rolodex.

He'd decided that, in the event of such a call, there was really only one person to contact first on the American side. The American president's chief of staff had once offered to volunteer for IDF. He was, more so than any other senior official in the administration, the most sympathetic to Israel and its isolation in the world community. Even if the U.S. and Israeli sides disagreed on Iran's intent, he knew the American president's chief of staff would at least assure that everyone would take the report quite seriously.

What happened after that was hard to predict. But he knew his duty, and he made the call. Others above his pay grade would make their own decisions, for their own reasons.

03

AIDA PALESTINIAN REFUGEE CAMP BETHLEHEM, ISRAEL

Dr. Elizabeth Thompson always considered it a blessing to visit Aida. She especially loved the sculpture of a large key over one of the entrances to the Palestinian refugee camp just north of Bethlehem. That key was a constant reminder to Aida's refugees that, someday, they hoped to win back their homes and a free country of their own.

The founder of the Aida camp liked to talk of a "beautiful resistance" to Israel's settlements in East Jerusalem outside the Green Line. That was one of the things Dr. Thompson liked about Aida. Unlike other Palestinian refugee camps, the thousands of residents in Aida resisted by building things of beauty with virtually no money or resources.

Children acted and danced at the Al Rowwad Children's Theater in the heart of the refugee camp. There was hope, not despair, at the theater. The women of Aida took part in sewing, aerobics, and yoga classes. They had computer labs and a library. Aida was one of the few truly peaceful enclaves of Palestinian refugees. Even the Pope had visited Aida.

Yet just a few blocks away stood the ugly retaining wall that surrounded Aida and separated the Palestinian refugee camp from both Bethlehem and East Jerusalem. Those who did not have proper Israeli passes, or yellow Israeli license tags, could not travel freely south to Bethlehem or north into East Jerusalem.

Off to the north, the people of Aida could see rooftops and parts of the two Israeli settlements—Gilo and Har Homa—that had been at the heart of an international conflict over Israel's insistence that it had the right to build anywhere it wished in East Jerusalem. But they could not easily reach either settlement unless they were willing to wait for hours at the one checkpoint that left Aida.

International Christian visitors had an easier time visiting Bethlehem—several hundred yards south of the camp—than the residents of Aida. It was one of the terrible ironies that bothered Elizabeth immensely when she made her rounds.

Dr. Thompson ran one of the few international Christian relief organizations, World Without Borders, that provided food, medical supplies, books, and equipment to the dozens of Palestinian refugee camps that had sprung up in East Jerusalem and on either side of the Jordan River. She traveled the West Bank extensively to keep track of supply chains and operations.

Aida was small enough that she knew every one of the residents, and they knew her.

Elizabeth climbed down from the beat-up, open-air jeep she'd used to travel the West Bank and Jordan for years.

"Dr. Thompson!" exclaimed the director of the Al Rowwad theater, Shira Dagher, a moment later.

"It's so good to see you, my friend. It has been too long!" Elizabeth took several long, purposeful strides toward the opening to the theater, where her friend was leaning up against the new pink and orange doorway that her NGO had helped build.

Shira Dagher was an elderly Arabic woman who now had six grandchildren living in different parts of Aida, all of them direct descendants of those who'd lived there before East Jerusalem had come under Israel's control. She was a permanent fixture in Aida. She knew everyone—

and everything. She embraced Elizabeth with no hesitation as a trusted friend.

"I am surprised to see you," Shira said. "I had not heard you were planning to visit us."

"I wasn't." Elizabeth gazed out over the courtyard, where children were playing happily in the bright sunshine and a yoga class was underway. "But I'd heard some things in Shuafat, after the arrests of the three men who've been accused of being part of the Tanzim. So I decided to visit a couple of the other camps in East Jerusalem."

Shira nodded. Between the two of them, they knew and heard things long before anyone else did in Aida. The Fatah trusted Dr. Thompson and her organization. And while she had no direct contact with the Tanzim—the unofficial military arm of the Palestinian Fatah that Israel and others considered to be terrorists—Dr. Thompson had friends who kept her informed. It never paid to be surprised in the Palestinian camps. Clashes and violence could break out easily. That rarely happened in Aida, but it was not impossible.

"So what have you heard?" Shira asked Dr. Thompson.

"That the Tanzim are *very* upset by the three arrests in Shuafat," Elizabeth added. "And that they are considering some sort of action to protest the arrests."

Shira squinted her eyes in surprise. "Here, in Aida?"

"Perhaps. But there's something else that disturbs me even more," Elizabeth said. "It's merely idle talk at this point, carried in the past twelve hours by some in several of the camps. It seems that some sort of word went out to cause trouble . . ."

"Trouble?"

"With the Israelis. The reports appear to be filtered from Hezbollah, through the Tanzim. They want Israel distracted."

Shira sucked in her breath quickly. They both knew what that meant. The surest way to distract Israel—and the world community—was an attack in East Jerusalem. An exploding bus or car bomb anywhere in the Israeli settlements of Gilo or Har Homa was certain to cause massive turmoil for Israel and attract worldwide attention.

Gilo and Har Homa were central to the indirect peace talks between the Palestinians, Israel, the United States, and others. The Palestinians wanted East Jerusalem as their capital. Israel considered East Jerusalem part of their own unified capital and the settlements in Gilo and Har Homa merely suburban expansion.

"But why now?" Shira asked.

"I don't know, but the talk is that they want trouble with the Israelis," Elizabeth said. "The arrests in Shuafat are an excuse."

"Well, that may explain it," Shira said glumly.

"What?"

Shira glanced around nervously to make sure no one was listening. "I have heard this talk as well," she said, her voice quiet. "Someone wants to cause very big problems for Israel right now, to distract them and the international community. This talk began in the past day."

Elizabeth always marveled at just how sophisticated her friend could be. If only Western leaders could understand, they would view people like the theater director as someone to be consulted, not shunned or penned up in a refugee camp with no resources.

She nodded. "An incident in either Gilo or Har Homa would trigger severe reprisals and international attention immediately."

Shira studied Dr. Thompson for several long, awkward moments. It was clear she was struggling with some bit of information. "A church bus left here with American tourists earlier today," she said finally.

Elizabeth's heart raced. "A church bus, with Americans?"

"They visited Bethlehem first," she said. "But they were going to come back through the Aida checkpoint, and into East Jerusalem after that. The driver . . ."

"What is it?" Elizabeth pressed anxiously.

"The driver—she has known the Tanzim for a long time now," Shira said, her voice nearly a whisper.

Elizabeth didn't need to ask any more questions. She knew what this meant. Her friend didn't have to tell her more. It was written between the words.

"I must go." Elizabeth turned quickly and began to hurry back to her jeep.

"May Allah guide your path," Shira told her. "Hurry. Perhaps there is still time."

Elizabeth nodded and quickened her steps. The possibilities—and the international ramifications—careened through her mind as she reversed the jeep and began to make her way through the bumpy, winding, open streets along the retaining wall that surrounded Aida, toward the one and only checkpoint into East Jerusalem from the refugee camp.

If a church bus with American tourists exploded in either Gilo or Har Homa, it would immediately ignite an international firestorm. Israel would be forced to defend its actions and settlements in East Jerusalem fiercely—as it had for years—and it would trigger anew the old angers and furies that had surrounded peace talks almost since the end of World War II.

It would also, Elizabeth knew, distract Israel and the United States for an extended period of time. That was the other piece of the talk she'd heard in Shuafat—that orders had come down through Hezbollah to provoke the Israelis in a big way. *An exploding church bus in one of the two most prominent Israeli settlements in East*

Jerusalem with Americans aboard certainly accomplishes that, she thought.

Her heart sank as she approached the last narrow, winding turn toward the checkpoint. Something had already happened. This particular checkpoint, normally busy with traffic, was relatively quiet. Today, though, more than a dozen Israeli soldiers had taken positions atop the retaining wall. Elizabeth hoped their rifles held rubber bullets, not real ones.

Children, and a few unemployed men, were tossing stones from the far side of a street. None of them landed near the Israeli soldiers. But, Elizabeth knew, it wouldn't take much to create a confrontation. Violence and conflict in and around the Palestinian refugee camps was always just a stone's throw away.

Elizabeth studied the line of cars in front of her. She knew, from long experience, that it could sometimes take hours for a car without yellow Israeli license tags to clear the Aida checkpoint into East Jerusalem. But the road narrowed here and took a sharp, left-hand turn before straightening out to enter the checkpoint. There was no way to see the cars toward the front of the line.

Elizabeth closed her eyes for a moment. At times like this, she had always trusted that still, small voice to guide her. She did so now.

Without another thought for her own safety, she put the jeep in park, grabbed the keys, and nearly jumped down from the vehicle. She hit the ground running, making her way along the stranded line of cars, up the winding street. She had no real plan.

As she turned the corner, the checkpoint came into view. There, just three cars away from it, was a church bus with chipped, blue paint and a faded white cross on the back. It was full of tourists, anxiously waiting to leave Bethlehem through the Aida checkpoint and make their way north toward Jerusalem.

Elizabeth slowed to a walk as she approached the bus and the checkpoint. She had no idea what might happen next, or how she could possibly determine if this was the bus her friend had mentioned. But as she walked, a certainty grew. This *was* that bus.

She knew she had to do something. Beautiful resistance was one thing. Cold-blooded murder of innocent American tourists who merely hoped to see Bethlehem and Jerusalem on vacation was another thing entirely.

Elizabeth glanced toward the window on the driver's side of the bus as she passed by. Her heart nearly stopped as she recognized the driver—a young woman Elizabeth had known for years, first as a child dancing happily at Al Rowwad and, later, as an active student in the yoga and aerobics classes at the theater.

The young woman, though, had her gaze fixed intently in front of her. Her hands gripped the steering column tightly. She didn't look down as Elizabeth made her way past the bus to the checkpoint.

As she neared the checkpoint manned by Israeli soldiers and officials, Elizabeth thought about what she would say. Was it possible that a woman such as this had talked and schemed with the Tanzim for years and now was prepared to take part in a suicide mission? Yes, she knew, it was possible. But would the Israelis believe her?

Thankfully, because some of them were now atop the retaining wall keeping a watchful eye, no soldier approached Elizabeth. She was able to walk inside the checkpoint building without incident. Once there, she moved quickly and deliberately toward two soldiers standing off to one side.

She pulled her papers out as she approached them. She flashed them to both soldiers, holding them steady so they could see she was an American citizen.

"Can we help you?" one of the soldiers asked casually.

Elizabeth took one more step, drawing close enough to them that she would not need to raise her voice. "My name is Elizabeth Thompson, and I run World Without Borders." She could see the name of the NGO meant something to them, which helped. "And I believe there is something quite dangerous about to happen near this checkpoint. Something you can help with."

That got their attention. Both soldiers stood up straight instantly. "Where—"

Elizabeth held up a hand. "Easy. Don't move quickly." She did not look over her shoulder. She didn't want the driver of the church bus to see any unusual activity inside the checkpoint building. "I've just been told in the camp that there might be a bus—a church bus with American tourists—that could be on a suicide mission toward either Gilo or Har Homa."

The soldiers glanced out the window at the church bus less than one hundred feet from the checkpoint. "That bus?" one of them asked.

"I do not know," she said, "but it fits the description. Is there a way a few of you can come up from behind, enter the bus, and detain the driver before she knows what's happened? You can search the bus after that."

The soldiers nodded. They were professionals. "We can," one of them said. Without moving, he turned his head ever so slightly and spoke softly into some sort of communication device attached to the left side of the uniform. He spoke quietly for several minutes, then turned back to Dr. Thompson.

"Just sit tight," he said to her. "This should take only a few minutes. I don't want you to turn back toward the bus. Keep chatting with us. I'll tell you when it's safe to turn."

Several long, tedious minutes passed. Elizabeth didn't remember anything they discussed. Her mind was a blank.

Then, as horns began to blare loudly, the two soldiers suddenly rushed past her and bolted through the doors of the checkpoint. Elizabeth whirled in time to see two Israeli soldiers pulling the driver of the bus from her seat and out the entrance. She was wailing loudly. She tried, unsuccessfully, to bite one of the soldiers but managed to deliver a swift kick to another.

The blaring of the horns was deafening. But the Israeli soldiers knew their jobs and did them efficiently and quickly. Within five minutes, they'd discovered the explosives carefully wrapped inside dirty, greasy cloths and wedged inside the bus engine—in a place where neither dogs nor an undercarriage visual search were likely to find them.

Elizabeth stared in shock at the chaos unfolding a few feet from her. Stones tossed by men and boys from the refugee camp were starting to rain down on the heads of the Israeli soldiers as they made the American tourists leave the bus and continued to check for additional explosives.

Elizabeth was glad her deep connection to the Aida camp and her quick reaction to the news she'd heard had made a difference. No one would ever acknowledge or report her help. But that didn't matter. It had never mattered to Elizabeth.

She wanted peace as badly as the Palestinians she served.

She was simply glad she'd managed to help avert a terrible event—one that made virtually no sense to her, but which had been designed to bring the world's attention back to Israel and their settlements in East Jerusalem.

She couldn't begin to guess why the shadowy networks that linked the likes of the Tanzim and Hezbollah might wish to distract Israel and the international community right now. She just knew that there would be no violence at this particular checkpoint or near this refugee camp on this day. And for that, she was thankful.

04

WASHINGTON, DC

The helicopter lifted off, lurched hard to the right, then flew like a banshee for a few feet before crashing, hard, against the wall at the far end of the room. The peals of laughter that erupted from the other end of the room seemed strangely out of place.

"No, Hannah, you have to pull back quickly on the throttle," Anshel Gould said, trying to keep from laughing. "You have to keep it in the air long enough for it to hover, then make the turn through the doorway."

"I tried," Hannah said. "It didn't fly right."

"Try again," Anshel said gently.

Anshel's middle daughter, Hannah, turned to the task again. She moved quickly to retrieve the small, battery-powered replica of the American president's helicopter, Marine One, from the floor at the other end of her dad's corner office in the West Wing of the White House. She returned the helicopter to its base, charged it for a moment, then tried again.

This time she was able to control the model of the helicopter as it lifted off. She kept the small blades whirring long enough for it to hover in the air a few feet over her dad's extraordinarily cluttered desk, then inched the throttle forward on the remote that controlled the helicopter. It eased forward, clearing the doorway by mere inches.

"It works!" she shrieked.

Anshel smiled. His daughter was persistent.

Hannah ran from the room quickly and followed the helicopter down the hall. The Secret Service agents milling around the Oval Office smiled. The president was still in the residence in the East Wing, so they let the helicopter pass by.

Hannah, still keeping the replica of Marine One hovering in the air, managed to make the turn into the Oval Office. The Secret Service agents let her through to follow the helicopter. It made one pass of the room, pausing briefly over the president's immaculate desk, then settled down on the carpet with the enormous presidential seal.

Anshel managed a crooked smile for the agents as he ambled quickly up the hallway to retrieve his daughter and her helicopter. They were used to Dr. Gould's kids early in the morning. This was the one time of the day that he had a chance to see them, before they went to school with their driver.

"We'll be out of your way soon," Anshel called out to the agents.

"No worries, sir," one of the agents answered. "POTUS is still in the East Wing."

"But he's headed this way soon?" Anshel asked.

"Soon enough," said the first agent. "But your daughter still has some flight time left."

Anshel tried to bring at least one of his three young daughters with him occasionally before he started his day at the White House. They would sit at a table next to his desk, finishing up home-work or occasionally terrorizing junior staff in nearby offices. Everyone was tolerant. The pace was brutal in this White House—just as it was in any White House. They all stole moments like this with family when they could.

Anshel was fond of saying that this White House was absolutely "family friendly"—just not for the families of the White House staff, who regularly put in eighteen-hour days, seven days a week. They'd all done everything they could to kid-proof the West Wing for the two young children of the president.

The White House was, in fact, a wonderful place for the president and his family. His two children—a boy and a girl both still in elementary school—had the run of the place, both inside and out. The White House staff made sure the media left them alone. There were never any photos of the president's two kids at play in the White House.

Anshel's boss had changed the political rules on his way to the Oval Office. He'd tackled every big issue thrown at him during his first year in office—from a looming economic depression, to national healthcare and the move to a clean energy future to head off the devastation of global warming—and had walked through that fire unscathed. He was, arguably, the most powerful presidential reformer on a grand scale since FDR.

Both Anshel and his boss visited the Capitol dome as much as possible. In fact, they'd been there more frequently since taking office than any previous chief of staff or president in recent history. Every part of the president's agenda was calibrated with Congress in mind.

But one rule had not changed. Family came first, whenever possible, and everyone who worked in the White House had to respect that. That meant Dr. Gould's kids could run along the corridors of power near the Oval Office at 6 a.m.

on a Thursday, and staff were expected to be tolerant and understanding.

Anshel Gould was an enigma—an unusual sort in Washington. Yes, he'd once earned a doctorate in social psychology. But he'd never put that degree to any use whatsoever, other than to torment the right wing of the Republican Party. He'd entered politics long before he'd ever earned that Ph.D., running state campaigns in New York while he was going to school at Columbia.

He'd never really gotten comfortable with the academic world. He much preferred the raw combat of politics. And Anshel learned early on that he was very, very good at politics—so good, in fact, that he'd won a seat in the New York congressional delegation at thirty-two and was the majority whip within four years. He'd barely finished his doctorate degree at Columbia by the time he'd packed his bags for DC.

There was no doubt, in anyone's mind, that Dr. Gould had given up a very promising career in the Democratic Party in Congress to join the president at the White House as his chief of staff. But Anshel never looked back in his life—not now, not ever.

He'd long ago created his own, unique brand of something his friends likened to a sort of Zen Judaism. Take each step along the path with fierceness and joy. Never fear that your next step is incorrect. Focus every fiber of your being on that next step. And then the larger goal is achieved.

That approach to life had always served him well. Anshel felt blessed and happy with his lot in life. He didn't worry about what might have been. He took each step along the path with the confidence that he was doing the right thing, for the right reasons. Where that path ultimately led him was not his concern. Others could judge his success or failure along that path. Content to make the right choice at each and every step along that path, his steady gaze was always forward. He was a relentless, positive storm. Others chose to be swept along—or get out of the way.

Anshel rarely had time to go to temple any-more, not with the seven-day weeks he was putting in. But his wife managed to convince him to spend time with friends from their temple, and that sufficed for now. To Anshel, the temple was a community, not a place of bricks and mortar.

His faith was a way of living and acting, not of internalizing. His belief in following the still, small voice was like breathing—a natural part of everything he said and did. It was ceaseless prayer, which infused his every action.

Today, though, would clearly be a test more unusual than others he'd encountered since taking over the chief of staff's office in the West Wing of the White House. He'd been avoiding the name near the top of his call sheet from the instant he'd spotted it as he entered the White House complex at the crack of dawn. The deputy head of the Mossad rarely called him—or anyone else in the U.S.—unless it was something important. Anshel knew, instinctively, what it was about. A steady parade of senior officials in the United States—from the secretaries of defense and state to the vice president and national security advisor —had been to Israel in recent months for quiet, but insistent, talks with the Likud government, Israel's major center-right political party, about the largest threat ever to face the nation of Israel.

Iran's nuclear program was at the top of everyone's list of problems in both the United States and Israel. What made the situation both difficult and intense was the nature of the leadership in all three countries. Iran's theocracy lurched unevenly between moderation and radicalism, almost on a day-to-day basis. The U.S. leadership had been trying, unsuccessfully, to engage with the religious head of that theocracy for months. Israel's conservative government, meanwhile, felt that talk with Iran was pointless and, perhaps, even dangerous.

"They're just running out the clock," the deputy head of Mossad had once said bluntly to Anshel. "Diplomacy serves their purpose. We talk while they build. We'll all wake up one day and discover that they've built a hundred thousand centrifuges underground somewhere, and they're enriching uranium before we know it. And then it may be too late. We were almost too late in Syria."

Anshel knew Israel would never let that day happen. The IDF had kept its hand on the trigger for months, waiting for even the first hint of a move toward a nuclear weapon in Iran. The Israelis grew more impatient with each passing day. If there was any sign that Iran was accelerating its weapons program, he was certain Israel would not wait.

The American president's secretary of defense had recently delivered a blunt, insistent message to the Likud government: give the United States time to negotiate a firm, verifiable nuclear inspection program on the ground in Iran, or else the U.S. would stand on the sidelines during an attack by Israel directed against those facilities in Iran.

It was an extraordinarily difficult position for the United States. The Pentagon and IDF had shared tactical air exercises for years. The Israeli Air Force's F-16 fighter jets, in fact, had just finished a "Red Flag" exercise at Nellis Air Force base in Nevada. The entire world had known about the joint exercise. Israel had made sure of it.

The IAF's own fleet of C-130 Hercules transport aircraft, meanwhile, had taken part in a competition at McChord Air Force base in the state of Washington. Clearly, the Israelis were looking for almost any excuse to test their long-range aircraft, refuelers, and transport planes with the U.S. military.

But things were much different now for Israel

and the U.S. During a previous American administration, under a conservative Republican president, Israel had enjoyed the ability to train in Iraqi airspace, with landing and takeoff privileges at American bases in Iraq. Israel could prepare for a staged attack against Iran's bunkered nuclear facilities from positions in nearby Iraq. But not now.

Though there remained deep, endless support for Israel on both sides of the aisle under the Capitol dome, America's stance had toughened. Virtually every American leader in the administration and Congress had made it quite clear that Israel would be on its own if it chose to attack Iran's nuclear facilities. The U.S. would not hinder those attacks, but it would not actively support that engagement, either.

There had been one—just one—concession to Israel and its military leadership in the current era. But it was a big one, known only to a handful of powerful members of Congress in the leadership and on the armed services and foreign policy committees. Everything had been handled at the highest levels in both the administration and Congress.

Anshel had quietly maneuvered the deal into place—based on a long-standing agreement that the U.S. would do its best to assure that the Israeli Air Force retained superiority in the Middle East region—and then hand delivered it to his boss, the president. The world did not yet know it, but the U.S. had secretly given Israel's air force an enormous edge in the region, and a slim thread of hope that it could take out Iran's nuclear facilities if that time should arrive.

Anshel had first broached the idea with the House speaker and the Senate majority leader. When they'd given their approval, in principle, he'd widened the circle to the chairmen of the Senate and House Armed Services committees and, eventually, to the Group of Eight in Congress.

The Pentagon had already made the decision to mothball its first-ever Stealth fighter—the famous, awkward-looking F-117 fighter developed in secret at Skunk Works—to an air base in Nevada. The planes, while still fully capable, were simply put on the shelf—despite pleas from pilots that the planes could still fly and fight as well as anything in the world. But the Pentagon leadership already had two much more advanced and capable Stealth fighters in production and in the field, so they'd taken the F-117s out of service.

Israel and Japan had put in bids for export versions of the newer Stealth fighters. Both Congress and the White House had signaled that they were open to considering the sale of export models of the newer Stealth fighters. Israel had already made plans to pay for the new Stealth fighters years from now. In that debate, a path forward for Israel had emerged—for the U.S. to simply sell the old F-117s to Israel now while decisions were made about export models of the much newer Stealth fighters.

The F-117 was still an incredible fighter plane—better than anything any Middle Eastern nations currently had in their inventory. And even though it was nearly three decades old, it was a fully capable Stealth fighter and could defeat any air-defense system in place in Iran—or anywhere else in the Middle East, for that matter.

The F-117 Stealth fighter was, in fact, a silver bullet for Israel.

In the end, the transaction to Israel had been an easier sell than Anshel might have imagined when he'd first set off on the quest. Congress and the White House needed something—anything—to indicate a show of support for the hawkish Likud government in Israel. The secret sale of the moth-balled F-117s to Israel made strategic sense on many levels. Anshel had been able to close the deal quickly.

Today's call from Israel, though, was one that Anshel had hoped he would not have to take. Before making the return call, he quickly thumbed through the folder that contained some of the most urgent parts of the president's national security briefing for the morning.

With some difficulty, Anshel had secured the ability to see an abbreviated version of the security briefing early in the morning, before it was actually delivered to the president. He never walked into any meeting cold, and national security matters were no different. Seeing the headlines at least gave him a chance to prepare before the meeting.

It was just a paragraph about two-thirds of the way through the briefing, but Anshel's heart sank when he spotted it. He knew, with a dread certainty, that this item was the reason for the call from the deputy head of the Mossad. A drone, part of a shared mission, had finally detected highly elevated levels of uranium hexafluoride in the atmosphere above one of the sites long suspected to be an enormous covert centrifuge facility near the holy city of Shiraz.

Anshel glanced through the background. Not surprisingly, no IAEA inspector had ever come close to visiting the suspected site. It wasn't on any of the published lists. But it had been involved in Iran's nuclear program before Iran had announced to the world in 2003 that it had ended its program. Most likely, Anshel knew, the Iranians had never shut down the facility—they'd simply poured more concrete on top of it and moved the centrifuges deeper into the earth.

But the elevated levels of uranium hexafluoride were unmistakable—irrefutable proof of action that almost surely involved tens of thousands of centrifuges. Based on what he was reading, Iran had made the internal decision to manufacture enough highly enriched uranium for at least one nuclear weapon. It would only be a matter of time. Iran was racing to the finish line.

Anshel looked over at the world clocks on his wall, then back at his call sheet. It was just after the lunch hour in Israel, and he'd put off calling back long enough. It was time to learn the grim truth—and prepare for what would probably be one of the longest days of his life.

"Ah, my old friend," the deputy head of Mossad said to Anshel when they'd connected. "I've been waiting for your call."

"I'm so sorry," Anshel said. "There were pressing matters."

"I can't imagine that anything will be more pressing than the news I'm going to share."

"You'd be surprised," Anshel answered.

The Mossad deputy paused briefly. "Can I assume you've seen the report?"

"The drone?"

"Yes, the drone. But there's more. We have reports out of Iran—"

"The arrests on their campuses," Anshel said quickly. "Yes, we know. We've heard. But is there any word yet of Razavi?"

"No, but we're checking now. We hope for news soon. Razavi hasn't been seen."

"Which means he's likely under arrest . . ."

"Or worse."

Anshel grunted. "I doubt they'd do much more

than place him under arrest. They'd need to fabricate a trial first before they do anything to him."

"Perhaps. I suppose time will tell," the deputy chief said. "But there is one other piece of news I wanted to share."

"As if this isn't enough?" Anshel said, laughing tightly.

"There was a suicide attempt in East Jerusalem a short time ago. We got to the driver of the bus just in time, thanks to information from an American doctor who'd picked up news in the refugee camp."

"Which camp?"

"Aida, near Bethlehem."

Anshel sat back in his chair. "Someone was playing for keeps if they were staging a suicide attempt from Aida. That could have triggered an international incident if it was aimed at either of the two big settlements in East Jerusalem."

"That appears to be the aim," said the deputy chief. "It was a church bus—full of American Christian tourists. They were planning to blow it up in either Gilo or Har Homa."

"Which would have kept both of us—not to mention the United Nations—busy for a while cleaning things up."

"And so the picture emerges," the deputy chief said slowly. "They round up opposition leaders to keep the lid on things inside Iran. They send word through Hezbollah to cause trouble in the settlements in East Jerusalem, keeping us both thoroughly distracted . . ."

"Buying them some time to enrich uranium as quickly as they can manage and sprint to the nuclear finish line," Anshel concluded.

Both men said nothing for a while as they played out the scenario.

"You know what we must do," the deputy chief said finally. "You will discuss the available options with your president?"

"I will," Anshel answered. "You know I can't promise full cooperation."

"I do. But I also know you will do your best to be persuasive," the deputy chief said before hanging up. "Be well, and wish us success, my friend."

05

WASHINGTON, DC

"You can't stop me. No way," Adom Camara said calmly, almost clinically. Sweat dripped off his brow, into his eyes, and down both sides of his cheeks. His gray University of Chicago T-shirt was already completely soaked.

He bent at the waist and held the basketball low in front of him. He started to swing the basketball from side to side, forcing his opponent to guess which way he was going on his drive.

He always played basketball early in the morning, before the day started. He'd tried running on the treadmill, or biking in the elaborate, private gym near the residence in the East Wing of the White House. He hated both. They bored him—even with the chattering talking heads screaming at him from MSNBC and CNN about the latest "big thing" engulfing DC.

Basketball was different. You had an opponent. You were constantly moving, and every shot, every drive to the basket, every defensive effort was different, unique.

President Camara's top aides had learned early on that he couldn't sit still inside the White House complex. He was always moving from office to office. His desk in the Oval Office was immaculate. There was nothing on it, save the phone he occasionally used to make calls his staff required of him.

Meetings with the young American president always happened in offices throughout the complex. If he wanted to talk to someone, he was just as likely to go find that person and hold the meeting in the staffer's office. His handlers were constantly trying to keep track of him. He walked the complex constantly, seeking out people to talk through an issue.

If it was a truly important meeting—with a head

of state, the chairman of the joint chiefs, or a Cabinet secretary—then, sure, they'd meet in the Oval Office. It was expected. But other meetings took place all throughout the West Wing, the Eisenhower Executive Office Building, or, occasionally, outside at the playground with one of his two kids playing on the swing set in view of the Oval Office.

But his favorite part of the day was right now, on the basketball court around the corner from the Oval Office at the start of the day. He'd sneak his first cigarette of the day, then play one of his staff aides to fifteen. They were all younger than him, which occasionally made him feel old, but it was always a test on the basketball court.

One of his first moves as president was to pave over part of the tennis courts that former President Jimmy Carter had built and replace them with a lighted basketball court. He'd played basketball with friends his entire political career, and he wasn't about to stop now that he'd become the leader of the free world.

Finding suitable opponents was difficult now, because his entire staff would have volunteered for time with the boss. In fact, some of them had undoubtedly read books on basketball on the off chance that they'd get time with the president on the basketball court. So he'd quickly settled on a few regulars, and that was just the way it was going to be.

His secret favorites were the press office guys. They were direct, almost profane. They didn't mince words and were loyal beyond belief to the president. Mirror images of the national media they coddled, held off, fed, and generally danced with twenty-four hours a day, they could also move easily from a discussion about some fight on Capitol Hill to an injury to one of their starting wide receivers on their fantasy football teams—a talent the president admired and emulated. In fact, the president had his own fantasy football team and often swapped political and football gossip in the same text messages with his press office staff.

The guy he was playing against right now was a good example.

Daniel James—DJ—was in his early thirties, married, with a young kid in preschool. His wife held a global health political job at the Department of Health and Human Services. DJ had been one of the press aides on the long presidential campaign and had been rewarded with a job as one of the White House deputy press secretaries after they'd taken office.

DJ lived and breathed politics and picked up on issues rapidly. He'd earned the respect of the older crowd who handled national security issues and had become the principal White House spokesman on national security issues. In fact, he'd earned enough respect to become part of discussions at the front end of a crisis.

He'd also adapted immediately when President Camara had collapsed the Homeland Security Council into the National Security Council soon after taking office. DJ, like his boss, recognized that foreign affairs and homeland security issues were tied together, so he thought it made sense to deal with the issues under one entity—not parsed out to different, sometimes warring, factions of the White House staff.

DJ was also a good athlete. He'd played soccer in college. But he'd also managed to squeeze in the occasional pickup basketball game and had run track in high school. He was a good match for the president.

In fact, DJ was up on the president right now, 14–12. He'd hit a few easy jumpers, but he'd also driven around the president on more than one occasion. DJ knew the president wasn't happy right now. But he wasn't about to let up. That wasn't right—even if he was the president.

The president swung the ball right, then left, then right again. He bobbed his head one way, then cut back to his left. DJ concentrated on the president's feet and ignored the head and hand fakes. He glided to his right quickly and cut off the president's path to the basket. Frustrated, the president pulled back quickly and fired off a fade-away jumper. It rattled off both sides of the rim, then fell off to one side.

DJ retrieved the ball quickly and pulled the ball back out. He dribbled easily at the top of the key. "You know you're about to lose," he said, trying his best not to smile broadly.

"Bring it," the president said, pulling on his shorts.

He looked tired but determined. He'd never been able to beat DJ in one of these games. He'd gotten close at times, like today, but DJ always managed somehow to drive past him when he had to.

DJ took a stutter step to his left. The president didn't flinch and held his ground. He put his right hand out, daring DJ to go to his right.

"Okay," DJ said and took the dribble hard to his right. The president put both a body and a hand on the drive, but DJ still managed to get within a few feet of the basket. He went up high and put the ball up against the backboard just over the president's outstretched hands. The ball banked off the backboard and settled easily inside the rim. It fell softly through the net and then to the court.

"Fifteen, and game." DJ couldn't hide the smile this time. He'd been forced to work hard this morning to beat the president. But it was one of the things he most admired about Adom Camara. The president didn't choose opponents for these morning games who were slouches. He played opponents who were younger, and better, than him on the court. DJ was impressed by that.

"Huh," the president said with a grunt. "I'd say you were lucky, but I know better."

"You were strong this morning," DJ answered. "You hit a few from outside."

"Not enough to make a difference." The president massaged the back of his neck. "I'm gonna learn to drive on you. You'll see. I'll take you one of these days."

"I believe you," DJ said. And, in truth, he did.

They grabbed two of the chairs courtside and sat down. The president finished off a small bottle of water in one long drink and wrapped a towel around his neck.

DJ caught the movement out of the corner of his eye. Other aides usually left the president to his basketball in the morning and didn't assault him with the day's work until it was finished. But something was clearly up, because Anshel Gould was striding across the White House lawn with unusual purpose.

"Mr. President," Anshel said quietly when he was within earshot, "I'm sorry to bother you, but I need a moment of your time. I need to talk to you about Iran . . . and Israel."

"Sure," the president said with a tight laugh. "It must be important. This is the closest you've come to this basketball court—and real exercise—in weeks."

Anshel ignored the dig. DJ started to get up from his chair, but Anshel motioned him back down. "DJ, you can stay. This one will end up in your lap."

DJ settled back into his chair. While he never said much about it—and never brought it up in even casual conversation in the White House—he'd always paid close attention to Israel and issues surrounding its national security because of his own personal Christian beliefs.

Grabbing another water bottle, he opened the cap quietly while awaiting the news. DJ admired Dr. Gould almost as much as he admired the president. The country—and the world—was lucky to have them as leaders. DJ couldn't think of a single situation or crisis that they couldn't handle.

They worked well together and complemented each other enormously. Dr. Gould could be abrupt, but DJ knew it was a single-minded drive to get any job done quickly, efficiently, and with the least amount of collateral damage. The president used that to his advantage, sending Anshel into situations when the outcome had to be success—or else.

"Mr. President," Anshel said, his tone more somber than usual, "a situation is developing in Iran. It's moving very quickly, and I think we have just a matter of hours until Israel takes action."

"Iran has made a move?" the president asked.

Anshel nodded. "One of our drones—one that shares data with Israel—discovered the activity overnight. The levels of uranium hexafluoride are at astronomical levels."

"How astronomical?" the president asked.

Anshel frowned. "Perhaps one hundred times beyond what you might expect from background noise."

The president grimaced. "Above one of the sites they'd identified to the international atomic agency?"

"No," Anshel said. "It's above another site—one that we've suspected but never proven conclusively to the UN Security Council. No inspector has ever been to this site, near Shiraz. It's an old site, from pre-2003 times."

"But we're sure it's HEU from centrifuges?"

"We'll confirm it absolutely with other sources, but there's no question. The levels would indicate they've moved tens of thousands of centrifuges into production almost overnight. They've made their decision. Most likely, they're producing it for a test."

"But the Israelis won't wait, will they?" the president asked almost rhetorically.

"No, they won't," Anshel answered. He told the president quickly about the opposition leader arrests in Iran and the attempted suicide bombing in East Jerusalem that were designed to buy Iran time.

Adom Camara had sent every emissary he could possibly think of to Israel in the past few months to hold them off while he pursued direct, bilateral talks with the religious theocracy that truly controlled the political apparatus in Iran. But he'd known, in his gut, it was only a matter of time before Iran made its move—and Israel its counter-move.

Israel's national security team had briefed the Knesset—the Israeli legislature—three months ago that Iran had crossed the technological threshold on nuclear weapons. Israel's national intelligence team confirmed to the Knesset that Iran had secured the warhead technology from North Korea. Russia, North Korea, and even China had helped the Iranians create missile capabilities—including a space launch capability that could put a satellite (and an ICBM) in orbit. And, thanks to help from North Korean scientists, they had the technical ability to produce enough highly enriched uranium to equip a nuclear weapon.

Russia had always been interested in the Middle East. It had a well-established trade relation-ship with Iran. But it had begun to discuss oil exploration with Israel as well in recent years as rumors circulated about the possibility of major oil finds in northern Israel and, possibly, beneath the Dead Sea.

All that remained was the decision to move. Iran's conventional military forces might have been twenty years old and out of date, but it would only take one nuclear weapon to slip through the Arrow defense system in Israel, and the world would likely see a second Holocaust.

The president's team had made some headway in the move to direct talks with Iran's religious leadership. But, in just the past few weeks, the talks had begun to grind to a halt. That meant one thing, and the news this morning confirmed it. Iran had made the decision to join the nuclear club.

"How much time do you think we have?" the president asked Anshel.

"Not much," Anshel replied. "Hours, maybe. They'll want to go tonight. As we know, the Israelis have been ready for this for months. They won't wait."

The president took a deep breath. He'd discussed this situation with Anshel and others on the joint chiefs and the national security team almost from the moment they'd entered the White House.

Israel's national leadership had moved to the right just as the U.S. leadership was moving to the left. The United States was still Israel's most trusted and invaluable ally in the world, but the rules had changed. Israel's national security team and leadership thought the United States was naïve in believing that direct, bilateral talks with Iran could forestall their inevitable move to nuclear weapons.

But President Camara was committed to a diplomatic course—one that did not automatically side with Israel when it made unilateral military decisions in its own national security interests. He and others on his team truly believed they could change the game, and the equation, in the U.S. relationship with Russia, China, North Korea, Iran, and the moderate Arab world.

Camara's first speech to the Arab world had taken place, strategically, in Cairo, Egypt. It was a brilliant first move in the dangerous, endless world of Middle East politics and intrigue. The speech had reassured moderate Arab nations that the Camara administration was committed to rebalancing equations in the center of the world, where hostility and violence were everyday occurrences.

He'd followed that speech with meetings with the Russian president and, the next day, with the Russian prime minister—the country's real leader and someone who was rapidly consolidating power in ways not seen since the days of the tsars.

President Camara had sent an ex-president to meet with the leadership of North Korea. He'd dispatched no fewer than six Cabinet secretaries to meet with Chinese leaders, paving the way for progress on global warming and international security issues. He'd made significant progress in both Afghanistan and Pakistan. He'd fulfilled his campaign pledge to dramatically scale back the U.S. military presence in Iraq, even as democracy was beginning to flourish there.

But Israel had remained at the center of the equation, even as chess moves were made elsewhere. The American president had not officially denied a direct request for IAF planes to fly through at least some part of Iraqi air space—but neither had he said that he would allow Israel's planes to move through Iraq on a mission that both countries knew was almost inevitable.

The American president had hoped that delaying a response to Israel would give the U.S. time to open and conclude direct talks with Iran's theocracy. He knew he was racing against the clock, but he'd still hoped to make it work.

And now—the decision was here. He'd made very little progress with Iran.

"Anshel," the president asked softly, "have they made the request?"

Anshel didn't answer right away. He glanced over at DJ, who was still sitting quietly, sipping on his water and taking in the conversation and its implications. The president glanced over at DJ as well, and nodded.

"I can leave, if you need . . . ," DJ offered quickly.

"No," the president said. "I want you in on the front end of this. When it comes time to characterize our decision on how much we cooperated with Israel, I want you to know where the decision came from."

"It's fine," Anshel said.

DJ sat still.

"So, has Israel made the request?" the president repeated.

This time, Anshel didn't hesitate. "Not officially, but I just spoke to the deputy head of Mossad. They're going to ask for permission to land at our three bases in western Iraq sometime in the next three hours. They'll refuel and take off immediately."

"How many targets?"

"He wouldn't say, but it's at least a dozen, and probably closer to twenty. They're using every single one of the Bandits who trained with our guys at Nellis and Tonopah."

"And your position hasn't changed on this?" the president asked.

Again, Anshel did not hesitate. He was the most pro-Israeli member of President Camara's inner circle. But he was also a political realist and knew how far he could push his boss. "We must allow their planes to fly over Iraqi airspace unimpeded, Mr. President. To do anything less would be unconscionable, given our relationship with them. But we also cannot allow them to land at our bases. The consequences of that, down the road, would undermine everything we're trying to do."

"And if we deny landing rights, how will Israel finish the mission?" asked the president. "Have they made their own decision on that question?"

"I believe they have," Anshel said. "It places them at enormous risk, but they've apparently

70

made the decision to strike first and then refuel outside Iranian air space. The planes that will be central to the mission have a range that's a few hundred miles beyond their targets. The planes—the ones that have a chance to make it back—will land either in Turkey to the north, or try to refuel out over the sea and land on the one carrier they've acquired."

The president cringed. He knew that success for those pilots—in either case—was difficult. "They won't try to make it all the way back to Israel?"

Anshel shook his head. "They don't think it's possible. They don't have any with the range to make it all the way back once the targets are hit. They will need to land somewhere first, or re-fuel. When we deny landing rights in Iraq, Turkey and the sea are their best options."

"Even with the tactical Stealth fighters we sold to them, with extended range? The ones you pushed me on relentlessly?"

"Those planes will allow the IAF to make it into Iran through the air defenses, Mr. President," Anshel answered. "They won't allow the pilots to make it all the way back to Israel. But I'm still grateful that you made the decision you did."

"And you?" the president asked, smiling. "You've made your own decision, then? No landing rights in Iraq? We're going to sit on the sidelines?"

Anshel didn't blink. He knew it was, in fact, a

serious question. "You know me, Mr. President. If it was my call, and I had no other considerations, I would make Israel's mission as easy as possible. I would let them take off from Iraq and then land there as well after the bombing raids are finished. But I know that position isn't tenable, and that it would actually jeopardize our own security. So, yes, that's my recommendation. We can't allow them to stage this mission from Iraq."

The president looked over at DJ. "So?" the president asked lightly. "What do you think of that decision? Can we defend it publicly? Will Egypt, Jordan, Russia, and others buy it?"

DJ looked thoughtful. "We can defend it publicly. We have to. There's no choice. We need to make sure all of the other nations that have a stake in this know we were not partners with Israel in the attack. We have to make sure everyone knows, quickly, that this was Israel's own decision."

"But letting them fly through Iraqi airspace?" asked the president.

"We have no choice there, either," DJ said. "Israel is our ally. It's not like we're going to shoot down an IAF plane as it flies over Iraq. If we can't stop this mission, and their decision, then we have to let their planes through. From the way it sounds, they won't be coming back through Iraq to get home. So we can explain what happened."

"Can you defend it publicly?"

"Yes, Mr. President, I can," DJ said. "We must make it very clear that this was Israel's own, unilateral decision. We did not facilitate the mission. I'll emphasize—strongly, and on background—that we denied landing rights in Iraq. I'll stick to that position, no matter what. And I'll point to the fact that IAF planes did not return through Iraqi airspace. I believe I can drive both of those points home. I'll make sure they're out there by the time you talk to the press. I'll run interference first."

The president nodded. This was the decision he'd wanted, and he was glad to have aides around him who knew him well enough to understand where he was likely to wind up on a question such as this. They would defend it with everything they could muster. There wasn't much that any of them could do, not at this point. "When will Israel begin?" he asked.

"In truth," Anshel answered, "they've already begun. Their refuelers are out over the water, and their tactical fighters will be in the air shortly."

"I see," the president said thoughtfully. "Well, then, we'd better prepare."

A threshold was clearly being crossed here. Regardless of the relative success or failure of Israel's mission, the world would be forever changed. How nations—and their leaders—responded in kind would make all the difference.

06

Lilongwe, Malawi

Nash had been stunned by one of the mVillage network messages addressed to him. It was from a student leader from Tehran University he'd met twice at international conferences. They'd exchanged network addresses.

The MMS message had been sent to Nash's personal account with mVillage, which he gave out selectively. In this case, he was glad he had.

The message contained a video—and a message about what it meant. It clearly showed Reza Razavi, the opposition leader who'd allegedly been denied the presidency in Iran—being placed under house arrest. Nash didn't guess what it might mean, but he had called his staff in London to make sure it received proper treatment.

"Can you post it right away?" he had asked before setting out on his travels for the day.

"Sure can," said one of the young staff in the London office.

"Give it prominent placement on the boards," Nash said. "We want people to see this one."

"We will," his staff aide replied. "There are other

reports, about student arrests in Iran. But this one will go big."

Satisfied, Nash had set off for a quick visit with a local pastor of a small church near Lilongwe. Over the years, the two had become friends. Nash was always traveling, but he tried to stop by his friend's house whenever he was in Malawi.

As he navigated his borrowed motorbike around the deep ruts in the road, he almost missed the sign that was tacked, lopsided, to the side of a shanty on the way into town. Nash had plenty of time to read and translate it. The road didn't allow him to go much faster than twenty-five miles an hour here.

Chokani kunyumba yanu, Madonna, use musabe ana anthu! the Chichewa words said. Loosely translated: "Go home, Madonna. Stop stealing our babies!" The message had been scrawled with some sort of dark, burnt stone. The next good rain would wash it away. But no matter. The point was clear to those who understood—even if the author was powerless to do anything about the issue.

There was an orphanage around the corner, on the outskirts of Lilongwe, where the aging pop star Madonna had adopted her first Malawi child, David. The adoption had created international furor at the time with children's welfare groups, who were concerned that Malawi officials had bent the rules because of her celebrity status.

Malawi, one of the poorest countries in the

world, was landlocked and somewhat isolated. AIDS, malaria, and tuberculosis had done their damage, as they had in other African nations. Madonna had created a charity, Raising Malawi, years earlier to help feed and care for the orphans. During one of her visits to the country, she'd arranged to adopt one of those orphans.

The adoption made news across the globe. But, in Malawi, the reaction was much slower. Word of such things often traveled the country by word of mouth. Many of Malawi's villages had no power and very little contact with the outside world. It was only in the cities, like Lilongwe, that people even grasped the concept.

When Madonna tried to adopt a second child from Malawi—a girl whose eighteen-year-old mother had died, unmarried, shortly after giving birth—a local court tried to block it. Madonna had first discovered Chifundo "Mercy" James at the Kondanani Children's Village, an orphanage just south of Blantyre, another Malawi city. But Malawi's high court had overturned the ruling, and Madonna's new daughter left the country on a private jet for London.

The sign alongside the road intrigued Nash. It took a lot for a Malawian to write such a thing. For those, like Nash Lee, who spent time working in the country, Malawi was really the "warm heart of Africa." The people welcomed *azungus*— white people—everywhere in the country. Yes, they were mostly a curiosity, but they were always welcomed with open arms.

Every village adopted orphans when it could. There were caregivers, maternal grandmothers, and others who took on babies whose mothers had died of AIDS or other afflictions. A person was an "orphan" in Malawi only in the strictest sense of the word. You were orphaned when you were isolated from your community.

The first time Nash had come to a medical clinic in rural Malawi to set up one of his global health projects, there had been kids everywhere. He'd had no idea who was an "orphan" and who was not. He'd pulled a Snickers bar from his backpack and handed it to one of the kids trailing behind him.

He'd watched, fascinated, as the kid stopped, unwrapped it, and then waited patiently as eleven other kids joined him by the side of the road. They'd carefully separated the Snickers bar into twelve roughly even pieces. There had been no fighting—just an easy willingness to share with those in the community.

When you took a bus in Malawi from one place to another, the bus stopped to pick up everyone and everything, including the chickens on their way to an uncertain fate somewhere. As many as fifty people might pile onto the bus. Everyone, and everything, was welcomed. The bus arrived at its destinations along the way when it could, with as many people as it could hold.

This was the "warm heart" of Malawi that Nash had grown to love and admire in his work. It took people awhile to recognize it, though. Americans and Europeans who flew into a place like Malawi, trying to do good and help out, would often miss this sort of thing.

Nash rarely saw this sort of generosity in the United States, a nation that liked to call itself a Christian nation. But here, in Malawi, it was as natural as breathing. Nash always marveled when he traveled to Malawi and other countries in Africa where people lived their faith and beliefs on a daily basis. Most people in America would never recognize such generosity in the face of utter poverty.

In fact, one of the things that always bothered Nash was the way in which even faith-based international relief organizations played up tragedy and despair to raise money for their work in Africa. Yes, there was despair in Africa in the face of hunger, drought, and AIDS—but there was also laughter, warmth, hope, and, yes, even happiness.

Nash was profoundly comfortable living his Christian faith in a place like Malawi. Here, he could simply do good without explanation. He came to help, and he helped. He didn't need to explain why his own personal Christian beliefs led him to Africa. He was just here to help. That was good enough for the people in Malawi, and elsewhere in Africa. He didn't need to be a celebrity, and he didn't need to be recognized for his actions.

Nash didn't want to judge Madonna, and heaven knew that Mercy and David would have much better lives in London as the son and daughter of one of the world's richest and most famous pop star icons. But, to Nash, it all sort of missed the point.

The point, as he saw it, was to work from the absolute epicenter of the need—the community. Everything in Malawi, and other African nations like it, revolved around community. Tens of thousands of African villages had legions of volunteers who had dedicated their lives to helping others. Nash's bond, and life, was dedicated to that community—and to those who served it. He was their connector, one of the *azungus* who under-stood how their world really worked.

His very first global health project, while he was still an undergraduate at Harvard, had been a simple one that embodied this worldview. He'd spent the summer going from village to village in rural Malawi, watching closely how the volunteer community and village health workers went about their business.

Those villages were all isolated from the rest of the country—and from the rest of the world, for that matter. There was no electricity, no power, in those villages. When someone got sick, there was no way to call 9-1-1 and ask for an emergency vehicle to show up at your door. You either walked to the clinic to seek medical care—which could take days—hitched a ride on the back of a bicycle, or waited until the nurse from the hospital eventually made his way to your village.

But Nash had noticed there was one thing available to each of those villages. In fact, it was the one thing that was ubiquitous in Africa: the cell phone. If you could keep a cell phone powered, and you had money to pay for service, then you could connect to the clinic and the rest of the world.

When Nash returned to Harvard, he did what came naturally to kids of his generation. He put the word out on his blog, his Twitter feed, his Facebook page, and elsewhere. *Help me,* he wrote in so many words. *How can I solve this equation?*

And the answers started to arrive. He borrowed an open-source, text-messaging software platform that had been developed to monitor democratic elections in countries where the media was largely controlled by the government in power. He borrowed another open-source software platform from a system that had been generated at Harvard to create really simple electronic medical forms. And he finished the project off with a third open-source software system created at UCLA that allowed the simple cell phone to plug into a diagnostic kit and test for AIDS, malaria, and TB—right there, at the point of care, in the middle of any remote place on earth.

Next, he'd invited those who'd shown an interest in the project to join him. They did. Half a dozen kids in various science, engineering, and computer science fields from other rich universities like Stanford, Yale, and elsewhere started talking. They crashed all the systems together to create a unique cell phone system that could do what sophisticated mobile health systems could do—but at a fraction of the cost.

Nash had secured a grant from a global health center at Harvard, which paid his travel back to Malawi and allowed him to buy enough text-messaging service for one hundred cell phones for ten years. He tested his pilot. He trained one hundred community workers to use the phones, connected them to donated solar panels to solve the power problem in the villages, and then sent them back out to their villages.

Within three months, the results were in. The number of people diagnosed with TB—and, ultimately, treated—doubled. The reason was simple. When a community health worker saw signs and symptoms, he or she would send a text message to the hospital, which then allowed the medical personnel there to move into action. The communication was instantaneous, and the response was equally quick. Nash had connected one hundred villages to the hospital—at a cost of perhaps $2,000.

And, from there, Nash and his team had taken the NGO and global health world by storm. Everyone signed up for the low-cost, high-impact mobile health solution—WHO, the United Nations fund, UNICEF, Save the Children, Partners in Health. What had started as a project while Nash was studying for finals at Harvard had, almost overnight, turned into a global public health concern.

Nike's global advertising firm had adopted Nash's project and created a charity for him and his team to encourage millions to send in their used cell phones for recycling in African villages. They won global health tech competitions. Foundations started giving money. And, before he'd known it, Nash was racing around the globe, implementing community-based health solutions as fast as his team could create them. There was nothing the team wasn't willing to try.

It had all happened so fast that they'd created a name on the fly that aspired to greatness and their game-changing goal: Village Health Corps. Nashua Lee—whose father was an icon of the Democratic Party in the United States, had raised millions for three different U.S. presidents, and had culminated an illustrious career with two ambassadorships to South Korea and presently in

Japan—made himself the executive director of VHC more on faith than anything else. Now, four years later, at the ripe old age of twenty-six, Nash was the master of a global public health empire that operated in more than one hundred nations around the globe.

Curiously, though, it was their latest technology twist at VHC that was starting to create highly unusual and mind-bending possibilities. One of their founding partners—an open-source software genius type from Cambridge in the UK—had set about to make the simple SMS, text-messaging system an actual media delivery platform.

The concept, while modest at first, had proved revolutionary. The team had developed the ability to compress and embed video files directly into text messages. Any cell phone equipped with the ability to view videos—and most could now do that—became a mobile TV, of sorts.

Then they'd adopted Google's operating system for mobile platforms, cut a deal to network through the ubiquitous computing cloud, partnered with Apple for delivery of media, and finished it off with a deal with Nokia to pilot test a new mobile phone.

Once upon a time, America Online had taken its modest text-messaging concept and created an Internet revolution. Other companies like Google and Microsoft expanded that revolution even further. Such technology changed everything in countries like China, which at first could not control the flow of information directly to its citizens through the Internet. They could control the media, but not the Internet.

But, over time, China and others did learn, in fact, how to control information on the Internet. They'd learned how to block searches and displays of certain types of information. They'd also been able to maintain control of information delivered via Internet-like media services on cell phones.

But they could not control text messages, which hide within the data on cell networks. They could not control that one-to-one system of data delivery. And Nash's VHC team had perfected the art of one-to-many SMS systems, which allowed even the smallest NGO to communicate with a far-flung network. A new form of communication was born that could operate within closed, controlled systems. They called it mVillage.

For the first time in a generation, dictators, despots, and totalitarian regimes could not control or manipulate information that had the ability to migrate and circulate among its citizens. Overnight, mVillage had enabled entire networks to communicate directly to people in countries like North Korea and Iran.

Global institutes, NGOs, and others with a stake in talking to the people in countries where the media was under tight control adopted this new mobile technology. In a very short time, they were bombarding the landscape with video messages and stories that carried truth into places where lies and distortion were the coin of the realm. It was a breathtaking, dangerous world that Nash and VHC had created for themselves and others.

This third wave of information delivery was confounding totalitarian regimes. Once there had been radio and television to the masses. Then there had been the Internet, also to the masses. Now there was IT via single mobile devices, delivered to the masses on a one-to-many basis. . . .

Nash shook his head to focus his thoughts on the present. He was late for his visit with his pastor friend. As he returned his concentration to the road to make sure he got there as quickly as he could, he almost missed the small, global satellite cell phone ringing and vibrating loudly on his belt.

Easing up on the throttle of the motorbike, he slowed enough to pull the phone from his belt to glance at the message. He received so many SMS messages and calls that he'd set his phone to both ring and vibrate loudly only when messages and numbers came in from a handful of carefully selected people.

He glanced at the caller ID. It had just one word —*DAD*. Nash came to a complete stop on the side of the dirt road. His father almost never called, so it had to be something important. Nash couldn't guess what it might be, but he knew he needed to listen to the voice mail.

His father operated in a world that Nash didn't really understand and largely avoided. But their work occasionally intersected—and was about to again.

07

RAMAT DAVID AIRBASE
SOUTHEAST OF HAIFA, ISRAEL

The plane was as ugly as it was black. The prototype of the plane—built at Lockheed Martin's infamous Skunk Works—had been nicknamed the "Hopeless Diamond" because it jutted out in strange places and looked like an oversized replica of the Hope Diamond. The actual planes in production weren't any prettier. They almost didn't look like they'd fly right.

But Ben Azoulay knew that those strange angles and odd shapes gave the plane its marvelous, almost unexplainable, ability to avoid the most sophisticated air defenses ever built. Even now, twenty-five years after the first F-117 came off the assembly line, those few American pilots who'd put enough hours on the plane to become "Bandits" swore by it as the best plane ever.

Azoulay, a second-generation Israeli Air Force pilot, was the first Israeli Bandit certified to fly the F-117. He was Bandit 1 for Israel. He was followed shortly by the other twenty-three IAF pilots—all rated as Bandits.

When the word came through that Israel, the Camara administration, and Congress had come to terms on a quiet, secret sale of twenty-four F-117s, the new, elite corps of IAF Bandits was ecstatic. They knew precisely what this meant.

The American F-117s were as close to a silver bullet to their country's Iran problem as they could imagine. Thanks to technical modifications made to the plane by Lockheed engineers, the F-117s could now extend their range without refueling to well beyond the public estimate of 1,070 miles. With adjusted payloads, the planes could now strike any target in Iran, avoid the new Russian air defenses in place, and get back to either Turkey or elsewhere without landing or refueling. Air strikes deep into Iran with F-16s and F-15s were suicide missions. The F-117s made the mission possible.

One by one, the new IAF Bandits piloted the newly acquired F-117s across the Atlantic to the First Air Wing at Ramat David to the north of Israel. There was no announcement, no ceremony, no fanfare. The planes simply arrived, one by one, at Ramat David.

Now, many months later and with enough training in hand, Ben felt that he was prepared for the mission he was about to undertake. His F-117 was one of only four equipped with something the Israel government would deny immediately after the strike. His plane carried a tactical nuclear payload designed to obliterate the entire site and everything in it. But Israel and the four Bandit pilots carrying the tactical nukes would never talk about these payloads and the damage they would inflict. To the world, the damage inflicted by their payload would look quite similar to what might be inflicted by a series of high-explosive bombs.

But Ben had been briefed enough to know that his payload was almost the only way Israel could take out the extensive underground networks of HEU, warhead and missile facilities that had been spread around Iran's countryside. He tried not to think about the moral implications of dropping a tactical nuke on a target. He had a job to do, one that was at the heart of his country's ability to protect itself. To Ben, that was all that mattered.

It wasn't that Ben didn't care about the implications. He cared deeply. Everyone who'd ever met him knew that he walked securely on the straight and narrow path. He was confident in his God and held strongly to faith, family, and country in a seamless fashion.

For all of these reasons, Ben knew precisely what this mission meant—to Israel, and to the world. And it was precisely for this reason that he would give his life for it, if need be.

As his crew secured the canopy that surrounded him, Ben closed his eyes briefly to say a prayer, touched the Star of David lightly beneath his jumpsuit, then moved his hand to the controls of the Stealth fighter. It was time.

A moment later, the F-117—the silver bullet so recently acquired from the U.S.—was in the air and on its way to Iran.

08

TEHRAN, IRAN

Reza Razavi was beside himself. It was bad enough they'd stolen the presidency from him. But to snatch him from the street and place him under house arrest?

He'd never felt so isolated. They'd stripped the house of every computer and landline. Thankfully, they hadn't checked for the cell phone he kept in a drawer in the bathroom.

Using the phone, he'd been able to check the mVillage boards for the past two hours. His own house arrest had even been captured somehow and posted on mVillage. Dozens of threads were starting to attach themselves to the outrage building over his house arrest.

"This is madness," Razavi muttered. He hadn't been able to stop pacing for the past two hours. He knew what was happening. He *knew*. He'd heard from dozens of his peers, colleagues, and friends in the opposition movement that had grown by leaps and bounds in recent months—literally from the day the conservative, messianic president of Iran had stolen the election.

The word was everywhere. The president—and the religious leaders he answered to in many small, but important, ways—had made the political decision to enrich enough uranium to test a nuclear bomb. The MMS and SMS text and video bursts were screaming through the cell phone media network that served as the only way for news to escape the borders of Iran.

Thank goodness for mVillage, Razavi thought.

Reza had always assumed it would only be a matter of time before the Revolutionary Guards created some excuse to place him under house arrest. It's why he'd hidden the cell phone. He and a second candidate who'd run unsuccessfully against Iran's president, Nassir Ahmadian, had been accused by Iran's Revolutionary Guards of leading a "soft" revolution against the government.

Ahmadian had rolled into power with the blessing of Iran's Supreme Leader, Ayatollah Amir Shahidi, and had promptly electrified the world with apocalyptic speeches at the United Nations and elsewhere that predicted the imminent return of the 12th Imam—the Mahdi—and the imminent demise of Israel.

"I will wipe Israel off the face of the map,"

Ahmadian had said on more than one occasion. Ahmadian's actions and words had taken a toll on the sensibilities of Iran's moderates, and several important clerics had quietly withdrawn their support of him over the years. The "principalist" clerics had pressed the Supreme Leader to disown his hand-picked president. But Shahidi had remained steadfastly behind Ahmadian and embraced him publicly after a highly contested national election that had led to violence in the streets of Iran and hundreds of arrests.

Iran's Revolutionary Guards had long targeted Razavi as the leader of a velvet revolution, accusing him of working with British and American operatives to incite violence and turn the people against Ahmadian and the elected leadership of Iran.

There was some truth to it, of course, though it was much more complicated than it appeared. Yes, Razavi was deeply involved in opposing Ahmadian and had the backing of the West in that opposition. But Razavi also had the blessing of several Grand Ayatollahs who were appalled at the bluster and naïve insensitivity of Ahmadian. Many of them would be outraged when they learned of Razavi's house arrest.

A split had grown in the religious leadership of Iran, and Razavi had worked hard to win the hearts and minds of senior clerics who hoped to see Iran move back into the good graces of the world community. He'd come close to reaching a majority among those clerics—but not enough to convince Iran's Supreme Leader to back him.

Reza was an enigma to some. He was very political—and adept at dealing with the highest levels of power and authority in Iran. But he was also just as comfortable dealing with the religious leaders and hierarchy. And, at an even deeper level, Reza was comfortable in his own skin, with his own beliefs.

It was obvious to even the most casual observer that Reza Razavi was a man of deep personal beliefs and convictions. He never defended his religious beliefs—he lived them.

That belief—and his willingness to act forth-rightly based on it—was what allowed him to operate in both the religious and political spheres in Iran. He was at home in many worlds. It also allowed him to very clearly see the current president for what he was—a political leader with very little real substance, but who was adept at saying things the masses adored.

The irony, Razavi knew from several sources, was that the Supreme Leader was no longer enamored of Ahmadian and hoped to see him removed from office eventually. But neither could the Supreme Leader afford to let the West dictate Iran's leadership, so he had swung the full force of his office behind Ahmadian after the contested election.

The senior commander of the powerful Guards —who also controlled Iran's covert nuclear weapons program—had gone on the offensive within weeks of the election, repeatedly condemning Razavi on Iran's state-controlled television for inciting unrest in the country. He'd demanded a trial by the judiciary. It was for this reason Razavi had known it would only be a matter of time before the Guards found a reason to arrest him.

But Razavi had prepared for this day well. And, since his arrest, he'd spent his time productively, monitoring world events through mVillage— now the principal way in which many Iranians received and sent real-world news of events and stories in Iran.

Razavi was amazed at the simplicity and elegance of mVillage. It rivaled the creation of the Internet once upon a time. With just a cell phone, Razavi could now create and send video messages that completely bypassed the state-controlled media to millions of followers.

More important, millions could continue to take part in democracy in Iran through mVillage, despite the government's attempt to control access to the Internet and media from the West. Iran's Revolutionary Guards had almost shut down the cell networks in the country to block mVillage but had quickly learned that doing so would end cell coverage in the country. That alone would likely be a tipping point and turn the country permanently against the ruling leadership, so they backed off from that threat. The mVillage network remained.

Razavi had taken a momentary break for a snack. But now he turned on his cell phone again and logged into mVillage. The video of his house arrest had triggered a tidal wave. There were dozens of media-rich text messages from all over the country in his inbox. Nearly all were from well-wishers and others in his immediate network who urged him to remain strong. More than a few promised to sound the alarm.

Iran had made the political decision to test a nuclear weapon, and people were beginning to broadcast this to the world through mVillage. No one had hard proof of the decision, but enough had heard from dissidents within the government's ranks to know it was likely true. Iran had gambled that silencing opposition and student leaders would buy them time. The exact opposite appeared to be happening, thanks to the video of his house arrest.

Based on what he was seeing in mVillage, Razavi knew it must be true. He was surprised Rev. Shahidi had blessed Ahmadian's decision to let the Revolutionary Guards go critical and cross the nuclear threshold. But it was a curious time in Iran, with Ahmadian predicting chaos that would usher in the return of the Mahdi and at least some part of the clerical theocracy buying into that political philosophy.

Troop activity on the western borders, read one mVillage message. Razavi opened the message and watched a video taken with a cell phone that clearly showed grainy images of jets taking off in the gathering darkness of dusk at an airbase somewhere in Iran.

Late night for the Supreme Leader, said another. The video embedded in that message, also shot with a cell phone, clearly showed Shahidi with an entourage entering a building somewhere in Tehran long after the sun had set.

Revolutionary Guards mobilizing, said a third, with the accompanying mobile video showing a montage of activity in and around the Guards' national headquarters.

Security tight around Kahrizak, said a fourth, with video showing troops mobilizing to fortify around the detention center in south Tehran that held many of the dissident leaders accused of fomenting the soft revolution.

It was enough, Razavi knew. The day he'd feared for some time had, in fact, arrived. Ahmadian and the Revolutionary Guards were making their move, and it would only be a matter of time before the Israelis responded. Perhaps they were on the move even as he viewed these messages through mVillage.

Razavi pulled out the portable keyboard he'd managed to secure from a friend and plugged his cell phone into it. There may have been no computers in the house, but he didn't need one. His mobile was more than enough to send a message out to his followers through mVillage. He would do so as a "friend of Razavi." But those who paid attention would know.

Be strong, Razavi began to type. We will face a test in the coming hours and days. We must remain firm in our commitment to usher in a new era of democracy. We must not respond foolishly, or in anger, as the world rushes again to our doorstep. . . .

09

LILONGWE, MALAWI

It always humored—and often exasperated—Nash that his father almost religiously refused to answer his cell phone. Nash had built a global public health empire around the use of mobile technology, yet he couldn't get his own father to answer a call—even when his dad had just left him a voice mail.

Yeah, he knew his dad was an ambassador for one of the United States' most important allies, but he could still take a call from one of his kids, for crying out loud.

Nash had tried his dad's cell several times

before arriving at his friend's house, then gave up. He finally excused himself, stepped outside the pastor's modest one-bedroom apartment, and called the after-hours number at the embassy. He eventually tracked down his dad's executive assistant.

"Cynthea, is my dad around?" Nash asked, trying not to let the exasperation he felt bleed through. "He sent me a text on my mobile."

"He's just finishing up a call."

"You're still in the office?" Nash asked, surprised. He glanced at his watch. It had to be almost midnight in Tokyo.

Cynthea sighed. "Yes, still here. Your father has been on the phone the entire evening."

Nash couldn't help himself. He was intrigued now and wondered why in the world his father would track him down in the middle of the night.

"What's up, Dad?" Nash asked when Cynthea finally connected him. "You called?"

There was a brief pause at the other end of the line. When Ethan Lee—Ambassador Lee to everyone but his kids and a few friends—finally answered, Nash could hear the exhaustion in his father's hoarse voice. He was obviously nearing the end of a very long day.

"I did call," his dad said. "By the way, where are you, anyway?"

Nash chuckled. Just like his dear old dad not to know where, exactly, his son was. "Lilongwe.

I'm testing a new project with the new diagnostic kit."

"Ah, the one you've been bench testing at UCLA," his dad said. "So you're taking it into the field?"

"That's right, Dad. Good for you." Nash laughed.

"Hey, I try to keep track of what you're up to," his dad said. "How's it look?"

Nash leaned up against the tree and glanced out over the gathering darkness of Malawi. He loved this country. He always returned to the warm heart of Africa whenever he could to test new parts of VHC.

This new project was revolutionary, and he'd wanted to get it right before rolling it out to hundreds of clinics. VHC had developed a mobile diagnostic kit that could take high-resolution images of blood work—at the point of care, anywhere in the world—and run analytics right there, on the spot. The mobile diagnostic kit, a cell phone, and a personal solar panel would allow a village health worker to estimate CD4 counts in order to titrate AIDS therapy or test for malaria or TB.

The entire mobile health system was a game-changer. NGOs previously had to roll expensive mobile clinics into remote and rural areas to test for such things. The new mobile VHC kits would be able to handle the same scenarios previously covered by the mobile clinics—at a cost of thousands of dollars per test—for just pennies.

Of course, Nash's non-profit company made no money on the new system. But that wasn't what mattered, as far as Nash was concerned. VHC was all about social innovation and solving global health problems. Spin-offs of the tech solutions more than covered the costs of doing good globally.

A good example was mVillage. Pieced together from multiple open-source systems and then wrapped together with some software development paid for by a foundation grant, mVillage had begun to eclipse Twitter and some of the other more popular social media tools in global use and bandwidth.

Nash knew, of course, that mVillage was just the new toy, and that something else would come along shortly to replace it, which was fine. He had no grand illusions of serving for very long as a tech industry titan straddling the world of media, finance, and technology. He was more than happy to do his thing and move on to the global public health pursuits that had gotten him involved with such things in the first place.

"The mobile diagnostic kit's going to work, big-time," Nash answered. "The first tests are confirming exactly what we'd hoped."

"You can get accurate CD4 readings, enough to estimate the right therapy?"

Nash grunted. So his dad had been paying

attention when he'd talked about this with him in past conversations. "Yep, we can."

"The pixel and image resolution is good enough?"

"It is. Depends on the cell phone, but the newer models work just fine."

"Any false positives?"

"None yet. We're keeping our fingers crossed."

"Good, good," his dad said. "Your kit is going to help millions out in the field. It sounds like you have something, then."

"I believe we do," Nash said. "Time will tell."

His dad paused. "But that's not why I called, though I'm always interested in what you're up to, of course."

"I know, Dad," Nash said, smiling to himself. "No worries. So tell me what's keeping you—and your staff—working at midnight there in Tokyo."

"Have you had a chance to monitor any of the mVillage traffic today?" his father asked.

"Not yet," Nash said. "I haven't checked with the staff in DC or London at all. I've been on a motorbike here in Malawi, going from village to village. I'm at a friend's house right now. Is something going on?"

"Actually, yes, there appears to be," his dad said. "My guess is there's an enormous spike in traffic in Iran. . . ."

Nash sighed. "You know I can't look up personal or confidential information," he said quickly. "That wouldn't be right."

"I'm not asking you to do that, or break any sort of confidences. But your staff analyzes traffic and trends and will be able to tell what's driving the spike."

"True. And the media produced in the system is generally available for everyone. . . ." Nash thought for a minute. It was a point-to-point peer system for MMS and SMS, but most of the users made their content available for others to distribute through the mVillage database out to mass media outlets on several aggregate Internet sites.

"Can you do me a favor, then?"

"Shoot."

"Can you check and see if you've gotten a post that's headed out to those public-facing community portals? Specifically, can you see if Reza Razavi has contributed anything yet to the mVillage community—"

Nash interrupted. "The ex-president in Iran who's now under house arrest, courtesy of the Revolutionary Guards? That Razavi?"

"You've heard?" his father asked, no trace of surprise in his voice.

Nash smiled. He wondered if his father had known. His dad seemed to know everything. But he doubted even his famous father would know the video of Razavi's house arrest had been sent to Nash's personal mVillage account, and from there to the world.

"Did you know that mobile video of his arrest

came to me first, and that I had it posted?"

"No, I didn't, but good for you," his father said. "It's not surprising, though. The only videos that ever make it out are coming through mVillage now. What I'm hoping is that Razavi still has a mobile with him—and the ability to reach out."

Nash glanced again at his watch. It was now too late for someone to be working in London, and too early for anyone in San Francisco. But he had a chance in DC. "Hang on. Let me text DC and see if I can find someone who can check the mVillage server."

Nash typed in the message and hit SEND. It always tickled him that he could connect with anyone from places like this, at any time of day. He got a return text seconds later. Someone was working in DC, and was checking. He waited half a minute and got a second text. Yes, Razavi had just posted a message to the mVillage servers, from a mobile he was obviously using at his house. The person in DC sent Nash the text, which he glanced at quickly.

"Razavi has sent something to the mVillage community portal." Nash scanned the words. "He talks about a coming test in the next few hours, and not responding foolishly."

"Good," his dad said. "That will help."

"It hasn't gone out yet to the community portals, but it will shortly. It will go out as a friend of Razavi's—not from Razavi himself. He seems to be masking the fact he can communicate directly through mVillage—for obvious reasons."

"Great. Glad to hear it."

"So what's he talking about? What test?"

"If you looked at the MMS videos coming out of Iran right now, you'd see them cataloguing military movement, Revolutionary Guards mobilization, heightened security, that sort of thing."

"Which means Iran's leadership has made the political decision to go nuclear?"

"Most likely."

"And Israel will respond," Nash said softly. He'd listened to his dad talk about global politics—and the way leaders in each nation shaped and fashioned the course of human events related to those politics—enough to know what was at stake.

One of his father's passions was Israel. Nash had never shared that passion—or abiding interest—in the fate of Israel on the world stage. He cared much more for the immediate needs of the people in Africa and developing nations. He had no time for a country like Israel, which had much going for it already.

In fact, he and his pastor friend had been engaged in a friendly, but heated, discussion about that very topic this evening. His friend had taken the position that global events were moving rapidly in a direction that placed Israel in the midst of many enemies, and that biblical prophecies centered on Israel were starting to make a great deal of sense.

Nash had never paid much attention to biblical prophecy. His own Christian faith led him much more in the direction of social justice and helping the poor. Events on the world stage held little interest for him—which was odd, considering what his father did for a living and the household he'd grown up in.

To Nash, Israel was a special country with quite a heritage and an uncanny knack for defending itself in the middle of a very dangerous region. But, he'd argued, it was not more special than or different from any other developed country. Nash had argued with his friend that evening that there simply had to be a better way to deal with Israel's enemies, and that none of it had anything to do with biblical prophecy. Nash and his pastor friend often argued about this point.

"Yes, Israel will respond, sooner rather than later," his dad said. "There's no question about that, in my opinion. Depending on their success, how certain nations and leaders respond following that action is what will matter."

Nash nodded to himself. "Got it. So you said there were two things?"

"Yes, well, I'm actually looking several steps beyond what might or might not be happening in Iran right now or the next couple of days," his dad said. "If Israel does act, the world will be riveted on that action, even if it's only partially successful. They'll be watching the Revolutionary Guards' next steps with the nuclear question, the response from Iran's surrogates, like Hezbollah . . . that sort of thing."

"But you're not so much interested in that, are you?" Nash asked. He knew the way his father thought.

"No, I'm not," his dad said. "I'm much, much more interested in what the next line players will do—especially North Korea, because they can act right now."

Nash knew, immediately, what his father was really looking for. He didn't even need to hear the question, because he could guess the direction his father was headed.

While Nash had never thought much about Israel, he did have a deep, abiding interest in another country—North Korea, the most secretive totalitarian regime on the planet. His fiancée was the daughter of a past president of South Korea, under the United New Democratic Party that had merged with the Democratic Party to become the United Democratic Party. They were now the opposition party to the more conservative Grand National Party in power.

Nash had met the girl he planned to marry at Harvard. Kim Su Yeong had grown up in the shadow of North Korea. Su and Nash had talked for hours and hours about the highly secretive, paranoid government in North Korea.

After Harvard, Su had gone to work at the State Department in the Camara administration. She logged a lot of hours during the day for the Korean desk, while she went to law school at night at Georgetown. Now Su was almost finished with school.

The two of them talked via Skype constantly. Nash hated that he had to travel as much as he did, but it was the cost of doing business.

"You know our mVillage network is only just beginning in North Korea," he said. "They've blitzed and re-blitzed the cell networks there. They've thrown everything they have at it to block any sort of communications in and out of the country."

"But I'm guessing they haven't been completely successful in blocking everything, have they?" his dad asked.

"No, in fact, they haven't. They tried targeting individual SIM cards to get at sources of MMS and SMS texts. But a black market of inter-changeable SIM cards with topped-off community accounts solved that problem. SIM cards are being passed around, along with cell phones. People are communicating. An mVillage net-work is starting to form. North Korea's only choice will be to completely shut down the state cell network—which is something it doesn't want to do."

"So there is an mVillage network database, one that feeds the community portals?"

"Yes. And we've been told the folks in Pyongyang pay really, really close attention to the mVillage community portals."

"I'll bet," his dad added sardonically. "Can you ask your staff to check on something? I know you can't look at any one individual, but we've heard that MMS reports have made their way out of all five of the major political prison camps in the country."

"Yes, that's true," Nash said quickly. "I was shocked when I first heard about it. I didn't think it was possible. But we just got a report out of Camp 14, where people work until they die. I was stunned that an MMS video of working conditions made its way out of there and to the community portals. I can only imagine what must have happened after that."

"So you've gotten reports from all five—including Camp 16, near Chongjin?"

"Yes, I'm certain. We've gotten reports to mVillage from all five."

"Wow," his dad said. "I'm amazed."

"So are you looking for anything specific from Camp 16?"

"Eventually," his dad said. "Camp 16 is where they send purged government officials and others. We've heard, very recently, that some interesting folks were just shipped there."

"Like?"

"Like the lead negotiator we've been trying to deal with, unsuccessfully, on their nuclear program. I guess they didn't like how soft he was becoming in his discussions with us."

"Wow."

"And the number two from the National Defense Commission, who tried to block the third son's succession to the Dear Leader's position."

"Wow, again."

"So we're looking for anything from Camp 16. Anything at all."

"Hang on," Nash said. He fired off another text, then waited. The answer came back a minute later. "Nope, nothing from Camp 16, not in a while."

"But you'll let me know right away if you hear anything?"

"Absolutely. No worries."

"And you're being careful out there in Africa, right?"

"You bet. Always," Nash said.

As Nash ended the call to his father, he couldn't help but wonder which direction things might turn. He'd have to check in with Su later, as well as the mVillage portals. It sounded like the world was in for a wild ride in the next few days. Nash was personally more interested in the Korean aspect of it all, but he couldn't help but wonder what might happen to Israel in the coming days.

10

MOSCOW, RUSSIA

It always amused him. The sycophants and hangers-on who trailed in his wake seemed perpetually worried—so sure his next adventure would be his last.

But they worried needlessly. His time was far from over. There was still much to do, places to see, and mountains to climb. Plus, what was life without great risk and great reward?

When Andrei Rowan had taken a mini-sub to the bottom of the world's deepest lake to tag a whale, his aides were certain that, somehow, the sub would malfunction, and he would be trapped at the bottom of Lake Baikal. When he'd embraced a tiger or flown one of Russia's bombers himself, they were certain each adventure would end badly.

"There is still much work to be done on earth," he was fond of saying.

What no one ever seemed to grasp was that the people demanded a level of risk and vision in their leaders. With great power came great expectations —and Rowan's many adventures in the world reinforced an image he'd carefully crafted on his rise to power as the prime minister and chairman of the United Russia Party.

Rowan lived with the certain, unwavering belief that the collapse of the People's Republic of the Soviet Union was the single most tragic event of the twentieth century—greater, even, than the slaughter of six million Jews in the Second World War or the beginning of the atomic era with the explosion of nuclear weapons in Japan at the end of that war. He believed with that same certainty that it was his destiny to return Russia to its rightful place in the world, and he lived every aspect of his personal and political life with that in mind.

Most people in Russia never gave any thought to their country's place in the world order. Few cared for the rule of principalities and powers or the interplay of nation-states. They were content to see bread on the table and a roof over their head. But Rowan thought of nothing else. He would not rest until Russia straddled the world again as it had under the former Soviet Union. And near the top of Russia's list was oil. Rowan was willing to pursue it, from Iran to Israel if need be.

While he rarely spoke of it, Rowan thought often of the great calling and mission of Lenin. The people of Russia had all but forgotten what Lenin had achieved in his time—what he had done for his countrymen and his fight to establish a governing principle for the rights of common men and women.

The West always underestimated Rowan—the lieutenant colonel in the KGB who'd been rescued from obscurity by Boris Yeltsin. They thought less of him when he rode bare-chested on a horse while vacationing or dressed all in black to ride, helmetless, with the Night Wolves through the streets of St. Petersburg.

But Rowan had learned much from Lenin, who had lost his humanity in his tireless, brilliant pursuit of revolution. Lenin had led the people of Russia out of the wilderness. He'd been utterly committed to revolution and had demanded equal obedience from others to that cause.

In the process of his servitude, though, Lenin had almost written himself out of the hearts of the people. They knew Lenin as the figure at the helm of the revolution—not as a great, human leader who could relate to their dreams, their visions, and their hopes for a better future.

Rowan would not make that same mistake. He was every bit as committed to the ideals carried by Lenin—and, later, by Stalin—but he would never make the fatal mistakes they'd made. History condemns those who do not learn from its mistakes. Rowan had studied, and learned, from those mistakes.

Making oneself human and open to risk was necessary in the pursuit of the people's support for a leader, he believed. Would they trust a man who hid behind bulletproof glass walls, with guards armed to the teeth to protect their leader? Or would they follow a man who was unafraid to take personal risk in order to see and touch the world? The answer, to Rowan, was obvious.

There was a knock on the door. Rowan looked up from the desk in his private study, where he had been meticulously poring over reports from two of Russia's principal intelligence agencies—the GRU and the SVR. As always, he'd spent considerably more time with the SVR reports, which he instinctively trusted. He'd learned, long ago, that it made sense to demand both a report at the close of the day and then a new round of reports at the start of the day to reflect what had occurred elsewhere in the world while Russia slept. It drove the intelligence agencies insane, but he slept better with this system of reporting.

"Come in," Rowan said loudly.

His top aide, Nicolai Petrov, leaned in through the doorway. "I just thought you would want to know that the activity has begun," he said softly.

"Yes, I know," Rowan said, glancing down at the SVR report he'd just been studying. "It appears that our friends in Tehran have progressed."

"And Israel is about to act," Petrov answered, nodding.

"Are we ready? Have you told the leaders in Duma of the events?"

"Yes, Mr. Prime Minister, I have informed them. They are ready to accept you in the morning."

"And do we know what we are going to tell the Duma in the morning?" Rowan asked.

Petrov nodded once and returned a level gaze at the man who would fill the shoes of Lenin and Stalin. "That it is an historic moment for Russia, that we must not miss this opportunity, that in times of chaos and turmoil, the cause of the revolution can be furthered."

"Or something to that effect," Rowan said, smiling easily.

"Yes, something to that effect," his aide said. "I am certain you will find the appropriate words for the leaders in Duma—as you always do."

Rowan cocked his head to one side. "And, Mr. Petrov, do you believe that?"

"Which, Mr. Prime Minister? That you will find the words to soothe and direct the leaders of Duma, or that out of chaos a greater, stronger Russia will emerge?"

"The second, Mr. Petrov," he answered smoothly. "There can be no doubt of the first proposition."

In fact, Petrov had long thought of what a day such as today would mean to Russia. He did believe that Andrei Rowan was right about the opportunity it presented to Moscow. "Without question, Mr. Prime Minister, it is an opportunity."

"A chance to begin to correct one of the great wrongs of the twentieth century," Rowan said.

"Yes, a great chance."

"It is the return of the great cause of revolution, on a world stage," Rowan said quietly. "The West has given us this chance, at long last. We must not let it pass us by."

"We will not, Mr. Prime Minister."

"No, we will not, Mr. Petrov. History will judge us badly otherwise."

11

WEST OF THE EUPHRATES RIVER NEAR AL HILLAH, IRAQ

"Identify yourself!" the voice commanded.

Israeli Air Force pilot Ben Azoulay reached over to the F-117's controls and turned the knob to the right to decrease the volume on his headset. He was surprised that, in fact, it had taken the U.S. bases this long to spot him over Iraqi airspace. After all, it was their own Stealth fighter, created by their own military-industrial complex.

Still, it had been the best Stealth fighter for a generation. The Russians and Chinese, especially, had thrown everything they had at systems to detect the ugly, black plane in the sky. Unless you had some idea where the plane was in the sky, you had no hope of spotting it.

"I said, identify yourself!" the voice barked again.

Ben was almost to the Euphrates. From there, he would follow the river southeast, almost to Kuwait, and then move into Iran near Khuzestan. He didn't dare go farther south, over the water of the Persian Gulf. There were too many threats there. He needed to make the straight shot into Iran from Iraq's southeast border, then head toward Shiraz.

Ben had been coached and coached on what to do in this scenario. IAF leadership had determined that they were going to take the most direct route to Iran, and risk action by either Jordan or the U.S. if they were detected. They would ask for permission after the fact.

Jordan had been no problem. He was in and out of Jordan's airspace in almost the blink of an eye. But Iraq? That was a different matter, and Ben had been certain he would encounter something, at some point.

"This is Bandit 1," Ben said finally. "We're on a friendly training mission."

Ben waited for several long seconds. He glanced to either side, then down at the ground. The night air was clear. Ben could see for miles in all directions. He kept his eyes peeled for the telltale signature signs of either a plane chasing him or a surface-to-air missile starting its chase. He saw neither.

The voice came back on. "Do you mean IAF Bandit 1?"

"Yes, IAF Bandit 1," Ben said, smiling to himself. He was Bandit 1 in Israel. But there was an *American* Bandit 1 somewhere—and the U.S. side wasn't too keen on having two Bandit 1s flying around on the plane they'd built for their own pilots.

"You said you're on a friendly training mission?" the voice asked.

"Yes, that's right. I will be out of your area soon."

There was another pause. "You're solo?"

"Yes, I'm solo."

"Where are the other IAF Bandits? The same training mission?"

Ben knew he had to be careful here. He was instructed not to lie—but to remain firm in his own situation. "I am solo. I do not know the status of the other IAF Bandits."

"Are they in your area?"

"No," Ben answered. "I do not believe they are in my area."

"Do you wish an escort?" the voice asked after another pause.

"I don't believe that's necessary," Ben answered. "I'll be gone from your area soon."

Which was true, of course. At the speed he was traveling, he'd be out of Iraqi airspace shortly— and headed toward his target.

There was a very long period of silence as the

F-117 hurtled through the night sky. He could see the outline of the Euphrates just ahead. Ben could imagine what was happening on the ground, wherever the voice came from. They were probably racing through all sorts of protocols. Ben hoped they arrived at the right answer.

"We don't have a training mission logged," the voice said finally. "Why is that?"

Ben answered immediately, with the script. "Sorry about that. We all got yanked out of our beds for a mock, surprise exercise. None of us knew about it. We were just told to scramble, in real time, as a test."

"A test?"

"Yes, sir. A test. Just to see how quickly we could get up and out. In case we had to."

By now, Ben was certain they knew where he was, his rate of speed, and his direction. They also probably knew he was carrying a payload. If they knew that one of those bomb bays carried a tactical nuclear weapon, they might have reacted a little differently. But even with that information, they'd still have a tough time shooting him out of the sky—if, of course, they decided they needed to do that.

"You said you'd be gone from the area soon," the voice said. "What's your destination?"

Again, Ben followed his script. "I'm to meet up with others in Kuwait, re-fuel, and then head back."

After the last, final pause—during which someone obviously made a decision—the voice came back online. "All right, IAF Bandit 1. You're clear. We will not engage. Good hunting."

"Thank you, sir. Appreciate it."

Ben turned to head southeast as he came across the Euphrates. Even now, at night, he could see the great river had all but dried up in parts. A sustained drought had created long patches of dry land throughout the course of the river.

Ben wondered how the other IAF bandits were faring in their missions. They were all consigned to radio silence until they'd hit their targets. The IAF leadership had not wanted to risk a breach, so all of the pilots were flying on their own, with pre-set missions and computer controls.

There were a handful of critical missions. One was at Natanz, where the first of Iran's centrifuges had been installed for uranium enrichment. The Mossad believed that, in fact, Natanz had been designed to draw the attention of the IAEA inspectors, and that it had never truly been designed for mass production of highly enriched uranium. Nevertheless, it was a high-priority target just in case.

A second target was a uranium conversion facility near Isfahan where gas for the uranium-enrichment process was stored in tunnels. The IAF believed that conventional bunker-busting payloads would destroy those tunnels and everything stored in them.

A third target was the heavy water reactor at Arak. This was a difficult target, especially since the Russians had moved in to secure it. The site was designed to produce enough plutonium for a weapon. HEU was an older technology and easier to produce. But plutonium was the way most modern nuclear weapons were produced, and Iran was intent on finding a path to the production of enough plutonium to arm a nuclear weapon.

A fourth was headed to the reactor at Bushehr, on the coastline of the Persian Gulf waters. Ben knew at least one other Bandit was flying near him, on his way to that site.

A fifth was at the enrichment facility run by the Guards near Qom that Iran had kept secret for years.

Ben's mission, though, was by far the most critical. His F-117 was targeted on the covert, underground site near the Guards' missile plant at Shiraz, where the U.S. drone had detected the massive amounts of uranium hexafluoride in the atmosphere above the site.

The site, south of Shiraz and near Fasa, contained tens of thousands of gas centrifuges, in full production, according to a human intelligence source the Mossad had worked inside over the previous years. Now that Iran had made the political decision to move into production, this site became the only one that mattered for the near future.

The problem was that the site had been secured under nearly one hundred feet of concrete and rock. It was virtually untouchable with even the most sophisticated conventional bombs.

Ben's F-117 was equipped with two sets of weapons. The first set contained conventional, laser-guided bombs. The second set contained nuclear-tipped missiles, with a kiloton yield. That yield was considerably smaller than the nuclear weapon that had exploded at Hiroshima in World War II, but they were still nuclear weapons.

The tactical nuclear-tipped bomb, if it worked properly, would explode well underground, with very little radioactive fallout. Still, for those looking down from satellites, there would be enough of a signature to hazard a guess as to what had just happened.

As Ben neared the end of the Euphrates and Khuzestan, he instinctively gripped the controls a little harder. The next few minutes, though, passed uneventfully. He knew from his pre-mission training that the reactor at Bushehr was likely under attack right now, drawing the Iran air-defense system away from him. As he crossed the border into Iran, he was relieved to see that nothing was showing up on any of his instruments.

As he neared his target, he flew west and then south of Shiraz to avoid even possible visual sighting from anyone on the ground.

The target was inconspicuous—just a few one-story buildings spread apart over about an acre. But Ben knew that underneath the buildings were a series of tunnels that worked their way down to a facility large enough to contain tens of thousands of centrifuges.

Ben released his conventional, laser-guided payload first. There was no sound inside the cockpit as it fell to earth, and no discernible sound as it struck. But an instant later, Ben spotted the puffs of dirt cloud kicked up by the strike.

He banked and then returned to deliver the second, final payload. Ben would have no way of knowing the success or failure, once he'd dropped the final weapons from his bomb bay.

After releasing them, he pulled away from the site rapidly. He thought he detected a muffled blast and looked down at the site. All of the buildings on top of the site suddenly collapsed in an immediate pile of rubble.

Ben pushed the plane to almost six hundred miles an hour and climbed to thirty-five thousand feet as quickly as he could. Based on the damage he'd been able to see firsthand above ground, he was fairly certain he'd succeeded in destroying whatever was beneath those buildings. Others, though, would judge the ultimate success of his mission—and, more importantly, what might happen next.

12

SOUTH OF THE LITANI RIVER
LEBANON

The young teenage boy flipped through the dog-eared pages of the cheap novel again, as he had for weeks on end. He loved the book. It gave him great comfort in a confusing world. Many of his friends had read the book. It was hugely popular among the masses of people who moved in and around the highly secret compound his family called home.

The book had just one picture—of a fat, olive-skinned man with a dark beard, an ugly, mis-shapen nose, and a blind right eye. The man—the Dajjal—stared out at the readers of the book with a leering confidence. He seemed like evil incarnate to the young boy.

The flowery Arabic script within the book moved along quickly. It told the story of a coming age in which the Jewish Dajjal—the Antichrist—would rise somewhere in either Iraq or Syria and rule for a time. Then it spoke of the coming of Issa, who would defeat the Dajjal and usher in the age of Islam throughout the world.

Stories of the Dajjal showed up like the old

cheap, dime-store novels about the American West in bazaars and outdoor malls all throughout the Middle East. The young boy had seen many such books, all with the same fat, leering Jew who would someday rise up from the lands of Iraq or Syria to take control of some shadowy Western army—only to be defeated at the hands of the triumphant forces of Islam.

But Ali Nouradeen wasn't just any young, impressionable teenager, curious about the politics of the world in which he lived. His father, Sa'id Nouradeen, was the secretary general of the Lebanese Islamist Party.

But, more than that, Ali knew from all the stories he'd heard for years, his father was the only Islam leader to defeat the Israelis on the field of battle. His father had led the victorious Hezbollah forces that had defeated Israel's ground troops and caused them to flee from southern Lebanon.

Ali believed his father was the man of destiny for Islam and would, someday, be central to the armed forces that would rise up to defeat the Dajjal, the Jewish Antichrist supported by the morally corrupt powers of the West.

Ali hoped to be part of that destiny, but his father was hesitant to bring the family into the struggle. The Israelis had murdered his older brother, Abdul Nouradeen, years ago, when Ali was just a young boy. He could still see the pain in his father's face when Abdul's name came up in conversation. Ali knew that his father would avenge his brother's death one day.

The killing of the eldest Nouradeen boy had compelled his family to move to a highly secure compound south of the Litani River in southern Lebanon. Friends and supporters had bought up much of the land south of the Litani after prolonged battles with the Israelis had rendered the area a perpetual war zone.

But the Nouradeen family members were welcomed throughout the lands in southern Lebanon as conquering heroes, and they were able to travel safely throughout the region. Ali had grown up surrounded by supportive families.

Ali closed the book and looked up at his father, who had been unusually pensive this morning. "Tell me the story of the Dajjal again, Father, and how we will defeat him one day," Ali said. He never tired of hearing his father's mellifluous voice, which could weave tales of wonder and awe on almost any subject under the sun.

Sa'id Nouradeen sighed. He had many things on his mind this morning. "Not now, Ali," he told his son. He was weary. He had been up all night, monitoring the reports.

"Please, Father," Ali begged, "there are parts of the book that you can help me understand."

The phone attached to Sa'id's belt rang, saving him from any further pleading. Sa'id glanced at his son, told him to be quiet, then answered the

Iridium 9555 phone. For years, he'd been forced to communicate with his network in person, without the use of phones. But Russian and North Korean scientists had taught them how to safely communicate via secure lines, and they cautiously stayed in touch. Still, they were always careful with their words and only confirmed what would otherwise be known. He always assumed the NSA was listening. When they needed to discuss anything secure, his network still did so in person.

Ali was an inquisitive, talented youth, Sa'id knew. Under usual circumstances, he enjoyed casual political banter with his youngest son about the Dajjal, the Mahdi, and such things. But today was not usual, and he could not afford to be distracted.

"Yes," Sa'id said, speaking softly into the satellite phone that served as his secure lifeline to a far-flung global network. He moved into the next room, out of earshot. "Remember that we are likely being recorded on this call. Mind your words."

"I understand. But I wanted to inform you that it is confirmed," said the voice at the other end of the phone call.

"They destroyed the entire compound near Fasa, at Shiraz?" Sa'id asked.

"Yes, all of it. There is nothing left but a pile of rubble above ground."

"They were able to get inside the concrete?"

125

"Yes, they opened tunnels, and then used a very large bomb to finish the job."

"So they used a tactical nuclear weapon?"

"It appears so. We won't know for sure for a little while."

"Is there any usable uranium left?"

"Not from Fasa. We needed several more days of work there."

Sa'id Nouradeen was quiet for a moment. "And the other sites—did we get what we needed from any of those sites?" he said finally.

The voice on the other end of the line hesitated. "Yes, we did obtain some from a second site, before the attack. It is being loaded onto a truck."

"Will it be enough?"

"It will be enough."

They both knew what that meant and did not need to elaborate for the benefit of NSA ears.

Sa'id nodded to himself. "So it will be a question of what they wish to do in Tehran."

"I believe we will get what we need," the other person said. "And we will strike back. We must."

"Even though it may not make it to Israel," Sa'id said. "Perhaps. We shall see. We must be prepared for other contingencies."

Iran's Revolutionary Guards had shown the Shahab 3 missile to the world in the fall of 1998, at a ceremony in Azadi Square in Tehran. More than half a dozen test flights had been conducted since then. Most of the tests had been failures, with mid-air explosions the end result.

But in recent months, with North Korea's help, the missile's power and accuracy had been vastly improved. It could reach Israel from Iran—barely. Whether it could, in fact, make it through Israel's emerging third-generation Arrow air-defense system was an open question—one that would apparently be answered shortly.

"You know, we might be better served to let you deploy there," his contact said at the other end.

"Without question," Sa'id answered. "We would ensure success."

But the Revolutionary Guards and Iran's leadership had said for years that they would retaliate against an attack by Israel with the Shahab 3. *So attempt to retaliate they must,* Sa'id reasoned. Anything short of that would show weakness at this crucial juncture in history.

"So what will you do?" his contact asked.

"Nothing yet," Sa'id answered. "But we will act quickly—when it is time. Let us see what Tehran decides, and the success of the mission they choose."

"And if it does not make it through the Israeli defenses?"

"Do not worry," Sa'id said, his voice full of confidence. "There is much that we have prepared, and much we can do. Israel will taste our revenge."

"Such as?" His contact, as always, was impatient.

He demanded action, as well as loyalty, from those who had joined the cause.

"Patience, my friend," Sa'id answered. "And remember that our enemy is always listening. All in time. Let us see what we will see today. And then tomorrow will bring another effort. We will continue until we have succeeded."

Sa'id Nouradeen hung up and replaced the Iridium 9555. He walked back into the room where his son was still studying the book about the Dajjal.

"I must leave for a time," he said to Ali. "Tell your mother not to worry."

"Where are you going?" Ali asked. "Can I come with you?"

"Not today," his father said, smiling at his young son's eagerness. "Another time. I have many people to see today. There is much to be done."

He strode from his family's compound, purpose evident in every step. There *was* much to be done on this day—the day that he and others had anticipated for years. When Israel had attacked the nuclear facility in Iraq—and in Syria more recently—the world had not reacted. But they would react this time to the attack in Iran. And Sa'id wanted to be ready when his own time to act arrived.

13

LILONGWE, MALAWI

Nash had been able to sleep for only a couple of hours. The sun was just coming up on the horizon. As much as he liked to do his own thing, he couldn't help himself. His father's world—and interests—had pulled him in. He'd logged onto his mVillage account from the guest house at the private hospital on the outskirts of Lilongwe. He'd read every piece of traffic through mVillage that was coming out of Iran. It was all unbelievable.

The moderate opposition movement in Iran was going crazy. They'd known, almost from the minute the Revolutionary Guards had moved into high gear on the nuclear HEU question, what was going on—and had reported it frantically to the world through mVillage. Their reports were absolutely dead-on accurate, from what Nash could see.

The reports tracked the movements of the two Revolutionary Guards leaders who acted almost autonomously—Ali Zhubin, the overall commander of the IRGC, the Army of the Guardians of the Iranian Revolution, and Hussein Bahadur, who

129

commanded the IRGC's air force and missile command.

Zhubin was Iran's master of asymmetrical warfare. He was close to the conservative clerics who ran the country and was influenced only by them. Bahadur was known for his successful ability to recruit fanatical loyalists to IRGC and the cleric leaders. Those two alone made the key military decisions, and spoke for the clerics, which was why the opposition tracked their actions closely.

Both Bahadur and Zhubin had threatened for years to respond immediately to an attack of its nuclear facilities with the launch of nuclear-tipped Shahab 3 missiles at Israel and U.S. ships, and efforts to shut down oil traffic through the Strait of Hormuz. Much of the world's oil flowed through this narrow passage. Iran controlled the north side of the Strait and had always threatened to exert military control over the world's oil if provoked. Even now, some of the mVillage reports were beginning to track Bahadur and Zhubin and focusing on what might happen next.

In just the past two hours, the mVillage system had doubled back on itself as reports of the Israeli Stealth attacks had begun to sweep across the countryside. The people in Iran were waking up to a nightmare scenario. Israel's planes had hit at least a dozen targets, from what Nash could see in the mVillage reports. They'd hit all the big ones—Isfahan, Bushehr, Arak, Natanz.

Amazingly, contributors to the mVillage network had already uploaded unclassified satellite images to Google Earth of the before and after pictures of well-known sites like Isfahan. It appeared that GBU-28, deep-penetration, bunker-busting bombs had done considerable damage at all of the well-known sites. There were no reports about use of tactical nuclear weapons.

The Google Earth pictures—obviously obtained from some country's military leaders—revealed that the tunnels had all been caved in, which meant the GBU-28 bombs had done their jobs. All of the buildings above ground at these sites were now piles of rubble.

Nash studied the Isfahan site, where Iran had been processing uranium and had secured a storage facility beneath a mountain. Google Earth pictures from just a few years ago clearly showed no buildings of any significance above ground. But by 2006, two tunnels had been built from several new buildings. Now, after the Israeli attacks, those buildings were gone, and the tunnels had caved in.

The site at Natanz was even more telling. Several years ago, Google Earth photos showed a few outbuildings. But then Iran had built underground cascade halls, covered by concrete, and co-located a pilot fuel-enrichment plant. The IAF planes had thoroughly destroyed the enrichment plant, and the cascade halls had fallen in on themselves. The centrifuges stored below that concrete were now trapped or covered in piles of rubble.

Other sites circulated by Google Earth links through mVillage were showing similar levels of devastation. The IAF planes had done a thorough job. Nash was amazed they'd been able to fly in under the cover of darkness to so many locations, and then get out. It was clear to Nash they'd been planning these strikes for some time.

They'd also hit sites the world had not known or cared about as well, places Nash did not recognize. He could only assume these were covert military sites that intelligence sources had targeted.

One of them, near Shiraz, was attracting a few posts, speculating that the destruction there was much more extensive than other sites. But no one knew much about the facility—in fact, it had never shown up on a single unclassified report as a possible site for nuclear activity—so there wasn't much to go on beyond speculation.

There were also no reports—at all—of any downed Israeli planes. Somehow, miraculously, the IAF planes had managed to fly into Iran without detection, drop their payloads, and then leave. The posts were evenly split—with half attributing it to the IAF's air superiority, and the other half to God's protection of the Jewish people. A few mVillage reports were already starting to speculate that the IAF had somehow gotten their hands on

Stealth technology and Stealth planes. At this point, there were only rumors.

As the young CEO of VHC—which ran mVillage—Nash had a unique view of everything coursing through the mVillage system. Reports were coming in quickly from all parts of Iran. Thousands and thousands of reports entered the mVillage system from everywhere.

Since it was impossible for the Revolutionary Guards or the clerics who ultimately ran the country to shut down the traffic, Nash wondered if, perhaps, they would eventually go after the hardware behind mVillage. But Nash's systems engineers had long ago cut a deal with Google and had embedded everything deep within their highly secretive cloud-computing network that spanned the globe. Google's cloud was virtually impervious to attacks because its whole was made up of the sum of its parts. There was no killing that system, short of some sort of global government con-spiracy.

So if Iran's Revolutionary Guards could not shut down the hardware or end mobile coverage in the country, then their last resort was to target well-known people who were on the mVillage network and prosecute them.

But history said this wouldn't work, either. After Ahmadian had stolen the past presidential election, the moderate opposition in Iran had not been intimidated and had not backed off.

When IRGC put nearly one hundred of its leaders on trial—in front of a hard-line cleric newly appointed as the head of the judiciary system—and then sentenced all of them to prison, they had not backed off. If anything, the traffic on mVillage only increased after both events. And when the clerics ordered two dozen of the opposition leaders hanged as "drug traffickers," the mVillage reports also did not cease.

Nash's mobile buzzed. He glanced at it. It was his dad again. Nash wondered if he'd worked through the night. "Hey, Dad. What's up? Have you gotten any sleep yet?"

His father ignored the question. "I assume you've seen all the reports out of Iran?"

"Yeah, I've been up most of the night reading through the mVillage reports on the portals."

"Anything about the attacks yet south of Shiraz, near Fasa?"

Nash remembered the few posts he'd seen. "A few, wondering about the extent of the damage. But no one seems to know much."

"I see," his father said. "Well, stay tuned. There will be more."

Nash knew enough not to ask his father more questions about this. "So what's your guess on Iran's response?"

"That's why I'm calling."

"I'm not sure there's much I can do from here in Lilongwe."

"There is, though. Remember when I asked you to check and see if Razavi was posting anything?"

"Yeah. His post from 'a friend of Razavi' started showing up on the community portals early in the morning."

"Good. I'm glad to hear it. So . . . can you send him a text back, just from you?"

Nash sat up straighter at his desk. "You're looking for back-channel discussions into Iran?"

"We *all* are right now, Nash, at every level," his father said quietly. "The next twenty-four hours will be critical. None of us know who will be making the decisions. It could be their Guardian Council, or the Supreme Leader consulting with a few of the clerics, or Ahmadian. Or, heaven forbid, the Revolutionary Guards. If Zhubin and Bahadur get their way, we're in trouble."

"If it's the Guards, then they're—"

"Yes," his father said quickly. "They're likely to retaliate with a medium-range missile, armed with a nuclear warhead—one that can reach Israel."

"That's assuming Israel didn't take all of the HEU out of the system. I've looked at the Google Earth pictures circulating through mVillage. The damage was pretty extensive."

His father sighed. "There's no way they could have taken it all out of the system. Absolutely no way. They slowed Iran down, perhaps for a few years. But they didn't stop them."

"So that's a problem?"

"Yes, a problem . . . which is why I need your help with Razavi."

"He won't know who I am," Nash said. "Why would he respond to my text?"

"He might not. But it won't take him long to figure out who you are, with your last name and the position you have with VHC and mVillage."

"And why would he trust the text if it came from me, and not someone inside Iran's government?"

"He won't, necessarily," his father said. "But we have to try. If he responds, he might be able to help. If he doesn't respond, then there's no harm in having tried. We're trying to get to everyone inside Iran as quickly as we can."

"And there's no other way to Razavi?"

He could almost see his father shaking his head at the other end of the line. "No, there's not. The IRGC has him under very tight house arrest. They can't afford to throw him into prison—not yet. But no one is getting in to see him, and they've pulled all of the computers from his house. Obviously, they don't know about his mobile yet. Which is why you can get to him."

"Okay," Nash said. "I'll give it a shot. What do I say?"

"Tell him he has to get to the moderate clerics around the Supreme Leader."

"The Supreme Leader—you mean Amir Shahidi?" Nash interrupted.

"Yes, Shahidi. We know he has questions about Ahmadian. He's had them for some time now. Tell Razavi that he probably has only a few hours, at best. The Revolutionary Guards, Ahmadian, the Guardian Council—there isn't time. He has to get to some of the moderate clerics who can talk to Shahidi. He has to make the case."

"Anyone in particular he should try to get to? Is there anyone Shahidi will listen to?"

"Yes, urge Razavi to try to get to Ayatollah Ahura Ehsan."

"I haven't heard of him."

"Most of the West hasn't. He's a senior cleric. He's consistently said publicly that Iran is not a threat and is willing to engage in direct talks with the U.S. He always maintains that Iran's actions are defensive, not offensive, and that they don't wish a war with Israel. But he's also conservative enough to earn Shahidi's trust, and has said that Iran will launch a retaliatory strike if it has to."

"So if he's in favor of a retaliatory strike . . . ?"

"He has to say that publicly. It's the only way he can stay credible. But he may be our only hope, if Razavi can get to him."

"And if he does, what does Razavi tell him?"

"That they cannot, under any circumstances, launch the Shahab 3 as retaliation. We'll deal with the Strait of Hormuz ourselves," his father said. "They have to give the United States more time to deal with this, with the world community.

We will organize sanctions against Israel—"

"The U.S. has never done that," Nash said quickly.

"We will now. We have no choice. If we don't act, others will. If just one Shahab 3 makes it through, none of us want to consider what happens next." His father paused. "Nash, I can't emphasize this enough. I'm not big on end-of-the-world scenarios, but if a nuclear weapon lands in Israel, it will set things in motion that we can't reverse."

"Okay, got it," Nash said. "So I'm delivering the message to Razavi that he has to get someone like Ayatollah Ehsan to weigh in with Shahidi on the missile."

"They have to keep the Guards from launching that missile. We don't have much time. The U.S. will intervene on Iran's behalf, in some fashion. But we have to keep that missile out of the air. If it launches, everything changes."

"Okay." Nash was already thumbing through his iPhone's directory. "I'll try. But you know this is a long shot."

"I know." His father's voice was grave. "But we're trying everything we know. We have to do what we can to keep Iran from launching that missile."

"And if they launch it?"

"First things first," his father answered. "I'm always hopeful that rational actors will emerge in times like this."

14

WASHINGTON, DC

Anshel couldn't believe it had only been twenty-four hours since he'd taken the call from the deputy head of the Mossad. The world had changed in those twenty-four hours.

They'd held briefings at the Pentagon, the Capitol, and the situation room almost around the clock. They'd sent more than a dozen stern messages to the Israelis. None of it had worked. Israel had gone ahead with the attacks. And now the various heads of state were starting to react in both predictable and irrational ways.

Anshel had been in and out of the Oval Office so many times in the past twenty-four hours that he'd hard-wired the path in his brain. He could probably make the trip with his eyes closed at this point.

The U.S. media was just now waking up to the story that Anshel had known was about to break from the moment he'd read about the drone's finding of highly elevated uranium hexafluoride in the atmosphere above a covert site south of Shiraz in Iran.

He looked up from his desk. He'd been there

since five o'clock that morning, poring over the scattered intelligence reports from around the world.

"You've been here all night?" DJ asked, leaning up against the doorway. Only his head actually entered the room. His own tie was slightly askew, and his eyes were every bit as red as Anshel's.

"Just about," he answered.

DJ glanced around the room. "No kids with you this morning?"

"Not today. Way too much going on."

DJ nodded, taking a tentative step into the office. DJ was one of the few aides on the White House staff who did not live in mortal fear of Dr. Gould. Other aides tended to arrive at Anshel's office in the safety of a group. Not DJ. He preferred wading right into problems headfirst. That's why Anshel respected him.

"Um, so . . . I was wondering," he said, easing into the conversation.

Anshel looked up again. "So you're not here on a social visit? You have something on your mind?"

"Yes, I do," DJ said firmly.

"And?"

"And . . . I was wondering how it is that Israel was able to fly in, bomb more than a dozen sites overnight, and get out without a single plane detected."

Anshel almost smiled. "You don't think their F-15s and F-16s are up to that fight?"

"They're up to a fight," DJ answered. "Just not *that* fight. The media are going crazy on me. They know the IAF doesn't have that sort of ability. They're speculating that maybe the U.S. jumped in with our Stealth fighters."

"We didn't," Anshel said softly.

"But they're talking to everyone they can about the IAF's ability to get there and back, without even as much as a shot fired at an IAF plane. It isn't possible. They're all saying that only the U.S. fleet of F-22s and F-35s can carry out that sort of mission."

Anshel held a hand up. He knew where DJ was going with this, and that both he and the media would eventually run this to ground. He'd been prepared for this for weeks, in fact. Only a handful in government knew about the secret sale to the Israelis months ago. But it was time to confirm the sale. They just had to be careful and make sure there was a huge amount of distance between the sale and Israel's own decision to act.

"There's another Stealth fighter that can handle that mission," Anshel said.

DJ stared at Anshel Gould. Anshel's expression confirmed what DJ had suspected since the middle of the night, and what some of the media were starting to ask about. "So it's true? We sold the F-117s to them?"

"About six months ago. It *is* a silver bullet for them. It's the only plane that could have handled such a mission. Anything else is just a suicide mission for the Israeli pilots."

DJ took a deep breath. "I don't see how this is possible," he said finally. "How could we make a decision like this without anyone knowing?"

"The Group of Eight knew and pushed it through as part of the black budget," Anshel said. "I talked to all eight of them personally. They all approved. More than that, most of them were advocates of the sale."

"Really? Both parties?"

"Really. We were going to sell them modified F-22s and, eventually, F-35s anyway," Anshel said. "Selling them the F-117s was just an extension of that."

DJ was surprised that the Group of Eight knew and that details of the secret sale had not leaked. The Group of Eight included the leadership of both the House and Senate, from both parties, who were always informed of anything significant on national security. But the White House had long ago learned that nothing remained secret for long once it had gone up to the Hill. And, DJ knew, Anshel visited the Capitol almost on a daily basis to consult with them.

Still, this was different. Support for the defense of Israel was so strong in both parties that neither side ever used Israel's defense as a political football. It just didn't happen in the United States, for any reason. So it was possible they could keep this particular secret.

"And the training?"

"Done as part of our regular joint training with them out at the Nevada bases. We flew the F-117s out there for years when they were black projects out of Skunk Works, and no one knew."

"Wow," DJ said. "Well, that would explain it."

"You seem surprised."

"Yeah, I guess I am." DJ shrugged. "I know we've denied Israel landing and takeoff rights in Iraq. So why sell them a Stealth fighter?"

Anshel sat forward in his chair. The world would never know this, but he'd been the strongest internal advocate for the sale, right from the beginning. It made all sorts of sense, both politically and from a national security posture. They had to give the Israelis something to defend themselves.

"Look, as I said, we were going to sell Israel— and Japan—planes out of our Stealth line. That was a given. The timing of those sales—that's the question. The F-117s were available now."

"And the sale allowed this administration to show its support for Israel, early on, even as we were changing the nature of our military and diplomatic relationship with them in Iraq and else-where," DJ said, warming up to the task at hand.

"There you go," Anshel said. He could always rely on DJ to get right to the core. He did it quickly.

"So will the leadership in Congress confirm the sale?"

"They will."

"Good. That will take some of the heat off the White House."

Anshel turned back to his intelligence papers. There was a lot to get to before they briefed the president that morning. But DJ didn't leave the office—not just yet.

"Yes? There's more?" Anshel asked.

"The media is wondering about some of the other reports."

"Other reports?"

"That Iran is preparing a second strike because Israel used a tactical nuke on a site in Iran."

"If Israel used a tactical nuke, that's their business," Anshel said brusquely.

"We urged them not to, right?"

"Of course. But what they choose to do in their own defense is their own call."

"And a second strike from Iran?"

Anshel sighed. It had been a very long night. "We are doing everything in our power—and I mean absolutely everything—to convince Iran's clerical and political leadership that a second strike would be an enormous mistake."

"Has President Camara weighed in?"

"He spoke to Rowan in Russia late yesterday. China's scheduled for this morning. They've convened an emergency meeting of the UN Security Council this morning as well. The president will talk to them by phone for a few minutes."

"What about Iran?"

Anshel shook his head. The silence had been deafening from Iran, on all fronts of their leadership. "We're trying to get to Shahidi. We haven't had any luck."

"And Ahmadian?"

"A waste of time," Anshel said dismissively. "The clerics are making the calls right now. We'll see how much rope they give the Revolutionary Guards."

"Do we have any ties to Shahidi? Any hope there?"

"Not much, to be honest. All back-channel stuff. But we're throwing everything we have at it. We've asked for formal talks at every level."

"And no response?"

"None to speak of," Anshel answered. "Shahidi's going to let the Guards do something in response. He has no choice. He cannot simply do nothing."

"So a second strike is possible?"

"Sure," Anshel said, almost casually. "If they have enough enriched uranium left, they'll probably launch something."

"The Shahab 3?"

"That would be my guess." A dark smile lit up Anshel's face. "If they do, we'll get our answer after all these years."

"Which one?"

"Whether defenses are any good against missiles with that sort of range," he answered. "We'll see if the emerging third generation of the Arrow missile defense system we've built for Israel is any good. For Israel's sake, I hope so."

15

LILONGWE, MALAWI

Nash was stunned. He'd gotten through to Razavi almost immediately. His father had been right. Razavi must have seen his last name and chosen to respond.

Nash had written in his text:

Mr. Razavi,

My name is Nashua Lee, and I am the creator of mVillage. That is how I was able to secure your number for this text. If you are able, can you call me on my mobile? I am in Malawi, Africa. I need to speak to you immediately about the events happening in your country, if you are able.

When Nash had pushed the send button on his text to Razavi's personal mobile number in Iran, he had not expected a response. When Razavi had responded just minutes later, Nash was left shaking his head at how small the world could be at times—and how technology had created one large community in many ways.

Yes, I will call, Razavi had responded. Nash's phone rang a moment later.

"This is Nash," he'd answered.

"Nashua Lee, the person who contacted me?" The voice on the other end of the line had a distinct Persian accent, but the English was impeccable.

"Yes, this is Nash."

"Your father is an ambassador of the United States, and you run mVillage?"

Nash smiled. It always amazed him that strangers could summarize your life in a matter of seconds. "Yes, I run mVillage, as part of the Village Health Corps—"

"Yes, yes, I know," he said, cutting Nash off. "But mVillage—"

"I run mVillage," Nash said softly. "So is this Mr. Razavi?"

"It is. But, please, call me Reza."

"Yes, sir, Reza," Nash said politely. "I'm calling at the request of my father—"

"The ambassador, in Japan."

"Yes, Ambassador Lee. He asked me to call you, to see if you might be able to help."

"I am under house arrest," Reza said, his voice calm. "There is very little I can do."

"My father believes you can help," Nash said firmly. "He believes that your voice can bring calm to certain people."

"Yes, but it brings violence to others," Reza said evenly. "It depends upon the audience."

Nash forged on. "My father believes that you can help with someone close to Ayatollah Shahidi."

Razavi laughed. "That would be nice—if it were true. But I am under house arrest under orders directly from the Rev. Shahidi."

"I understand," Nash said. "And I'm sure it's complicated. But there are people he listens to, who might be able to reason with him."

"Perhaps. But history, so far, would seem otherwise."

"But we have to try," Nash said, beginning to think his quest was hopeless. "People will make decisions in the next few hours . . ."

"Yes, they will. But I am powerless to prevent them."

"Mr. Razavi, I do not believe that is true," Nash said with resolve. "There are times when you must simply do the right thing. No matter what. And this is one of those times."

There was silence on the other end of the line for a few moments.

"And what would you—what would the

American government—have me do from inside the walls of my home, where I am imprisoned?" he said finally.

"My father believes the Rev. Ehsan might be in a position to influence the Supreme Leader."

"Ahura Ehsan?"

"Yes, the Rev. Ehsan."

"That's what your father believes? That he might listen to my words?"

"Yes, he does."

"Do you know why he believes this?"

"No, I don't, honestly," Nash said. "But I know that my father always has his reasons, and I trust his judgment. If he believes it will help, then I do too."

"I see," Razavi said. "Ahura is a good man. He is close to the Rev. Shahidi. He is no fool. But he is also every bit as conservative as his leader. I'm not sure it would make much difference."

"But will you try?"

"If I do," Razavi asked, "what must I say?"

"Please ask him to intervene, right now, on the Shahab 3. Please ask him to give the United States time to act, to organize sanctions against Israel for their strike—"

"The U.S. would sanction Israel?" Razavi asked, surprised. "It has never done that before."

"My father says it will, now. But only if the Rev. Shahidi is able to forestall the launch in retaliation."

"And he believes Ahura can help persuade the leader of this course of action?"

"He may be our only hope," Nash said. "If just one Shahab 3, with a nuclear warhead, should reach Israel, everything will change. We both know that. So, will you make the call? Can you ask him to intervene with the leader and stop the missile launch?"

"Yes, I will," Razavi said after a few moments of hesitation. "For you are right. It is the right thing to do."

16

Camp 16
Near Chongjin, North Korea

Kim Grace had heard rumors over the years that her entire family had been moved to various camps. None had ever come to Camp 16, though. Once interned, her life was effectively over. She would never be given a chance to know what had happened to her family—until the day a new political prisoner had arrived with a mobile phone miraculously secured with his personal possessions.

Kim Grace had lost nearly all of her teeth. Her gums had long ago turned black from a diet of just corn and salt. She had been unable to stand straight for the past year and regularly hunched over at the waist as she spent almost fifteen hours each day in the nearby mines. The one set of clothes she'd received when she'd first arrived at Camp 16 had become rags. She no longer had socks.

But she still had hope that, some day, she would see her children again. Despite the desperate odds, she held her children close to her in ceaseless prayer to God. It was the reason she woke up each morning. Her deep Christian faith helped her believe that, one day, she would see the faces of her two daughters and the young son she'd been forced to leave behind when she became a political prisoner at Camp 16.

The world had long ago forgotten about Camp 16, and Kim Grace. They'd once risen up in horror to protest the Nazi concentration camps and the Soviet Gulag. Yet literally hundreds of thousands of prisoners had died in the North Korean camps over the years from malnutrition, torture, or execution. No one cared.

There were two nuclear test sites west and south-west of Camp 16 in the mountains near Chongjin. Kim Grace knew that because, once, she'd been a highly trained and valued nuclear engineer. She knew what took place at the nuclear test sites near Camp 16, south of both China and Russia.

But there was very little she could do, or say, about those tests near Camp 16. The proof of the knowledge she'd brought with her to Camp 16 had vanished without a trace from the planet. It was, in fact, why she was at Camp 16 in the first place.

When she'd first arrived at the camp, the guards had promised her that her family would eventually join her there. Others had family members there—top government officials who'd fallen out of favor with the Dear Leader and, then, with his third son, Pak Jong Un, who would soon succeed his father as North Korea's leader.

But her family members had never arrived at Camp 16, and her hope had waned to next to nothing over the years. She was resigned to her daily fate. But, still, she kept both eyes wide open as each new batch of prisoners arrived at the camp, and her prayers to the God she served never stopped.

She'd been accused by the Bowibu, the country's national security agency, of passing nuclear secrets to South Korea and the West. The charge was ludicrous, of course. Kim Grace knew virtually no one associated with anyone outside North Korea. She'd devoted her life to helping create North Korea's civil and military nuclear capability.

But a coworker who knew of her growing unease at the way in which her civil nuclear engineering work was converted to military purposes—and who also had an irrational hatred of her Christian beliefs—had turned her in to the Bowibu. The trial had been quick, and absurd.

She'd been sentenced to one hundred years of hard labor at the camps—which the North Korean government consistently denied even existed.

In her "interview" before coming to Camp 16, she'd had both legs and her right arm broken. Two hammer blows had broken the teeth on the right side of her face. All of her fingernails had been removed. She'd lost a toe on one of her feet. She'd weighed just seventy pounds when she'd been allowed to leave her interviews. After six months—and after she'd already been convicted of high treason for passing nuclear secrets to the West—Kim Grace had finally admitted to being a spy.

When the young man had arrived at Camp 16, Kim Grace had paid no attention to him. She made very few friends at camp. The days were much too hard for that. You had to meet your work quota or face reduced corn rations. If you consistently failed to meet your work quota, you were sent to the prison within a prison, and there was no returning from that second prison alive.

So Kim Grace made certain she met her work quota each day, no matter what. She rarely talked to anyone throughout the day and was much too tired to speak to anyone at night. Sleep was too precious to waste even a moment on idle chatter. It was all she could do to spend time on a Bible verse, and a prayer, at the end of each day.

But the young man who'd arrived at Camp 16

several months earlier was hard to ignore. He worked with energy and always had time toward the end of the day—once he'd reached his quota —to talk to his fellow prisoners on breaks.

At first the guards had paid close attention to the young man, who was in his midtwenties. But, over time, as the young man went about his daily routine with energy and purpose, they'd turned their attention elsewhere. The young man was a model prisoner and never caused any trouble. He helped others do their work, always smiled at the guards, and generally made life better for every-one at Camp 16. It was hard not to like him.

Kim Grace had been unable to muster enough energy to talk to him initially. When she did talk to him at last, the knowledge of who he was and what he had been simply stunned her.

You Moon was a boyhood friend of Pak Jong Un—the young man about to become the new Dear Leader in Pyongyang. He'd grown up play-ing Nintendo fighting games with the leader-to-be. They'd played basketball together. Pak Jong Un had always worn a replica Chicago Bulls jersey when they'd played on the glittering basketball court built at the southern end of the Dear Leader's palace complex northeast of Pyongyang. You Moon claimed to have spent time with the soon-to-be Dear Leader at all seventeen of their different palaces and residences over the years, including a private resort near Baekdu Mountain and a lodge along the sea at Wonsan.

You Moon also said that he'd regularly beaten Pak Jong Un on the basketball court and in Nintendo games. But, officially, the young man about to become North Korea's Dear Leader always won his games 15-0 and had set every world record imaginable for each Nintendo game they'd played.

In fact, the official biography of his friend stated unequivocally that he'd first learned how to master computer science through his Nintendo gaming and had later translated that passion and love into the ability to direct the nation's most sophisticated high technology systems run by the National Defense Commission. His biography said that he was now the world's most gifted, proficient, and skilled master of high technology anywhere in the world.

It also said that he'd once made 8,776 free throws in a row, shattering the previous world record of 5,221 set in 1996. Unable to confirm the report, the Guinness Book of World Records did not recognize Pak Jong Un's free-throw record.

You Moon had lost touch for a couple of years when his friend went overseas to a private school in Switzerland. They'd stayed in touch via text messages and through mVillage. Most of their talk was about the Chicago Bulls, or the NBA, or some celebrity in the West who'd done something stupid or ridiculous. They never talked about politics, the government, world events, or his father. When Pak Jong Un had returned from Switzerland, everything changed. He began to spend considerably more time away from the various palaces and residences. He attended many, many official meetings with his father. Eventually, You Moon only saw his friend during private, arranged vacations. His friend was quite clearly being groomed to take over for his father. Any fool—and You Moon was no fool—could see that.

As they'd entered adulthood, his friend had helped You Moon secure a job as a mid-level bureaucrat with the General Staff of the Ministry of People's Armed Forces. You Moon had no real knowledge of how the highest executive organization in North Korea's military affairs actually functioned. All he knew was that he made plenty of money, by North Korea's standards, which left him plenty of time to do almost anything he wanted to do in Pyongyang.

When his friend became the supreme commander of the People's Armed Forces and the chairman of the Military Committee, it was obvious to You Moon that Pak Jong Un had assumed overall command of the North Korean military apparatus. The generals all reported to his friend.

But You Moon was also smart enough to see that it was mostly an exercise in shadow authority.

The generals did what they wanted. His friend may have been the Supreme Commander—and his father may have been grooming him to become North Korea's next leader—but the generals clearly told the Supreme Commander where to go, what to say, and how to act in public.

You Moon knew this because his friend would occasionally complain, privately, about the noose around his neck when they were together on a vacation. His friend did so very discreetly and swore You Moon to secrecy. But it was obvious that his friend had quite a distance to travel before he could assume his father's mantle as Dear Leader. Perhaps time would change this. But, for now, Pak Jong Un was a puppet as his father's health failed.

Kim Grace and You Moon became friends over time. For the first time in her miserable existence at Camp 16, she actually looked forward to the end of the day. She found that she could sit and listen to You Moon for hours. He was like the son she'd never had a chance to know.

When she'd finally worked up the courage to ask You Moon how he'd managed to come to Camp 16, a dark shadow fell across his face. That was rare, because he was usually so full of energy and enthusiasm—even here in this place that God and the world had seemingly forgotten. The sudden change in his demeanor was unmistakable. There was real sadness in his voice as he told the story.

You Moon had made a mistake. It had been an understandable one, made by many young men. But, in You Moon's case, it had been catastrophic.

A young woman You Moon had been dating had joined them for a private, four-day weekend at Wonson a year or so after Pak Jong Un had taken the helm of the defense commission. She also worked at the General Staff of the military armed forces. You Moon felt blessed to date her. Bright, funny, and stunningly attractive, she was—almost—enough to convince him to stop visiting other places in Pyongyang in the evenings.

The three had enjoyed jet skiing, drinks at night, long talks on the beach, and gorgeous sunrises. In just two days Pak Jong Un had grown infatuated with the young woman. It was hard not to be drawn to her. She was a blazing light in the heavens.

On their third day at the seaside residence, Pak Jong Un had kissed the young woman as they were sitting on a veranda overlooking the sea. You Moon had seen it from a distance. Later that evening, he'd confronted his friend. The conversation had grown heated, and You Moon had shoved his friend in anger. It was their first real fight—and their last.

You Moon was arrested that night. His friend, in the heat of anger, had ordered him detained. He was tried for treason against the state the very next morning and shipped off to Camp 16 immediately. It had all happened so abruptly that You Moon had been unable to tell his family, or anyone, about the incident.

He'd been a trusted friend of the young man waiting in the wings to become the nation's next Dear Leader one moment, and a political prisoner and enemy of the state the next—all because he'd objected to his friend's advances toward his girlfriend, the type of dispute that young men had been involved in for ages.

But these were no ordinary young men, and their friendship was more than just a little unbalanced in the great equation of life. You Moon knew that now, but it was too late to correct his mistake. He wondered if his friend would, one day, show some sort of mercy and bring him back from the purgatory of Camp 16. He doubted it, but hope was all that he had now.

Because the entire incident had happened so quickly—and because Pak Jong Un had ordered his friend banished immediately—You Moon had only managed to leave with the possessions with him at the seaside resort. All but one of those possessions had been taken from him as he'd arrived at Camp 16. The one possession he'd managed to hide from the guards was a slim Nokia mobile phone and two spare batteries that he taped to his body and managed to sneak in undetected.

The phone, thankfully, had been fully charged when he'd arrived at Camp 16. He'd carefully monitored the power on the phone and only checked world events and messages on mVillage occasionally, late at night. The phone's power was now about three-quarters diminished. Even with the spare batteries, it would be completely drained, and worthless to him, in less than a year at the rate he was using it.

You Moon told no one about his phone after his arrival at Camp 16. He knew one slip would mean that his phone would be taken from him. So he told no one—until, late one evening, when he'd finally decided to tell Kim Grace about it.

You Moon instinctively trusted Kim Grace. She had no reason to turn him in at Camp 16. Her life was over, save for her last, flickering hope of seeing members of her family one day. He knew, in his heart, that she would not violate his trust.

She'd told him everything she knew and believed and, over time, he'd reciprocated. That included the knowledge of the secret cell phone, the first lifeline to the outside world that had ever managed to make its way into Camp 16.

As Kim Grace and You Moon learned of each other's lives and work, they slowly realized that they had something in common—a bonded knowledge and a path to the outside world that the North Korean government would have stopped at all costs, had they known about it.

In fact, they both came to realize that they shared secret knowledge that no one outside of North

Korea grasped—knowledge that the world likely should know about. But there was no one to tell, and they were both effectively gone from the face of the earth. They could tell their stories to each other, but to no one else. And they were not certain anyone would care, even if they could reach outside the forbidding walls of Camp 16.

Because of her former work as a civil and military nuclear scientist, and her knowledge of what was really being tested at the two nuclear sites near Camp 16, Kim Grace had a fairly clear idea of what North Korea was capable of with weapons of mass destruction. She knew the world would be surprised to know North Korea's true intent.

Because of his privileged status as one of Pak Jong Un's closest childhood friends, You Moon had been granted access to the most secret workings of the General Staff and also knew what the North Korean military considered important. What's more, he and his friend had quietly talked about some of the tests during late-night Nintendo sessions. His friend had been guarded, but You Moon was astute enough to grasp what he was hearing.

In fact, You Moon's friend had boasted about how stupid the West was with their seismic monitoring of the first four tests at sites near Camp 16. The United States had sent their modified Boeing jet, the Constant Phoenix, near the tests to monitor the seismic levels.

When the blasts had indicated they were testing an atomic bomb of only four kilotons or so, the Western media had rushed in to declare that North Korea hadn't quite reached the "real" nuclear club yet. They belittled North Korea's progress in joining the nuclear club. The yields were too small to do much damage, they all said.

"How stupid the Western leaders are!" You Moon's friend had said one evening, laughing. "If they only knew that we have perfected the atomic bomb!"

The generals of the Korean People's Army, though, had given Pak Jong Un only part of the story. They told the Dear Leader's son only what he needed to know—which was that the West was wrong, and that they had, in fact, perfected an atomic weapon.

Kim Grace's knowledge of the field and what was being tested near Camp 16—and You Moon's knowledge of what the high echelon of the military was spending money on, and what his friend had told him during their late-night Nintendo sessions —allowed them to collectively understand the real picture emerging near Camp 16 and in the halls of the nuclear research centers Kim Grace had once roamed.

The truth—built on the backs of political prisoners from Camp 16, who'd been marched to the nearby underground facility to build it and then served as human guinea pigs for the tests—was a much more complicated one.

The North Korean leadership genuinely believed the United States would one day invade their country as they had in the 1950s. North and South Korea were still technically at war, and American military troops were only a stone's throw away from Pyongyang.

They believed, passionately, that it was only a matter of time before the West returned and overran North Korea—the way they'd gone into Iraq, Afghanistan, and, now, Iran.

What Kim Grace and her colleagues had been searching for with every fiber of their being for years was a way to keep the Western principalities and powers at bay. They needed an equal, opposing force that could not be resisted. And, Kim Grace knew, they had likely found it.

North Korea had long ago crossed the nuclear threshold. Kim Grace knew they were fully capable of detonating a twenty-kiloton atomic bomb, or greater. They'd long ago mastered the fission part of the equation. That was no longer what they were interested in, however. One atomic bomb—or six of them, for that matter—would not change the game.

What North Korea was now testing, or perfecting, was a much different version of a weapon of mass destruction. There was some reference to it in the old literature—the scientific papers that

Kim Grace and others had read and re-read until every copy in the libraries at the Yongbyon nuclear research center was dog-eared with use.

They were now looking at something that could only be characterized as a fission-fusion-fission bomb—a weapon that would, in stages, unleash the strong nuclear forces and energy of multiple isotopes. And they weren't even all that concerned about whether it could be carried on a plane, truck, or boat to a remote location.

It could sit there, right near Camp 16, and affect half the world's population in Japan, China, Russia, and even India.

Nuclear scientists had been experimenting with different atomic isotopes—and their interaction with each other in fission and fusion processes—for a generation. There were three isotopes of hydrogen, for instance. Two of them are stable and not radioactive, but a third—tritium, with one proton and two neutrons—is unstable.

Nuclear scientists had long ago perfected the fission process—the splitting of the atom to create an enormous release of energy. That was the atom bomb. Next, they produced a fission reaction in a tightly controlled, closed system in order to generate enough heat and might to fuse two atoms together and release even greater energy. That led to the hydrogen bomb, which had the capacity to make entire local regions of the world radioactive.

Over time, they'd made the process of fission leading to fusion simple. They didn't need underground tests for that part. The technology for a closed system with uranium or plutonium surrounded by a dry, solid powder of lithium-deuteride was so simple that it did not, in fact, require testing.

Once North Korea had perfected the small kiloton fission bombs, Kim Grace and her colleagues were certain they could, in fact, create a hydrogen isotope bomb that allowed the small fission explosion to trigger a thermonuclear fusion release of energy.

The fission tests near Camp 16—the ones that had been dismissed and ridiculed by the Western press and intelligence analysts—were actually the final phase of a process that created a thermonuclear hydrogen isotope bomb.

But the next part was what had begun to frighten Kim Grace and had sent her to Camp 16 when she'd begun to express misgivings privately to a colleague. While the hydrogen process was being perfected, they'd begun to test two other isotopes —cobalt-59 and cesium-137. Cobalt-59 was easy to test. Cobalt-60 was widely used in nuclear medicine throughout the world. Non-proliferation groups had been worried for years that terrorist groups would create dirty bombs by exploding easily obtained cobalt-60 sticks with dynamite, irradiating a neighborhood. Cobalt-60, which was highly unstable and radioactive, had a half-life of five years or so.

Cesium-137 was even more unstable—and more dangerous. With a half-life of thirty years or so, its release into the atmosphere could have devastat-ing, long-term consequences for an entire genera-tion. Cesium-137 was available through nuclear medicine as well.

Kim Grace and her colleagues had been told to look at ways in which cesium-137 could be stabilized long enough to salt a nuclear weapon— to surround the fission-fusion process of a hydrogen isotope bomb with cesium-137 released in a final fission process.

This fission-to-fusion-to-fission process was what the nuclear research center at Yongbyon had been focused on for years. They were creating a weapon that had, at its core, a four-kiloton fission atomic bomb. That, in turn, triggered the fusion process with the dry lithium-deuteride powder. And, in rapid succession, that fusion process created a final, devastating fission process, releasing cesium-137 into the atmosphere.

It was the most wicked doomsday device Kim Grace could imagine. There was no upper limit to the size of a hydrogen bomb you could build if you had no intention of placing it on a mobile missile warhead or even the back of a flatbed truck.

You could, in fact, build one large enough—and

salt it with enough cesium-137—to irradiate nearly half of the world's population with just one fission-fusion-fission detonation. A cesium bomb could potentially wreak havoc and decimate half the world for a generation.

No rational political or military leader would ever deploy such a weapon for the simple reason that it would irradiate and sicken every man, woman, and child in a country—and those in every surrounding country, for that matter—if the cesium bomb was large enough in size.

But, Kim Grace and You Moon both knew, North Korea's leadership was not entirely rational. They'd been isolated and living in abject fear of Western invasion for a generation and counting. They clearly felt the need to create something that would give them the upper, final "dead hand" in a military confrontation with the principalities and powers that surrounded them on all sides.

North Korea had Russia and China to the north. The United States patrolled their southern border. And they had Japan to their east. It was hard for You Moon's friend—and the permanent military leadership that surrounded him at all times—not to feel a little intimidated by their neighbors.

As Kim Grace and You Moon became fast friends and talked of such things in hushed whispers at the end of long, horrible days at Camp 16, they sometimes despaired. They had no friends to talk to about this knowledge. No one cared about them, or their desperate situation at Camp 16. They had been forgotten, discarded, and consigned to the trash heap of history.

Despite her faith, Kim Grace couldn't help but think that she would die, alone, with her secrets. She couldn't even write a note to pass on to the world. There was no pen to write with, and no paper on which to record her thoughts.

You Moon still clung to the hope that his friend would come to his senses and pull him back from the abyss opening up now at his feet. But he, too, had doubts that consumed him each day.

And even if someone should find them, and ask to hear their stories, what would they both say? How would they explain their secrets—the knowledge they both shared—in a way that would impress the leaders of the powers surrounding them on all sides?

It seemed hopeless.

17

TEHRAN, IRAN

Ahura Ehsan folded his finely embroidered prayer rug carefully and returned it to the closet after finishing his morning prayers. The house was quiet this early in the morning. But Ehsan knew the quiet was deceptive, and that it would not last long.

He'd gotten almost no sleep that night. Almost every manner of council in Iran had met throughout the night as the reports of the Israeli attack began to come in. Ehsan had attended as many of them as he could manage before returning to his modest home in a Tehran suburb shortly before dawn.

Ahura was worried, which was unusual for him. He was not one who ever worried for the future. He followed the still, small voice in all things, in all ways. He was a relentless, positive storm. He believed that every action demanded careful attention to detail and a strict observance to his own beliefs.

Those who followed his writings and talks could feel his deep passion. Everything he said and wrote followed the scriptures carefully and methodically. But those who knew him well also had long ago come to believe that Ahura was so much more than this careful script—he was a walking, living, breathing testament to the way of God.

It was strange to Ahura to think that his country had been under attack just twelve hours earlier. There was virtually no sign of the attacks in Tehran. The Stealth planes from Israel—and they had, almost assuredly, been Stealth fighters developed in America—had attacked sites all around the country, at locations where the IRGC's nuclear efforts had been underway.

But Tehran had not seen the attacks and had no visual knowledge of them. Like many others in his country, Ehsan was relying on reports from people near the sites who were filing virtual multimedia reports with portals like mVillage.

It always amazed Ehsan how mobile technology had changed everything. There were people in rural parts of Iran—and throughout the world, for that matter—who spent nearly all of their disposable income on mobile phones. It was their central link to the rest of the world. It also ensured that nothing happened unnoticed. No trees fell in the world without observation any longer.

Ehsan had ignored nearly all of the incoming text messages on his own phone throughout the night. Dozens of people were trying to reach him, and he had chosen not to respond.

But there was one that kept returning to his mind's eye. He could not turn away from this one message, no matter how hard he tried. He settled into his study, composed himself, and turned on his laptop. He could not avoid the message any longer. He knew the risk he was taking by responding . . . and the risk being taken by the sender.

My dearest Reza, he wrote. Greetings and peace. I hope you are well? He hit the send button and wondered, as he often did, what the digital journey was like for messages that went from his office to the rest of the world. He also wondered, vaguely, if the IRGC would someday be able to track such messages in the mobile world.

The reply was virtually instantaneous. Clearly, the former president had been waiting for his reply. I am well, Reza wrote in his text. I wish the circumstances were different. I am managing in my unjust imprisonment, which I'm certain you must have heard about by now. I hope it is a temporary thing, my arrest.

Patience, my friend, Ehsan wrote back. We are all working through these very difficult times. We are all doing our best.

I know you are, Ahura. I will not write what I know to be true in my heart, for that would put you in a difficult place.

Thank you. So what did you write about?

Reza replied immediately. I write to urge you to do whatever is in your power to intercede with the Rev. Shahidi on the question of retaliating against Israel for their unjust and unprovoked attacks.

That is well beyond my reach, and not something I know anything about, Ehsan wrote back.

I understand. Nevertheless, decisions will be made very, very soon. The Rev. Shahidi will be in a position to keep a missile from being launched at Israel—a missile that cannot be recalled once it is launched.

They both knew precisely what was being

discussed—and what was being asked. Should there be enough highly enriched uranium left for a nuclear warhead that had been created with extensive help from North Korean scientists in recent months, it was certain that the IRGC leadership would move to launch it at Israel.

Ali Zhubin, especially, had been adamant on this point for months. The IRGC's military commander had briefed the Guardian Council in the past few days that Iran's leadership had a moral and legal obligation to respond to an Israeli attack with a second strike.

Zhubin claimed that North Korea's scientific help with the Shahab 3—a nearly identical replica of North Korea's own intermediate-range missile —had perfected both the guidance system and the ability to fly through Iraqi airspace. President Ahmadian had confirmed Zhubin's claim in several briefings with the political leadership.

Whether it could penetrate the emerging Arrow 3 air-defense system that was being deployed with U.S. assistance was another matter. But Zhubin had been quite forceful that Iran had no choice but to respond, regardless of the consequences. Doing nothing was simply not an option, he had argued quite forcefully.

The Guardian Council had not ruled yet, and neither had the Rev. Shahidi. But they would very soon, perhaps even as the two of them were writing to each other. Some sort of a response was imminent, and the options ranged from a return strike at Israel and pre-set targets like the USS *Abraham Lincoln* somewhere in the Arabian Sea, to a decision to deny oil to the West through the Strait of Hormuz.

I cannot say what the Rev. Shahidi is considering, Ehsan wrote. I have not been involved in those discussions.

But this wasn't entirely correct. Ahura Ehsan was close to Shahidi. He was the Supreme Leader's lifeline to some of the more moderate clerics, who were still united in their support of Shahidi and his agenda. Ehsan had the ability to tell Shahidi when he had gone too far and was about to lose critical support of the mainline clerics he could not afford to lose.

Yes, I know, said Razavi. But should you have the opportunity, I would urge you to consider this. The U.S. has pledged that it will sanction Israel for their actions. It will take definitive action against Israel, something it has never done in a generation—but only if we do not strike back in anger with a nuclear missile attack.

And how do you know this? Ehsan wrote back, mildly surprised.

I know this. And I know it to be true.

Ehsan sat back in his chair. He did not doubt the words he was reading. He also did not wish to probe this further, for to do so would jeopardize his own position. If this is true—if the

United States will take action against Israel—
what might that action look like? he wrote.

I do not know, exactly, Razavi wrote. But I know
that it will be significant, public, and definitive. It
will be action that could finally separate the
United States from Israel, in a way that can be
demonstrated to the world.

Both Razavi and Ehsan knew there were many,
many leaders in the Arab world who had worked
for a generation to build some sort of diplomatic,
political, and military distance between the United
States and Israel. To date, all such efforts had been
failures. There was an opportunity now, but it
was linked to Iran's response to the Israeli attack.

Ehsan was growing uncomfortable with the
nature of the discussion. It was dangerous. He
understood the thrust of Razavi's message. It was
a credible back-channel effort. But he did not wish
to get more explicit in his writing.

I see, and I understand, Ehsan wrote back. But
I must go now. I will do what I can to discuss
this, if it seems appropriate to raise it.

That is all I can ask, my friend. This is an
important time, and all considerations must be
on the table. We have an opportunity, if we
choose well.

Ehsan closed his laptop. His mind was already
turning, wondering how he could safely carry this
message forward with the Supreme Leader—or
whether it was simply too dangerous to raise it.

18

GILAN QARB, IRAN

The truck had rolled down out of the mountains during the night, along the historic trade route linking Kermanshah and Baghdad. The Kermanshah-Baghdad route had been ill-used for years, but the route still existed, and it was the safest way through the mountains to the plains to the west. There was also just enough truck traffic on it to mask the truck's covert mission.

It was only one, plain-looking flatbed truck and very difficult for any satellite photos to isolate. There were no other vehicles with it. A convoy would have attracted attention. They'd managed to fit a dozen people into the cab of the flatbed and benches on either side of the back of the truck, which had been fitted with a light canopy to mask its true nature.

It was headed to a remote location that had never before been used for military purposes. It wasn't on anyone's tactical military map. No computer model, no matter how sophisticated, could have possibly guessed at this site as a starting point for the purposes of plotting arcs and distances.

The truck arrived at its destination without

incident as the sun was beginning to make its presence known on the other side of the mountains to the east. It drove past some ruins in the ancient village. The locals had always claimed the ruins were from a large fire temple, attributed to Hercules and known as the God of Hunting. It was well-named, some of the truck's occupants had joked.

Gilan Qarb was more than four hundred miles from Tehran to the east, in one of the westernmost provinces of Iran. The level plain of Gilan Qarb was west of the Kalhor Mountains. It was a calm, peaceful land, irrigated by the Gilan Qarb River and several others.

There was a square castle with trenches in the corner on a nearby hill. This is where the truck settled. A few crows protested their arrival as the truck took its position within the crumbling walls of the ancient castle.

The truck's driver and the other occupants from the cramped cab space scrambled down and began to unhinge the canopy on both sides. Once the canopy had been removed, the occupants in the back began their work quietly and quickly.

This was the first time this team had been assembled—and it was a highly unusual team. The team was split between North Korean scientists, who'd arrived in the country that day, and Iran's leading nuclear and military scientists, who had been mentored by the North Korean team for some time now.

And leading both factions was Hussein Bahadur, the outspoken chief of Iran's air force who had personally recruited loyal fanatics into the IRGC. Bahadur had made the decision to oversee this operation himself. He did not want any last-minute changes. This particular mission was too important to entrust its leadership to a subordinate.

The North Koreans were extraordinarily efficient. Because it was so close to the design of their own intermediate range missile, they knew precisely what to do with both the sequencing and the setup. They had checked the chambers before leaving, and double-checked them now. It was second nature to them.

They secured the missile's launch position and its target coordinates within an hour. Bahadur had said very little while the North Koreans did their work. He said almost nothing to the Iranian part of the crew with him. They were intently focused on watching the North Koreans do their work. It was one thing to do this part during an exercise. Now they were in the field, and this was not a test.

He'd been on his secure Iridium 9555 satellite phone just twice in the past hour—once with Zhubin, who'd told him that Tehran's political and religious leadership was close to deciding on a course of action, and a cautious call with his longtime ally with the Hezbollah in southern Lebanon.

His Iridium phone vibrated softly. He pulled

the phone from the holster. It was Zhubin. "Yes?" he said, anxious to know the answer.

"Something new has entered the discussion with the Guardian Council. The Rev. Shahidi is meeting with his inner cleric council," the IRGC military commander said.

"Something new? What can it possibly be?" Bahadur was impatient. He wanted to act.

"News that the United States will act against Israel if we do not launch a return strike with your missile," Zhubin said.

"And you believe that? It's talk. It has always been talk. We both know that."

"Yes, we do."

"Will it keep the Rev. Shahidi from allowing us to act?" Bahadur asked, dreading the answer.

"It has . . . delayed things. They are not quite certain what to do. They want more time to discuss this new offer from the Americans that has arrived from somewhere."

"It is a lie!" Bahadur exploded. "They only wish to keep us from doing what we must. They will find us, this truck, and they will finish the job here before we can launch. They could have a cruise missile coming at us even as we speak, despite the care we have taken."

Zhubin did not respond for a few moments. He had just emerged from a meeting with the Rev. Shahidi and President Ahmadian, and he needed to be very careful here. It had been just the three of them. No one else had been involved in the discussion.

"You have your orders," Zhubin said. "Those orders have been in place for months, in preparation for an Israeli attack. Nothing has changed—yet."

Bahadur blinked, once, and allowed the words to register. The standing order was to launch a second strike missile once it was in place if Israel had attacked. Unless that order had been replaced with a new one—which had not yet occurred—then his duty was clear. He was to launch.

"I understand," Bahadur said, nodding once. "I must go. We have work to do."

"Act quickly, my friend," Zhubin said. "New orders could arrive at any moment."

Bahadur ended the call and replaced the satellite phone. He turned to the lead military scientist who'd been standing nearby, waiting for his own orders. "Are we ready?" Bahadur asked. "Is the missile ready for launch? Are the coordinates in place?"

"Yes, sir," the scientist answered. "We are ready."

"Then it is time. Launch the missile," Bahadur ordered. "Now."

Moments later the Shahab 3 was airborne, moving across the plains of Iraq toward Tel Aviv on a gentle arc. It would arrive in Israel with the first light of the morning sun.

19

WASHINGTON, DC

Adom Camara had just fallen asleep after the longest day of his presidency when the phone rang. He grimaced. There could only be one reason for such a call, after midnight.

He picked the phone up beside the ornate bed after just one ring. He was already alert and wondering where he'd placed his secret pack of cigarettes his wife and others hated to see him carry around. He spotted the windproof butane lighter on the nightstand. The pack of menthol cigarettes couldn't be far away.

"Yes?" he answered softly.

"Sir, the satellites have just picked up a flash," the voice said on the other end. He recognized it as General John Alton, the first army general to become vice chair of the joint chiefs. Vice chairs didn't have any command authority, but they served at the pleasure of the president. Alton had been at the White House for the past twenty-four hours.

"When?" the president asked.

"Two minutes ago. At least three of our early warning and signal intelligence satellites picked up the launch. The SIGINT operators believe the burn has just finished, and the warhead has separated and is now on its way to its target."

"Which is?"

"We believe it's headed toward Tel Aviv," General Alton said promptly.

"Is it on course, or is it falling off, like some of their earlier tests?"

"It appears to be on course."

"Where was it launched?"

There was a slight pause as the general consulted his terrain map. "A remote village, Gilan Qarb, in a western province of Iran. It's close to the Iraq border."

"Have the Israelis locked onto the ballistic trajectory?" asked President Camara. He'd been briefed so thoroughly on this subject that he felt like he could practically see the missile's arc in his mind's eye. He knew the emerging Arrow 3 system could handle a single warhead. A multiple launch, from many different locations, was a completely different story.

"Yes, sir, they have," the general said.

"Have we moved our own ships out to sea?" Bahadur and others had vowed to target and burn American ships in the Persian Gulf after an Israeli attack.

"Yes, sir, the USS *Abraham Lincoln* is well out to sea in the Arabian. The other ships are also well out to sea, and moving. They can't reach us from the shoreline, and there's no way their planes will get anywhere close to our fleet."

"And we're sure that Arrow has locked onto the trajectory?" the president asked, returning to the urgent problem at hand.

"We're on, live, with IDF now. They're ready. They've already committed with Arrow. They'll wait to see the success there and correct if they need to at the next level down."

Alton and other leaders at the Pentagon were fairly confident of the Arrow system's capabilities. Of course, there was no way to know if the North Koreans had modified the guidance system to the point that it could elude the system. But they would know shortly.

"Do you have real-time tracking on a monitor?" the president asked.

"Yes, sir, we do. It's on a closed-loop, on the monitor in your study. It'll be all over, one way or another, by the time you get to the Situation Room. So you might as well watch from your study."

The president grabbed the University of Chicago sweatshirt at the foot of the bed, pulled it over his head, and moved briskly to his study.

An aide had already put the live satellite feed up on the monitor. The president sat down at his desk. They both watched in silence.

They had multiple views of the trace signals of the warhead by now, from different satellites. President Camara was surprised that Shahidi and the others had made the decision to launch. If the missile somehow made it through the emerging Arrow 3 system, Arrow 2, and then the Patriot low-orbit system and actually hit Tel Aviv—and if it did, in fact, have a workable nuclear payload—he wasn't entirely sure what might happen next.

The joint chiefs had predicted that Iran would launch at least one missile in retaliation. They had no choice, the generals had argued. Doing nothing was not an option, and they weren't actually prepared for a full-on war with the IDF. So a launch would show their willingness to respond—without an actual full-scale response.

And if, by chance, the missile stayed on its trajectory, the warhead survived separation, it made its way through the Arrow system, and then exploded a nuclear payload on impact in Tel Aviv—well, then, the balance of power would be forever changed in the Middle East.

Despite approaches from every conceivable angle, they had been singularly unsuccessful opening any sort of direct dialogue with Shahidi or any of the leading clerics associated with the Guardian Council in Iran. Camara knew that dealing with President Ahmadian was hopeless and an utter waste of time. But Shahidi and his inner circle were still an enigma as well.

The president's aide handed a telephone head-set to him. General Alton was still on the line. "Mr. President, while we wait—there is one other thing," the general said.

"Yes?" the president said, his eyes transfixed on the satellite video images on the monitor in front of him.

"Our satellite photos confirmed those who were responsible for the launch. We picked up markings and signatures on the truck and equipment from low-earth, so the resolution is good—enough to confirm that the North Koreans were there, helping them set the system and launch the missile."

The president shook his head. "That will make this more difficult," he said quietly.

"Yes, sir, it will," said General Alton.

The warhead was now nearing its apex. An instant later, there was a slight burst of light as the Arrow missile hit its intended target. None of this could be seen from earth—only satellites were able to pick up the explosion.

Israel's new, emerging Arrow 3 anti-ballistic missile defense system—parts of which had been deployed with U.S. help just months earlier—had worked. Iran's second strike had failed.

20

Moscow, Russia

It was his second talk to the Duma leadership in as many days, but Andrei Rowan never failed to find the right words. The 450 representatives of the state Duma were his people. He'd hand-picked most of them over the years. They'd supported his seamless transition from president to prime minister with almost no opposition. They belonged to him in a way that rivaled the power of the old tsars.

Rowan enjoyed his talks with the Duma leadership. They always asked intelligent questions, and he liked the interplay. They alone carried the torch for the greater Russia. They understood the need for Russia to deal smartly with the nations of the former Soviet Union at their border and to pay very close attention to what happened in the regions closest to Russia.

The Duma leadership was supportive of Rowan's quest. They did not understand all of its many-layered aspects, to be sure, but they recognized Russia's historic place in the interplay of nation-states. And they appreciated Rowan's consummate leadership skills on the world stage, and his ability to recognize strategic opportunities and take advantage of them.

There was no question that the events of the past two days in Iran now presented a clear opportunity. Rowan had been preparing the Duma's leadership for just such an eventuality for months. He had accurately predicted that Iran's leaders were so hungry for empire in the Middle East that they would accept Russia's leadership and pay enormous sums for the knowledge that it could provide.

The strategic relationship between Iran and Russia had been wildly profitable for Russia. Iran had paid billions for the right to develop a robust civil nuclear capability. Russia now had an intimate knowledge of all aspects of Iran's nuclear capabilities—including their plans and desires to enrich uranium, create plutonium, and become a world superpower by joining the nuclear club.

What the Duma leadership did not know—and, really, could not appreciate—was the depth of commitment on the part of Iran's reining cleric. Amir Shahidi was a driven, ruthless man who had calmly dispatched all of his past and present rivals.

Rowan had watched with some admiration as Shahidi had worked his way to the top of the Revolutionary Guards—and used that post to vault to the top of the clerics as the Supreme Leader over more learned clerics with a much deeper understanding of the judicial aspects of the Koran.

In fact, Shahidi had not really been qualified to take up the mantle of Supreme Leader after the death of Ayatollah Khomeini. But he was now the highest-ranking political and religious leader in Iran for a simple reason—he understood the levers of power at the highest levels and wielded them with ruthless efficiency.

Soon after seizing power, Shahidi had removed Khomeini's son from power—largely because he was a rival for the loyalty of the leadership of the Revolutionary Guards—and then had him poisoned. And when the son-in-law of his closest rival cleric began to gather popular support shortly after Shahidi had been named Supreme Leader, he'd been arrested for treason. The IRGC had him executed. Shahidi had moved similarly against anyone who had opposed him, especially in the early days of his reign.

Rowan appreciated the Rev. Shahidi's willingness to do whatever was necessary in order to consolidate power—including the lawless execution of rivals. Rowan understood Shahidi's ability to use the Revolutionary Guards to dissect the lives of his potential rivals and remove them when necessary.

Rowan himself had miraculously jumped from a lowly lieutenant colonel to the leadership ranks largely through a deep, interlocking network of spies who supplied him enough information on Boris Yeltsin's personal life to enable him to move to the head of the class. Rowan understood the value of a loyal, trusted intelligence network that could act with impunity and ruthlessness on one's behalf.

Shahidi had been forced to move more slowly of late against the likes of Reza Razavi and the more moderate clerics who'd quietly been lining up behind Razavi's bid for power. But Rowan knew that Shahidi would act—when the time was right. And he would not allow Razavi or his followers to alter Iran's march toward superpower status in the Middle East.

In fact, Rowan knew that Israel's actions in the past two days would permanently end the moderate uprising within Iran. While the attacks had clearly set Iran back for years in its quest to develop a deep nuclear weapons capability, the actions also strengthened Shahidi's hand. There would be no opposition to his ambitions in the short term.

It was the moment Rowan had hoped for, and anticipated. Iran would act through proxies as it had for years. Iran virtually ran Lebanon, and it was very close to establishing a permanent Shi'a leadership by proxy in Iraq as the U.S. military slowly left the country. Iran was poised to move into any Arab country the moment it recognized weakness, and the moment that chaos dictated action.

"My fellow comrades," Rowan said evenly at

the head of the ornate table in a conference room where he regularly met with the Duma leadership. Nearly a dozen top Duma officials were gathered around the table to hear the latest from their leader. "I bring you interesting news today of events in Iran and Israel."

"We have seen the televised reports," one of the officials said. "We understand that Iran's second strike failed."

"Yes, the American Arrow system in Israel worked as they'd hoped and took Iran's intermediate range missile out," Rowan said.

"And most of Iran's nuclear facilities are gone," a second Duma official said.

Rowan smiled. "That is not all bad for us. Iran will spend billions more in the coming years to build their capabilities back up."

"Does Iran have any remaining uranium? Will it launch more strikes?" asked another official. "What does the GRU say?"

"The GRU and SVR have conflicting views," Rowan said, laughing. "So you all are free to choose the intelligence you'd care to believe."

"But what do you believe?" another asked. "And you said you have news. What is it?"

Rowan leaned forward at the head of the table. "Here is the news, which we alone have and which the world has not yet learned of. I have just spoken to the Rev. Shahidi of it, moments ago. Israel may have achieved a victory of sorts in Iran with its use of the American Stealth fighters. But we have proof of something at one of the sites that Israel attacked. Their pilot used tactical nuclear weapons to reach beneath the earth. We have the proof."

"What does that matter?" one of the Duma leaders asked skeptically. "Iran has already launched a nuclear weapon in retaliation. Who will care that Israel deployed nuclear weapons first?"

Rowan leaned back in his chair. "Oh, the world will care, my friend. The world will care that the United States helped Israel carry out a nuclear attack on Iranian soil. It will set the Arab world on fire, once the world learns of it. Israel's first use of nuclear weapons will more than justify Iran's response and will set in motion many new actions."

"Such as?"

"Give it time, my friends," Rowan said. "We are only at the beginning of what may happen. The Americans will not have the stomach for what will occur in the coming days. Their people will demand that they leave the battlefield in Iran and all other parts of the Middle East once reprisals have been carried out, leaving it to us."

"How do you know this?" one of the Duma leaders demanded.

"Because I know the Rev. Shahidi—what is in his heart and, more importantly, what is in his mind as he plans his next course of action,"

Rowan answered calmly. "Iran will act, in many different quarters. Israel may have achieved success in the past two days, but Iran has many proxies that will act now."

"And what of Israel?"

"Israel will not be forgotten. I can assure you of that. There are plans for them as well."

21

TEHRAN, IRAN

Ali Zhubin was beside himself. He could barely contain his anger as he waited outside the Rev. Shahidi's private quarters in a quiet part of Tehran, where Shahidi preferred to do business.

How could the Israelis have intercepted their intermediate-range missile so easily? It should have been a shining moment for Iran's nuclear program —the day Iran arrived on the world stage, finally, as a nuclear superpower. Yet the world had hardly reacted to the defeat. It was just one more in a series of victories by Israel's military forces.

But the Rev. Shahidi had noticed and was already talking about bringing Bahadur up on charges before the Guardian Council. Ahmadian had noticed and managed to say something colossally stupid in public about it—something to the effect that God had guided the missile directly into the path of the Arrow interceptor to allow Iran to test their system. He'd then vowed that the clock was now ticking and that the 12th Imam was waiting in the wings, ready to take the stage to challenge the Dajjal, who would appear shortly. Zhubin just wished Ahmadian would learn to keep quiet.

He also wondered why the Rev. Shahidi kept Ahmadian around. Perhaps he needed a useful fool, someone who uttered ridiculous things in public. Ahmadian distracted the Western press with his pomposity, his rantings about the 12th Imam, and his constant drumbeat about the coming Apocalypse.

Zhubin was a realist and quite practical in his views about politics.

He knew precisely where Shahidi had come from, what he stood for, how far he would go— and how he would sacrifice even friends when necessary to achieve his larger geopolitical goals.

Shahidi was the driving force behind Iran's quiet, steady march toward empire in the Middle East. The truth was that Shahidi would have vastly preferred to avoid a military confrontation with Israel. It was a much more certain route to empire through proxies in Iran, Iraq, Pakistan, and Afghanistan, along with economic and military help from Russia, China, and North Korea.

It was only a matter of time before the Sunni

regime began to crumble and fall away in places like Saudi Arabia. Iran's Shi'a leadership was poised, and ready, to move when such events presented opportunities.

Iran's nuclear weapons ambitions had always been something driven by the Revolutionary Guards' leadership—and Zhubin had been forced to carry their arguments to Shahidi's chambers. Zhubin knew the very careful line he walked with Shahidi, who was ambivalent at best about the utility of pursuing nuclear weapons. One misstep and Zhubin's career—and perhaps his life—were over.

Today would be a crucial test with Shahidi. The first test of the Shahab 3 had been both a victory and a very public failure. The missile had made it to Israel, but not its intended target. Zhubin could not predict Shahidi's reaction to the events.

He'd studied Shahidi for years. The enigmatic cleric who refused to travel outside of Iran or meet with leaders from the West still confounded Zhubin on occasion.

The door to Shahidi's study opened. Zhubin rose from his seat and took a step forward.

"My friend," the Rev. Shahidi said softly, extending his left hand, "God grant you peace. We have much to discuss."

"Yes, we do." Zhubin grasped his left hand firmly. Shahidi's right hand had been paralyzed in a terrorist attack decades earlier. The incident had left his right hand permanently disabled and had shaped his personal views in ways that Zhubin still struggled to understand.

They walked into the study, which was furnished largely with books, a smallish table, and very little else. His prayer rug was carefully folded to one side of the bookshelf. It was a quiet, peaceful place—a place where revolution, chaos, and apocalypse seemed out of place. Talk of missiles and war seemed foreign here. Shahidi's white robe swished as they walked.

Shahidi rarely spoke in public—and only in broad generalities when he did venture into those waters. He made everyone come to him—even the likes of Andrei Rowan from Russia or the North Koreans. They all made the trek to Tehran and, eventually, to this quiet study.

As they sat, Zhubin watched as Iran's Supreme Leader stroked his now-graying beard gently, easily. That was a good sign. Zhubin had watched his leader in many meetings such as this. Stroking his beard meant he was in a thoughtful, deliberative mood—and was not preparing for some precipitous action.

"Let me congratulate you, my friend," Shahidi said as they settled into their chairs at the small table. There was a plain brown folder on the table. Zhubin did not reach for it. If Shahidi wanted him to see its contents, he would offer it.

"Your kind words are always welcome."

"Today was a great victory for the Guards," Shahidi said. "This day has long been anticipated, and we achieved much."

Zhubin just nodded and waited before engaging. "We serve at your pleasure."

Shahidi looked off into the distance, through the nearest window. "There is much good news in the events of the past two hours. The world now knows that we can respond to Israel. The missile worked, as it was intended. Had it reached its target, the weapon would have given us a great victory. That is important. It is a good thing. We always anticipated that Israel could intercept a lone missile. Its defenses are much too sophisticated to allow a single missile to make its way through."

"Yes, that is true."

"We will not speak again of the decision to launch the missile. It was the right decision. It achieved what we'd hoped. Israel knows, now, what its adversary is capable of—and that we are willing to strike back at their very heart."

"Yes, the world knows that we can reach into Israel with our longer-range missiles."

Shahidi looked back. His eyes were shining with an intensity rarely seen as he looked directly at Zhubin. For a brief moment, Zhubin could see what Shahidi must have been, once, as a battlefield commander. "But that is not enough, is it, my friend?"

"No, I do not believe so," Zhubin answered cautiously.

"No, it is not."

Shahidi moved his left hand toward the folder and slid it gently toward his military commander. "Please, look inside."

Zhubin opened the folder. It was a brief military report of both on-site and remote reconnaissance of one of the sites Israel had attacked near Shiraz—the site where the Guards had been covertly enriching massive amounts of uranium. Zhubin glanced through the satellite photos, the printout of atmospheric readings, and the conclusions in both Russian and, now, Farsi.

The report's conclusions were clear and would undoubtedly be communicated to the United Nation's Security Council members shortly. Israel had used tactical nuclear weapons—in fact, a clear first strike—against Iran's facilities. Once this was known to the world, things would change.

Shahidi leaned forward. "We have two tasks that we must begin today. They must be done. There can be no failure. We have prepared for this day. We know what we must do."

"The Strait?" asked Zhubin.

"Yes, and their carrier, the *Abraham Lincoln*. Both must be achieved. From the mountains, the air, and beneath the waters, turn all of it on the Americans and the Israelis. Do you understand?"

"I do," Zhubin said firmly. "And we will not fail. I give you my word."

He pushed his chair back. He had his orders, and he would not fail, not today. Both of these objectives were within his grasp.

22

NEW YORK CITY, NEW YORK

He made sure he was on time today. He could afford to be late to most meetings in New York. But not this one, not today. The black town car pulled up to the curb behind several other nearly identical black town cars parked outside a side entrance to the New York headquarters of the United Nations.

It was hard to tell, from the cars, who was here today for a special convening of the 1540 Committee. The Russian ambassador to the United Nations, Grigori Ulanov, had not made it widely known to others in the tight diplomatic community that operated in and around the UN what he was bringing to the 1540 committee today. Ulanov had merely promised that it would be interesting.

While the 1540 Committee was well known to those who labored in the dark, complex worlds of nuclear non-proliferation, the public had no idea what it did and likely did not care. It was chaired by Costa Rica—hardly known for its leadership in stopping the export of nuclear weapons technology around the world. But the membership of the 1540 Committee included China, Russia, the United States, and a few others, like Japan and the United Kingdom. The membership was enough to make it the right place for Ulanov's message.

Ulanov double-checked the contents of his briefcase before exiting the town car, just to make sure he had enough. There were nearly twenty identical envelopes in the briefcase—more than enough to pass around the table of the committee.

The 1540 committee rarely met. The name came from Resolution 1540 adopted by the UN Security Council in 2004. It was set up to enforce export controls on nuclear technology to "non-state actors." The 1540 Resolution required the member nations of the UN to refrain from supporting such "non-state actors"—otherwise known as terrorists —in their efforts to acquire chemical, biological, or nuclear weapons.

The 1540 Committee had released its first report to the UN in 2006, and then a second in 2008. The Security Council had extended its charter on several occasions.

Ulanov and the leadership in Moscow knew it was not the right committee at the UN for the envelopes and the information they contained. In fact, someone—either the UK or the United

States, most likely—was likely to object on protocol grounds.

There were other venues and meetings that made more sense. The Security Council was meeting later that day in closed session, in fact, to discuss the series of events of the past forty-eight hours. But Ulanov would never have an opportunity to present envelopes such as these at the full Security Council, or even in the smaller subset of that panel with the superpowers. There were too many roadblocks.

The United States had vetoed virtually every resolution ever brought before the UN Security Council that contained language critical of Israel. While the Camara administration was clearly in the process of reconsidering policies at the heart of the Israel-Palestinian conflict, it was still U.S. policy to oppose any Security Council resolution that condemned Israel without also condemning terrorist groups. As a result of this longstanding U.S. policy, it was difficult to bring any issue before the Security Council that dealt only with Israel.

This was why Russia had opted for the somewhat obscure 1540 Committee. It was an asymmetrical move, diplomatically. Russia was sending a message by bringing their news to this particular committee, which had largely come into existence to put a spotlight on rogue nations that might consider handing the technology for weapons of mass destruction to terrorists. But, more importantly, it would put the issue squarely on the UN agenda at a critical moment.

When Ulanov entered the vast hall, the seats around the outer, semicircular table where staff and observers sat were completely full. Every representative of the committee membership was at the actual committee table in the center. The word had clearly gotten around—despite Ulanov's efforts to keep it quiet—that Russia was dropping a bombshell at today's meeting.

Ulanov glanced at the American seat and was pleased to see that his counterpart, Peter King, was there. They exchanged quick nods as he took his seat. He had not spoken to King about this meeting, which had been called on just twelve hours' notice, but King no doubt knew what it was about. The American was not smiling.

Ulanov wasted no time. Shortly after being recognized by the Costa Rican ambassador, Ulanov rose from the table. The cavernous room grew quiet. More for effect than anything else, he walked around the table, personally delivering each envelope to the members of the 1540 Committee. This was a closed session—as were most of the sessions of the 1540 committee—but Ulanov knew the contents of the envelope would make it into the international press very quickly.

"Mr. Chairman," he began, even as he was still handing out the envelopes, "let me say at the outset that the Russian Federation recognizes that the content of these envelopes is troubling. But we felt, given the events of the past forty-eight hours, we had no choice but to bring it to the committee's attention. This may not be the best forum, but I will explain our rationale shortly."

Ulanov glanced at his U.S. counterpart, even as he continued walking back to his seat. King had merely glanced at the contents and then closed the folder. He either knew what it contained—or didn't care. "As you read through what I've provided," Ulanov continued, "please bear in mind that we bring these facts to light reluctantly. But, as I said, we felt like we had no choice."

King raised his hand. Ulanov glanced at the chairman, who nodded quickly. Ulanov turned back to his American counterpart and recognized him. "Mr. Chairman, I have examined the contents of this envelope," King said, choosing his words carefully, "and I can tell you with absolute certainty that the 1540 Committee is not the place or time for this information. My friend from the Russian Federation knows this. It is more properly a matter for the Security Council, which meets later today."

"Perhaps," Ulanov said. He slid his chair out quietly and took his place at the table. "But my American friend knows full well that long-standing U.S. policy in these matters would, by necessity, require him to do everything in his power to keep information such as this from being presented to the Security Council."

"The past is the past, and I cannot change that," King said evenly. "But we are here, today, in the present, and we have difficult issues to address shortly at the Security Council. We all know what's at stake right now." He glanced down at the envelope. "And I can say that what the Russian Federation is presenting here today is not helpful."

Ulanov smiled. "Are you saying that the United States would have an interest in joining us for a presentation of this information to the Security Council?"

"You may be surprised at what the United States is willing to present to the Security Council, on this and other matters," King said.

"Are you saying that the United States would condemn Israel for its recent actions?" Ulanov raised one eyebrow. This was a new, unexpected development.

"I am saying that my friend from the Russian Federation should have consulted us before bringing the information to the 1540 Committee," King answered. "He might have been surprised at our reaction—and what we are willing to consider—if he'd pursued that course."

It almost stopped Ulanov. But Russia was committed, and they had to proceed. Ulanov looked away from the game within a game that had just occurred between the two superpowers and addressed the full committee. "My American friend's words notwithstanding, this information is highly relevant to the committee's work. It speaks directly to the 1540 mission—which is to stop rogue nations from willfully delivering nuclear technology into the hands of non-state actors.

"As you will see as you look through the contents of the envelope," Ulanov continued, "I have presented clear evidence to the committee. The envelope contains satellite and other scientific evidence that clearly shows Israel recently launched a nuclear first strike against Iran. It is the first use of nuclear weapons in a Middle East conflict, and it is unacceptable. It shows that at least one IAF fighter used tactical nuclear weapons against Iran facilities—using American technology."

There was an audible gasp from some of the observers gathered at the outer table. King raised his hand again but did not wait to be recognized. "I will say again," he said, his voice rising above the buzz growing in the cavernous room, "that this is not the proper place for this discussion. The 1540 committee is designed to keep technology out of the hands of terrorist groups—not to discuss military options by sovereign nations."

Ulanov shook his head. "No, my American friend is wrong—and for this reason. By using nuclear weapons in a first strike against Iran,

Israel has done the unthinkable. They have changed the playing field. They have now made it acceptable for others—especially the non-state actors and terrorist groups we often discuss here—to quickly seek to retaliate. It has escalated the stakes substantially, and that makes this a matter for the 1540 Committee."

Peter King pursed his lips. He had clear marching orders—delivered by phone from Dr. Gould at the White House just minutes before this committee had convened—to forcefully push this informa-tion off the agenda of the 1540 Committee as quickly as he could. Dr. Gould had been quite clear—get this issue moved to the full Security Council as quickly as possible.

But he also knew that Russia had already succeeded with at least one strategic objective. Israel's calculated decision to use tactical nuclear weapons to penetrate deep underground into the hardened bunkers to destroy Iran's covert centrifuges was now an open issue—and would be known to the world shortly. The debate would now quickly shift toward universal condemnation of Israel. It was inevitable. World opinion worked this way, King knew.

"It is *not* a matter for this committee," King said. "Israel is not a non-state actor. It is not a terrorist organization. This committee is not commissioned to deal with military actions taken by sovereign nations in defense of their own national interests. The 1540 has one clear, unambiguous mission, which is to do everything we can to keep technology from being transferred to terrorist groups. If the Russian Federation wishes to raise this, it needs to come before the Security Council. So I would ask the chair to refer this matter to the Security Council—which is where it belongs."

Ulanov looked toward the committee chairman and nodded once, signaling that he would not object to the U.S. motion. The Costa Rican ambassador, who'd spoken to King prior to the meeting, made the motion quickly to refer the matter to the Security Council. The matter was referred moments later.

But, from the American perspective, the damage had already been done. Israel was now the bad actor—the nation that had first used nuclear weapons in the Middle East, which would trigger an immediate escalation on the part of Iran and its proxies. Forces would be unleashed.

From the Russian perspective, Andrei Rowan had gotten what he needed. Ulanov knew he would be pleased.

23

Aboard the USS Abraham Lincoln
The Gulf of Oman

"Get them here!" he barked. His voice echoed loudly in the command and control center, the nerve center of the Nimitz supercarrier. He didn't care who knew that he was angry. He needed the ships in the vicinity, and he needed them here yesterday.

The executive officer of the USS *Abraham Lincoln*—the ship's second-in-command—took a step forward to address his superior officer. "Sir, are you sure—"

Vice Admiral Asher Truxton turned abruptly. "Yes, I'm sure. We need all four of them here, and we need them now. We're going to need everything we have." Everyone else in the command and control center listened intently as the vice admiral spoke.

"Sir, we have our full complement of eight supporting ships, and we're loaded to the gills with the aircraft we need," the executive officer said. "We have four other carrier fleets ready to support us. We'll be fine."

"I know," Truxton said sharply, "and we have eyes in the sky looking out two hundred miles, targeted EMP ready to shut down their systems, and the next-gen blue-green lasers looking for midget subs. Our Sea-RAM system is ready. I know! I've been briefed more times than you can imagine. But we still need those LCS ships— we need ten times the number we have."

The crew on the *Abe* was universally perplexed about why Truxton was on their ship and running the show for the time being in place of their captain, Dewey Smith. But Truxton was not your typical vice admiral and fleet commander. He'd visited the USS *Abraham Lincoln* twice before during operations and maneuvers in the Persian Gulf region.

So it wasn't unusual for Truxton to be on board. It was just odd, and out of place.

What none of them knew was how gravely concerned Truxton was at the moment. He had always paid close and special attention to Israel. And, right now, Israel was at the center of a storm that could shortly engulf the world.

Truxton was also plain mad at the way his own leadership wasn't prepared. He'd fumed, cursed, and boiled over with rage at Washington, DC, and the procurement bureaucracy that had botched several key acquisitions. That ineptitude was about to see its consequences near the shallow waters of the narrow strait of water responsible for the passage of 40 percent of the world's oil.

He was angry, too, that the leadership at the Pentagon was still mired hopelessly in the past, and the notion that a show of huge projected force with massive carrier fleets in the water would always get the job done. Times had changed, and Truxton was worried that they simply were not prepared for asymmetrical concepts that could confound even the best and biggest they had to offer.

Truxton knew precisely what he needed in the Persian Gulf—and specifically what he needed in the shallow, coastline waters south of Iran and the Strait of Hormuz. These were the most treacherous waters anywhere on the planet, and he wasn't convinced they could handle a coordinated, all-out attack.

He knew this, in his bones, and it angered him to the depth of his long career in the Navy that they weren't prepared right now, at a critical moment in time. There was a way for Iran to strike—and temporarily cripple—Western forces trying to keep the Strait of Hormuz open for the passage of oil.

Iran's military was second-rate. There was no question of that. The Iranians lied through their teeth, bluffed, and pretended at every turn. They announced prototypes and make-believe weapons systems whenever possible. They projected force that simply did not exist. They had very little ability to build anything that could significantly threaten the U.S.—or Israeli—military. U.S. military forces crushed Iran in every war game scenario that had ever been conducted.

But Truxton knew this was not the full story—not by any means. Russia, China, and North Korea had been advising the leadership of Iran's Revolutionary Guards for years now—and selling them weapons systems behind this advice. The Iranians had learned a great deal by watching and listening. They'd learned how to be smart about what they were buying with their vast oil wealth. Iran used its oil wealth to keep Russia interested and at the table.

And they were buying systems that could exploit vulnerabilities. Truxton and the Pentagon leadership knew that Iran had purchased dozens of SS-N-22 anti-ship cruise missiles—the so-called Sunburns—that had been developed in Russia and modified in China, and most probably the sister, Russian-made SS-NX-26 Yakhonts missiles that could nearly hit Mach 3 and had a range of 180 miles. Both the Sunburns and the Yakhonts could carry a nuclear payload, if need be.

The Sunburn was twice as fast as any comparable American anti-ship cruise missile. The Sea-RAM "just in time" system consistently knocked them down in drills, but Truxton knew that any sort of swarm attack was a different scenario entirely. What's worse, China had developed an even more advanced cruise missile

—the Anjan, or "Dark Sword"—and they weren't sure how many had made their way yet to Iran's Revolutionary Guards.

For all they knew—and the Pentagon knew a *lot*—hundreds of Exocets, Sunburns, Yakhonts, and even Anjan Dark Swords could be tucked away in the mountains up and down Iran's southern coast. Truxton drew some comfort in the knowledge that the U.S. had developed the ability to track, target, and shut down the individual guidance systems on all of these cruise missile systems. But a swarm attack, from many different directions, could still create problems for the American ships in the Gulf.

What worried Truxton just as much was their relative inability to track and fight in the shallow waters of the Persian Gulf if they had to close in on the waters just south of Bandar Abbas. They needed fast ships that could reach forty knots, draft in shallow water, and deal with coastline threats.

They had such a ship—the Littoral Combat Ship —that had been in development by both General Dynamics and Lockheed Martin for years. But the Pentagon had been forced to cancel both programs due to massive, almost inexplicable cost overruns at both defense contractors and then restart the procurement. As a result, they only had four LCS ships, when Truxton knew they needed ten or twenty times that number in the Persian

Gulf region. But four LCS ships were better than none, he knew.

Truxton had ordered all four LCS ships there immediately, and they would arrive within a day or two. But, for now, the 5th Fleet stationed at Bahrain was responsible for the Persian Gulf and the Strait of Hormuz, and they would simply have to deal with whatever happened in the region.

All the NSA traffic said something was imminent. Iran had chosen not to track the Israeli planes out over the sea, or over Turkey, immediately following the attack against Iran's nuclear facilities. They'd chosen to retaliate with the lone Shahab 3 strike and to muster concerted forces elsewhere.

The Pentagon leadership now presumed that Iran's next effort would be to close the Strait, as it had vowed. Truxton was not convinced that U.S. and Israeli forces were ready, and he had made the last-minute decision to run things from aboard the *Abe*. He was worried about the possibility of swarming threats—from midget and swimmer subs or speedboats deployed on suicide missions.

The USS *Abraham Lincoln* was a Nimitz-class supercarrier. It had been to the Gulf region several times. The officers on board knew what they were up against. They'd left the Naval Station in Everett, Washington, only two months ago for a seven-month deployment to the Persian Gulf.

Captain Smith opened the door to the command

control center and stepped in smartly. Whatever emotions he felt about the vice admiral showing up on his ship were hidden well. "Sir, the ships are in position," Smith said. "The AWACs are up, satellites are real-time, eyes and ears are open, and the aircraft are ready to go." An outstanding captain, Smith deserved his command of the supercarrier. But he also respected the chain-of-command. If Truxton felt he needed to be here, then Smith was apparently willing to accept his superior's presence without question.

"So we can move in, if need be?" Truxton asked.

"At your command, yes," Smith said. "We are 150 miles out from Bandar Abbas. We can move at any time. We can deploy whatever we need. We stand at ready."

"Good." Truxton nodded. "And the Aegis system?"

"Running. No threats observed," Smith said.

"Sea-RAM?"

"Tested, and ready."

"And the four LCS ships?"

"They will be here within the day," Smith said.

"I wish we had more of them." Truxton frowned.

"You and me both."

"It's a shame we botched the procurement so badly. We need as many of those ships as we can get our hands on, right now."

"We're ready, sir," Smith said firmly.

"I believe you, Captain," Truxton murmured. "I do. But we may yet be surprised by what we see."

24

JASK, IRAN

The nondescript, twin prop jet landed without incident at the tiny airport on the outskirts of Jask. No other planes had landed at Jask that morning, so it made its way to the end of the single runway and turned into the flat, tin-roof hangar without much discussion on the airwaves.

Jask was a quiet, sleepy resort town on the coast of the Oman Sea, south of the Makran Coast mountain region. It was a tranquil, beautiful resort area, with a budget hotel, a lone gas station, a mosque, and a hospital. There was only one main road into the town. Jask's historical site was on the western side of the coastal town, and its square ran alongside the eastern shore.

Iran's leaders had long ago established a pretense for visiting the area. Several of them had purchased resort villas and regularly visited there with an entourage. The local Jask community had grown accustomed to visits from Tehran officials and their retinue over the years. It was not out of the ordinary to see a group from Tehran.

But twenty miles inland, at points where the mountains climbed up and away from the coastline, the Guards had systematically built a number of sites to launch the anti-ship Sunburns they'd acquired from Russia, through North Korea, and elsewhere.

They'd also managed to conceal hangars for dozens of attack helicopters and small planes that were prepared to join a firefight one hundred miles or so offshore at a moment's notice. There was the risk, of course, that some of these planes and helicopters—which had been parked there, idle, for years in some cases—would be unable to take off and join a fight.

But it was a risk the Guards were willing to take. There had been no training exercises anywhere in the Jask area for years—merely visits from officials who were there to vacation and make regular trips up into the mountains a short distance away for sport and fun.

None of the local residents at Jask knew that, fewer than thirty miles away, the Guards had a full-fledged listening post capable of tracking movements of carrier fleets up to two hundred miles out to sea from that location. They had no knowledge of the cache of the Russian Sunburns or Dark Swords obtained from China that were armed, waiting for a launch order.

They couldn't possibly realize that—within a sixty-mile radius—there were three separate hangars built into the side of the Makran Coast mountains, hiding secret runways roughly the length of a large naval carrier designed to allow small fighter jets and attack helicopters to take off quickly.

All of this had been built carefully and meticulously over the long history of the Guards' control of the military in Iran for just this day, when they needed to exert temporary control of the Strait of Hormuz at a critical moment.

What the Americans, Israelis, and others failed to grasp about Iran's theocracy and the Revolutionary Guards was that they took a very long view of their steady march to empire. They were content to rule, build, and grow over decades—not years. Though the Western press often had difficulty tracing their strategic intent, they weren't hasty, crazy, or wild-eyed. Far from it.

No, in fact, they had exhibited patience around the region, allowing proxies in Lebanon, Iraq, Afghanistan, and elsewhere to do their bidding. They were content to build and wait.

Hussein Bahadur had wasted no time getting from Gilan Qarb south to Jask. In fact, he'd left the moment the Shahab 3 had been fired at Israel. Zhubin wanted him to personally oversee the battery of anti-ship missiles, speedboats, attack helicopters, and small planes the military had strategically arranged up and down the southern coastline of Iran.

The more logical strategic headquarters for this mission, of course, was Bandar Abbas at the narrowest point of the Strait of Hormuz. But the entire world expected Iran to operate from there. So it did not operate from there.

Asymmetrical warfare dictated that one came at one's enemy from many different, unexpected directions. Who in their right mind would attack an enemy's greatest strengths head-on—especially when that enemy had the collective might and power of the United States and Israel?

The American Navy's projected force was the greatest any navy had ever shown in the history of the world. Their Nimitz-class supercarriers were virtually indestructible. Short of a small nuclear explosion onboard one, the carriers that served at the core of their fleets were unsinkable.

But, Bahadur knew, they were also very big targets—ones that the Russians and Chinese had spent tens of thousands of man-hours studying and plotting against. Iran now possessed the fruits of that long study.

The entire world knew Iran had every intention of shutting down the Strait of Hormuz in retaliation to an Israeli first strike. Shutting the Strait down would effectively stop the flow of most of the world's oil, bringing the entire global economy to the brink of collapse.

Iran, alone, held the key to control of the shallow waters and shipping lane through the Strait of Hormuz. It wasn't as if the United Arab Emirates was going to stage counter-attacks from Dubai.

No, there was just one navy—the American Navy—that could prevent the closure of the Strait. And Bahadur had a plan to keep it out for weeks, and possibly months.

In truth, shutting down the Strait was not in Iran's own national interest. It would hurt its own exports as well as others, but there was very little choice in the short term. The leadership of the Guards had won their argument. If they did not respond to the Israeli attack with some sort of military success in the region, their cause would be harmed for years, if not decades. They needed a critical, strategic success, and they needed it immediately. The Strait was their best hope.

Several of the Guards' leaders were waiting for Bahadur in front of the budget hotel as his car turned left off the main road into Jask. They'd been there for the better part of a day.

"God grant you peace," Bahadur said as he stepped from the car.

"Upon you be peace," responded the senior-most official.

Bahadur wasted no time with pleasantries. "Have you visited the three hangars already? Are they prepared?"

"Yes, sir, they are," the official answered.

"Our pilots? The submarine crews? They are all here?"

"All of them drove through the night to get here. They are all in place."

"And the missiles? They are ready as well?"

"Armed," the officer answered. "We will fire on your command."

Bahadur nodded. All was well. It was almost time. There was only one other thing to check on, and it was something he wanted to do personally.

The Guards had also built a secret facility on the western side of Jask, north of the old historical site, to allow midget submarines to set out to sea. There were a dozen speedboats secured there as well, underneath a tin roof that ostensibly had been built to protect luxury boats from the rain.

Every defense think tank in the world believed that Iran had only a handful—fewer than ten—of the essentially worthless midget and "swimmer" submarines. But the Guards had purchased every midget submarine that had ever become available, and had, in fact, built two dozen of their own over the years, modeled after North Korea's Yugo sub. North Korea had given Iran four Yugos as repayment of debt, then had taught Iran how to manufacture more of them.

Most of them worked—thanks to the North Korean military leaders and scientists who'd helped them acquire much of their arsenal and hardware and showed them how to operate all of the various moving parts—and were now ready to be deployed on suicide missions. The old and new Yugos were parked near Jask.

The truth, which the world would learn very

soon, was that North Korea had equipped and trained Iran's Revolutionary Guards. The Iranians had learned—and learned quickly. They were excellent students and more than willing to take everything North Korea had been willing to give.

It was time to set the trap for the Americans. Bahadur needed the Americans to think that the Iranian navy was projecting a show of force south of Bandar Abbas. One of his lieutenants was in command of a small fleet of Corvettes and Tir class attack craft. They were waiting on Bahadur's order to leave port at Bandar Abbas and head in the direction of the American supercarrier fleet two hundred miles away, in the deeper waters of the Gulf of Oman.

At the right moment, Bahadur would call his lieutenant from an unprotected phone, over an open satellite channel, and give the order to move the fleet of Corvettes and Tirs out to sea. The NSA would pick it up, relay the order instantly, and, most likely, act on the intelligence.

Once engaged, all of the American ships and fighter jets attached to the supercarrier would leave the USS *Abraham Lincoln* to head toward a seemingly inevitable confrontation in the Strait. It was the logical thing to do—meet force with force. It would, of course, leave the mother ship unprotected out at sea in the Gulf of Oman.

But the American Navy, arrogant as ever, would have no worry about their Nimitz supercarrier sitting comfortably 150 miles away from the fight near Bandar Abbas.

Bahadur knew the Americans believed their Navy was invincible and operated their ships in international waters with that in mind. And, of course, they were almost invincible in a direct confrontation. But Bahadur had no real intention of meeting the mighty American Navy head on.

The world was, in fact, waiting for this show of force. This battle for control of the Strait was what military planners had feared for years—and had hoped would never happen.

But Israel's strike in Iran had changed the equation, forever. There was no turning back. Too much was at stake, on all sides.

25

SAVANNAH, GEORGIA

The place was a crummy hole-in-the-wall, just off I-95 at the north end of Savannah. It had no regular patrons—just truckers, mostly, who stopped for coffee, cigarettes, and gas. Some of the locals occasionally drifted by for the cheap cartons of cigarettes.

There were always trucks at the place. Big ones, small ones. The place smelled of diesel. Every parking space had a permanent oil and gas stain. There was plenty of traffic in and out of the Quick Value Stop (QVStop) pumps.

None of the patrons knew, or cared, who owned the gas/beer/cigarette hole-in-the-wall. Had someone bothered to point out to them that it was one of fourteen thousand QVStop stations in the U.S., and that QVStop was owned by an indirect, wholly owned subsidiary of Venezuela's state-owned oil company, they'd have received blank stares in return.

The fact that QVStop's U.S. corporate headquarters in Dallas, Texas, had bulletproof and bomb-proof glass around it, as well as other state-of-the-art security measures, might have caused them to raise their eyebrows a little. That was a little unusual for a corporate complex in the United States. But no one cared. The QVStop had really cheap cigarettes, a wide selection of beer, and competitive gas prices.

The owners appeared to be a local guy—somebody who'd grown up a few miles from the QVStop—and his live-in girlfriend at a nearby trailer park. The couple put in long hours and had big dreams of branching out to other QVStops in Savannah and, eventually, the rest of Georgia. They were always there bright and early in the morning and also late at night. They seemed to be there twenty-four hours a day.

But the local guy and his girlfriend weren't the

actual owners. They merely had a stake in the QVStop, a percentage, and were given promises of being franchise owners of this particular QVStop and others. The majority ownership was held by someone else, in partnership with other regional managers who made infrequent appearances at the store.

The couple didn't see more than one or two of these managers at a time. They just went about their jobs, collecting the cash and disbursing it as they were told. They didn't skim, largely because they desperately hoped their good faith and straight dealings with the owners of the QVStop would reward them with full franchise ownership.

They also didn't ask too many questions. Trucks rolled in and out of the place all the time. They barely paid attention to the traffic outside the building. It wasn't their business what the regional managers moved in and out of the back room of the building.

They were never there for very long anyway. When one of the regional managers showed up, they invariably came in a truck, stopped by for a cup of coffee, and chatted for a few minutes while other workers out back did whatever they were doing.

The couple didn't care. They knew their place and had a job to do. They did their jobs very well. Both knew this was their big chance to bootstrap their way out of the trailer park, and they weren't about to jeopardize it by asking too many questions.

The couple had no idea who these regional managers were, or where they came from. The man had asked once in passing, and the regional manager had simply shrugged and laughed.

"I'm from Georgia," the regional manager had said with a smile and a slight British accent.

"Georgia? Here, in Savannah?" The local guy had been thoroughly confused.

No, the regional manager had said politely, from the Georgia that had once been part of the old Soviet Union. He'd come to the United States after the breakup. He was part of a Muslim community that had started to drift to the West from his homeland after the breakup.

The local guy had nodded politely and said nothing further. He wasn't exactly sure where Georgia was, whether there was even a significant Muslim population there, or whether what the man was saying was possibly true. But it didn't matter to him—just like it didn't matter to him who owned QVStop. He had a future and a good job. The gas came to the pumps regularly, and the regional owners provided the store with a steady supply of cheap cigarettes. Not much else mattered.

But there was someone, in fact, who cared. He cared a great deal. The FBI field agent assigned to Savannah had been watching the creation of the leadership team and the truck movement in and out of this particular hole-in-the-wall for some time. It had become a particular passion of his, and he'd put in quite a lot of time on its profile.

The agent had learned, early on, that the local guy and his girlfriend were sham owners. The real owners were an older couple who'd migrated to the United States from Iran after the fall of the Shah. They'd been in the United States for some time and were respected leaders in the small circle of Shi'a Muslims who regularly worshipped together in the Savannah area.

From there, the agent tracked down some of the "regional managers" who showed up at this particular QVStop on a regular basis. They were young guns, direct from Iran, given plenty of latitude by the QVStop franchise to make money with cigarettes, beer, and gas.

What bothered the FBI agent, right from the outset, was the fact that a couple of them had come to the U.S. through Venezuela instead of coming straight from Iran. They'd spent some time training at the state-owned company's headquarters in Venezuela first. It made sense, of course. QVStop was closely held and followed by the leadership in Venezuela, including its president, Victor Ramirez. And Ramirez had a special place in his heart for Iran.

The ties between Ramirez and Iran's leadership were very strong. Ramirez had been to Iran no less than seven times in the past decade to put together more than $20 billion in deals. Ramirez had welcomed Iran's president, Nassir Ahmadian, to his own country several times.

So it was quite natural for Venezuela's state-owned oil company to entertain bright, energetic, ambitious Iranian men and then send them on their way to the United States to make their way in the world. It made a lot of sense. Ramirez and the state-owned company regularly moved money, materials, and people around to all of their fourteen thousand stations in the U.S. These young men were part of that system.

But something about the setup had bothered the FBI agent from the first moment he'd started to look more closely. He hadn't yet been able to convince many up the chain of command about his belief, but he hoped he could soon. He was waiting for something—a thread of some sort that he could follow—to help him make sense of the picture.

When he could, the agent ran license tags of interesting-looking trucks that made their way through the hole-in-the-wall station. Nothing suspicious really hit. It always led back to cigarette wholesalers, or beer wholesalers, or oil and gas distributors.

Until one day, when the license tag of a

particular flatbed connected not to one of these wholesalers but to a recent shipment of more than a dozen containers labeled as tractor parts. The containers had made their way from Iran, to Venezuela, and then through customs at the port of Savannah to begin their journey into the heart of America. The first stop was the hole-in-the-wall QVStop just off I-95 north of Savannah.

The FBI agent had moved quickly, obtaining a search warrant as fast as he could. This was the sort of anomaly he'd been looking for. A team of agents descended on the gas station and seized the truck before it could leave and head out onto the interstate system. They'd discovered plenty of tractor parts inside—and other parts as well. As best as the agents could determine, there were enough parts inside to set up an explosives lab. They arrested the driver, who'd been hired by someone else to deliver the tractor parts.

The agent began the time-consuming and arduous task of connecting this driver back to the original source of the tractor parts. It would take time, and heaven only knew if he would ever find the true origin—and owner—of the shipment. He filed his initial report and sent out an alert.

QVStop's leaders at corporate headquarters in Dallas quickly disassociated themselves from the owners of this particular hole-in-the-wall station and told authorities that it was unfortunate and sad that someone had been trying to use the station to smuggle in illegal parts for some sort of illicit enterprise. They made a point of firing and disenfranchising the local guy and his girlfriend and told the authorities that they would get to the bottom of what happened.

The regional managers who had been involved with the local couple during the past few years simply vanished into the mist. The older couple who held the ownership papers to the QVStop knew nothing about them, or where they'd gone. They also claimed to know nothing about this particular shipment, or who had even ordered it.

The only signature on the truck's shipping manifest belonged to the local guy who ran the QVStop. He didn't remember signing it, but it was most definitely his signature.

But while the ghosts who'd operated in and around this QVStop had left for another place, the FBI agent had his answer. He believed there were other Iranian young guns, at other QVStop stations in the United States, waiting for a day and a time. They'd been given a reason to be in the United States and safe passage into the American economy by the state-owned oil company in Venezuela.

Iran and Venezuela were closely aligned and shared much. It was only natural their subsidiaries employed young men from both countries in their American outposts.

The question, for the FBI agent, was their

ultimate aim. Were they here to make their fortunes in a land of opportunity, as it seemed? Or were at least some of them practicing *taqiyya*—merely disguising their true beliefs and intentions —while waiting for a day and a time?

26

THE WHITE HOUSE WASHINGTON, DC

DJ looked over at the world clock on the wall of his tight, cramped, windowless cubicle office off to one side of the press secretary's office. He couldn't believe it was nine o'clock in the morning and he'd already been there for almost five hours.

He hadn't been able to sleep. His wife had essentially kicked him out of bed in their small, two-bedroom loft apartment ten blocks north and west of the White House. She had a big day coming up, so DJ crawled out of bed, crept around the apartment quietly so he didn't wake up their son, and began to troll through the news reports coming in from all over the world. There were hundreds of news reports related to Iran, Israel, and the growing conflict that now threatened to engulf the world.

Finally, after staring at the glowing monitor in the study off to one side of their small apartment for the better part of an hour, DJ had given up, taken a shower, and headed to the White House. He'd walked the entire ten blocks because the Metro wasn't operating, and he'd been unable to find a cab.

DJ couldn't help himself. He was worried. Israel was in a lot of trouble, with enemies closing in on all sides. It wasn't just Iran—it was Iran's proxies in Lebanon and Gaza as well. Russia was showing an interest in the region again, and countries like Syria had not abandoned their hatred of Israel. Israel seemed to be squarely at the center of a growing conflict on all sides that threatened to overwhelm it.

He trusted President Camara implicitly, and he believed with every fiber of his being that the world was very, very fortunate that someone like Adom Camara had assumed the presidency at this particular moment in history. If anyone could walk the straight, narrow path through the very difficult times they now faced, President Camara could.

Camara had earned back the trust of most of the world's leadership. He'd largely been able to isolate Iran's leadership from the rest of the world. He'd brought Egypt, Jordan, Saudi Arabia, and others in the Arab world firmly to one side, away from Iran. He'd re-engaged with the Russian leadership, and both sides now regularly talked about global geo-political strategy. China was now engaged on global warming and other items of mutual interest with the U.S. He'd repaid the American debts owed to the United Nations, and the UN leaders now paid close attention to what the Americans had to say.

While Camara had been unable to pull Russia and China out of Iran's economic orbit, which had always been an impossible task, he'd been successful in isolating Iran from the rest of the world community. At a critical moment, he'd convinced the five permanent members of the Security Council at the UN, including Russia and China, to impose several harsh sanctions against Iran.

Thanks to Camara, the United States was no longer isolated in the world community. Its leadership was respected. Iran, North Korea, Venezuela, Libya, and a few others were now the isolated ones, their actions watched closely by the world community.

DJ knew all of this and regularly made sure the international media knew it as well. But this conflict between Iran and Israel seemed hopeless —and headed toward a truly horrific military confrontation that had real potential to set off conflicts that could extend beyond the Middle East. Iran wasn't about to back off. Neither was Israel.

And because of the United States' long, close

relationship with Israel—which was not about to change anytime soon—DJ knew in his heart that Americans would shortly be drawn to the center of the conflict. There seemed no way to avoid it. DJ also couldn't help but wonder if Israel wasn't being pulled into a global conflict that had been prophesied for thousands of years. It wasn't the kind of thing he'd talk about out loud, but the thought did enter his mind from time to time.

The president had allowed DJ to get his Top Secret clearance, which gave him access to many of the military briefings and material. The reports he'd seen had made it very clear that the Israelis were deadly serious about removing or substantially delaying Iran's nuclear threat. There was no getting around that fact—or the certain knowledge that the U.S. would be heavily involved, whether it wanted to or not.

DJ had sat through any number of discussions with the president about the situation. In every instance, the president had been intently focused on doing the right thing and still achieving the necessary strategic goal—and balance. Camara was unwavering: do what's right for the United States, and then the world, with as little damage as possible.

Isolate the bad actors, the president always maintained, and the world will understand. Truth is a powerful weapon.

But this situation with Iran and Israel seemed

impossible to deal with, even for someone as disciplined, strategic, and thoughtful as Camara. There was just no easy way to confront this problem, DJ believed. He always listened for a way out of the quagmire. But none, as yet, had emerged.

Still, he had faith in the president and the leaders he'd assembled. If anyone could find a safe path forward, it was this president.

"How long have you been here?" a friendly voice asked from the doorway to his office. DJ looked up from his desk to see Dr. Gould leaning up against the side of the doorway.

"Five hours," DJ answered without looking at the clock again.

Anshel nodded. "I couldn't really sleep either. I got maybe two hours last night."

"I couldn't stop reading the news reports." DJ shook his head. "They're endless. It seems like the entire world is paying attention, and writing about it."

"They *are* paying attention," Anshel said. "People are funny like that. They can go for years without paying much attention to something. But then, when it's time, they focus in like a laser. It's why you get mass audiences for things like the Super Bowl or the Olympics."

"But the Iran problem has been around for years!"

"True. But did it matter—until now?"

"I guess not." DJ shrugged. "But it should have mattered, long before now."

"Trust me," Anshel said, "some very smart people have been working away at this problem for a long time. This isn't a surprise. We know what Iran is going to do. We've known their intentions for some time. So do countries like Egypt, Saudi Arabia, and Jordan."

"And Israel? Do we know what they're going to do?"

Anshel managed a crooked half smile. "We know what they just did, don't we?"

DJ swiveled around in his chair. "But, seriously, do we know what they're going to do if this goes further? If this escalates? What if that ballistic missile with the nuclear warhead had landed in Tel Aviv? What then?"

"But it *didn't* land," Anshel said quietly. "We need to keep that in mind. Israel's defenses worked, just as planned. And we need to take advantage of that and act accordingly."

"How? That's what I keep asking myself. How do we find a way through this mess? Iran will respond. Israel isn't going to back down. They can't. How does this end? How do we—"

Anshel held up a hand. "I get it," he said, more forcefully than usual. "But there are ways to deal with this, once we get through the immediate confrontation. We'll do what we need to do in the short term. We have no choice. We'll get the situation under control, militarily, in the region. And then we'll move toward a permanent solution that will isolate the bad actors from the world community for good. We can take control of the situation and build a solution that should keep Iran and others from constantly exploiting the never-ending conflict with Israel."

"You really believe that's possible? A solution? Because it doesn't seem possible. Iran won't give up their path to a nuclear state. And Israel can't afford to let that happen."

"Yes, I do believe it's possible." Anshel moved into DJ's office and pulled a chair toward his desk. He sat down sideways, casually draping his right arm over the top of the chair. "Listen. Keep this between the two of us, for the time being. I'll brief you more fully when the time is right. But I've been working on something, a new plan, for months."

"A new plan?" DJ couldn't help himself. A flicker of hope emerged where none had been before. He trusted Dr. Gould as much as he trusted the president.

"Something I've been working on quietly with the Israeli government, ever since they released their plan for a Palestinian state."

"But that plan was absolutely insane!" DJ exploded. "No one thinks it will work, because it won't. It's the craziest plan I've ever seen. A superhighway running under the Negev, connecting the West Bank to Gaza? With both Israelis and Palestinians running around with monitors that identify their nationality? Three different parts of a Palestinian state, none of them connected? The West Bank taking most of the land mass right out of the center of Israel, dividing it in half? Relocating one hundred thousand Israeli settlers from the Jordan River to other parts of Israel? No way. It won't work. Not in a million years."

Anshel smiled at DJ's passion. "You're right. It's an insane plan. It's completely unworkable. It's unacceptable. It doesn't solve the Palestinian refugee problem. There isn't enough land to take in several million Palestinians from all of the refugee camps in the region. You can't keep one section of a country, Gaza, disconnected from another section in the West Bank. And, you're right—the West Bank, as it's currently defined, practically cuts Israel in half."

DJ considered Anshel intently. Once upon a time, in a former life as a member of Congress, Dr. Gould had been quite adept at the tricky art of political gerrymandering. In fact, he'd managed to pull off the impossible—creating a political map that protected members from both parties and wasn't so crazy that it couldn't survive a court challenge.

And, in one sense, this was gerrymandering—on a world stage.

"So you have an idea in mind?" DJ asked.

"Something that can end most of the conflict with countries other than Iran?"

"I do. It could calm things down with almost everyone outside of Iran's immediate influence."

"A peace process that could isolate Iran?"

Anshel's eyes sparkled. "Precisely."

"And you think the Israelis will go for it?"

"Some will—hopefully enough of the right parts of their leadership. The ones who are reasonable and understand that we need a solution."

"It's the kind of plan that might bring along countries like Egypt and Jordan?"

"Especially Egypt and Jordan," Anshel answered. "And it will give Israel a fighting chance against Syria and Lebanon—something they don't have if they give up land in the West Bank in the north."

DJ sat forward in his chair. "Absolutely! It's why the Israelis don't want to give up the northern land in the West Bank—why they're allowing the settlements to go forward there. If you give up that land, and establish a new Palestinian country that practically comes right up to the northern part of Jerusalem, you might as well allow Syria and Lebanon to camp out on your front porch. . . ."

"Which Israel will never allow," Anshel finished quietly. "A free-standing Palestinian country north of Jerusalem in the West Bank puts it just a stone's throw from Tel Aviv, Haifa, and Jerusalem and gives Syria and Lebanon easy access to every major population center in Israel."

"Not to mention you'd have to move all of those settlements along the Jordan River north of Jerusalem. You'd have civil war on your hands in Israel."

"So we don't move them." Anshel peered directly down at DJ, as if waiting for the plan to sink in.

"But if you don't move the Jewish settlements, then what's left as an important centerpiece in a new Palestinian country? What's their capital city?"

"Beersheba."

DJ just stared back. The concept was almost unthinkable. But everything about Israel seemed a little surreal on the world stage. "Beersheba's a real city," he said finally. "It's one of the largest in Israel."

"You're right. It is. But it was always planned as part of an Arab state. In fact, it was central to the original UN partition plan for a new Palestinian country right after World War II," Anshel explained. "It was supposed to be included—until the IDF kicked the Egyptian forces out in 1948. If you look at the old discussions, right after the war, the UN meant for Beersheba to be the capital city of a new Arab state. It should have been— and could be today."

"Beersheba belonged to the Arabs after World War II?" DJ asked. "I didn't know that."

"Most people don't," Anshel answered. "But a Palestinian historian, Aref al-Aref, was actually the governor of Beersheba during the British Mandate after the UN partition plan in 1947."

"Hamas loves to lob bombs from Gaza out toward Beersheba," DJ mused.

"So take away their target."

"Israel would never let Hamas get near Jerusalem," DJ said.

"Hamas would lose its power in a free Arab state," Anshel shot back. "They flourish only because Gaza is completely isolated from the rest of the world."

"So you would unite Gaza with parts of the West Bank in the South, and make Beersheba the capital?"

"Exactly."

DJ sat back in his chair. He was stunned. It would actually give something of value to a new Arab state—and end forever the constant drum-beat of criticism that Israel was an aggressive nation-state intent on taking land in Egypt, Jordan, Syria, and Jordan.

DJ called up a Google map of Israel on his computer monitor and examined it, connecting the dots. It was a radical solution—one that had not been considered since the chaotic days right after World War II.

It was radical—but also held out the possibility of a sustainable solution. If you created a real capital city at the heart of a new Arab state, surrounded by a valley fed by water from the Hebron mountains, the land would actually have value as a home for the millions of displaced Palestinians. It was a true measure of land for peace.

"You're talking about giving Israel's Southern District to the Palestinians," DJ said.

"Yes, I am."

"You'd give up the South—all of it—to create a free, united Palestinian country?" DJ asked finally. "And force both Egypt and Jordan to make sure it worked?"

"It's in their interest to make it work. Both of them once went to war with Israel for the South."

DJ looked back at the map. The Southern District of Israel formed a perfect triangle, wedged in between the Mediterranean to the west, Egypt to the south, and Jordan to the east. Jerusalem was at the top.

"What about Ashdod, north of Gaza? It's Israel's largest port city."

"It stays in Israel. It's almost directly west of Jerusalem anyway."

"And what about Ashkelon?"

"A bargaining chip," Anshel said. "It's changed hands so many times in history it might as well be on the table one more time, in the interest of a permanent solution for peace. But, most likely, it remains in Israel as well. The key is Beersheba. The new, united Palestinian country will need a capital, a center—with a real economy and a chance to succeed."

DJ pursed his lips. "Israel would never give up their access to the Red Sea at the southern tip. It allows them to handle oil tanker traffic to and from the oceans to the south. Israel is counting on bringing in oil traffic through their pipeline from Ashkelon to Eilat, and then out through the Red Sea. They've been negotiating with Russia, Georgia, and others over that for years—ever since they took it over completely from Iran after the Shah fell."

"Yes, that's potentially a problem," Anshel mused. "It *is* odd to think that Israel once had a fifty-fifty partnership with Iran to secretly bring in oil through the Eilat-Ashkelon pipeline—until the Shah fell and the partnership went away—and that this same pipeline may now make Israel the key exchange point for oil from the north to the Far East."

"So how do you solve that problem?"

"Obviously, Israel would own it," Anshel answered. "But the new state would guarantee its security—much as Iran and Israel once held joint ownership of the pipeline. Oil pipelines run through many countries, with joint ownership and security considerations. This one would be no different, in the end."

"Israel would never give up Eilat," DJ said

flatly. "It's a popular resort—not to mention key as a port for oil tankers someday."

"True. But pirates are making it less attractive as a resort," Anshel said. "And we'll need to negotiate the oil pipeline question. Peace only comes along once for Israel. Everything needs to be on the table."

"The Negev desert is a harsh place. It isn't worth much."

"The United States can change that," Anshel said. "Massive irrigation and water storage can change anything—even the Negev. And we would obviously commit to those sorts of big terraforming construction projects there, in the interest of permanent peace."

DJ shook his head in awe. "It would give the Palestinian refugees a real place to migrate to—not a make-believe land with cobbled together, half-baked, piecemeal, scattered plots of property with gates and walls, barbed wire fences, and permanent Israel military outposts everywhere."

"Yes, it would."

"And you think the Palestinians in the northern parts of the West Bank would move there?"

"They would if they had a real country to go to. They have no home right now. The West Bank isn't a real country. Never has been—and isn't likely to be any time soon."

"And Jerusalem? There's no way that ever gets sorted out."

Anshel smiled. "Don't be so sure of that. You might be surprised."

"I'm not surprised by anything these days," DJ said. "So?"

"I believe the original Green Line, from 1949, is possible—Arab to the west and south, Jewish to the east and north. We can bring everybody except Hamas on board, and we isolate Hamas from everyone else to make it happen."

There was only one other piece of the most complicated peace puzzle the world had ever known—the Temple Mount.

"There are some parts of Israel that will never give up the dream of building a third temple on the Temple Mount," DJ said. "It's one of the reasons they keep control of the overall city."

"A small, narrow group—not in the mainstream, much too conservative for the majority of Israel," Anshel said. "But there's a solution there as well, which everyone can buy into."

"Which is?"

"The Israeli government has been quietly studying the grounds south of the Dome of the Rock for years now, in concert with some of the archaeologists from American universities who've received permission to dig outside the Temple Mount area for comparison purposes," Anshel said. "They've reached some fairly concrete conclusions, which they're willing to go public with soon."

"Let me guess," DJ said, laughing. "The original temple was never where the Dome of the Rock is currently located?"

"Never," Anshel answered. "That ground is too high. The temples were further south, closer to the City of David. They've concluded that the temples were sitting where the El Kas fountain is, halfway between the Dome of the Rock and the Al Aqsa Mosque."

"And there's proof?"

"The IDF has quietly conducted some ground-penetrating radar probes that clearly indicate there had once been vaults and arches beneath the ground to the south. It's solid rock to the north, where the Dome is—not a likely candidate for a temple structure thousands of years ago. Thermal infrared scanning also shows there were likely structures once to the south—not on the northern part of the Temple Mount, where the Dome stands."

"So the temples were south of the Dome?"

"And will be for a third temple, if Israel ever chooses to build one."

"Israel would sanction that location—south of the Dome of the Rock?"

"They will."

"So the Dome of the Rock could coexist, peacefully, side by side with the site of a third temple," DJ said in awe. "Both sides get what they need. If that piece works, you're talking about a permanent solution to the Palestinian problem and the potential for a lasting peace—"

"Potentially."

They both looked back at the Google map of Israel that was still up on DJ's screen. As he sat there staring at the screen, DJ vaguely recalled a phrase he'd once heard in his Sunday school classes. Something nagged at the back of his mind, something he knew he'd heard but couldn't quite recall. It had been years since he'd actually read parts of the Bible that talked about Israel and the Promised Land, but he knew the stories.

And then he remembered.

"From Dan to Beersheba," DJ said quietly. "That's what this is. It recreates the land that the Jews historically controlled and occupied. That phrase is used in the Bible quite often to describe the land that the Jews actually lived in for most of their history—from Dan to the north, to Beersheba in the south. It keeps Israel's enemies to the north, and creates a free, united Palestinian state to the south, where Egypt and Jordan can keep a careful eye on it. It's almost the only way to get to peace."

Anshel smiled. DJ was a smart kid. "There you go," he answered softly.

"It defines the land you're talking about here," DJ marveled. "You might even say it's a realistic description of a Promised Land—without all the aggressive, unrealistic military expansion notions that have gotten Israeli's leadership in trouble since the Second World War."

"Yes, you might." Anshel stood up. He had an endless series of meetings to get to throughout the White House complex, with the first starting in just two minutes. "But there's a lot of ground to cover between today and any sort of a permanent solution. We need to get through the immediate crisis, and then we'll see."

27

THE STRAIT OF HORMUZ
SOUTH OF BANDAR ABBAS, IRAN

Had anyone bothered to ask Hashem Sanjar, the commander of Iran's nearly worthless navy, he would have objected. It seemed like a suicide mission. But Sanjar was no fool. The rear admiral had risen through the ranks of the smallest branch of Iran's military by learning when to be quiet and do as he was told. And this was a time to be quiet.

When the Guards had told him to pull the navy's three destroyers out of mothballs at Bushehr a year earlier and move them to the port at Bandar Abbas—the Iranian navy's home port—Sanjar had dutifully dispatched the engineering and cleanup crews. The destroyers were more than half a century old and hadn't seen action for years. But no matter. They were now allegedly in service.

When the Guards told him to re-equip all five of their frigates with Chinese anti-ship missiles and move all of them to Bandar Abbas, he did so without question. He'd likewise pulled one of the Corvettes back from the Caspian Sea months ago, repositioned it at Bandar Abbas, and moved the rest of their Corvettes there as well.

In fact, Sanjar was more than a little surprised that the Guards had made such a great show of moving the destroyers from Bushehr to Bandar Abbas several months ago. They'd also made a show of consolidating their frigates at Bandar Abbas. Every intelligence network in the world had taken note of the movements. They were impossible to miss.

Had they forgotten Pearl Harbor at the start of World War II, when the Japanese had laid waste to American Navy ships sitting there in port? Moving so many of the Iranian navy's larger ships to Bandar Abbas was akin to that American mistake at Pearl Harbor. Their big ships were sitting ducks.

But when Sanjar had asked Bahadur, quietly, if he was sure about the move, he'd been assured that the relocation of the big ships to Bandar Abbas was a temporary measure as they evaluated all of their options. Sanjar had not pressed the issue further.

But those "temporary measures" had become permanent, and virtually every big ship and submarine under Sanjar's command was now stuck at port in or near Bandar Abbas at the most critical moment in Iran's military history. Sanjar was fuming, but he also knew his duty. He would go down with his ships in flames, if need be. But he would fight.

When he heard directly from the Rev. Shahidi in the past twenty-four hours that he needed to position all three of their Russian-built Kilo submarines just twenty miles or so away from Bandar Abbas, where the shallow waters of the Strait began to deepen as it became the Gulf of Oman, he almost said something. But, in the end, he did nothing to dissuade the Supreme Leader of the military strategy.

Those three diesel attack subs were among the quietest in the world. They were of much better use out to sea—not trapped near the Strait's shallow waters where they would be sitting ducks for the American Navy's massive fleet. It was an insane move.

Sanjar briefly considered making an end run through close associates of Reza Razavi to see what they thought of the suicide mission the Iranian navy was about to embark on in the Strait. But that was a very dangerous course of action. No matter how much civil unrest had grown within Iran's diverse population, Razavi was a long way from the presidency in Iran.

So Sanjar kept quiet and put the navy ships in

place. He was more than a little curious about one aspect of the military strategy that Shahidi, Bahadur, and the Guards were employing, but he had only raised this privately with two of his direct subordinates.

The Iranian navy had invested heavily in literally hundreds of fast patrol boats of all sizes and shapes, many of them equipped with torpedoes and even fairly sophisticated anti-ship missiles brought in around heavy embargoes from Russia, China, and North Korea. They'd also placed dozens of slightly larger gunboats in service in the past few years as well.

But almost none of those smaller boats were to be found at the moment. Sanjar had his hands full coordinating the big ships and submarines at Bandar Abbas and couldn't be troubled to deal with the tiny boats that were nothing more than fleas on an elephant. The Guards were undoubtedly deploying them somewhere, for some unknown purpose. It just seemed curious.

Sanjar's Iridium phone rang at his belt. It was Bahadur. It always bothered him immensely that some in the Guards, like Bahadur, were so foolish that they didn't realize these satellite phones were open lines to the Western intelligence community. Holding a conversation on these phones, Sanjar knew, was like telephoning the CIA and NSA directly. But he kept those opinions to himself as well. He answered his phone and reminded himself to mind his words, which would become part of intelligence community transcripts almost as he spoke the words.

"Admiral, is the fleet ready?" Bahadur asked without preamble.

"Yes, we are ready," Sanjar responded. "We await your command."

"Then move your ships forward. Position them behind the Kilos," Bahadur said. "The American fleet is on the move, and they will be in your area shortly."

"Sir, if I may?" Sanjar knew he had to be extraordinarily careful here, on many levels.

"Yes, Admiral?"

"I just wanted to be absolutely certain that this is what the Rev. Shahidi wishes. There will be casualties in a direct confrontation with the Americans."

"Your concern is duly noted, Admiral," Bahadur answered. "But let me ask you a question. Do you believe that you can hold the Strait, at least for a time? Can you do that?"

"Yes, absolutely," Sanjar answered promptly, taking care that his words conveyed confidence. No matter what his private concerns might be, he did not want intelligence transcripts circulating that conveyed those concerns. "We have more than enough to keep the Americans out of the Strait in the short term. We will be victorious. We can hold the Strait."

"Then that is all that should concern you," Bahadur said. "You have your orders. Keep the Americans out of the Strait. Order your ships out to sea, and join the Kilos."

After Bahadur had hung up, Sanjar turned to his second-in-command at the naval headquarters at Bandar Abbas. "It is time," he ordered. "Move the fleet."

"You're certain it's the best course of action? You don't want to wait to see what the Americans send forward first toward the Strait?" asked his second-in-command, who shared Sanjar's concerns. He'd tried to listen in on the recent conversation with Bahadur, but it had been impossible to discern the direction from just one side of the conversation.

"We have our orders," Sanjar said tersely. "We must move the fleet out to sea now. We will do our best, and may God grant us victory."

Moments later, virtually every major vessel in Iran's navy was on its way out to sea, toward the entrance to the Strait of Hormuz.

28

ABOARD THE USS ABRAHAM LINCOLN
THE GULF OF OMAN

It made no sense. Truxton had stared at the real-time intelligence communiqué for nearly three full minutes. He saw the words. He understood the words, the sentences, and the order in which they were arranged. He could see the semblance of an understandable military strategy behind them. But they still made no sense to him.

"Sir?" asked the junior officer who'd handed the communiqué to him. "Is everything all right? Is there some further clarification I can ask for?"

Truxton looked back down at the key phrase intelligence had gathered from the rear admiral of Iran's navy: *We can hold the Strait.* What did that mean? That they would camp out at the narrow entrance of the Strait, daring the Americans to come in and clear the Iranian ships out? Was it a reckless dare? Was it bravado? Was it desperation?

Truxton knew Sanjar was not a stupid commander. Iran's navy had shown some limited capability over the years. They had enough at their command, if they chose, to hold off virtually any fleet at the entrance to the Strait for a period of time. But, eventually, greater firepower would prevail. The Americans had too many fighter jets, too many frigates, too many submarines not to prevail.

So what was their aim? That was what troubled Truxton. Surely they didn't think they could hold off the Americans, and the other UN peacekeeping forces from other parts of the world, that would shortly show up at their doorstep to join the fight?

The world would simply not stand for a permanent closure of the Strait. Saudi Arabia, Iraq, and virtually every other oil producer in the region—except Iran, of course—was screaming at the United Nations even now to keep the Strait open. Iran could close it. But for how long, and at what cost?

The *Abe*'s captain, Dewey Smith, stood off to one side, studying the communiqué as well. They would receive orders from the Pentagon shortly. Captain Smith wondered how Truxton would respond to the orders, which would direct them to send all of their carrier ships forward to meet the Iranian navy south of Bandar Abbas.

Truxton could override the Pentagon and naval command—but at great risk to his career. If the decision were left to just him, Smith knew he'd likely have no choice but to do exactly as Washington directed. Now Truxton would need to make that call. Some part of Smith was glad.

"Captain, what do you think?" Truxton glanced up from the intelligence communiqué.

"I think it's pretty clear they're sending their ships out from Bandar Abbas," Smith said. "They've positioned everything they have around the world here, for a day just like this one. And now they're on the move."

Truxton nodded. "We've known that for months. They've pulled every big ship they have into Bandar Abbas. Virtually their entire navy is right there."

"Waiting for us," Smith said quietly.

"Exactly. Just waiting for us."

Smith had known the vice admiral for a long time. He could practically read his mind at this moment. "They want us to come after them," he said, echoing what he knew was likely on Truxton's mind as well.

"They do. It might as well be an engraved invitation. But why?"

"I don't know," Smith said, genuinely perplexed. "They must know that they can't win a direct fight."

"So why fight?"

"Because they have no choice." Smith shrugged. "They have limited options right now. They could pursue other targets—like Bahrain— to show the world they aren't going to stand by while Israel rips their heart out."

"I suppose," Truxton mused. "But going into Bahrain, or any other country, would make matters worse for them. We're right here. They know we're not going to just sit by and watch them walk through Bahrain or Dubai."

"So they take the fight to us, the one they know they're going to have anyway."

Truxton glanced back at the communiqué, the unanswered question still looming large in his mind. The conversation between Sanjar and Bahadur that NSA had captured and transmitted almost as it had happened was a puzzle. Its meaning was clear. Sanjar had gotten clear orders to move his forces out into the Strait, to meet the American Navy head on. But Truxton knew—with a certainty he wouldn't be able to articulate to DC—that there was more behind the conversation, something that all of the war planners who'd been up thirty-six hours straight at the Pentagon couldn't know, or anticipate.

The vice admiral looked over at the phalanx of junior officers who were standing off to the side, waiting for their orders. "What's the rest of our signal intelligence showing?" Truxton asked, the question directed at no one in particular. "Anything unusual? Any sub movement? Planes sighted anywhere on radar?"

Several of the junior officers glanced at each other. One of them finally volunteered. "Nothing, sir. No activity, other than the three Kilo subs we already know about. And no aircraft anywhere."

"Nothing?" Truxton asked. "No air cover for the ships moving out from Bandar Abbas?"

"No, sir," the junior officer responded.

"What about their speedboats? Or their Yugos? Any sign of them?"

"No, sir," said another junior officer. "We've been looking, from the air and underwater. We haven't seen anything."

Truxton looked back at Smith. "Captain, does that strike you as odd?"

"That we aren't seeing air cover?"

"Yes, and nothing else as well."

Smith paused. "Yes, it does seem a little odd. They send all those ships out from Bandar Abbas without air cover?"

"Or anything else, for that matter."

"We know they've got all those smaller boats in reserve," Smith said. "Where are they?"

They both walked over to the console that displayed every movement within two hundred miles of the *Abe*. There was a bright array of movement in and around Bandar Abbas. But farther out, closer to the supercarrier fleet, all they saw were friendly signs of activity. There wasn't a single piece of activity anywhere near them.

"So where's the rest of it, Captain?" Truxton asked quietly. "Where are they hiding?"

"Trying to protect the Silkworms, maybe?"

Smith waved his hand across a bank of hard targets along the southern Iranian shoreline that the Pentagon had long ago identified. Pre-set cruise missiles would shortly take out every single one of the Silkworms that had been positioned up and down the coast. The Pentagon was fairly certain they'd rounded up all of those positions over the years.

"That's a lost cause," Truxton explained. "Sanjar and the others know that. They can't protect those Silkworms. They'll try to get as many of them out as quickly as they can, but it's a waste of time to try to protect them. No, the rest of their forces have to be somewhere else."

"Closer to Bahrain, then?" Smith asked. "Further inside the Gulf, waiting to go after Bahrain, Qatar, or even Saudi Arabia?"

"Perhaps, but not likely. That opens them up to everything we have on the ground in Iraq."

Smith glanced back at the map and waved his hand over the country of Iran. "There's nowhere else they could be."

Truxton stared hard at the southern coastline, away from Bandar Abbas and closer to Pakistan. "Any chance Pakistan has let them slip in on their western border?"

"No chance," Smith said. "We've kept a close eye on the Pakistani ports. We'd know if they were staging something from there—and they're not."

"Then that just leaves one option, Captain."

"Which is?"

Truxton jabbed an index finger at the mountain ranges up and down the Makran coastline. "They're in there somewhere. They have to be."

"But we haven't seen any activity there, nothing to speak of," Smith said.

"That doesn't mean they aren't there," Truxton answered. "We've missed a lot of activity in Iran over the years—like uranium enrichment."

There was movement at the other side of the room. Truxton and Smith both looked over.

"Sirs," one of the junior officers called loudly, holding a new communiqué in his right hand, "we have orders from Washington. They want us to join the fight at Bandar Abbas with everything we have. They're asking you to give the order to move."

Truxton nodded at the junior officer, then eyed Smith. "Captain?"

"You have to issue the order." Smith met the vice admiral's steady gaze.

Truxton gazed off into the distance, weighing his options. He did have to issue the order, but he had some discretion. He could change the rules of engagement, on the margin. In his heart, he knew something was out there, waiting, in the darkness. He'd always trusted that still, small voice—and he'd trust it here.

"Hold a third of your ships and aircraft back, Captain," Truxton decided finally. "We're going to leave them here, at *Abe*'s side."

"Even though the Iranian ships are at Bandar Abbas?"

"Yes," Truxton said with finality. "We're going to see what else shows up to join the fight. Because, Captain, we both know there's something else out there, even if we can't see it yet."

29

BAQA'A, JORDAN

Dr. Thompson glanced at her GPS Garmin running watch, a present from her husband this past Christmas. She couldn't believe it was almost five in the afternoon. The day had just disappeared. She'd been running from clinic to clinic all day. She hadn't even stopped for lunch. She was, even now, fondly remembering her morning coffee and bagel.

So much had happened since Aida. She couldn't help but wonder if the events in East Jerusalem had, somehow, been connected to everything she'd heard about since. But she also realized she might never know the truth. Plus, she had her responsibilities in the many refugee camps. There was never time to rest, much less reflect.

Elizabeth loved her mornings. It was the only part of her day that she had to herself. It had been that way for years, from her days as a student at Baylor Medical School in Houston, Texas, until now. Once she got up from the table each morning, after having her first cup of coffee, she spent the rest of every single day in full service to others, seven days a week.

Dr. Thompson had driven herself hard in the service of others for as long as she could remember. From the time she'd become a Christian at the age of twelve by reading the Bible from cover to cover to see for herself what it was about, she'd decided to give her life in service to others. She didn't rest each day until every single task she'd set for herself was completed. And every task was always about someone else—never herself.

But that sort of single-minded service to others was why the volunteers and staff in her global health NGO—World Without Borders—loved her. They would all follow Elizabeth to the ends of the earth. They trusted her instincts and, more importantly, her heart.

It was impossible not to see Elizabeth's faith in blazing glory. She never talked about her faith. She lived it—in every act of compassion, every medical intervention with a refugee, every kind word to a stranger, every diagnosis of a new HIV patient.

Once World Without Borders had been nothing more than a good summer internship idea for students at Rice, Baylor, and several University of

Texas campuses. WWB was modestly funded and sent undergraduates to various underdeveloped countries each summer as volunteers to clinics created there by the Baylor Medical School and other Western entities.

But from the moment she'd graduated from medical school at Baylor, Elizabeth had set about becoming both a doctor and a global public health leader. She'd worked relentlessly to establish herself as someone who could simultaneously treat patients and create a compassionate, well-funded global health NGO that could deliver novel medical treatment in third-world countries.

One of her early breakthroughs had been the ability to deliver all of the necessary components of a mobile medical clinic in a backpack. The Lab in a Backpack could handle everything from the diagnosis of HIV, malaria, and TB to the delivery of vaccines anywhere in the world, no matter how remote the location. The cheap, but effective, backpack could go anywhere.

When the Gates Foundation scaled the program up at $50 million, World Without Borders was born. Running WWB was now Dr. Thompson's full-time job. It operated in thirty countries around the world, delivering low-cost medical care everywhere from clinics in Uganda to Palestinian refugee camps in Jordan, the West Bank, and East Jerusalem.

Elizabeth's husband, Jon, shared her passion and

heart for service to others. A senior finance official at the World Bank, he traveled nearly as much as she did and had a knack for creative solutions in underdeveloped nations. They would often meet in different parts of the world for a few days, then go their separate ways.

Elizabeth knew that, one day, she would also find time for a family. But not just yet. There was too much she wanted to accomplish before starting a family.

She'd just arrived at Baqa'a. The largest Palestinian refugee camp in Jordan, it had almost twice the population of any of the other refugee camps in the country. Hard numbers for refugees were difficult to come by in Jordan. The government hated to count them, because that simple act inevitably led to Jordanian citizenship, but Elizabeth knew there were easily one hundred thousand refugees in Baqa'a.

WWB now operated in dozens of the Palestinian refugee camps—even in Gaza, where the raw, systemic violence was unrelenting. The fact that Elizabeth rarely traveled with an entourage and never with any semblance of a security detail made the staff and volunteers of WWB exceedingly nervous. But Elizabeth was one of those rare individuals who genuinely believed that her life was in God's hands—and she lived each day in recognition of that belief.

Her husband had tried on more than one

occasion to convince her to travel with at least a personal bodyguard or two, but to no avail. She always answered that she didn't walk alone, no matter where she was in the world. And no security detail could absolutely guarantee her safety—not in the parts of the world where she and WWB operated.

The truth was that Elizabeth had earned respect almost everywhere she went—respect of the Palestinian leaders in the refugee camps, respect of officials at ministries of health in African nations, and respect of leaders in developed nations such as Israel and the United States. She could walk freely in crowded streets or hallways of power.

Baqa'a, though, was different than most Palestinian refugee camps. Elizabeth actually felt safe in Baqa'a. It was a lot like Aida in that respect. It operated almost the way a city would in a free, united Palestinian state. It had a camp TV station, of sorts, that people could watch on YouTube. People wrote local news stories about the camp that they posted online. They talked of soccer around the world, raised families in relative peace, and traveled to other parts of the country with ease.

At the center of Baqa'a was one hope—that someday there would be peace with Israel and a new, united Palestinian nation. They lived each day with that hope of a new Arab nation with money, power, dignity, and independence from controlling nations such as Syria or Lebanon. It had been the hope for a generation.

The Palestinian refugees of Baqa'a and elsewhere were tired of never-ending wars and conflict. They hoped for peace in their time. Elizabeth and the staff and volunteers of WWB lived this hope in every encounter with refugee families who flocked to the free WWB medical clinics that operated throughout the region.

Elizabeth had been in and out of the region for almost a decade. And, for the first time that she could ever remember, hope was beginning to replace despair. She heard it in dozens of hushed, fervent conversations in the camps WWB operated in. The refugees themselves could sense that something was happening. They had begun to talk, openly, of a new, emerging Arab state. They all believed that their long journey in the wilderness would be over soon.

They didn't know, yet, where exactly it would be located, who would run it, how its economy would function, or what it might be called. But Elizabeth could see—and hear—the confidence in the voices of the people she cared for and listened to on a daily basis. They knew somehow that a free, united Palestinian state—and a peace with Israel—was coming soon.

The inhabitants of Baqa'a had much in common with other people throughout history who'd spent a generation wandering in wilder-nesses, waiting patiently for the day that the great principalities and powers of the earth would grant them safe haven back to a homeland. The people of Baqa'a had almost infinite patience. They would wait until that day arrived, and rejoice when it did finally appear.

In fact, just that day, Elizabeth had received a most curious invitation that somehow seemed connected to these hopes and dreams for a real, new nation for the Palestinian nations—one that had taken up most of her day. She'd been invited to meet with senior officials of Jordan's Ministry of Health about plans for a new teaching hospital that would also include a medical school.

Elizabeth had been thrilled to learn of the plans and had pledged her organization's full cooperation toward its creation. In fact, WWB had already created modified courses for various public health professional training efforts. This would be bigger, but not all that different from what they'd already done.

When she'd asked about the prospective location, though, the officials had been strangely reluctant to reveal it. They'd talked vaguely about a new location, somewhere else. Elizabeth had decided not to press them. She'd learned long ago that it was better to just wait. Most things were revealed over time.

But she'd managed to steal a glance at one of the

blueprints the officials had brought with them and was surprised to see that they included plans to convert existing buildings in an established city. And, if she wasn't mistaken, the city looked an awful lot like Beersheba, in Israel. She wondered, privately, why Ministry of Health officials in Jordan were thinking about a city in what was clearly, and firmly, part of Israel.

It was all very curious. But Elizabeth knew that, in good time, she would learn more. And, until that time, she would do her work as she always had—and always would.

30

SOMEWHERE IN THE ARABIAN SEA

Ben Azoulay hated waiting. He'd never been any good at it. His teachers had been forced to find ways to keep him occupied in school. He'd fidget endlessly in his seat all day long, waiting for the moment he could leave his desk and jump into action.

It was ironic that his job now was to sit and navigate. But Ben didn't view his job that way. He was at ease in the air, with a throttle in his hand and bright, flashing scopes before him. He was at his best when the world was flashing by him on all sides, an enemy to be confronted out in front of him.

But there was no enemy in front of him just now. Israel's prime minister, Judah Navon, had ordered all of the IDF to stand down for the moment. They were on the sidelines, waiting for the inevitable next shoe to drop.

Azoulay and the other Israeli Bandits who'd managed to navigate the newly acquired F-117s in, around, and over Iran's air-defense systems to their targets had all managed to make it out of Iran safely. Half of them, including Azoulay, were on direct orders from Navon to stand down and wait to see what Iran would do next.

So Azoulay could do nothing more than pace back and forth on the lone carrier that Israel possessed, which was deployed three hundred miles away from the fighting that was almost certain to erupt in the Persian Gulf.

Israel had gone back and forth for years about the need for a navy carrier. Shortly after Navon had become Israel's prime minister for the second time around, he'd ended the speculation and discussion by committing to the purchase of an American-built carrier. Navon knew where the IDF was weak, and he moved to shore up those areas immediately after taking office.

A carrier was one of his first purchases. It was done quietly, without fanfare. Unlike Iran, which boldly proclaimed prototypes or weapons development that was years away from reality, Israel under Navon went about its business with no public pronouncements. The carrier purchase, one of those efforts, went almost unnoticed outside of publications like *Jane's Defence Weekly.*

Navon was a fighter. He'd come up through the ranks of the IAF and had been one of the most decorated fighter pilots in Israel's post–World War II history. He was just nineteen, and a brand-new fighter pilot, when the Six Day War remade Palestine and the Middle East landscape.

Navon had been one of those pilots who'd made run after run every day during the war that had allowed Israel to seize control of the Sinai Peninsula, Gaza, the West Bank, the Golan Heights, and eastern Jerusalem. He'd emerged from that war as a hero, and later parlayed that into a career as one of Israel's most successful, conservative members of the Likud Party.

Realizing that the United States was important to Israel's own national security interests, Navon had studied at Harvard and had worked for several years in both Boston and New York. He understood American political viewpoints quite well—even though he was rarely in sync with them.

Past American presidents had often been at odds with Navon's blunt, opinionated style. One American president had called Navon a liar and cheat in private, only to watch in horror as his private assessment became quite public when someone who'd overheard it relayed it to a *New York Times* reporter.

But none of Navon's political or personality traits mattered in the slightest to Azoulay and the IAF Bandits. To them, Navon was fearless, their leader and someone they would follow to the ends of the earth. They knew with certainty that Navon wanted only to protect Israel. Everything he'd done in his life had been with that end in mind, and the IAF Bandits all knew it.

Navon's history was so well known to the members of the IAF—and Navon himself took such an active interest in the IAF's missions—that Azoulay and the other IAF Bandits almost felt like they worked directly for him. That's what made this current wait so difficult. They were itching to get back in the fight. But Navon had made it quite clear. They would let the Americans engage first in the Gulf.

More than a dozen IAF Bandits, fresh off their bombing runs to Iran, were on board the carrier. They'd all made it safely to the carrier in the dead of night and, like Azoulay, were anxious to get back in the air as quickly as they could. Each knew what was at stake and didn't want to be stranded on a carrier at sea if Israel was attacked.

When the confidential Mossad communiqué finally came through that Iran's entire fleet at Bandar Abbas had moved out to confront the

American 5th Fleet, there was almost a collective sigh of relief among the fighter pilots. They would be engaged in the fight—and soon. They all knew it.

Iran's strategy seemed odd to Azoulay, though. First, they had not pursued Israel's planes—not out to sea or into Turkey. And now, against all odds, they were stacking all of their ships near Bandar Abbas for a hopeless confrontation with the mightiest navy the world had seen. It made no sense.

But Azoulay also knew that the greatest military strategists on the planet had studied the situation and would shortly tell them where to engage. As always, he would follow orders, and pray that those in command knew what they were doing.

31

JASK, IRAN

It was too good to believe. Bahadur had delivered the good news to Ali Zhubin via a secure terrestrial network, and Zhubin had in turn relayed the news to both the Rev. Shahidi and Ahmadian.

America had taken the bait. They had deployed most of the ships attached to their Nimitz super-carrier to the narrow waters south of Bandar

Abbas. They were moving quickly to confront the Iranian fleet that had just left port. They were already seventy-five miles away from their carrier and closing in on the Strait. By the time the Americans realized their error, it would be too late.

True, the Americans had inexplicably left some of their ships behind. But it was pointless, Bahadur knew. Their swarm would overwhelm the *Abraham Lincoln*, and there was very little the Americans could do to protect their floating target 150 miles out from the Strait of Hormuz.

With most of their ships moving toward a fleet in the Strait, Iran's Revolutionary Guards would shortly launch an all-out, full-scale attack behind them against the *Abraham Lincoln*. Using dozens of the subs, fighter jets, and attack boats that had been pre-positioned along the southern coast over the years, the American fleet would suddenly have a ferocious, unexpected rear-guard fight on their hands.

By the time they could react and turn around, the fight would be over—and one of America's Nimitz carriers would be headed toward the bottom of the sea. Bahadur knew they only needed to buy time and win a fight. The Guards couldn't defeat the American Navy over the long term, but if they won an early fight, the balance of power would shift. Iran would no longer be on the defensive and could shift into a full diplomatic offensive to make up at the United Nations and elsewhere what they'd lost on the battlefield in the past few days.

Bahadur stood at the end of the small, wooden pier that extended out to sea on the western side of the resort isthmus. He looked out over the water, wondering what the Americans would think shortly once they'd realized their mistake.

"Are we ready?" he said, turning to one of the aides who was waiting by his side for orders.

"Yes, sir," the aide answered. "All pilots are in place."

"The Yugos and mini-subs are ready?"

"They are running, sir. Waiting on your command."

"The Sunburns?"

"In place, sir," the aide said smartly.

Bahadur smiled. It was a good day to be alive. His only regret was that he would be unable to see the victory firsthand out over the waters of the Arabian Sea. But the reports would be enough for him—reports that would confirm this victory as the greatest in Iran's history.

"It is time," Bahadur said, turning back to his aide. "Send everyone out. Launch the missiles. Now."

An instant later, doors to hidden hangars in the Makran mountains flew open. Jet after jet emerged from the hangars, headed out to sea, their bomb payloads armed and ready. Iran's secret fleet of Yugos, mini-subs, and attack boats moved out from their concealed positions. Silkworms began to emerge from their positions. And the array of Sunburn and Dark Sword anti-ship missiles began their very rapid journey out to sea, all of them with just one large target in their sites.

Iran was taking the fight to the Americans, in a way they'd never anticipated.

32

ABOARD THE USS ABRAHAM LINCOLN

The scopes all lit up at once. There were so many blinking lights on the various pieces of equipment, from so many directions, it seemed surreal to the observers in the command and control center. At first, the junior officers who'd trained for years for this sort of combat thought that it had to be a mistake. Within seconds, they realized it was no mistake.

"Find the vice admiral and captain!" one of them yelled, almost at the top of his lungs. "We have a full-scale attack coming at us!"

Truxton burst into the room an instant later and took up a position just over the junior officers' shoulders. He said nothing and only stared at the scopes grimly. He knew precisely what the blinking, moving lights meant.

The Pentagon leadership had vastly under-estimated Iran's force—and their strategy. Every single one of these targets coming toward them had emerged from the southern coastline of Iran one hundred miles outside of the Strait of Hormuz.

They were appearing out of thin air, which meant they'd been in place for some time. And there were dozens of targets, all coming right at them.

The anti-ship cruise missiles would arrive first, Truxton knew.

And they were arriving at almost Mach 3, a terrifying speed that would overwhelm the ship's anti-missile computer system.

But he also knew something Iran's Revolutionary Guards did not. America had not been idle as Russia had developed the Sunburn missile and then its successor. And when China had developed the Dark Sword, the Pentagon leadership had gotten very serious about meeting the threat.

In a rare show of procurement common sense, all branches of the American military had quickly finished researching, developing, and deploying a highly classified system that could generate high-power microwaves over a wide area and destroy electronic equipment controlling the individual cruise missile guidance systems.

The research had begun years ago in the U.S. Department of Energy's nuclear weapons laboratories and had then moved over to the Pentagon once the architecture had been studied. The system had been originally designed to destroy incoming Soviet ballistic missiles.

But at the end of the Cold War, it became obvious that they would no longer need to worry as much about ballistic missiles launched at the U.S. continent. The much greater threat, the Pentagon had correctly assessed, was the new generation of fast, highly maneuverable cruise missiles from Russia and China.

The high-power microwave weapons system had emerged as the single, best counter to those threats and was now in place on all carrier fleets.

Captain Smith joined Truxton and stood off to one side. Neither of them said a word. They were both looking, and waiting, for confirmation that all of Iran's anti-ship cruise missiles had been launched. Once they'd confirmed that, then they could deploy the countermeasures.

The seconds seemed like minutes. The Dark Swords would arrive first, followed shortly by the Sunburns. But neither Truxton nor Smith would wait for that moment.

One of the junior officers turned to Truxton. "No other missiles in the air, sir."

"You're certain?" Truxton asked.

"Yes, sir. Everything else from the coastline is confirmed at much slower speeds. The computers have confirmed this as well. There are no new missile threats coming at us."

Truxton turned to Smith. "Captain?"

Smith simply nodded in return and gave the order. Without preamble or fanfare, a series of switches were flipped. The high-power microwave beams were sent out, and all eyes turned back to the scopes. They watched as several dozen lights almost instantly disappeared from the scopes.

Satellites picked up the video real-time as the cruise missiles that had been accelerating to speeds approaching Mach 3 suddenly took an abrupt nosedive and disappeared into the murky waters of the Arabian Sea, no longer threats.

The few remaining cruise missiles not caught in the wide-area microwave blast were detected moments later by the ship's Sea-RAM computer system. All eleven of the ship's RAM nine-foot-long missiles were locked and loaded, but they'd only needed a half dozen of them. They launched and intercepted the remaining anti-ship missiles six miles away from the *Abe*.

"All missiles down," one of the operators said.

Truxton looked back at the scopes. They were still facing a massive threat from a horde of suicide bombers and attack boats. Truxton cursed to himself that they had so few LCS ships in service right now, and the four they had were still not within range of the fight. They could use those LCS ships right about now, especially along the coastline.

Smith stepped up to one of the screens, the one that used the latest generation of extended blue-green lasers to track underwater threats. "Is that right?" he asked quietly, pointing to the screen.

The officer nodded. "We've counted fifteen of them, sir."

"Fifteen of what?" Truxton asked.

"They have to be Yugos," Smith answered. "We knew of the four from North Korea. But, obviously, they have more of them, and I'd be willing to bet my paycheck the North Koreans built them for the Guards. They're moving too fast to be submarines. They have to be minis."

Truxton shook his head. They had no subs in the area, and most of the ships that could meet the mini-subs were headed to Bandar Abbas. The Yugos were small—fewer than one hundred feet —and could likely get close enough to the *Abe* to crash into it, especially if their sole intent was a suicide mission against the carrier.

"Make sure we have the nuclear power plant covered," Truxton said to the ship's executive officer. "Nothing gets through. This is your only assignment. If they're able to get any suicides near the plant, we're in trouble. So make sure it doesn't happen. Understand?"

"Yes, sir," the executive officer said. He was gone a moment later.

"Captain Smith, do we have anything else we can call in?" Truxton asked.

"Not in the immediate area. Just the ships we have left."

"Those are deployed, and will get much of what we have coming in. But we can't handle all of their fighters."

"No, we can't," Smith said soberly.

Truxton pursed his lips. "What about the Israelis? Don't they have that carrier nearby?"

"Yes, just fifty miles out from here."

"Make the call," Truxton ordered. "Get their fighters here, right now."

"What about channels?" Smith asked.

"I don't care!" Truxton exploded. "Get those IAF planes here now!"

Smith turned to another officer. "You heard the vice admiral. Make the call to their ship's captain."

"The LCS ships?" Truxton hardly paused to take a breath.

"Two are within range and will be here shortly," an officer answered.

"Better than none, but we still need more," Truxton said. "What do we do about the attack boats that will be here any moment?"

"Our guns will get most of them," Smith answered.

"But not all of them," Truxton said.

"No, probably not all of them."

"And the fighter planes?"

"Our planes are already turning around, coming back from Bandar Abbas," Smith said. "And because you left some behind, we can engage the first to arrive."

"How soon can the Israelis get here?"

"They'll get here to meet the second wave."

"What about the subs?"

"We have enough laser-guided missiles to go after all of them. Just barely."

"So if we don't get them all?"

"We'd better brace for some direct hits," Smith said.

Truxton sighed. "Okay, then. Settle in, boys. We have a long day in front of us, and we'll need all hands on deck. We just need to keep the *Abe* afloat. I don't intend to be the first commander to see an American supercarrier sink to the bottom of the sea. That's our goal, until the cavalry arrives."

33

THE WHITE HOUSE SITUATION ROOM
WASHINGTON, DC

The room was quiet. Everyone at the table knew the stakes—and what their beleaguered 5th Fleet carrier faced in the next hour or so.

General Alton had briefed everyone, including the president, as quickly as he could once they were assembled around the table in the Situation Room. The news was grim.

It wasn't the nature of the swarm attack that had taken the Pentagon by surprise; it was the sheer numbers coming at the *Abraham Lincoln* in waves less than one hundred miles off the southern coast of Iran.

Just as the intelligence community had been surprised by the depth of the covert uranium-enrichment facilities and nuclear warhead development in the Revolutionary Guards' military facilities spread across Iran, it was now equally surprised at the raw numbers of fighter jets, missiles, subs, and attack boats that had descended on the *Abe* like an angry swarm of bees.

The satellites had picked up the fighter jets the instant they left their concealed hangars in the Makran mountains near Jask. The Pentagon had already locked in coordinates, and a barrage of cruise missiles would shortly level each location.

But that's like locking the proverbial barn door after the cows have wandered outside, DJ mused to himself from his straight-backed staff chair at the side of the Sit Room. *Doesn't do the* Abraham Lincoln *much good right now.*

General Alton had been given the raw numbers from the staff to the joint chiefs just a couple of minutes earlier, and he'd quickly summarized them for President Camara and his senior staff. The supercomputers had crashed all of the different detection nodes together to produce a snapshot of what the *Abe* was facing.

It was a nightmare scenario, far worse than anything they'd ever simulated in their many—and expensive—war games on a battle for control of the Strait of Hormuz. Clearly, Iran's Revolutionary Guards had meticulously prepared for a day such as this one, and the Pentagon had not done all of its homework.

It wasn't the first time the American intelligence community or the Pentagon's leadership had been surprised by capabilities in the volatile and highly unpredictable Middle East. *But it will be the last time,* Dr. Gould thought darkly from his seat to the right of the president. *Never again.*

"So," the president said, "we weren't quite prepared for this sort of attack?"

"We anticipated a swarm," General Alton said quickly. "What we didn't anticipate is that it would come at us from so far south, so close to Pakistan."

"We had no idea they'd built hangars there, or placed subs and boats at Jask? Is that right?" asked the president.

"Yes, sir," Alton answered. "That's correct. We did not know those hangars were there, or that they'd pre-positioned so many boats and subs at Jask."

Anshel leaned forward in his chair. He was seething, and the veins seemed ready to burst on both temples. "Tell me how this is possible!" he said, his voice rising with each word. "We've had the entire southern coastline under surveillance for years! How did we miss what they built at Jask, right under our noses?"

Alton didn't duck the question. "We missed it, Dr. Gould. That's all I can tell you. All of our intelligence said that Jask was a resort area for the Guards' leadership, nothing more. They've been going there for years, and we never detected any sort of activity. They concealed it very well."

"We can get into all of that later," Camara said, cutting him off. "Right now, I want to know what Vice Admiral Truxton needs to turn back this threat—or, to put it more bluntly, whether he *can* turn back this threat."

Everyone instinctively turned back to the many satellite videos running in real-time on a half-dozen display monitors around the room's periphery. At the center of all of them was the Nimitz super-carrier, sitting there like a massive floating target.

"I can at least tell you that we took out all of the Silkworms we've had system coordinates for. None of them got off the ground. That's made it easier to take on the rest of the threat."

"Good," Anshel said.

"There is one saving grace." Alton paused. He knew Vice Admiral Truxton had been harshly criticized by some on the joint chiefs for his decision to hold back a third of the 5th Fleet when he'd been ordered to send everyone forward to meet Iran's navy south of Bandar Abbas. Right now, though, Truxton looked like a genius.

"Which is?" Camara asked.

"Vice Admiral Truxton did not deploy the entire fleet to Bandar Abbas," Alton said. "He kept a third of the planes and ships back, for some reason. If he'd sent everything forward to Bandar Abbas, Iran's move coming in behind us would meet almost no resistance. The *Abe* would be under water by now."

"So Truxton knew something?" Camara asked.

General Alton grimaced. "It was intuition, on his part. Something didn't feel quite right, so he kept part of his fleet in reserve."

And they'd probably raked him over the coals for it, DJ thought.

There had been a steady stream of explosions apparent from the satellite images on several of the screens, even as they'd discussed the situation in just the past few minutes. Everyone, even DJ, could see the *Abe* was under a constant wave of attacks from all sides. It was impossible to tell, though, what was going on with only the naked eye. Only the computers knew the score for sure.

"So does Truxton have what he needs?" Camara asked again.

"We have enough jets, barely, to take on their

fighters—but only for the first wave. We've asked the Israelis for help. Their IAF Bandits will be there in a few minutes."

"The same ones that flew in and out of Iran?" Anshel asked.

"Yes, the same ones," Alton said. "They've been on a carrier since finishing their mission. They all just took off and are headed toward the *Abe* even as we're talking here."

"Do we have enough ships to counter their attack boats?" asked the president. "They have so many of them, how can we possibly deal with that swarm?"

"Truxton says he kept enough ships back to take them on, and two of our LCS ships will be there for the second wave as well. We just need to hold them off initially, until reinforcements can get there."

"And the subs?" asked Anshel.

Alton looked over at the Navy contingent at the table. None of them moved. They'd been completely unprepared for the number of ninety-foot Yugo submarines that Iran had managed to build with North Korea's help in the past five years. It was a wildcard that no one had anticipated and left the *Abe* wide open for a successful suicide attack.

"We thought they only had four Yugos," Alton said quietly. "It turns out they have a dozen of them now—or more."

"Built for them by North Korea?" Anshel demanded.

"We presume so," Alton answered.

There was an awkward silence in the room. They'd made considerable progress in recent years with strategic blue-green laser communication between orbiting satellites and submarines, which gave them a decent chance of detecting even a large number of underwater threats.

But the sheer number of Yugos advancing on the *Abe*—combined with the fact that two of the American subs needed for closer triangulation had initially deployed to Bandar Abbas—would overwhelm even the redundant computer system, leaving detection in some cases to a person looking at a scope.

There was the very real possibility that a seven-person Yugo sub, carrying a tactical nuclear payload developed in North Korea, could make its way through the *Abe*'s defenses and cave in the side of the ship if it came in behind a successful fighter jet bombing run.

"Mr. President, I can assure you that the vice admiral has every hunter at his command out looking for those Yugos," Alton said. "He's doing his best, with limited resources at his command right now."

"But his best might not be good enough, General," Camara said. "And if we lose the ship?"

"We will not lose the ship," Alton said. "The vice

admiral has surrounded the nuclear power plant with almost everything he has on board. It would take at least two direct hits to get to it."

"But if the *Abe* is out of commission, for any reason?"

"We'll have given the Strait to Iran—for the time being," Alton answered grimly. "At least, until we can regroup."

There was a sudden commotion at the other end of the room. Something had just happened. They all looked over at one of the monitors. Balls of flame had erupted from the center of the *Abe* and had been picked up by the satellites instantly.

"The *Abe* has been hit by a suicide plane," one of the officers announced. "Three missiles took the plane out of the sky, but it was already headed toward the power plant. It was a direct hit."

34

THE GULF OF OMAN

The captain of the midget submarine built in just the past two years in Iran—under the direct supervision of North Korean military advisors at a covert shipyard southeast of Bandar Abbas, near Minab—was proud of his command. In the past two years alone, his own sub had taken on any number of covert missions in the Strait of Hormuz.

They'd already planted dozens of mines in strategic locations throughout the Strait, for instance, making it difficult for any combat ships to navigate the Strait during a conflict. They had also successfully tracked more than a dozen commercial ships through the Strait, preparing for the day they might be called on to sink one of those ships in a war of attrition.

The sub had virtually no ability to contribute in any sort of combat scenario, but the North Koreans had been able to modify the original design of the midget sub enough to give it a much longer range than the West believed. Through a combination of battery conservation, surface maneuvers, and occasional dives, it could make a one-way trip out to sea.

The Yugo captain was on just such a one-way mission right now. The crew aboard the sub knew there were only two options at the end of their journey—they'd either reach their target, or they would be forced to surface and wait to be captured by the Americans.

They did not communicate with anyone on their trip out to the deeper waters of the Gulf of Oman. They had no way of knowing the fate of any of the other Yugo subs. The sub was a mere ninety feet in length and barely handled a skeleton crew of seven people, including the captain.

This particular Yugo was just one of three in the Iranian navy that carried a tactical nuclear missile on board. The crew knew it would need to get quite close to its target, the American Nimitz super-carrier, in order to fire a torpedo at close range. They knew it was a likely suicide mission, but they were prepared for it—and for their fate.

The captain did his best to scan the horizon for any sign of activity on each trip to the surface, but the trip had been quiet. He'd heard nothing from the sub's surprisingly robust passive sonar system near the surface, and he'd seen nothing visually with the naked eye.

As he neared the coordinates on his map—and the very large target—the captain was careful to come up from the depths. The United States ran a worldwide underwater surveillance system in all of the world's oceans, including the Gulf of Oman, but Iran had long ago discovered the nodes' locations and charted paths through the passive sonar network.

No, the captain knew that only a fairly specific sonar sweep would pick up their sub as they approached the supercarrier. But that would be difficult. The North Koreans, for instance, had shown them how to mill their propeller blades so they were extraordinarily quiet, and the energy system contained components mostly developed in the United States.

The captain appreciated the irony. The technology for the blades had come from a Japanese company, Toshiba, via the former Soviet Union, to North Korea and then to Iran, and the highly efficient energy storage system had largely emerged from Western technology.

The Yugo crew didn't need a sonar system to recognize their target. They knew where it was in the open water, and it wasn't moving. The crew grew anxious as they drew very near their target and began to ascend toward the surface of the sea. They expected to pick up the telltale signs of an approaching torpedo at any moment. At two other times, they'd heard nearby sounds from their own simple passive sonar system, but they were more likely actions taking place elsewhere.

At one point, they did pick up the sounds of some sort of approaching weapon, followed an instant later by the clear signs of a direct hit. The captain knew, with some certainty, that a Yugo very close to them had been hit.

He saw the opportunity. The destruction of a sub so close to theirs would create a cornucopia of noise in the vicinity for the next few minutes. He pushed the engines to their maximum speed and took direct aim at the target just above them.

Without thinking, or telling the crew about his endgame, the captain made the fateful decision to use the Yugo sub as its own torpedo. He would get as close to the supercarrier as he could and wait until the last possible moment to release his torpedoes.

The captain knew the supercarrier was dealing with so many threats—most of them on the surface or from the air—that they were overwhelmed by the swarm tactics. There was a good chance he could come up right under the target undetected. At least, that was his hope.

As he neared the surface, his passive sonar system started going haywire. There were dozens of objects all around him in the water. Many of them, he guessed, were recent casualties. The captain pressed forward. There was no turning back.

An instant later, the Yugo crashed into the hull of the ship. Without hesitation, the captain released the torpedo that contained a small nuclear payload. It detonated on impact within seconds, blowing a massive hole in the hull of the ship and obliterating the Yugo and its crew at the same time.

35

MOSCOW, RUSSIA

The courier hand-carried the latest SVR briefing report to Rowan's private quarters. Once he'd been briefed on the latest actions near the Strait of Hormuz, the SVR's director of intelligence had ordered the report sent to the prime minister immediately. It contained information that he knew would be of immense value to Rowan and the Duma leadership.

Rowan thanked the courier and opened the briefing report. He smiled as he read through the top sheet, summarizing the current situation in the Persian Gulf. The satellite pictures were especially telling.

Just as his military staff had predicted, the Americans had managed to minimize the damage from the anti-ship missiles developed once upon a time in the former Soviet Union. Despite the cruise missiles' enormous speeds and ability to evade detection, the Americans had used their next-generation electronic counter-measures to literally turn their guidance systems off. The damage had been nil.

But, also as his military staff had predicted, Iran's Revolutionary Guards had managed to surprise the American Navy's leadership with a massive, asymmetrical attack behind their fleet's main strike force.

There had been two direct hits on the Nimitz supercarrier positioned at the opening to the Strait of Hormuz as a show of force to keep the Strait open. The satellite pictures clearly showed the aftermath of a plane crash near the ship's power plant and a second huge gash in the ship's hull near the power plant.

The SVR report predicted that the carrier might

actually sink, but Rowan knew that wasn't likely. Nor did it matter to Rowan or Russia. Iran had achieved what it had needed with its attack. It had shown that the Americans were vulnerable and had forced the fleet's forces to pull back from the Strait to protect their flank. There would be no immediate battles south of Bandar Abbas.

For the time being, the Strait of Hormuz would be closed to ship traffic. And, as he always did, Rowan saw a clear opportunity in the face of the panic and chaos that would shortly begin in the world economic markets as the price of oil inevitably began to spiral upwards. What's more, Iran's temporary military victory at the Strait also presented an opportunity. And Rowan was always eager to take advantage of any opportunity when it came to oil.

He leaned across his desk and pressed the inter-office intercom. "Nicolai, come in here for a moment," he said quietly. "We must talk."

Petrov glided through the doorway a moment later. He settled quickly into one of the two chairs positioned sideways across from the prime minister's desk and waited.

"Has the Duma leadership been briefed?" Rowan asked his chief of staff.

"Yes, moments ago," Petrov said.

"Their reaction?"

"They were pleased and not surprised. We've done a good job of predicting events so far.

However, I think they were somewhat surprised that Iran's strategy in the Strait worked and took the Americans by surprise."

Rowan nodded. It was time to move on.

"We can assume the Americans will gain control of the situation shortly, and that the Israeli military forces will come to their aid," Rowan said.

"Yes, most likely." Petrov knew from many such conversations that it was always best to agree with Rowan.

"So it will only be a matter of time before the Americans manage to move into the Strait and take control of the situation," Rowan said. "Which means we need to act on the Baku pipeline, right now, while the world oil economy is reeling. We must seize this opportunity, while the world's attention is directed elsewhere. It is in Russia's national interest. We must protect that pipeline. We must take every opportunity where oil is concerned."

Petrov smiled. He could clearly see where Rowan was going. "We'll need to commit some of our own military to it."

"Of course, but they'll largely be under NATO's authority—to protect the pipeline."

"The presidents of Georgia and Azerbaijan will protest immediately to the UN Security Council."

"They'll get nowhere. With oil supplies closed through the Strait, we have no choice but to secure every other route for oil to Russia and the

West. The Security Council will agree with us. We cannot allow Russia to go without oil, and we will argue that the Baku pipeline is critical to our own national security."

"Yes, absolutely," Petrov said.

There had been a time, before the fall of the Soviet Union, that all oil from the rich fields just below the Caspian Sea was shipped via pipelines through Russia. But the Baku-Tbilisi-Ceyhan pipeline changed all that and had permanently altered the balance of power in Russia and countries in the former Soviet Union like Georgia and Azerbaijan.

The Baku pipeline stretched from the landlocked Caspian Sea through Azerbaijan, Georgia, and then Turkey to the Mediterranean. While only a small fraction of the world's oil was shipped through the BTC pipeline, it was a massive thorn in Russia's geopolitical side.

Russia had insisted at the outset—when the pipeline was first proposed—that the BTC pipeline be constructed through Russia like every other pipeline running from the Caspian to the Mediterranean. When it became clear that this scenario wasn't likely, Russia withdrew all of its support for the pipeline.

The United States had quietly encouraged all three countries to move forward with the pipeline, despite the Russian protests. The pipeline gave both Georgia and Azerbaijan some measure of independence from Russia, and they made no secret of it. Two different U.S. secretaries of energy had been present at dedication ceremonies when different parts of the pipeline had opened.

But both Petrov and Rowan could see that the current situation presented a unique opportunity to gain control of the pipeline. They would move military forces in, for now, to help protect the flow of oil. And if those Russian troops stayed there for a time to ensure the pipeline's protection, then so be it.

"But we have another opportunity as well," Rowan said. "I saw it quite clearly in the satellite pictures, and the SVR director confirms it in his report."

"From the fight in the Persian Gulf?"

"Yes, from that fight," Rowan said.

He leaned back in his chair. He was enjoying the fact that Russia was able to wait at the edges of these confrontations and take strategic advantage of them when it made sense to do so.

"There was a second nuclear detonation. That makes two nuclear strikes in the Middle East in less than a week—first, Israel, and now this strike against an American ship." Rowan continued. "The hole in the side of the U.S. carrier was clearly caused by a tactical nuclear warhead from one of the new Yugos. Nothing else could create a hole that size."

"The North Koreans built those subs for Iran," Petrov said, eyes wide. "Which means the nuclear warhead came from them as well."

"Its design, at the very least," Rowan said. "But that's all we'll need with the Security Council and the media. In effect, North Korea was responsible for the first nuclear strike against an American military facility. The game has just changed, and we cannot miss the chance to move in behind this."

36

ABOARD THE USS ABRAHAM LINCOLN

The nuclear power plant was in chaos. Black smoke billowed everywhere. Sailors ran through the smoke, patching everything in sight. Sirens pierced the air, drowning out the shouts.

But, despite the chaos, the sailors still managed to come to attention as the vice admiral arrived at the power plant to personally inspect the damage. The sailors were stunned. There was no need for the vice admiral to be here, personally, to see the damage. The ship's computer system told him everything he needed to know from the highly sophisticated command and control center. He didn't need to actually visit the power plant to know the extent of the damage.

But Truxton wasn't your average vice admiral and fleet commander. That was crystal clear to the sailors, and it gave them considerable security to know that their commander was fighting here with them, side by side. It meant a great deal to them, in fact.

Truxton immediately sought the plant's operations manager. "Are we functional?"

"Yes, sir," the operations manager answered promptly. "Thanks to everything you threw up around us, the plane only managed some partial physical damage when it landed."

"The explosion from the Yugo?"

The manager grimaced. "I won't lie. It did some damage. We've got some containment issues right now."

"How serious?"

"We need to get it under control. I'll know shortly."

"But you believe we can contain it?"

"Yes, sir, I do. Thanks to your order, we had enough in place to protect the plant, even with the damage from the Yugo."

"So the plant won't go critical?" Truxton already knew the answer to the question, courtesy of the ship's computers, but he wanted to hear it for himself.

"It will not go critical," the operations manager said. "We have it contained."

Truxton nodded. He was pleased. The *Abe* would not sink. It was in bad shape and wouldn't move anywhere anytime soon, but it would not sink—and that was all that mattered right now. As far as he was concerned, the mission was a success. They would deal with Bandar Abbas and the Strait of Hormuz in time.

Truxton turned back to the executive officer who had remained at his side throughout the battle. "Are the IAF Bandits close?"

"They've just engaged." The executive officer smiled. "The first reports are that the IAF F-117s came up on every plane in the sky and took them all by surprise. Half of them had enough left to keep going after the remaining attack boats in the area."

"So the threats are gone from the air and sea around us?" Truxton was mildly surprised and every bit as pleased as the ship's executive officer.

"We believe so," he answered.

"And the Yugos?"

"We believe the one that crashed into us was the last in the area."

It was all good, then. The *Abe* was stable, and the immediate threats had been neutralized. They were not able—yet—to deal with the Strait of Hormuz. For the time being, Iran controlled the Strait. Truxton knew there were serious geopolitical, economic, and diplomatic conse-quences of the situation now.

But the *Abe* was still floating, and the American Navy's 5th Fleet still had the opportunity to take back control of the Strait at some point. To Truxton, nothing else mattered. Others would have to deal with the aftermath. He'd done everything he could, for now.

37

NATIONAL SECURITY COUNCIL
THE WHITE HOUSE
WASHINGTON, DC

The receptionist had no idea what to do with the call slip. It had been more than three decades since anyone from Iran's Interests Section at Pakistan's embassy in Washington had felt compelled to contact someone senior at the White House.

There were no diplomatic relations between the U.S. and Iran and no personal connection. All the receptionist knew was that someone who said he was the head of the Interests Section from Iran was on the line, asking to speak to the head of the National Security Council at the White House. It seemed bizarre.

"Give it to Dr. Wright," the second receptionist said when she was consulted about the call. "She'll know what to do with it."

The receptionist nodded. The entire administration staff was thrilled the day that Susan Wright showed up at the office as the president's deputy national security advisor and chief of staff to the NSC. She'd brought relative peace to the embattled NSC staff office, which had been in turmoil for more than a year over the consolidation of national security and homeland security staff at the White House.

Dr. Wright oozed calm, if such a thing was possible. She always had a smile and a ready laugh in almost any setting. No matter the circumstance, Dr. Wright managed to find a way to be patient. Nothing seemed to faze her. Part of it had to do with her quiet, unassuming faith. She was a peacemaker at heart and in practice.

President Camara's NSC leadership was, by and large, dominated by retired military. The president's national security advisor was a retired four-star general, and the previous NSC chief of staff had been a close military advisor as well.

When the NSC staff structure had been completely reorganized to recognize the plain and simple fact that homeland security and the nation's foreign policy interests were largely cut from the same cloth, there had been some serious infighting for months as dozens of smart and talented people jockeyed for position and power.

But then Dr. Wright arrived on the scene as the new NSC chief of staff—and things began to change in subtle but important ways. Susan Wright firmly believed in chain of command, and the need for a clear management system for important policy decisions, but she also believed in seeking diverse views in a team-building environment. She wasn't afraid to let opposing voices enter debates.

Part of the reason for her flexibility was her long career in academic life, which encouraged healthy intellectual debate. She'd somehow managed to convince two different schools at Harvard to allow her to pursue simultaneous degrees—a J.D. from law school and a Ph.D. in foreign policy. She'd managed to obtain both within four years, which was almost unheard of. No one knew how she'd managed it—and Dr. Wright never talked about it.

She'd almost immediately jumped onto the tenure track at Harvard and had secured her first large government research grant to study the role of American-styled democracy in the Middle East before she'd turned thirty. She'd always taken a special interest in Israel. Her star in academia had risen in meteoric fashion, and everyone knew it was only a matter of time before she was named president of an Ivy League school.

Her colleagues at Harvard were mildly surprised when she'd chosen to take a leave of absence from her duties and research to become the president's deputy national security advisor. But, in truth, it made perfect sense. She would undoubtedly parlay her DC experience into an even larger role in academia when she left politics in Washington.

Her job at the NSC was difficult. The national security and military superstructure in Washington was heavily dominated by men. But Dr. Wright was no shrinking violet, and she had no trouble at all going nose to nose with senior officials from the Pentagon when necessary.

The front office NSC admin staff, though, didn't care about any of this. They were just glad to have a friendly face to talk to when they had issues they didn't understand.

"He says he's the head of the Interests Section of Iran," the receptionist said. She clutched the phone slip in her hand.

Dr. Wright swiveled her chair away from her computer monitor and held out her hand. "Let me see the name," she asked calmly.

The receptionist gladly handed over the phone slip. "He's on hold."

Susan recognized the name. He was, in fact, the head of Iran's Interests Section, which represented Iran's interests from the embassy of Pakistan in Washington. It was as close to an Iranian ambassador in Washington as you could get.

Susan thought for a moment. The call really needed to go to the State Department. It made no sense for her to take it. But she also knew that, if she referred him to State, he might bounce around there for a few calls. She decided to take it and worry about the consequences later.

"Okay, tell him I'll be with him in just a second," Susan said.

The receptionist breathed a sigh of relief and left the office quickly.

Susan turned back to her work on the computer screen, minimized the windows to her work, and waited. The intercom buzzed a moment later, and the receptionist told her which line to pick up.

She picked up the line. "This is Dr. Wright. How can I help you?"

"Oh, wonderful, Dr. Wright," said the caller. "We were hoping to speak to someone at your level." The caller paused, clearly uncomfortable.

"Is there something I can help you with?" she asked again.

"I would like to know if you would be willing to speak with Ali Zhubin," the caller said finally. "He would like to speak to you. It is urgent. You do know of Major General Zhubin?"

Susan closed her eyes. This was a diplomatic nightmare. She had no business, at all, even thinking about taking such a call. It was, without question, more appropriate for the folks at State. But she'd never shied away from difficult calls, and she wasn't about to start now—not with the American Navy in the middle of a confrontation with Iran's navy near Bandar Abbas. She could at least hear what Zhubin had to say, then pass on that news to others.

"Yes, I know of General Zhubin," Susan answered. In fact, she'd met him on two occasions, at academic conferences. Zhubin was a general and the commander of Iran's Revolutionary Guards, but he'd also studied at Tehran University and had some academic credentials.

"And would you be willing to speak to him? I can connect him, if that is acceptable."

Susan hesitated just a moment more. "I will speak to him," she said finally, fully cognizant that the conversation would become a transcript circulated through intelligence circles—on both sides of the ocean—within a matter of minutes.

There was a brief pause, a series of clicking noises on the other end, and then Zhubin came on the line. "Dr. Wright, how nice to speak to you again!" he said exuberantly. "It has been, what, three years since we last saw each other?"

It had been exactly three years. They'd exchanged words briefly at a conference in Geneva. At the time, he had not yet taken over the Guards. And she was at the conference representing a United Nations working group. But he'd remembered the meeting, and so did she.

"Yes, three years. So, what have you been up to since then?" she asked, laughing lightly. "Anything you'd care to share with me?"

Zhubin chuckled. "Ah, Dr. Wright, perhaps we

can share stories at a later date. But, today, I have a pressing matter I wish to discuss—one I wanted to convey with a personal call."

Susan sat forward in her chair and pulled a notepad toward her. She knew she'd have the benefit of transcripts at her disposal following the call, but it gave her comfort to jot notes as she talked. "All right, General, what is it?"

"As you know," Zhubin said, "we have just achieved a great and important victory over your American Navy in the Gulf of Oman—"

"General Zhubin," Susan interrupted, "please spare me the histrionics. There was no great victory. Two suicide missions came at the *Abraham Lincoln* and did not achieve a thing. We both know that."

"You may characterize it as you wish," Zhubin responded, "but the fact remains that your 5th Fleet has stalled in the Gulf and cannot advance. Your carrier, the *Abraham Lincoln*, is dead in the water. I believe any reasonable observer would call that a great victory."

"General, we will make sure that the Strait is open for passage shortly," she said forcefully. "We both know that it's only a matter of time."

"Perhaps. But I have additional information I wish to convey. That is why I am calling today—to convey that information."

"Which is?"

"You *are* aware that there are many more targets in the Gulf region, beyond the military targets. I wanted to make sure that you are aware of this."

Iran had made veiled threats for years regarding taking out various oil production facilities in the region in retaliation against any military action by Israel. But taking out those facilities might likely do more damage to Iran than others. Iran was a net importer of refined gasoline, and shutting down the Strait of Hormuz would do serious damage to Iran's economy. Compounding that with a slow-down in oil production—from Iran and others—could do irreparable damage.

"Yes, General, I am aware of the range of possibilities. But OPEC is prepared to pick up whatever slack occurs if Iran stops producing oil. You know that as well as I."

"I am aware of OPEC's position. But OPEC does not make sovereign decisions for Iran. And OPEC also cannot protect Bahrain, Kuwait, Qatar, the United Arab Emirates, Oman, or even Saudi Arabia. We alone control access to facilities from those countries—now and into the foreseeable future."

Susan took a deep breath. They were headed into very dangerous waters. "General, I want to make sure I do not misunderstand what you are saying. And I want to repeat what I said earlier. It is only a matter of time before our 5th Fleet re-opens passage through the Strait of Hormuz."

"And as I said—perhaps that is so," Zhubin answered. "But that is not important now. What *is* important is that we control that passage right now. And, unless the United States is willing to take certain actions and repair the damage that has been done, we are prepared to do what we must do."

"General, what actions would you have us take?"

"We would like you to condemn Israel's actions, in the strongest possible language. We would like you to stop arming Israel. We would like you to help us repair our civilian nuclear facilities—those that Israel just attacked—and supply us with the enriched uranium we need to operate those peaceful facilities. We would like the United States to permanently relocate the 5th Fleet away from the Gulf of Oman, where it consistently threatens Iran. We would like the United States to give up its mindless allegiance to the corrupt Sunni monarchies in Saudi Arabia and other countries. And, of course, we would like a permanent, free Arab state on the lands illegally seized by Israel— one that is not cobbled together with useless pieces of land—that gives the dispossessed Palestinian peoples a real homeland."

Susan almost laughed. "Is that all?"

"It would be a good start," Zhubin answered.

"Is there something from that list that would help ease tensions right now?"

"Dr. Wright, I want to be clear," Zhubin said, deadly serious. "We are prepared to act against any and all targets—military or otherwise—in the countries that rely on the Strait of Hormuz if you do not move the 5th Fleet away from the Gulf of Oman immediately.

"We both know what happens to the price of oil if there is a serious, permanent disruption in facilities and traffic. Neither of us, I can assure you, wish for that to happen."

"So that's what you're asking? You'd like us to move the 5th Fleet away from the Strait?"

"Yes, that would be an excellent place to start a discussion. We would also like Israel to remove their Dolphin submarines from the Suez Canal as well and return to port in the Mediterranean."

"Israel is a sovereign nation. They make their own decisions about their own national security interests."

"Yes, but they listen to the United States."

Susan chose to ignore that line of reasoning. "And if our 5th Fleet continues to move forward, toward Bandar Abbas?"

"You do not want to do that, Dr. Wright," Zhubin answered. "Trust me. No one will like what happens next if you do not withdraw the 5th Fleet immediately. We both know that we have the capability—and the expertise—to do what is necessary."

"You would target oil facilities in other nations in the region?"

"There are many targets and many opportunities. Neither of us wishes to test further the possibilities or suitable targets of opportunity. Withdraw your 5th Fleet, Dr. Wright, before it's too late."

38

JERUSALEM, ISRAEL

Throughout the course of his life—first as a pilot and then, later, as a politician in the rough-and-tumble world of consensus-building politics in Israel—Judah Navon had come to believe that there was just one way to live your life. You charted your course, and you never deviated from it.

There had been times, as a pilot, that he'd questioned the mission. But he'd never deviated from the mission or from the target that had been set. It had become ingrained in him. Once the path was set, you followed it. He viewed politics much the same way. Once you'd decided on a plan, you didn't move away from it.

It had always served him well. Political fads came and went, but Navon always believed there was only one purpose to politics in Israel. You were there to serve the national interests of Israel—to protect it against enemies on all sides intent on destroying the country and its people—and nothing should ever move you away from that mission.

Navon feared no one—at least no human being on earth. He was willing to engage with any leader, anywhere, for the sake of Israel.

But in all his years of blunt dealing with both enemies and friends, Navon had never seen a time such as this. He'd never felt so alone in the world, so dependent on the strength of the Israeli people, and so vulnerable to attacks from neighbors who grew stronger on a daily basis.

He'd always been able to look over the horizon. It was his gift—the ability to see a threat even before it had made its appearance. This time he could not only see, but *feel,* the threats starting to accumulate just over Israel's horizon.

Despite the successful F-117 raids into Iran, Navon knew that Iran's military would return at some point in the coming years, stronger than ever. It was inevitable. Iran was intent on building an empire, and it had the resources to do so. Iran would, at some point, be a regional superpower.

Russia's interest in the region was also becoming palpable. Israel had recently discovered one of the world's largest natural gas fields in the Mediterranean west of Haifa—a find that held the potential to make Israel energy independent for decades. Russia was mildly interested in a joint venture to fund development of the field. What's more, Russia was also interested again in the possibility of a joint effort to ship oil through the Eilat-Ashkelon pipeline in Israel to the Far East. Navon knew it was only a matter of time before Russia reasserted economic and military interest in certain parts of the Middle East. They'd already committed to deepening and defending a port for Syria. Once Russia entered the picture, choices would be narrowed.

It was also just a matter of time before the long Sunni hegemony ended in Saudi Arabia and elsewhere, triggering political earthquakes that no one could predict at this time. What was certain, though, is that the turmoil would create opportunities for Israel's enemies.

Hamas, Hezbollah, and Syria were all much stronger, and much more willing, to test Israel at every turn. The Palestinian Authority peace process had turned to a shambles and was nearing collapse.

And the United States? Who could predict what it would do? True, the U.S. military occupation forces in Iraq had allowed the IAF to fly through its airspace, but it had offered little support beyond that. Navon had heard rumors from the United Nations and elsewhere that the U.S. was considering condemning Israel in the strongest possible terms for its use of tactical nuclear weapons in the bombing runs in Iran.

For Navon, that would set an historic—and dangerous—precedent.

The United States had always been Israel's strongest, closest ally. With the U.S. no longer firmly by its side, Navon wasn't sure where else to turn.

For these and many other reasons, Navon was

coming to a difficult realization. Israel was moving into a brave, new world—one in which it would either adapt or perish. Israel simply could not defeat all of its enemies indefinitely. Some would need to be turned into allies or, at the very least, neutralized and forced to the sidelines.

Navon had yet to communicate any of this with the Knesset or his top aides, but a new path was beginning to emerge. Israel would need to make peace with certain neighbors and offer up something of real value to solidify a new peace. Otherwise, Navon believed, there might not be a viable future for Israel. At some point, Israel's enemies would overwhelm her.

Navon had to maneuver Israel toward peace. He had no choice.

In fact, he was considering raising the issue for the first time at his weekly cabinet meeting in Jerusalem that Sunday. Navon glanced at the latest message on his desk, from the head of Israel's permanent mission to the United Nations, Ambassador Isabella Jaffe. Her message was clear and blunt. The UN Security Council was about to make life extraordinarily difficult for Israel.

Russia was about to bring news of Israel's use of tactical nuclear weapons before the council, Jaffe had learned. What the Security Council would do with that information was anyone's guess—but it couldn't be good for Israel.

Navon had addressed the Security Council

within the past year in an effort to move them toward a condemnation of Iran's nuclear ambitions. It hadn't worked. The UN had remained intent on pursuing diplomatic solutions in Iran. Navon had short-circuited that process, and the Security Council was now looking for any excuse to condemn Israel for its unilateral actions. The only remaining question, in Navon's mind, was how the U.S. would respond.

Jaffe, though, said she had a thought—and an idea—she wanted to share with Navon. He returned her call.

"Ambassador Jaffe. So . . . you have news for me?" Navon said once they were connected.

"I do, Prime Minister. I believe we have an opportunity with the Russian ambassador here," Jaffe answered. She'd been educated in the United States, with a doctorate from Princeton. Her immediate family was now in its third generation in Israel. But she still had deep roots in Russia, with other relatives still living in various parts of Russia. That connection helped her now.

"I can't imagine what that might be, given that they are about to bring up a condemnation for our strikes in Iran," Navon said.

"Yes, they do intend to pursue that," Jaffe said. "But they might also be willing to bring up something else at the same time. And it could make matters, well . . . interesting."

Navon sat forward in his chair. "What is it?"

"I've been told that the Russian ambassador might also be willing to bring up the Yugo suicide attack against the *Abraham Lincoln* in the Strait."

"You mean, make it public knowledge that it was a nuclear strike against an American ship?"

"And that it was manufactured for Iran by North Korea."

Navon was silent for a moment. That would raise the stakes. It also might be an opportunity to shift the spotlight away from Israel and toward someone else. "Why would Russia do that?" he asked finally.

"Honestly, I'm not sure, Prime Minister," Jaffe answered. "They have their reasons. But we'd be guessing at this point."

Russia had been pursuing an interesting geopolitical strategy for years in an effort to build itself back up to superpower status. Chaos and misdirection had been a staple of Russian politics for years. This could be part of that strategy. But, right now, this clearly helped Israel. And for that, Navon was grateful.

"No matter," Navon said quickly. "If it helps shift the attention away from us, then, by all means, we need to support what Russia is doing."

"It will put the United States squarely into the middle of things," Jaffe said. "We need to keep that in mind."

"They are already in the middle of things," Navon countered. "It is their 5th Fleet that will determine whether the Strait is open soon—or not. They may not like it, but the Americans are now in this fight."

"Agreed. But it will complicate things."

"Which may be precisely what Russia is hoping for," Navon said. "After all, they may see opportunity here that no one else is focused on just yet."

"So I have your permission to work with the Russians on their presentation to the Security Council?"

"You do."

"Including some of our own intelligence information on how the North Koreans built the Yugos and armed some of them with nuclear weapons?" Jaffe asked. "I would like to present evidence of the ship we seized flying under the flag of Antigua, the one that contained clear parts for a self-contained nuclear weapon aboard a Yugo. It ties North Korea to Iran—and now, of course, to the attack on the U.S."

"Yes, by all means. Just take the usual precautions, and make sure you've cleared your material with the deputy head of Mossad."

"It is a clear violation of UN Security Council Resolution 1747," Jaffe said. "We were going to present it anyway, but this seems like the best time for it."

"Yes, it makes sense," he said. "Use your best judgment."

But Navon's mind was already racing, moving to the next chess move on the board. With the Russian move, the next series of geopolitical moves would be led by the United States now. And it was difficult to know which way they would go.

Navon needed options. Forces were encircling his country, and he desperately needed an escape route for his people.

39

NEW YORK CITY, NEW YORK

Peter King couldn't remember the last time he'd seen so many people collapse themselves into the room that held the rectangle table for the Security Council members and the semi-circular table surrounding it for observers and staff. There was a sea of people and a loud, permanent buzz in the room. Rumors swirled through the crowd of onlookers and observers.

King had been forced to push his way through the crowd to get to his seat near the center of the rectangular table. He'd just finished conversations with President Camara, the White House chief of staff, Anshel Gould, and the new deputy national security advisor, Susan Wright.

This would likely be the most difficult Security

Council meeting for the United States in years. Not only was the Strait of Hormuz still closed, but, according to Dr. Wright, Iran was quietly threatening to take additional actions against non-military targets throughout the Gulf if the United States did not withdraw the 5th Fleet.

King's marching orders were clear. He was to do everything in his power to secure nine votes of support behind the continued presence of the 5th Fleet in the Strait. The world's economy rested firmly on the 5th Fleet's ability to reopen the Strait.

But, King thought privately, *at what cost?* If Iran followed through on its threats and did, in fact, attack non-military targets in the Strait, it could move the world economy to the brink of collapse overnight.

The price of oil could increase fivefold in forty-eight hours, crippling already fragile economies in some countries.

Russia would not tolerate threats to the flow of oil. It would take unilateral actions in its own national interest to preserve its ability to secure oil for its own domestic economy. Other countries—including the United States—would make similar determinations in their own national interests. Worldwide economic chaos would ensue.

No, there was really only one option, and King had to convince the Security Council of it. The 5th Fleet had to remain in place, and it had to open the Strait as quickly as it could. Everyone would just need to deal with the aftermath when, or if, it happened.

Thank goodness the *Abraham Lincoln* was still afloat. Had Iran's spectacular, asymmetrical attack succeeded in sending the *Abe* to the bottom of the ocean floor, things would be in a very different place today. But the *Abe* did not sink, thanks to the out-of-the-box, quick thinking of the vice admiral, Asher Truxton, who'd planted himself firmly on the deck of the *Abe* in the middle of the storm.

The United States would need to tread carefully today at the Security Council meeting. King had a prepared statement in his coat pocket that contained remarks he knew would take the permanent UN Security Council members by surprise.

But his orders here were clear as well. He would bring this particular card out only if necessary. King privately hoped that it wouldn't come to it. He glanced across the room. He spotted the Israeli ambassador, Isabella Jaffe, and their eyes met briefly. King looked away quickly. He knew that Jaffe, and the Israeli leadership, would not think much of the statement he carried with him in his suit coat pocket.

King stood off to the side and chatted amiably with several of the representatives of the new, rotating members to the Security Council from Brazil, Nigeria, and Bosnia. The Russian and

Chinese ambassadors had not yet made their way to the table.

The Chinese had been strangely silent during the chaos and turmoil of the past few days. It surprised King a little. But, at the same time, much of it was really not their fight. China had smartly positioned itself as a world leader in alternative energy in recent years, while also rapidly building many coal plants. China was moving away from an oil economy as fast as it could and was quickly approaching a point where it was not as dependent as Russia and the U.S. on the Middle Eastern oil reserves.

Still, King knew, there were parts of all of this that were of immense importance to China. China was paying very close attention to North Korea's role in Iran's ambitions for empire. After all, China was North Korea's closest and most important ally. It was also, by far, its biggest trading partner and provided Pak Jong Il's regime with arms, fuel, and food.

North Korea's recent nuclear tests had begun to sorely test the relationship, but China had still steadfastly suppressed any threat of international economic sanctions against North Korea. It would likely continue to do so for the foreseeable future.

Russia, though, was another matter altogether. King was struggling to understand what Russia meant to do and where it hoped to emerge at the other end of this crisis in the Middle East. As usual, the Russian leadership was playing so many different angles it was difficult to tell whom it supported—or why.

The visit that had most perplexed King was the one that Israel's prime minister, Judah Navon, and his top national security advisors had undertaken recently. They'd met with the Russian prime minister and then lied about the visit to the Israeli press. The truth of that visit had never really been explained, either in public or in private.

It was difficult to determine Russia's true motives in many things, King knew. So, as he always did, he watched what it did—not what it said.

And, King knew, Russia had quietly begun to mobilize troops on its southern borders with Georgia and Azerbaijan. That could only mean one thing—it meant to take advantage of the growing turmoil in the world oil economy and move on the Baku pipeline.

There was no doubt that the Russian ambassador, Grigori Ulanov, would present the same informa-tion—evidence of Israel's use of tactical nuclear weapons in Iran—at today's Security Council meeting, as he had earlier in the day at the 1540 Committee. But King also suspected that Russia had more in mind and would whack the proverbial hornet's nest more than just once.

The Chinese ambassador—Dr. Zhao Kuan—made his way into the room. One of King's aides said he'd been in almost constant consultation with Chinese Premier Li Chan, who had long ago mastered the art of using surrogates to do his bidding.

Ulanov appeared in the room an instant later. As both made their way to the table, the loud buzz in the room began to quiet. As they all took their seats, idle conversation in the room ceased.

Ulanov wasted no time. Within minutes of being recognized by the president of the Security Council—who, that month, happened to be from one of the new members, Herzegovina—the Russian ambassador promptly stood up from the table and circulated his first set of findings to the other members.

King barely glanced at the documents as they were delivered to his seat. They were, in fact, the same documents that had been presented to the 1540 Committee earlier that morning: a presentation of satellite and other evidence of the damage done to Iran's nuclear facilities near Shiraz.

"It is unmistakable evidence, Mr. President, of what Israel has done," Ulanov said. "They have deployed, and used, a nuclear weapon. It is a first use of nuclear weapons—something which this body must take action against at the highest possible level."

"Ambassador Ulanov, are you also prepared to show evidence of Iran's use of nuclear weapons, just twenty-four hours later?" King asked quickly.

"The world watched as Iran launched what can only be described as a weapon of mass destruction toward Israel. Had that missile struck home—which it did not—we can only imagine the repercussions. Surely you don't condone that?"

"Of course not, though we will never know for certain if it carried a nuclear payload," Ulanov responded. "But that is not the issue here. Iran was provoked by a clear, irrefutable first use of nuclear weapons by Israel."

"There is an immense difference," King responded. As usual, King felt compelled to defend Israel, which had never been allowed to argue its case on the Security Council. The U.S. and the United Kingdom had argued Israel's cause since the end of the Second World War. "If it is proven that Israel did, in fact, use a nuclear weapon, it was clearly contained, and tactical. What Iran launched was a weapon of mass destruction, aimed at killing untold millions of civilians."

"Perhaps," Ulanov mused. "But only if there was, in fact, a working nuclear warhead attached to the missile Iran launched. That is still not proven, by any means."

"I am certain those facts will come to light soon enough," King said. "But the intention is clear. Iran meant to fulfill its intended, announced mission, which is to wipe Israel off the face of the map."

Ulanov laughed. "Now, now, my American friend, not so quickly. Iran was merely responding to an unprovoked attack by Israel. I, for one, might argue that Iran was within its rights to retaliate."

"So will you argue that position?" King asked. "Or will you, in fact, see Iran's response as a serious and extraordinarily dangerous escalation of the situation—one that threatens others in the region beyond Israel and Iran?"

"We shall see," Ulanov said, smiling. "The U.S. position on the use of nuclear weapons in the region, especially, is likely to be tested with the next piece of my presentation."

Aides to Ulanov quickly passed out a second set of documents. King spent more time studying these. He'd not expected this.

The documents were from multiple intelligence sources, but King was fairly certain that he'd seen some of this from the Mossad before. It was clear evidence that a nuclear weapon had detonated aboard the *Abraham Lincoln*. There were further schematics that showed the weapon had most likely been engineered by North Korean scientists to work with a Yugo sub, built for Iran by North Korea.

King took a deep breath. The game had changed.

"So as the United States already knows," Ulanov said once the documents had been delivered to the Security Council members, "there has clearly been another use of nuclear weapons in the region. These documents show, with absolute clarity, that a Yugo submarine built for Iran by North Korea exploded a nuclear device—also provided by North Korea—in the vicinity of the American Nimitz-class supercarrier in its 5th Fleet. That the *Abraham Lincoln* is still floating—given this nuclear attack—is quite surprising. So my question for the United States is: what do you intend to do about this, now that North Korea and Iran have used nuclear weapons against an American ship?"

All eyes turned toward Dr. Zhao, the Chinese ambassador. China consistently defended North Korea and would again. But, for now, Dr. Zhao remained silent, so King decided he had no other choice but to enter the fray. The White House had only just begun to formulate a diplomatic response to the nuclear attack against the *Abe* by North Korea and Iran. But King could not walk away. He would simply have to ask for forgiveness later. He pulled his prepared statement from his suit coat and placed it in front of him. Given the evidence now on the table, he would need to modify his statement.

"Mr. Ulanov, I would have this to say," King said slowly. He glanced down at his prepared statement and began to read. "First, and importantly, the United States would like to go on record as condemning in the strongest possible terms the unilateral actions taken by Israel to use tactical nuclear weapons to attack a facility in southern Iran. There is no excuse for Israel's decision to use a tactical nuclear weapon against an adversary, and the United States will support strong, measurable UN Security Council actions against Israel as a direct result of its decision there."

There was an audible, collective gasp in the room. The United States had never agreed to even modest UN sanctions against Israel. That it was now willing to condemn its longest, closest ally in the Middle East had taken many in the room by surprise.

King looked up from his prepared text and spoke without notes.

"But, secondly, I must also add that the United States is currently assessing the truth of the attack in the Strait of Hormuz."

"I can assure you that what I've circulated is clear and verifiable," Ulanov said quickly.

King paused, scanned the room, and forged ahead. He would worry later about the consequences of the words. "While I cannot confirm that the attack against the *Abraham Lincoln* did, in fact, involve the use of nuclear weapons, I will say this." King's voice was steady, unwavering. "If it is shown that Iran and North Korea conspired to use nuclear weapons against a U.S. ship, we will take immediate—and appropriate—action in return. Everyone in this room can be certain of that."

40

BEIT LAHIA, GAZA

The flatbed truck was as nondescript as any other rumbling through the streets in the early dawn in Gaza. It had no markings. Its drivers joked with pedestrians as it wound its way north through side streets in Gaza toward an abandoned warehouse area north of Beit Lahia.

The back of the flatbed truck was covered with rough canvas and held in place with rope on all sides. Various things jutted up and off to the side. But it was largely ignored as it rumbled along. The drivers even took time to stop at a local café for a quick cup of coffee. It was, by all appearances, just another trip in Gaza.

But the pieces inside the truck had been carefully assembled over the previous months. The leaders of Hamas would never make the same mistakes they'd made in 2006, when their cache of rockets had been seized in a brutal month-long war with the IDF that had inflicted serious damage to Hamas' leadership.

Never again, they'd vowed. Since 2006, they'd forged a close working relationship with the Hezbollah leadership in southern Lebanon. They were learning to love and trust Sa'id Nouradeen, the only Arab to defeat Israel on the battlefield. They wanted to learn what Nouradeen knew and had chosen to drift within Hezbollah's—and Iran's—orbit.

Hamas' leadership still held press conferences with their faces covered. They still kept their actions hidden, from both the people of Gaza and the world. But they'd learned from their mistakes of 2006. They didn't keep their cache of weapons in central places.

They didn't ship just through the Mediterranean —they'd figured out routes through the pirates off the Somalia coast. They didn't bribe in small amounts at the Egyptian border—they'd established bigger bribes and more permanent underground tunnel routes from Egypt into Gaza.

Hamas had managed to send engineers to train with Hezbollah engineers in Lebanon. From there, they'd managed to learn how to break apart, ship, and then reassemble rocket parts and warheads. Pieces of rockets and warheads now came in through multiple sources—the Mediterranean, underground tunnels at the Egyptian border, even the Suez Canal.

Hamas had also learned that it made no sense to identify any single person as the leader. No imam or political leader publicly claimed responsibility for directing Hamas or its actions. It was easier that way, they'd learned. There would be time, at some point, for a single leader to emerge. But not yet.

As the truck left the cobbled streets of Gaza, several of the inhabitants sitting under the canvas in the back of the truck stopped playing cards long enough to check to make sure the truck's contents were secure. They needn't have worried. The Hezbollah and Iranian engineers who'd trained them had done a good job. The truck's contents were just fine. The various parts had been reassembled correctly and were secure.

There was actual joy on this particular truck. This would be an important day for the Hamas soldiers and engineers. They were better prepared, properly trained, and ready to see the fruits of their years of patience. Today would be a good test.

They'd chosen a cloudy, rainy day. It would be almost impossible for Israel's radar and satellites to detect them. But, in truth, the Hamas leadership was growing less concerned by Israel's ability to detect them. *Let them see! They should know what we are capable of achieving.*

The truck pulled into the barren parking lot beside an abandoned warehouse. They had an unobstructed view of the Mediterranean from this location, less than a mile from the coastline. It was a perfect spot. The truck's inhabitants scrambled and pulled the canvas down.

Acting quickly, the team assembled the parts they needed for the test. A half hour later, a satellite looking down would have seen a perfectly assembled Fajr-4 rocket recently acquired through Hezbollah from Iran, then re-engineered with a smaller warhead design.

The team locked the missile in place and, without preamble, fired it out toward the Mediterranean Sea. The missile flew and flew, and the team cheered loudly. Several checkpoint boats monitored the missile flight and reported back. The modified Fajr-4 rocket had easily flown more than fifty miles before disappearing into the sea.

The team quickly reported their findings back to others waiting for word on the test in Gaza. The success of the test flight cheered them all. They'd worked for three years to engineer and assemble just such a missile. For the first time, several of Israel's major cities—Jerusalem, Tel Aviv, and Ashdod—were within reach of their missiles. The terms of the conflict, at long last, had finally changed for Hamas.

Minutes later, classified communiqués and transcripts began to fly forward to capitals in and around the Middle East. Hamas' successful test-firing of a modified Fajr-4 rocket capable of delivering warheads into populated areas in Jerusalem and Tel Aviv—as well as sensitive military and nuclear facilities in Israel—quickly sent shockwaves through various quarters.

Israel had been severely condemned for its brutal 2006 war against Hamas. It would be much more difficult to contain them this time, the IDF leadership wrote in confidential, strategic memos for Navon and the Knesset. Any misstep by Israel could lead the United Nations to propose European peacekeeping forces in Gaza—permanently locking in Hamas' ability to do as they pleased in Gaza.

UN peacekeeping forces south of the Litani River in southern Lebanon had done nothing to stop Hezbollah from positioning rockets capable of reaching deep into Israel, and peacekeeping forces in Gaza would create an almost identical scenario for Israel.

If Israel was not careful, and strategic, they could soon have enemies capable of launching armed, short-range missiles from the south, north, and northeast at major population centers. They were deploying a laser-driven missile shield designed to deal with short-range missiles as quickly as they could, but the IDF had long ago concluded that such a shield could not possibly protect their major population centers from a barrage of missiles fired from both the north and south.

No, the IDF had concluded that Israel needed to reduce the number of fronts on which they were fighting. One front was fine. Three fronts was an impossible military task.

So, the communiqués concluded, the Hamas test of a missile that could fly farther than fifty miles was a watershed moment. Every major city, military facility, and nuclear center in Israel was now within reach of Iran's proxies in both the south and north. Some solution—political or military—to Israel's problem with Hamas in Gaza was needed—and soon.

41

SOUTH OF BURMA
THE INDIAN OCEAN

The old, creaking cargo ship made its way slowly out of port at Burma, where it had refueled and picked up some additional freight. The captain of *Kang Nam 5* knew that, within hours, he would be forced to make a choice.

The American destroyer, the USS *John McCain*, had shadowed the North Korean cargo freighter from the East China Sea, down the coastline of China, and past Vietnam and Thailand before the North Korean ship had made its way into port at Burma.

This particular *Kang Nam* was one of five such cargo ships that regularly made the passage from the Nampo port on North Korea's western coastline around the China coast to Burma—and destinations beyond. The U.S. Navy had shadowed all five of them for months but had yet to invoke the UN Resolution that allowed it to request to board the cargo ship to look for illegal nuclear weapons parts.

North Korea's military leaders had made it very clear that they had no intention of allowing anyone to board and search its ships. They had no use for the UN Resolution sanctioning a request to hail and search any North Korean ship at sea. What's more, they'd said that any move by an American ship to board one of the North Korean freighters would be considered an act of war.

Should the U.S. try to board a North Korean freighter, they'd vowed retaliation with nuclear weapons. It was not an idle threat.

American ships had come close to halting one of the five *Kang Nam*s on two occasions. In both cases, however, the freighters had returned home to the port at Nampo rather than risk a confrontation at sea or a possible search-and-seizure in an unfriendly port.

While it did not give an American ship the right to search a North Korean cargo ship with force, the UN Resolution did give an American destroyer the right to shadow a North Korean ship into port, where it could ask the port's government to grant access.

North Korea's leaders had quickly come to realize that, if it wanted to continue to ship illegal nuclear materials aboard the *Kang Nam*s, then they'd need a friendly port in which to dock and refuel. Burma had gladly obliged, and the two countries now enjoyed an alliance built out of necessity.

North Korea's five *Kang Nam*s now regularly refueled at port in Burma and then headed out again. The *Kang Nam*s had been able to regularly make the trip from Nampo to Bandar Abbas in Iran with just one stop at Burma. The U.S. ships could do nothing about it—unless they wanted to risk a confrontation at sea. And, to date, American military leaders had chosen not to confront a North Korea ship.

In the past ten months, all five of the *Kang Nam*s had made more than two dozen trips around the China coastline to Iran. None of them had been stopped. All of them had refueled at Burma before making their way again to the port at Bandar Abbas.

The U.S. suspected that all of the *Kang Nam* cargo ships contained illegal nuclear materials and other weapons parts for Iran. But there was very little the U.S. could do beyond shadowing the ships—as long as Burma was unwilling to allow a search-and-seizure in their own port.

Today, though, would be different. Russia's revelations before the UN Security Council had forced the United States into action. The very public news that North Korea was ultimately responsible for the first-ever nuclear attack against an American military facility had placed the American government in a no-win situation.

President Camara had consulted with the joint chiefs and the Group of Eight in Congress. In fact, he'd made three separate trips to the Capitol in just the past forty-eight hours to consult with Congress. All of them had come to one unmistakable conclusion: they had to confront North Korea, in some fashion.

The joint chiefs had decided, ultimately, that it was time to test the UN Resolution. It had sent five destroyers to shadow all of the *Kang Nam*s. Three of them were still at Nampo, and a fourth had been in the Bandar Abbas port since the beginning of the confrontation with the 5th Fleet in the Strait of Hormuz.

But *Kang Nam 5* was out at sea, and North Korea had decided that it, too, had no choice but to test the UN Resolution. Pak Jong Il himself had personally phoned the ship's captain and ordered him to leave Burma and make his way to Bandar Abbas. He was also told, in no uncertain terms, to resist any attempt by the Americans to board his ship.

North Korea's military leaders had decided to hedge their bets somewhat and had ordered the ship's captain to offload some of the questionable nuclear material cargo destined for Iran in Burma. It could always pick it up at a later date, when tensions had eased. But, for now, it made no sense to test fate more than it already was by sailing straight from Burma to Iran.

As the *Kang Nam* made its way into international waters, the USS *John McCain* made no attempt to hide its intentions. It steamed close and pulled alongside the North Korean freighter. The American destroyer had its guns trained on the North Korean freighter in the event that it opened fire on the incoming U.S. ship.

But the North Korean captain made no move. He didn't respond to ship-to-ship communications, and he didn't present even a token show of force. No guns were raised aboard the *Kang Nam*.

Instead, nearly every member of the crew of the North Korean freighter came on deck as the ship began to slow and come to a halt. They all watched impassively as the American destroyer pulled alongside, casting an enormous shadow over the much smaller North Korean ship.

The American destroyer's captain, Samuel Bingham, decided that he had no choice but to call out to the *Kang Nam*. Standing off to one side on the bridge, flanked by his second-in-command, Bingham pressed the call button on the ship's broadcast handset. "This is the captain of the USS *John McCain*," he said calmly, his voice reverberating loudly from the deck toward the *Kang Nam*. "We believe that you are carrying illegal material, and we are invoking UN Resolution 1874. We request permission to board your vessel, the *Kang Nam*, in order to search your hold."

Bingham waited for a minute or so. There was no visible response from the crew members of the *Kang Nam 5*. Many of them began to lean against parts of the ship, waiting for what might happen next. They didn't appear tense. If anything, they appeared resigned to whatever was about to happen.

Bingham had his orders as well. He was to insist that the *Kang Nam* agree to be boarded. If it refused, or did not respond, then he was to shadow the *Kang Nam* to its next port of call and ask the government there to allow it to be searched.

"I repeat, this is the USS *John McCain*," Bingham said loudly. "Under UN Resolution 1874, we demand the right to board and search your ship."

Still no response from the North Koreans.

Bingham turned to his second-in-command. "Now what?"

"We can wait," his second-in-command answered. "It's not like they're going to outrun us." The others on the bridge laughed. They all turned their gaze back to the *Kang Nam*.

There was no visible response from the *Kang Nam*. An instant later, however, there was a loud belch as the North Korean ship captain fired up the engines. The *Kang Nam* began to pull away from the American destroyer, almost in slow motion. The crew aboard the USS *John McCain* waited for orders from their captain.

Captain Bingham considered, for just a moment, how easy it would be to fire on the *Kang Nam*, force it to stop, and then board the ship. But he couldn't do that. That sort of confrontation would, without a doubt, trigger an immediate military response from North Korea—something both the White House and the joint chiefs had told him to avoid.

Bingham gave the command to his crew. They would shadow the *Kang Nam* at a safe distance, to its next port of call. Once there, they would make the formal request of the port's government to board the ship.

But one thing was now quite certain. The United States had confronted North Korea in international waters for its role in Iran's attack against the 5th Fleet near the Strait. The United States had sent an unmistakable signal to North Korea—and to the world—that it meant to respond to the nuclear attack against the *Abe*.

What came next, though, would be much, much more difficult. For, as both ship's captains knew, *Kang Nam* was headed toward the Strait of Hormuz, and for the port of Bandar Abbas in Iran.

42

TOKYO, JAPAN

Ethan Lee almost placed another call to his son but then thought better of it. He would need to work his way through, over, and around several diplomatic hurdles on his own first before he could ask his son to engage in back-channel discussions with Iran's opposition leaders.

Lee was deeply troubled—and not just because of the uncertainty that had literally exploded overnight in Israel, Iran, and North Korea. No, the longtime U.S. ambassador to Japan was worried that Japan's new prime minister, Naoto Tanaka, had gone around the bend and was, even now, throwing his country's lot in with China.

Ever since Tanaka had swept into power—removing the Liberal Democratic Party from leadership in Japan for the first time in decades—the rumors had swirled that Tanaka was moving Japan away from its historic, post–World War II security alliance with the United States and into a dangerous orbit with China.

What was most unusual about all of this was that Tanaka was a deep product of the American educational system. He'd received his Ph.D. in engineering from Stanford, one of America's most prestigious academic institutions. He'd met his wife at Stanford. So he knew, and appreciated, the United States—which made his deliberate move away from U.S. influence all the more curious.

Lee understood why Tanaka was moving in this new direction. The Japanese people had thrown the LDP out of power in Japan in a massive reform effort. Tanaka had no choice, in some respects, but to honor that reform tsunami. Moving away from its long dependence on the United States for security was a natural extension of that reform movement.

But moving directly into China's orbit was another matter entirely. It made Lee wonder if Tanaka hadn't lost his way as he struggled to master the world political stage.

Lee could see that Japan was moving inexorably into a permanent security relationship with China, which would make everything infinitely more complicated in the world. Japan was the foundation for the U.S. military presence in the East. If Japan moved toward independence from the U.S.—and into China's arms—it would make matters very complicated for the U.S.

Japan, under Tanaka's direct leadership, had hedged and almost denied U.S. military relocations in Japan. They had ended joint funding for certain projects. When the U.S. denied immediate foreign exports of its F-35 fighter to Japan, Tanaka had turned to China for its J-10.

Tanaka had then met with the IRGC in Iran.

Tanaka was playing a dangerous game with both China and Iran.

But now Lee had very specific information that Japan was about to cross a diplomatic line that would make it extraordinarily difficult to retreat from. Career diplomatic staff in Japan had provided him with the draft of a major new speech that Tanaka planned to give at an international conference soon. In it, Tanaka made clear that they were initiating a major diplomatic and policy shift—away from its historic reliance on the United States and toward an independent foreign and military policy.

Lee knew the speech would send shock waves around the diplomatic world. The timing was atrocious. Lee would need to move quickly to see if anything could be done to delay the speech, at least until things had settled some in North Korea and the Middle East. But Tanaka was an exceedingly smart man and not easily persuaded to move off a position once he'd settled on a course.

Lee had discussed it briefly with his son, if only because it was a safe harbor for some feedback. Nash had encouraged him to move quickly and bring the information to the attention of the president. It was that decision he was now wrestling with. But, he knew, he *would* need to move quickly, one way or another. Events were unfolding rapidly, in many directions.

43

JERUSALEM, ISRAEL

With everything happening in the world, Judah Navon knew that it was an odd time to focus on a press conference and the release of a scientific report. But this was no ordinary report, and the timing was now even more critical.

Navon needed this information available to Israeli citizens, and he needed it yesterday. Armed with the information from the definitive scientific report, Navon could safely address the most difficult issue at the heart of any future settlement of Palestine and the partitioning of Jerusalem—the fate of the most sacred site to Islam, the Dome of the Rock. He couldn't do this, though, if his back was against the wall.

Navon had not yet decided whether to take seriously the radical peace plan that his deputy chief at Mossad had presented to him—the plan essentially drawn up by President Camara's chief of staff, Anshel Gould.

Navon did not question Anshel Gould's motives. After all, he'd been an IDF volunteer once, and he'd always been a staunch friend of Israel. Still, it was an extraordinarily radical plan, one that might very well create rioting in the streets if the Israeli leadership indicated that they were taking it seriously.

But Navon always wanted options, and that was especially critical now. All of Israel's enemies appeared to be converging on the small nation at the same time, and he needed every possible scenario in front of him as events unfolded. If the situation got desperately out of hand, and Israel was forced to negotiate some sort of peace for its survival, he wanted to know what was possible.

A prominent Israeli architect had been funding his own studies of the location of the First and Second Jewish Temples. Using crude infrared, ground-penetrating radar and other methods, this architect had been able to show with some precision that the land south of the Dome of the Rock was a much more likely location for the ancient Jewish temples.

Over the years, others had begun to learn of this architect's various and studied approaches to the question. He'd built up a small but loyal following within conservative Jewish circles.

The Knesset finally decided to see if this architect's theories did, in fact, have any merit. It had commissioned a series of studies—managed by a consortium of research universities—to explore the theory from an historical, architectural, geophysical, and archaeological basis. The studies also took a serious look at the ground south of the

Dome of the Rock to see if, in fact, there was any evidence of past buildings in the rubble and trees that lay between the Dome of the Rock and the Al Aqsa mosque.

The studies had been highly secretive, and only a few had been given updates as the science proceeded. But, within two years of the beginning of the studies, all of the science converged on one inescapable conclusion. The First and Second Temples had, in fact, been on the ground south of the Dome of the Rock.

The various principal investigators, researchers, and study authors were going to publish a series of papers in leading peer-reviewed journals, but Navon had convinced them to release some of their findings at a press conference.

Their findings showed that the Moriah area was not the Temple Mount built by Herod. A later Roman temple had been built on the Moriah area by Hadrian, confusing things. The Al Aqsa Mosque and the Dome of the Rock were built upon the remains of that Roman temple. And remains of the original Jewish temples were actually covered now by debris and dirt between the Dome and the Al Aqsa mosque in the area of Al Kas fountain.

What's more, it appeared that the Western Wall—once known as the Wailing Wall—was never part of the Second Temple complex. The Western Wall most likely was a wall remaining from the Roman temple of Jupiter built by Hadrian—not from the retaining wall surrounding the Second Jewish Temple, as many believed. And, based on another temple of Jupiter discovered in Lebanon and some commentary from the fourth century, some believed that the Holy of Holies from that Second Jewish Temple had been covered by a statue of the Roman emperor Hadrian after the destruction of the Temple in AD 70 by the Romans and is now directly below a fountain named El Kas in that area.

While not definitive, the research was impeccable. The politics of whether a third temple could ever be built, of course, would be as intense as anything since the Second World War. But knowing the proper location would, at least, give Navon a chance to propose a partition location for the most sacred ground on the planet if that should ever be necessary.

And, right now, Navon was happy for small victories.

44

THE WHITE HOUSE
WASHINGTON, DC

She was nervous. It wasn't the person in the office. It was the actual office itself.

Susan Wright had been to many spectacular functions, in many wonderful and ornate places. She'd met privately with the Dalai Lama in the private office of the president of Harvard, where they'd talked of a guided trip through the foothills of the Himalayas. Nelson Mandela had once invited her to breakfast at a café in Johannesburg during an international conference. She'd met more than a dozen well-known international leaders privately at meetings of the Council on Foreign Relations.

It didn't matter. She was still nervous. It was the Oval Office, a place she'd only seen in photos, and she wasn't entirely sure that she'd be able to keep her composure during the meeting with the president and his chief of staff. She tried to remind herself that no person—and no office—deserved to be revered on earth. It didn't help.

She'd arrived in Washington and had quickly immersed herself in her job—so quickly that she'd never managed to make the customary rounds of the West Wing to meet everyone in their quarters. The president's national security advisor handled all the big meetings in the Oval Office. Susan kept the home fires burning and ran the staff meetings in another part of the White House complex. That had always been her nature—to shy away from the limelight, keep her head down, and get jobs done.

She'd met President Camara, of course—but not in the Oval Office. She'd been in several meetings with him in the Situation Room recently, and she'd been in a couple of meetings with big groups in the East Room. But meetings in the Oval Office with the president were reserved for top aides and for small meetings. This was her first trip there—courtesy of the unusual call with Zhubin.

Anshel Gould had called her shortly after the call, asking for a quick summary. He'd listened quietly as she recounted the story—and Zhubin's closing threat. He'd seen the NSA transcript, of course. But it was obvious he'd wanted to hear the story directly from her. When she'd finished, he'd asked her politely if she could repeat the conversation with the president.

The call with Zhubin was still reverberating in her mind as she made her way quickly through the halls of the West Wing. She glanced down at her lapel to make sure that her hard pin was still in place. It was. She checked the collar on her jacket to make sure it wasn't sticking up. It wasn't. She glanced in a mirror as she turned a corner to make sure that she hadn't smeared mascara as she'd rubbed her eyes from a lack of sleep. She hadn't.

She paused briefly in the foyer near the Oval Office and chatted quietly with one of the president's three secretaries. The side door to the office opened an instant later, and Anshel waved her in. Susan excused herself from the idle conversation with the secretary and followed Anshel into the room.

Susan was struck immediately by how clean and immaculate the office was. There wasn't a single thing out of place. Every chair, every table, and every lamp seemed to own a rightful place in the office. The floor was polished. The carpet looked as if it had been hand-brushed. The windows didn't appear to have a smudge or a blemish.

The president's desk was every bit as immaculate as the office itself. There was just a phone to one side, and an inbox. The inbox was empty. Of course, Susan had heard all the stories—how the president preferred to wander the corridors of the White House complex, seeking out meetings and quiet places where he could steal a quick smoke. She'd heard that his own, private office wasn't nearly as neat and tidy as the Oval Office. But, still, the orderliness of it all surprised her.

President Camara stood off to the side, gazing

out one of the windows, clearly lost in thought.

Susan and Anshel waited a moment. "Mr. President," Anshel said softly.

The president turned and fixed his eyes on Susan. She felt a brief panic. But, as she'd done her entire life, she quickly cleared her mind and focused on the immediate task at hand. There would be time, later, to reflect on what all of this meant. She had a mission and a duty to convey the nature of Zhubin's threat to the president.

"Please," the president said, "have a seat."

Anshel took a seat on one couch and motioned for Susan to take a seat on the opposite side. The president settled comfortably into a chair at the apex of the two couches, where he could look at both of them as they talked. Susan imagined that he'd done this sort of thing many times in this office.

Susan leaned on the couch's armrest briefly, then thought better of it. Pulling her notebook to her lap, she folded her arms over it and looked directly at the president, waiting.

"As you know, Mr. President, Dr. Wright received a call from General Zhubin," Anshel said. "I've had a chance to discuss the call with her, and I felt you needed to hear about it from her directly."

Camara looked over at Susan. "I've read the transcript. I thought you handled yourself quite well. You were polite but firm. I especially liked the way you moved him off his ridiculous claim to some sort of great victory."

Susan pursed her lips. She didn't take compliments well. "Thank you, Mr. President. I'm not entirely sure it was the right thing—taking the call, I mean. Perhaps I should have referred them to State once I knew about the nature of the call . . ."

"It was the right thing to do," Camara said quickly. "It's immensely helpful to know what people are thinking. I mean, *truly* thinking, not what their intermediaries put forward. I think you heard some of Iran's core intentions. And, believe me, that is extremely important right now."

Camara cast a glance in Dr. Gould's direction.

Susan had read all the intelligence briefings. She knew the scenarios the White House and the joint chiefs were dealing with, including the recent confrontation with the *Kang Nam* south of Burma and Russia's bombshell at the UN Security Council meeting.

"Yes, you did the right thing," Anshel said to Susan. "We're glad you opened up a dialogue with General Zhubin. As you know, we've struggled to engage with them directly."

Susan nodded. "Shahidi isn't an easy man to reach, or read. I've heard that they make even Rowan travel to Tehran if he wants to meet with Shahidi."

"That's true," Camara said. "All roads lead to

Tehran. Shahidi hasn't traveled outside the country for years. And very few from outside his inner circle meet with him. We've been trying for years to set up a face-to-face meeting, with almost no success at all."

"So hearing from Zhubin directly helps," Anshel said. "He has Shahidi's ear and is as close to a proxy as we can find."

The president leaned forward in his chair and eyed Susan directly. "Do you think he was serious? His threat to attack other targets in the Gulf, outside the military ones—d you think he was serious?"

Susan had replayed the conversation a hundred times in her head. She'd even reread her own words, and Zhubin's, in the NSA transcript just to make sure. "Yes, Mr. President, I *do* think he's serious. If we don't move our 5th Fleet, I think Iran will follow through."

"And the demand about moving Israel's Dolphins?" the president asked.

"I believe he's serious about that as well," Susan answered. "To me, it's a way for them to test how closely we're working with Israel."

Both Anshel and Camara nodded, as if they'd come to the same conclusion. "Which is why we'll get back to them immediately that we have no sway—none at all—over what Israel does with their Dolphins," Anshel said. "What Israel and Egypt do in the Suez Canal is between those two countries. We have no control over that."

"Absolutely," Camara said. "Israel is going to do what it's going to do. It will make its own decisions, with or without our input."

"Though," Anshel added, "I am going to make a call and discuss it with them. If moving those Dolphins eases things, then it might make sense—"

"They won't move them," the president interrupted firmly. "We both know that. Those Dolphins protect their carrier in the Indian Ocean, and they offer protection to their IAF planes as well. They won't budge."

"True enough," Anshel said. "But I'm still going to try."

"Knock yourself out," Camara shot back.

Clearly, there is some history between the two of them on this subject, Susan thought.

The president turned back to Susan. "What about the rest of the demands he made? It was a long list."

Susan smiled politely. "Yes, it was a long list. But, you know, we've already answered one of their demands."

"Yes, we have," the president said. "Peter King was wonderful at the Security Council. His statement condemning Israel's actions was pitch-perfect. I think people were surprised. What about the other demands?"

"Some of them are ridiculous, of course, and

simply nonstarters," Susan said. "We aren't about to stop arming Israel. We're not going to reopen Iran's nuclear facilities for them and supply them with enriched uranium. And we aren't about to speak ill of any of the Sunni states we've worked with for years."

"No, we aren't about to do any of those things—and Zhubin knows it," Anshel said.

"As for a free Arab state on meaningful land, well, you would know more about that possibility than me," Susan said. She'd heard about Dr. Gould's plan, which had been quietly circulating among top national security aides in the White House for several days.

"We'll see." Anshel shrugged. "People have tried to solve that equation for as long as any of us can remember, without much luck. Perhaps the time is right for a bold plan. We'll know soon enough if there's an appetite for peace."

The president settled back in his chair. "Which leaves the 5th Fleet, doesn't it? It really comes down to that, doesn't it?"

"Yes, Mr. President, I believe it does," Susan answered. She had her own thoughts on that subject, but she was curious where the president had come down on that question.

Camara reached up and massaged his temples. Susan could see that he'd wrestled with this decision already. "To be honest, I'm not sure we have much choice," he said softly. "We can't move the 5th Fleet away from the Strait. There isn't a country in the world—outside of Iran and North Korea—that wants us to do that."

"Have you heard from the Russians and Chinese on the question?" Susan asked.

"I have," the president said. "They want us to stay. They both believe that reopening the Strait is the only option. We can't move our ships away."

"Which means that we're going to test Zhubin and Iran?" Susan said. She did her best to keep her emotions in check. She knew what this meant.

"Yes, we are going to test them," the president answered. "As I said, moving the 5th Fleet away from the Strait right now is simply not an option. That would put every other country that moves oil through those waters at risk if we capitulate and move now."

Susan unclasped her hands on her lap. "Mr. President, I just want to say that I do believe General Zhubin is serious. If we don't move the 5th Fleet, Iran will take a next step. We can't be sure of that, but everything in his tone during our conversation leads me to believe he was deadly serious about that part."

The president nodded. "I believe you. But, as I said, I don't believe we have a choice. Our ships are going forward in the Strait—not backwards."

45

CAMP 16
NORTH KOREA

The day had been especially brutal. Despite her efforts to keep her spirit from flagging—and to stay focused on the day that she might once again see her family—Kim Grace was losing hope. Her body was failing her. The many injuries she'd sustained before she'd even come to Camp 16 were starting to take a permanent toll on her mentally and physically.

Intellectually, she knew that this was, in fact, what the North Korean leadership wanted at Camp 16. The prison camp wasn't a place where former government officials and political prisoners were reformed. It was a place where they were subjected to intense physical pressure and hard labor, where they were worn down until they literally died of fatigue and exhaustion.

Kim Grace knew that. Yet, she still persevered. The one flickering hope was that she could survive long enough to see her children again. That's all she hoped for—nothing more. She could die once she knew, with certainty, that her children were not wards of the state and sentenced to the same inexorable march to death she now experienced on a daily basis.

You Moon, her friend, had graciously given her precious minutes of text messages on the Nokia cell phone he had miraculously managed to steal into Camp 16. They'd spent days before that working on the exact wording of the texts and where to send the initial messages in the mVillage system.

In the end, You Moon had decided to send the question about Kim Grace's children to someone he'd met seven years earlier at a world student leader's conference in Seoul. Pak Jong Un, You Moon's friend, almost never traveled outside of North Korea, but his father had permitted it on this one occasion, and You Moon had accompanied the youngest son of the Dear Leader. No one at the conference knew who the two young men were.

While there, they met a young woman, Kim Su Yeong, from Harvard University in the United States. Kim Su had been friendly, and they'd struck up a casual conversation at a Starbucks after an evening session. Kim Su and You Moon had "bumped" their contact information together on their mobiles, exchanging mVillage account names with each other.

After an hour of discussion, You Moon and Pak Jong Un were both startled to learn that Kim Su Yeong's father had once been the president of South Korea. She didn't like to broadcast that fact, but their conversation had been friendly and meaningful, so she told them. Pak Jong Un said nothing about his own heritage and place in North Korea, and You Moon also kept it a secret.

Since then, You Moon had occasionally followed Kim Su Yeong through Google searches. It was amazing what you could find out about someone's personal life that way. Nothing seemed to be private anymore. He'd learned, for instance, that Kim Su Yeong now worked at the State Department in the United States and that she was engaged to be married to a young man who had created and now ran mVillage. He'd filed that information away.

Now, at Camp 16, You Moon had decided that Kim Su Yeong would be just the right person to send a message to, inquiring about the whereabouts of Kim Grace's children. If anyone could help, Kim Su could. So he and Kim Grace carefully formulated the message, then sent it to the mVillage address that was now seven years old. It did not bounce back.

Three days later, You Moon received a message. It contained only five words, but they were inscribed on Kim Grace's heart. *I will look into it,* Kim Su Yeong had texted back. Kim Grace was beside herself with indescribable joy. She prayed to God with every waking thought for an answer.

You Moon had grown close to Kim Grace in

the months since he'd arrived at Camp 16. He did not despair as she did. He still harbored hope, Kim Grace knew, that his childhood friend would free him from the prison camp once he assumed ultimate power from his father. It was an unrealistic hope, she believed, but she said nothing to her friend. Who was she to dash hope and a will to live?

So, during the long, 16-hour days, You Moon would join her as they slogged through the mindless, physical tasks of the day. They'd learned how to converse with each other, despite the guards' best efforts to keep the prisoners isolated. They carried on extended conversations as they walked by the other's station. In fact, it had become something like a game. They would start a conversation, and the other would carry it forward as he or she passed by. On the next pass, the other person would talk. And thus the conversation would progress. On some days, they'd made a single conversation stretch for the entire sixteen hours.

But this day had been marked by stern warnings from the guards, tense moments with a few of the prisoners, and a general uneasiness through-out the camp. Clearly, something was afoot. All of the guards knew something, and whatever it was permeated everything in the region. The tension had made it virtually impossible for You Moon and Kim Grace to carry on a conversation.

So they compared notes late that night. They'd heard bits and pieces of information passed between the highly knowledgeable political prisoners at Camp 16 throughout the day.

It turned out that the Dear Leader was nearby, to inspect the very facilities Kim Grace had helped engineer. She was certain, in a way she couldn't describe intellectually, that he was there to ensure the cesium doomsday device was ready and in place. There was no other reason for the Dear Leader to visit the nuclear facility in person, near Camp 16.

That evening You Moon used up precious battery time on his mobile to check the mVillage forums. With Kim Grace looking over his shoulder, they learned that North Korea was now at the very center of a growing worldwide confrontation with the United States over a nuclear attack against a 5th Fleet carrier near the Strait of Hormuz.

The Dear Leader and the North Korean military had made it very clear that they would consider certain moves by the American Navy an act of war. They were prepared to use nuclear weapons in defense of their country and military forces.

Kim Grace grew quiet and pensive as she read the accounts. She, perhaps more than anyone else in the world, knew what might happen next if the world's leaders were not careful. She'd helped engineer the device that the Dear Leader was, even now, readying for possible use.

"We must tell someone," Kim Grace had whispered to her friend in a corner of their dingy, cramped living quarters.

"Yes, but it will expose you here," You Moon had answered back quietly. "It won't take the security forces long to trace the information back to Camp 16, and then to you."

"We can be careful. I can make the information very general," she said.

"But how many people know of the cesium device?"

"Probably two dozen, maybe more," she'd said.

"And how many of them would reveal the information—knowing they would be executed immediately for revealing it?"

"None," Kim Grace had said grimly. "But I have nothing to lose. Not now."

"You have your children," You Moon had said.

Kim Grace had grown very quiet as she listened very carefully for the still, small voice that had guided her always. It was crystal clear right now. She knew what she must do. She knew what was right.

"I must tell someone," she'd said finally.

"Even if it puts you and your children at risk?" You Moon had asked.

"Yes. The world needs to know what North Korea possesses and is capable of," she'd answered, her voice steady and unflinching.

You Moon had nodded. They'd spent the next

thirty minutes formulating the message carefully. They'd described the genesis of the cesium doomsday device and how the underground atomic tests were the final confirmation of its capabilities. They'd then described the prison camp talk that the Dear Leader was on a final inspection of the device even now.

They'd added one final note, pleading with Kim Su Yeong to guard the source of the information as if her life depended on it. Kim Grace and her children would be executed, they wrote, if the information could be traced back to her and Camp 16.

As You Moon and Kim Grace sent the message, they both knew instinctively that they'd just placed their lives in the hands of someone half a world away.

46

BANDAR ABBAS
THE STRAIT OF HORMUZ

General Zhubin was impatient. He knew they had to move every ship and submarine still at their disposal, and they had only a couple of hours to do so. He wasn't about to wait for the U.S. reaction to his demands. He had to put their mine-laying plans into place, regardless of the U.S. response.

"Is everything in place?" he asked, careful not to let his impatience sound like panic to those around him.

"Yes, sir," one of his Revolutionary Guards commanders answered. "Two of our Kilos are ready to start laying mines. They'll need to re-load three times at Bandar Abbas, but they still should be able to put two hundred of them in place before the sun comes up."

"Some of them will be at the mouth of the Strait?"

"Yes, sir. They'll be at the narrowest part, east of the Tunb Islands and south of Larak Island."

"And how many of our smaller boats do we have still in operation that we can use?"

The IRGC commander glanced down at a sheet. "More than two hundred, which should allow us to put another six hundred or seven hundred mines in place."

"That includes Hovercrafts and Boghammers, along with the patrol boats?"

"It does. But we've also managed to outfit some fishing ships and other civilian craft to lay some of the older mines."

"So we have enough to close the Strait?"

"We have more than enough," the IRGC commander said confidently. "We will have more than one thousand mines in place at every chokepoint by morning."

General Zhubin smiled. "Which will greet the 5th Fleet when it arrives."

"You believe they will advance?"

"I do," Zhubin said. "I cannot imagine them retreating. So we must be prepared. We must assure that there are enough mines in place to send a clear message to every tanker that it is not safe to pass through the Strait."

"Will the MDM-6 mines be enough, do you think?"

Zhubin nodded grimly. "They will. No tanker will be able to withstand the detonation. They're much stronger than the old mines from twenty years ago. No tanker will pass once they know we've laid down the mines."

"How long will it take the Americans and the British Royal Navy to clear the mines, do you think?" the IRGC commander asked. He knew the planning scenarios, but he was curious what General Zhubin believed. He'd learned from long observation that Zhubin was a realist in private. He used bombastic language in public, but he was always candid with his own inner circle.

Zhubin didn't hesitate. "Not long, to be honest," he said calmly. "They've already taken care of many of our anti-ship missiles, and we just learned that they have the ability to shut them down electronically, in flight. So they'll move into the Strait as quickly as they can with their mine-sweepers, knowing that we can't directly challenge their ships. They'll be able to take out our mines within a matter of a week or so. That's why we're going to add to the equation."

Zhubin moved over to a large map of the Strait of Hormuz that he'd set out on the table in their own war room. He pointed to a spot on the map.

"What's there?" the IRGC commander asked.

"A weak point," Zhubin said. "One that will give the Americans and the British pause before they move their minesweepers into the Strait too quickly. We will strike here as well tonight, to make sure they understand our seriousness of purpose."

The IRGC commander looked back at the spot that Zhubin had identified—the city of Doha in Qatar. It had no military significance whatsoever. But Iran had long pledged to target economic sites, and this one would make a point well, Zhubin knew. There could be no mistaking Iran's inten-tions once they'd struck Doha and threatened to run over Qatar.

"The Americans think they can play their games in Dubai," Zhubin continued. "They think they can shut down our economy by bringing Dubai to ruin and keeping us from going around their embargoes. Well, we can play that game as well. Their allies will think twice about crossing Iran when they see that we are serious in Qatar."

The IRGC commander held up some additional documents. "The new J-10s we acquired from

China through North Korea are also headed toward Riyadh tonight?"

"Not Riyadh," Zhubin said. "They may be moving in that direction, but that isn't their target."

"What is?"

"They will close off the East-West pipeline long before they reach Riyadh," Zhubin said.

"Ah." The IRGC commander nodded. "To make clear they can't simply divert their oil through another pipeline, to the Red Sea, once we've closed the Strait?"

"Exactly. Not only will they have to contend with mines and our anti-ship missiles, they'll need to worry about Qatar and other vulnerable countries in the area. And even their backup plans to ship oil from the region will be crushed once we've disrupted the East-West pipeline through Saudi Arabia."

"And then?" his aide asked.

"Then we will make sure our allies and partners move on Israel," Zhubin said. "It is time to make sure they understand that we can strike at them, at will. We will unleash the storm."

47

EAST OF RIYADH
SAUDI ARABIA

The J-10 worked its way quickly and efficiently through the Saudi airspace. The pilot knew the lousy Saudi Arabian air force would scramble shortly, but he wasn't worried. The J-10 was quite a plane. He felt honored to be one of the few in Iran's air force to be given access to their newest fighter.

Iran had paid $1 billion for twenty-four of the J-10s from China, which had immediately and publicly denied the sale. But the Russians, who had seen several of the early prototypes, confirmed the sale privately to NATO sources. What's more, the Russians confirmed that the earliest prototypes in China came directly from Israeli defense firms trying to salvage work they'd lost when Israel cancelled the Lavi project. China denied that the J-10 was built from the cancelled IAF Lavi, but Russian engineers had seen the prototypes themselves.

The irony that the J-10 he was now flying was built from a cancelled IAF Lavi prototype was completely lost on the pilot. He had no interest in the J-10's unusual history. All he knew was that the plane was nearly as good as the American-built F-16s that Israel now flew.

China's Chengdu Aircraft Design Institute had been working on the J-10 for almost thirty years, but it hadn't admitted publicly that it flew the planes until just a couple of years ago. Again, the Iranian pilot didn't care. All he cared about was that it could outrun the Saudis and drop its payload at will on the East-West pipeline in the dead of night.

The J-10 pilot kept up a constant chatter with the other twenty-three pilots en route. For reasons he didn't understand, they were told to talk it up as they raced in and out of Saudi Arabia. Apparently the IRGC command wanted the entire world to know what they were doing.

So the J-10 pilots talked. And they learned—that Iran had struck various points in and around the city of Doha in Qatar through the night. As they were laying bombs along the East-West pipeline, rendering it inoperable for weeks and perhaps months, the J-10 pilots learned that Iran had effectively entered Qatar and was now making very loud noises that it would annex the small country if the 5th Fleet did not retreat from the Strait of Hormuz.

It was a shock to the pilots. They understood what they were doing here along the East-West pipeline. That made some sense to them.

But Qatar? Why would the IRGC and the Supreme Leader enter Qatar? There must be some point they were trying to make, because it surely made no sense to take on another front in an ever-growing war with the Americans and the Israelis.

As the last of the J-10 pilots dropped their payloads and turned to head home, they all heard the next piece of news. A midsize oil tanker flying under a Dutch flag—carrying oil from the Saudi fields out to sea through the Strait—had hit the first of the MDM-6 mines Iran's navy had secretly, quickly, and efficiently placed through strategic points.

The pilots learned, through quick chatter, that the world news media was reporting that the tanker had sunk almost immediately, spilling vast amounts of oil into the shallow waters of the Strait. The pilots had all cheered as one. Iran was succeeding, across the board, on this night.

By morning, the pilots learned that both the American 5th Fleet and the British Royal Navy had stopped their steady march into the Strait. Iran had succeeded—for now—in closing the Strait to oil traffic. It would take time to reopen it. A huge force of minesweepers was, even now, massing in the deeper waters of the Indian Ocean, planning for its entry.

The J-10 pilots didn't care how long that minesweeping effort might be. They simply knew that their mission that night—and the missions carried out by their counterparts in other parts of the IRGC and Iranian navy—had been successful beyond their wildest dreams.

48

LONDON, ENGLAND

The crude oil traders were beside themselves as the news crashed over them like a tsunami in the early morning hours.

Royal Dutch Shell reported the sinking of the mid-sized tanker in the Strait of Hormuz. That was followed in quick succession by the news that Iran had sent forces into Qatar, and then the news that the backup East-West pipeline through Saudi Arabia was now inoperable due to the J-10 bombing runs.

In the first hour alone on the ICE Futures Europe Exchange, oil prices had tripled. Crude oil was now trading at more than $200 a barrel. Bloomberg and Reuters were reporting that the steady march upwards in the price of crude would likely exceed that once electronic trading opened on the New York Mercantile Exchange in a few hours.

Iran had clearly made its point—and emphatically. Not only had it closed the Strait, for a time at least, but it had taken the fight to places not expected by the Americans. It had cast an enormous pall of uncertainty over the global economy in the blink of an eye.

Had Iran simply placed mines in the Strait as retaliation to Israel's military action, the oil traders might not have reacted quite so precipitously. They were used to threats to isolated pipelines. They'd grown accustomed to wars and rumors of wars.

But Iran's actions against another sovereign oil nation, and its brazen action against a major pipeline in Saudi Arabia, had created chaos unmatched in the history of the Middle East cauldron.

The White House had issued a statement at midnight East Coast time, as Iran's military intentions became clear. Washington was clearly trying to restore calm to the markets with an immediate pledge to use its own oil reserves to reduce its short-term need for oil from the Middle East region. Britain, Germany, Russia, and France followed suit shortly, pledging to use their own domestic reserves as the crisis unfolded.

Meanwhile, OPEC's oil ministers had already scheduled an emergency session by phone for midmorning London time. OPEC had signaled, even before trading began, that it would substantially ramp up production in every part of the world not affected by the conflict in the Strait.

None of it worked. Crude oil prices had moved

up in a steady march. They showed no promise of retreating any time soon. The oil price shock would almost instantly affect every sector of the global economy.

The only relative good news in the midst of the oil chaos was that Iraq had reopened its northern export pipeline to Turkey, which had been closed following recent terrorist explosions.

The pipeline, which connected the Ceyhan oil export terminal, carried a quarter of Iraq's oil exports. As long as it remained open, and oil-producing regions beyond OPEC remained stable, then the global economy would not go into a free fall.

But even OPEC's oil ministers—accustomed to dealing with terrorism, civil wars, border wars, economic sabotage, and high-level government deceit—were singularly unprepared for the shock that Iran had just delivered to the world economic system.

The OPEC ministers only had so many tools in their economic toolkit. To some, the spike in prices would be a short-term boon to their economies. But they all knew that sky-high prices would quickly destabilize an economy that ran on oil.

Even the hardest cynics hoped the Americans could figure a way, quickly, to open the Strait to safe passage of oil tankers, and deal with Iran on terms that would not engulf everyone in a third world war.

49

North of Tbilisi, Georgia

The Russian T-90 tanks arrived as a swarming horde. It was almost as if they'd known what was about to happen in other parts of the world—as if someone had anticipated the actions far in advance and had massed at the Russia-Georgia border for just such a moment in time.

The first of the T-90 tank commanders raced toward the oil pipeline that ran from Baku on the shores of the Caspian Sea to the Mediterranean port of Ceyhan in southern Turkey. They would arrive shortly and begin to take up strategic positions along the pipeline in both Georgia and just across the border in nearby Azerbaijan.

The pipeline—which ran through Georgia and Azerbaijan, two former Soviet states—was constantly under threats of sabotage. It was the second-longest pipeline in the former Soviet Union states. It was supported by Western interests—but not Russia. It was one of the few alternate routes out of the Middle East for oil.

It had been a thorn in Russia's side since it had first been proposed and built several years earlier. Speculation had been rampant for years that Russia would use any excuse to go after it and potentially open up a new southern front war with both Georgia and Azerbaijan.

Andrei Rowan, of course, could not have been more pleased. Virtually every geopolitical action he'd predicted to the Duma leadership had occurred—and presented him with precisely this opportunity and moment. He'd seized it vigorously and without any second thoughts whatsoever.

Rowan had first consulted with Grigori Ulanov, his UN ambassador, in the early morning hours before notifying the Duma of his intentions. He wanted Ulanov's assurances that the UN would not, in fact, make any moves toward Russia.

"Not now," Ulanov had said.

"You are certain?"

"Yes, absolutely," Ulanov had answered. "I have laid the groundwork for weeks that protecting the Baku pipeline is not only in Russia's sovereign interest, it is in the interest of the rest of the world that will rely on the flow of oil through that while the Strait is closed."

"What will Peter King tell the Security Council?"

"He will be careful. He cannot afford to challenge us too much. The U.S. needs Russia right now, more than usual."

"So as long as we don't deliberately provoke a military confrontation in Georgia, we will be able to act?"

"Yes, to protect the pipeline."

"And if Georgia military units engage?"

"As long as they act first, we are within our rights to respond," Ulanov had answered.

Both he and Rowan knew, of course, that it was almost inevitable that Georgia and Azerbaijan would respond. They could not simply allow T-90 tanks—and the rest of the Russian military—to enter by force without a response of some sort.

But the sudden conflagration in the Middle East had instantly changed the rules, and the Baku pipeline was precisely the excuse Russia had needed for years to extend its reach south again, toward the Mediterranean.

In fact, it was not out of the question for Russia to consider extending its military protection all the way to Ceyhan, just a stone's throw from Israel. Ulanov had already made it clear to the UN Security Council staff that Russia would volunteer to spearhead peacekeeping forces throughout Georgia, Azerbaijan, and Turkey in order to protect the Baku pipeline.

Rowan had finished the secure call with Ulanov satisfied that the United Nations would not interfere with his plans. He had called his aide, Nicolai Petrov, and the SVR leadership into his study within the hour.

"I want everything we have sent forward, toward Tbilisi," Rowan had told them when they'd gathered. "Get the tanks moving and bring the air cover in as quickly as we can."

"Georgia will act first, because we're moving right at Tbilisi," Petrov had offered.

"Let them act," Rowan had said. "We have prepared for this time. We cannot miss this opportunity."

"And when Camara calls you, and asks you to pull our troops back to the Russian border?" Petrov had asked.

"He can ask," Rowan had answered, smiling. "I will politely decline. I will point out to him what he already knows from his own national security staff—that it is in the West's interests to allow Russia to protect the Baku pipeline. With the Strait closed, they will need an alternate route for oil out of Iraq and other countries in the region."

"True enough," Petrov had countered cautiously. "But Georgia and then Azerbaijan will consider it an act of war."

"But it is not an act of war," Rowan had said. "It is an act in our own national, sovereign interest. We must protect the Baku pipeline—now more than ever."

"There will be casualties, once shots are fired," Petrov had said.

"We'll move quickly, and decisively," Rowan had said. "That will limit casualties."

"And what of Ceyhan?"

Rowan had simply smiled. His aide already knew the answer, because they'd discussed the scenario several times in the past week. The dialogue was for the benefit of the SVR leadership that had simply watched the discussion unfold.

Russia had already pre-deployed both submarines and ships in the Mediterranean at Ceyhan. Ulanov would seek UN permission to have peacekeeping forces in place to protect the terminus of the Baku pipeline in Turkey. The Americans would balk, but Russia would already have troops in place at the western terminus of the Baku pipeline. There would be little the Americans could do at that point.

Once Russia had troops firmly in control of the pipeline, from Baku to Ceyhan, then it was only a matter of time before circumstances allowed them to pursue Georgia and Azerbaijan.

Rowan was more determined than ever to correct what he believed was the worst tragedy of the past fifty years—the collapse of the Soviet empire. It was time to begin the process of correcting that horrible wrong. Protecting the Baku pipeline was the first step of many on that path.

And the fact that it would put Russian troops at Ceyhan, almost a stone's throw from northern Israel, was something that only a few in the world would worry about. Russia had no immediate interest in Israel. Rowan was interested in the land and states between the Mediterranean and its southern border. The raging wars against Israel were nothing more than a convenient excuse for Russia to extend its reach to the south.

Rowan's predictions proved correct. Its military actions had gone as planned. He was able to report to the Duma leadership by late morning that the T-90s and supporting air forces had taken control of key points along the pipeline. Its ships had just as easily moved into Ceyhan, and Russian forces were even now beginning to take up secure positions in southern Turkey under a NATO flag.

Georgia and Azerbaijan had moved parts of its military forward but not into direct conflict. No shots had been fired. But all sides knew some sort of conflict was inevitable.

50

ABOARD THE USS *ABRAHAM LINCOLN* NEAR THE STRAIT OF HORMUZ

"What's your recommendation, Captain Smith?"

It was a double-barreled question. The captain of the USS *Abraham Lincoln* was between the proverbial rock and a hard place. It was bad enough that they were forced to idle just at the entrance of the Strait of Hormuz, waiting for the minesweeping forces from the British Royal Navy, the 5th Fleet, and various other NATO allies to do their job.

Now they had a second confrontation coming up on them fast—one that they probably couldn't avoid. And the second, while much smaller and confined, had much greater potential to trigger an immediate threat to the planet.

The *Kang Nam 5* would arrive at the entrance to the Strait shortly and demand safe passage to Bandar Abbas. The United States had already made it clear that it would take some sort of retaliatory action against North Korea for its part in the successful nuclear strike against the *Abe*.

North Korea's cargo ship would be at the 5th Fleet's doorstep any moment. Vice Admiral Truxton knew the choices before them were awful. If they chose not to let the *Kang Nam 5* pass by, North Korea would take it as an act of war. If they boarded the ship, it would likewise be taken as an act of war, despite the UN resolution granting them the right to stop and seize what was obviously an illegal shipment.

But if they allowed the *Kang Nam* to enter the Strait—while the minesweeping operations were still underway—it could also be perceived as an act of aggression, if something should happen to the North Korean ship in the treacherous waters near Bandar Abbas.

There was no way to guess what the North Koreans might do if their ship was harmed—no matter what caused the damage.

"Captain Bingham says the *Kang Nam* has been

silent since they first approached it," Captain Smith answered. "They aren't likely to stop and ask for permission when they get here. Most likely they'll simply keep sailing toward Bandar Abbas and challenge us to stop it and board."

The captain of the USS *John McCain*, Samuel Bingham, was a topnotch sailor, Truxton knew. He'd done everything by the book so far. But he and his crew had grown increasingly frustrated as they'd shadowed the *Kang Nam* around the coastline and toward Bandar Abbas. They wanted to act.

"So do we challenge them?" Truxton asked.

"I don't see how we can," Smith answered. "The *McCain* already tried that. They didn't respond and forced our hand. We obviously couldn't board the ship, so they kept going."

Truxton shook his head. "As if we need this right now. With everything else that's happening, we could do without this confrontation."

"No question," Smith answered. "But we have to do something."

"And your recommendation?"

"That we let the ship pass, at its own risk," Smith said. "I don't see any other choice. It's not going to stop, regardless of what we do."

Truxton looked off into the distance. He didn't tell his captain or crew, but he was doing his best to listen to that still, small voice that never failed to guide him in situations like this. He just needed a little peace and clarity at the moment.

"No good will come of any action we take," he said finally. "So we might as well do the right thing. I'm going to instruct the *McCain* to follow it to Bandar Abbas. We'll clear the path there with our minesweepers."

Captain Smith's eyes widened. "We're going to *help* the *Kang Nam* through the Strait?"

"We are, Captain," Truxton said. "And, God willing, the *Kang Nam* will make it to port safely without an incident. The last thing we need right now is a serious nuclear threat to go along with the regional threats we're already facing."

51

LILONGWE, MALAWI

Nash checked with the headquarters of the Village Health Corps. The forums and bulletin boards on mVillage were melting down with the series of events rocketing around the globe. Thankfully, the servers that ran mVillage were distributed through the cloud. It would take an awful lot to crash their system. Nothing had ever come close, and Nash wasn't worried.

Still, Nash and his staff had never seen any-thing like the traffic on mVillage right now. There were millions and millions of messages and bulletins swirling around in the system.

Out of all of those millions of messages, his world-class staff had managed to filter out one of them. They'd flagged it for Nash's attention. There was a second message marked *private, urgent,* and *confidential* from his fiancée, Kim Su Yeong.

The first was a private message that had been routed and then rerouted directly to Nash. It was from an anonymous IP address somewhere in Iran. It had taken the VHC staff in New York a little bit of time, but they'd eventually been able to authenticate it. The message was not a spoof. It was real.

The purported author was Ahura Ehsan. The text read:

To my newfound friend, Nash. I hope all is well, and that this finds its way to you. I am sorry for the routes, but the leadership has begun efforts to close down and monitor even electronic communications. I fear that it is only a matter of time before we may be cut off from the rest of the world.

I have spoken to Reza. He was amazed and astonished that the United States has, in fact, fulfilled your promise that it would condemn Israel for its tactical nuclear attack in Iran. We have secured an audience, at last, with the Rev. Shahidi. We will follow up on the U.S. condemnation of Israel at the United Nations. I hope, and pray, that this will lead to a constructive dialogue that should have occurred a decade ago.

Nash was in a small bit of shock. While his earlier discussion with Razavi had not been able to stop the launch of the intermediate-range missile by Iran's Revolutionary Guards, it had clearly led to an opening. If Ehsan could manage an audience with the supreme, mysterious leader of Iran, there might be hope of settlement talks. Maybe even of peace.

The U.S. condemnation of Israel in such a public forum at the UN—the first since the Second World War—had clearly had an impact with Iran's leadership. The question now was whether there was enough time for it to lead to something meaningful before the world descended even further into chaos.

It was the second message, though, that had Nash reeling. He wondered why he and his fiancée, of all people, should be the recipient of such a message. But he also knew that, whether he liked it or not, he was in a position of authority in the brave, new world of instantaneous global communications. It was logical that such a message would find its way to his doorstep.

There was a very clear directive in the Bible. To those who are given much, much is expected.

Both Nash and Kim Su Yeong had been given much in their lives. They both lived their religious beliefs fiercely and acted every day on that guiding principle. So, without hesitation or concern, Nash knew that he would do the right thing by this message.

The message was short and in Korean. Actually, there had been several short texts, one after another, that told an incredible story. Kim Su Yeong had translated them into one note for Nash's benefit. She'd also passed on the plea to keep the source of the information highly confidential. Revealing its source, she said, would mean that a half dozen people would be immediately executed in the highly secretive, paranoid world that was North Korea.

Kim Su told Nash that she knew the author. She'd met him briefly at a world student conference years ago. She'd only learned later that this person's friend was the Dear Leader's son, and next in line to assume power. It was a stunning coincidence.

The note read:

To my friend beyond this place, I am unsure whether this will make a difference, or if anyone will take it seriously. But I believe, in my heart, that I must write this. I feel compelled to do so, in a way that I cannot describe.

I am a prisoner in Camp 16, in the mountains of North Korea. I have befriended one of our country's best nuclear engineers, who is imprisoned here because she argued against the decision to build and deploy a terrible, new weapon.

My friend says North Korea has created a doomsday device. It is so powerful that it could contaminate half of the world from its radioactive fallout, she says. She knows— she helped build this device, and she developed the science behind this cesium bomb. She says it is a fission-fusion-fission device.

The Dear Leader, even now, is inspecting the final activation of this device in the mountains near Camp 16. They are prepared to use this device if the Americans enter North Korea. I am writing because I wish to warn the world. I pray that you are in a position to tell others, and to help.

This text, too, left Nash in a state of shock. If true, it represented a terrible last gamble by the North Koreans. He and his fiancée had talked many, many times about how irrational the North Korean leadership could be. And now, with the United States forced to confront North Korea in a highly unstable set of circumstances, it was impossible to predict what they might do if backed into a corner.

If the message was true—if, in fact, North Korea did possess such an awful weapon capable of mass destruction—Nash would need to let someone know. He truly wished he could avoid the task. But, as always, he would follow his convictions. He would do his part, whether he wanted to or not. Doing nothing was not an option.

But first, before he passed both messages on to people who would know what to do with the information, he wanted to clear his head. The events of the past few days—and his own role in some of them—were starting to give him great pause. He needed a friend who would listen and provide some calm counsel.

He eased his motorbike along the dirt path and came to a stop outside the nondescript church at the outskirts of town. His friend, Asa James, lived in a one-room apartment above the church.

Everyone, Nash included, called the man Pastor James. They weren't sure of his denomination. Nash wasn't sure it mattered. He was just a Christian, running a church in the poorest country in the world.

James's great-grandparents had come to America from Malawi and had taken root. But, while he was finishing up a theology degree from Princeton, James had decided to make his way to Malawi. He was following the still, small voice. Once in Malawi, he'd never left. There was simply too much work to be done in the country for him to ever leave and return to the relative comfort of the United States.

Nash loved spending time with Asa. His sermons were simple and elegant. He spoke directly to the needs of his very local community.

And yet, over time, Nash had learned how deeply Asa understood the world, even if he did not venture into it very often.

"My friend, you look famished," Asa said as he closed the distance from the front door to Nash's motorbike.

"I am, in more ways than one." Nash pulled on the straps to his helmet, removed it, and slung it over the bike's handlebars.

Pastor James embraced Nash with his right arm and pulled him toward the church and his apartment. Nash was tall, but Asa was a big man. He swallowed Nash up in his reach as they walked along the dirt path. "You are always much too busy. You need to take time to listen."

Nash smiled. "That's why I'm here."

"And I am happy to oblige," Asa said, a twinkle in his eye. It was well known in the community that the good pastor loved to talk. He could sit for hours and opine. Nash appreciated it, because the man was so widely read. Even here, in Malawi, the Internet assured that the world's knowledge was only a keystroke away.

As they entered the sanctuary of the church, Nash stopped and looked around. Some of the parishioners had been busy since the last time he'd stopped by. Smooth, hand-carved pews had replaced all of the hard, makeshift benches. Three big panes of glass allowed light in. And a simple, elegant mahogany pulpit—adorned and elongated in true African style—was now at the front of the small church.

"I can see that you now speak in style," Nash said.

"A gift. It just arrived one day. I still do not know who carved it."

Nash looked over at his friend. "Really? No one has taken credit?"

"I have a good idea, but, no, I cannot know for certain. When I ask, everyone says it is a gift from the people of the church."

Nash loved that phrase, one that Asa used frequently. "People of the church." You rarely heard that concept in the United States, where churches tended to be more about buildings and structures and rules and ritual. Not in Africa. Here, the people of the church confronted poverty and pain by day, and demons and witches by night.

In Malawi, the warm heart of Africa, the people of the church faced all of this with power, joy, and an unimaginable sense of hope and belief that their needs would be met. They did not question the day, and what it had to offer. It just was.

An intense aroma drifted through the church.

Nash knew that smell, and he was instantly humbled. "That smell, is it . . . ?"

Asa nodded. "It is. One of my grandmothers caught a chicken and has prepared it for our meal tonight."

Nash closed his eyes. He was not prepared for such an honored gift. Chickens were a rare dinner. They were killed and eaten in many families just once a year. That they would kill one, in his honor, was almost too much for Nash. "You shouldn't have, Asa."

"Not true, my friend," Asa answered quickly. "You have always freely given of your time here in Malawi, and we are grateful for the gift. Chicken is the very least we can offer in return on those rare occasions when we can give something back."

"Well, I am truly honored, Asa," Nash said quietly. "Truly."

"Let us eat in joy, then. We have much to discuss. I have set a table out back, so we may watch the sun set while we eat and talk."

As they walked out the other end of the sanctuary, to the backyard, Nash was welcomed by an elderly woman preparing their evening meal. Nash had seen her on several occasions when he visited Asa and the church.

Her personal history was extraordinary. The simple fact that she was now in her seventies—in a country where the average life expectancy was forty—was in and of itself quite amazing. Asa had told Nash that, over the years, the woman had taken in more than one hundred orphaned children. Her extended family was enormous. She didn't distinguish between blood relations. She took in any child who had lost parents, regardless of circumstance.

Asa had long ago bequeathed an honorary title to the woman—matron of the church—even though she was not one in any sort of an official capacity. But Nash doubted that anyone much cared about that. She was a matron, and a mother, to the people of the church and its children.

"How are you, Matron?" Nash said as they walked to the simple table set before them out back of the church.

"I am well, sir," Matron answered, then returned to her task. Nash could see that fresh vegetables were cooking over the fire with the chicken as well. They'd truly prepared a feast for a king in his honor.

A stone teapot was placed in the center of the table, with two small stone cups. "Some tea?" Asa asked.

"Absolutely, thanks."

After Asa poured the cup of tea, his gaze lingered on Nash.

"So, let us be about our business of the evening," Asa said as he settled his considerable bulk at the table. Asa wasn't overweight. He was just a big man. "I have known you for many years, Nash, and I have never seen your thoughts so deep, and your gaze so distant. What is troubling you?"

The sun was beginning to set in the west, turning the entire sky orange. Such beauty was readily available in Africa. There was no need to pay for such things here. Nash was always grateful for the orange skies of Malawi and Africa.

"I am worried—for the world, and what I am being asked to do right now in these very troubled times," Nash said finally.

"Then tell me your worries, and we will see what God may have to say about them," Asa answered. "For, I can assure you, He knows your heart, your worries, and the path from both."

So, as they worked their way through the glorious chicken dinner prepared by the church's matron, Nash talked—about the explosion of worldwide interest in mVillage; the way in which it was central to information efforts in oppressed nations; his back-channel discussions with Iran's opposition leaders; his failure to stop a nuclear missile launch toward Israel through those initial discussions; the latest effort to see if some sort of a diplomatic meeting might be arranged in Iran; his father's role in the growing uncertainty in Japan as it moved away from the U.S. and within China's orbit; and, finally, the message from a political prisoner in a secretive prison camp in North Korea that said a cesium doomsday device would soon threaten the very survival of the planet.

• • •

Asa said very little as his friend talked. That alone was unusual. He was almost always asked to speak at gatherings. But that was not his place here, this evening.

It was a little surprising that a young man should be at the absolute center of so much drama on a global level, but God placed a great deal of responsibility in the hands of those who could be trusted to do the right thing even in the midst of chaos, uncertainty, immense pressure, and even terror. Nash was more equipped than most to handle such responsibility, Asa was convinced. Still, it was a heavy burden for someone so young.

"Nash, do you know where the phrase 'salt of the earth' came from?" Asa asked toward the end of Nash's long discourse.

"Vaguely," Nash answered. "I know it generally refers to people who do the right thing and keep things together."

"Basically, yes, that's right," Asa said, nodding. "Jesus was talking to His new disciples. He told them that they were, in fact, the salt of the earth. What He meant by that was that salt keeps things from going rotten, from being corrupted. Jesus was telling His disciples that they had a very high and noble purpose—to preserve the world from corruption. Because once something is corrupted, it's doomed and headed to destruction.

"But Jesus then added a very important caveat.

He also said that salt is worthless if it loses its qualities—its 'saltiness.' Once salt is no longer salt—if it's no longer able to preserve—then it might just as well be tossed to the ground so people can walk over it. Without its flavor, salt is worth nothing.

"In effect, when the salt of the earth loses the ability to preserve the world from corrupting, then the world itself is at risk. Without those in place —like you, Nash—who are called to be the salt of the earth to do the right thing, the world can very quickly become a vile, dangerous place and rapidly head toward doom and destruction. The end of the world, then, is literally at hand."

"But I *want* to do the right thing," Nash said softly.

"And you will," Asa answered. "You always do. But that is not the problem for the world right now. It is my belief that there is simply not enough salt on the earth to preserve it. A vast part of the Christian church is like the church of Laodicea from the Book of Revelation. It's lukewarm. God would actually prefer that you're either hot or cold.

"Either you're with God, or against Him. God can at least challenge directly those who are against Him.

"But huge parts of the Christian church— especially vast areas, denominations, and wings of the church that I'm intimately familiar with in the United States—are consumed with things of the world, of the flesh, of material wealth, of comfort and safety and security. *That* church is no longer concerned with the role Jesus assigned to it—as the salt of the earth.

"It is lukewarm. And, because it is lukewarm, Jesus has no use for it. The Christian church today is like the salt that has lost its flavor. It might as well be cast to the ground, so it can be trampled by men and cattle alike. It is good for nothing and will not stop the world from corrupting."

Nash was quiet. "That's a harsh judgment," he said after a while.

"I can't believe the entire Christian church is like that."

"It *is* a harsh judgment, reserved for a big part of the church—though not for all," Asa said firmly. "There are progressive pastors and church leaders who are doing their best to revive the church, to convince it to become the salt of the earth again, to encourage it not to be lukewarm. There are individual churches, where thousands gather to care for the poor and dispossessed and to have an enormous impact on their community.

"And I know there is a new movement in the next generation of Christian believers who are just now coming to power and positions of authority in the world to change course," Asa said firmly. "They want to be the salt of the earth. I only hope that they get there sooner, rather than later.

"There may still be time for the church to

return to the central role that Jesus assigned to it. There may yet be time to avert destruction. But, I must say honestly, I am not hopeful. I believe that too much of the church has lost its way. It is not willing to fight to preserve the earth. And, for this reason, the world is now in grave trouble.

"In America, especially, they've been pre-occupied with obtaining political power, and with issues that have nothing to do whatsoever with the original, core principle Jesus assigned to His disciples, His followers: to be the salt of the *earth*—to keep it from destruction.

"But now, at the moment of gravest concern and crisis for the planet—when extraordinarily powerful forces conspire in many directions to cause widespread destruction to the earth we are called to protect and preserve—the Christian church has abandoned its role as the salt of that very earth."

"Why is that, do you think?" Nash asked.

"To be honest, I'm afraid a nearly global movement has taken very deep root in the hearts of many Christians," Asa said. "They hope to see Jesus return again, to earth. And, for this reason, they do nothing to forestall His return to the earth. They do not act—in the hope that destruction will, in fact, descend on the earth, requiring Jesus to return.

"It is a terrible, terrible thing—this willingness on the part of the Christian church to do nothing so that destruction, corruption, chaos, and evil descend and take root on our planet. It is, in fact, precisely the wrong thing to do, and Jesus will take those to task who abandon His call to serve as the salt of the earth.

"For those in the church who sit, wait, pray, and do nothing in the hope that Jesus will return to earth and save it from destruction, they are like the salt of the earth that has lost its flavor," Asa said. "It is then worthless and will be cast to the ground.

"We—the Christian church—are called as a people to do everything in our power to preserve, lift up, support, and help the earth. We are the salt of the *earth,* of the world. We are not supposed to abandon our efforts to preserve and protect. We are commanded to do everything that we can to save it from corruption and destruction.

"If, at some point, even the salt of the earth are not enough to keep the world from destruction, then God will act. But not before then—and not while there are enough of us who are doing everything in our power to keep the principalities and powers from doing their worst to the earth they control."

Nash was again silent for a long time. He finished the last pieces of his chicken and cleaned his plate. The orange sky was slowly turning dark.

"So I guess it's safe to assume that your advice to me is to act, to do what I think is right, without fear," Nash said.

"You are the salt of the earth, my friend," Asa answered. "God does not want you to lose your flavor—and your ability to help preserve the world from corruption."

52

TEHRAN, IRAN

General Zhubin was prepared for his meeting this time. He'd brought his air force commander, Hussein Bahadur, with him for his meeting with Amir Shahidi. And, just for good measure, he'd secretly flown in the daring, highly respected Hezbollah leader in southern Lebanon, Sa'id Nouradeen, for the discussion. Nouradeen was important to their plans.

Zhubin had also invited three other representatives to the meeting—a top aide to the president of Syria, a leader from Hamas in Gaza, and the second-in-command from the new Hezbollah group in Venezuela that ran covert operations in the United States.

He had good news. They'd prepared for months for just this moment. While the world listened to Iran's president, Nassir Ahmadian, spout nonsense for public consumption, Zhubin and Bahadur had quietly gone about their business in Iran's national interest. Shahidi and the IRGC ran things—not Ahmadian. And anyone who knew anything about Iran understood this.

Yes, Israel's attack had hurt. It had set Iran's ambitious nuclear program back by several years, but Zhubin already had plans in place to rebuild it quickly. He was confident they'd be back in business sooner than the world expected.

But Iran's empire building wasn't front and center for Zhubin and the IRGC right now. Taking the next strategic steps in its direct confrontation with the United States was, and Zhubin's careful strategy was about to move to the next level.

Zhubin knew the plan was bold and somewhat risky. But it was also necessary. It was only a matter of time before the U.S. 5th Fleet and the British Royal Navy reopened the Strait of Hormuz. Their siege in Qatar was a public diplomacy message and wouldn't last. Saudi Arabia and Western forces would quickly rebuild the East-West pipeline. Russia would secure the Baku pipeline.

Oil would flow once again—and soon. So Iran needed to move quickly with its allies and global partners in new directions. They needed to change the equation, and he had just such a plan. It was time, at last, to draw Israel squarely into the very center of the conflict. It was time to force the United States' hand. Israel was the final chess piece that needed to be manipulated.

For years, the United States had been obsessed with al Qaeda, the shadowy, stateless confederacy of Sunni terrorists who were convinced that only a new Sunni caliphate could counter what they considered a Jewish-Christian alliance led by the United States and Israel.

Long forgotten, deeply buried, and generally not known to the public was the very real terror network that Iran funded on a global basis. But, over the years, the Iran-sponsored terror network had gone corporate. It had much bigger, more ambitious goals. It was designed to take over the hearts and minds of citizens and countries—not blow up single airplanes with crazy shoe bombers.

If the United States had any sense at all, Zhubin believed, it would have long ago recognized Iran's empire-building aims and its deep commitment to building a *real* confederation of global Shi'a partners that marched inexorably across countries. Even Iraq, which the United States had gone to great lengths to win, would eventually fall under Iran's reach, Zhubin believed.

America's obsession with al Qaeda fit per-fectly into Zhubin's and Shahidi's plans. While the U.S. focused obsessively on the al Qaeda Sunni caliphate conspiracy in Iraq, Afghanistan, Pakistan, Yemen, and elsewhere, Iran and its allies marched along with their own business.

But, much more importantly, al Qaeda would serve nicely as a foil in the next step in their confrontation with the United States and Israel. It was time to trigger certain events, and al Qaeda's leadership would likely claim credit for some of them.

Zhubin was playing to win, not just to cause harm. He wanted U.S. recognition of Iran's power and influence, and threatening Israel's existence in a tangible way was now firmly in his sights.

What was simply stunning was the West's seeming inability to recognize the real threats facing Israel and, by extension, the United States. While U.S.-led military forces ran around the globe chasing al Qaeda, shadows, and mythical caliphate conspiracies, real principalities and powers had taken root and now controlled actual nations that intended Israel's destruction.

Iran, Syria, Hezbollah-run Lebanon, Venezuela, and a new Hamas-run Arab state waiting in the wings in Gaza were sovereign powers that worked together, with common goals and purposes. Others were learning the nation-building exercise as well. Terrorist and guerilla groups in Latin and South America had learned their lessons of the 1970s and 1980s. Former terrorist and guerrilla leaders were leaving prisons and winning national elections.

Almost as one, nations were being formed and run by groups that formerly employed terrorist and guerrilla tactics for the purpose of intimidating states. Now they controlled some of those very same nations and states. It was as if someone, somewhere, had sent out a directive. Underground leaders had gone to school to learn a very valuable lesson. Terror tactics are no good without control of the state.

What this meant was that principalities and powers in control of a handful of nations could all act as one, with a single goal and a common purpose in mind.

"May God grant you peace," Rev. Shahidi said once they were all seated around his conference table in his study. He turned to his IRGC leader. "So, General Zhubin, is everything in place?"

Zhubin glanced around the table. He knew the American NSA would have gone apoplectic if it had detected such a group assembling in Shahidi's office. But Zhubin had been careful. Everyone seated at this table had taken deliberate, secretive routes. There would be no reports of this group assembling here. Zhubin was confident of that.

"Yes, Reverend, all is in place," Zhubin said.

"You're confident it will all take place at the same time?" Shahidi asked.

"It will." Zhubin turned to Nouradeen. "Sa'id, can you tell the Reverend of your plans?"

Nouradeen sat forward in his chair. He kept his back straight, his head high. He'd met with Zhubin many times in Tehran over the years, but this was only his third private audience with

Iran's Supreme Leader. He was deeply honored by this meeting. In all his years toiling in southern Lebanon, he'd hoped one day to have a seat at the table. And now he did. It was recognition of long years of struggle.

"As you know," Nouradeen began slowly, "you have graciously allowed us to stockpile nearly forty thousand Katyusha rockets directly from Iran's supplies. Those rockets are spread throughout southern Lebanon. Most of them are held in reserve. We continue to reach Israel border towns occasionally with these rockets. Hezbollah recruits, as you know, train at the intelligence academy here in Tehran. With the IRGC's help, we combine military and intelligence—"

"But none of this has had much of an impact on Israel," Shahidi interjected.

"No, sir, it has not," Nouradeen acknowledged, "which is why we have worked with the IRGC to acquire as many Fajr-5s as possible. Cargo jets have regularly flown from Iran to Damascus airport. Our agents and the IRGC have then taken them to the Bekaa Valley. Our training has been intense and successful. We are confident we can move the mobile launchers onto trucks and engage targets in Israel within fifty miles or so. That puts a number of major population centers there within range."

The Fajr-5 had changed everything for Hezbollah in southern Lebanon. Both China and North Korea had helped Iran design the rocket, which could carry high-explosive payloads. Haifa, Acre, and Nahariya in Israel were all now within range. Hezbollah had spent years filming, studying, and planning for a coordinated attack against Israel's major population centers. Such an attack would shock Israel, create mass casualties, and cause hundreds of millions of dollars in damage.

"But, now, Reverend, the IRGC has equipped us with the Zelzal-2 missiles," Nouradeen said. "This gives us the ability to strike Tel Aviv and even Jerusalem, if we wish. We can also deliver a chemical payload. We are ready to strike Tel Aviv and Jerusalem. We have been for two years."

"Very good," Shahidi said. "Your trucks and teams are in place? They are ready to deploy?"

"As soon as you direct us, Reverend," Nouradeen said. "We are ready." He watched the Supreme Leader closely. But Shahidi's face was a mask. There would be no discerning his thoughts through mere observation.

In rapid succession, Zhubin went around the table and asked each of the representatives to explain their careful, coordinated plans, how quickly they could deploy, and their probable estimates of success. In each case, deployment could be immediate, and each was confident of success.

Iran had waited patiently for this day to arrive. They'd supplied, trained, and financed proxies in Lebanon, Syria, the West Bank, Gaza, and Venezuela for just such a day. It was the moment at which Iran would seize the upper hand, finally, in the war with Israel that had lasted for a generation.

The Syrian official pledged intelligence and military support, where needed. The Hamas leader was similarly prepared to deploy rockets fully capable of hitting Tel Aviv and Jerusalem. West Bank insurgents would keep the IDF busy in many directions at once.

The last to speak was the Hezbollah representative from Venezuela. His mission was, by far, the most complicated—and the most dangerous. His teams in Washington, New York, and Boston were on the ground, armed with fully capable cesium-137 dirty bombs and ready to move as soon as the word went out to them. All of the teams had entered the country connected in some fashion to Venezuela's national oil company that sold oil to American consumers in almost every state of the U.S.

Positioning them in the United States—and arming them with a makeshift, dirty nuclear weapon capable of considerable damage in an urban setting—had been relatively easy. But making the decision to turn these teams loose was another matter entirely. It was, in many ways, a direct, sovereign attack against the U.S. on its own soil.

But, the IRGC leadership had argued, there was almost no choice at the moment. The U.S. Navy was engaged directly with Iranian naval forces in the Strait, and they were well within their rights to extend the war to the U.S. territory.

Still, there was one other piece to fall before Iran would authorize the coordinated attack by the Venezuelan, Hamas, and Hezbollah proxies—an attack that would, once and forever, shift the balance of power against Israel permanently in Iran's favor, the IRGC believed.

Iran needed a diversion—a very large one—that would consume the American leadership and take their eyes away from the direct confrontation in the Middle East. The option would, in effect, stretch conflicts around the globe.

Curiously, the option had rather casually been given to Shahidi in a private conversation recently with Andrei Rowan. The Russian prime minister had mentioned, almost in passing, that he felt the Americans would move away from their confrontation with Iran if a substantially greater threat presented itself.

It was an option, Rowan had suggested, that Iran should take a serious look at. Russia would, of course, disavow any knowledge of it, should anything occur. Still, he'd said, it was a thought.

That option was arriving at Iran's doorstep, even as this group met in Tehran. Within hours, North Korea's *Kang Nam 5* cargo vessel would begin to approach the American 5th Fleet and the shallow waters of the Strait of Hormuz that Iran still had a tenuous hold over.

If the U.S. Navy boarded the ship, then the U.S. would very quickly be at war with North Korea. The Iran threat would take a back seat to the sudden risk of a real nuclear confrontation. If the *Kang Nam* entered the Strait, and the Americans attempted to keep it from making port at Bandar Abbas, North Korea would also consider this an act of war.

And if the *Kang Nam*, for whatever reason, should somehow sink in the murky, treacherous waters of the Strait and never make port at Bandar Abbas, Rowan had mentioned in passing to Shahidi, well, then that would be most unfortunate.

53

ABOARD THE USS *JOHN MCCAIN*

The *McCain* destroyer's captain, Samuel Bingham, wasn't quite convinced of the decision that had been handed to him by the vice admiral. But, as always, he went by the book. If Truxton told him to shadow the *Kang Nam* through the Strait and make sure that it made it to port at Bandar Abbas safely, then he saluted and set about making sure he had the means necessary to make it happen.

The *Kang Nam* had almost dared the American Navy to board it. The North Korean cargo ship passed right by the *Abe*, within eyesight of the American sailors who'd gathered on deck to watch the drama drift by slowly.

It was an eerie scene—the much smaller North Korean freighter dwarfed in size and power by both the *Abe* and the *McCain*. But the *Kang Nam* just sailed right by, in radio silence, on its way to Bandar Abbas.

Bingham had exchanged a few terse words of instruction with Truxton and Dewey Smith as they'd begun to enter the Strait.

"Take great care," Truxton had ordered the *McCain* captain. "Do everything in your power to make sure that the *Kang Nam* makes it to port safely at Bandar Abbas. Make sure you've handed it off in line of sight to the Iranian navy. I will communicate our intentions to Hashem Sanjar."

Truxton had signed off and immediately sent an electronic message to Sanjar. The commander of Iran's navy did not respond, other than to acknowledge receipt of the message.

It seemed obvious to Bingham that Truxton was using the radio airwaves, which were obviously monitored by at least a half dozen foreign powers, including Iran, to make the American intentions toward the *Kang Nam* quite clear. He wanted the world to know that the 5th Fleet intended to allow the *Kang Nam* to pass by, unimpeded.

Still, both Bingham and Truxton knew the truth. Should something happen to the *Kang Nam* here, in the open waters, no amount of diplomacy or persuasion was likely to deter North Korea's unstable, paranoid leadership. By the time everyone sorted out the truth, both North Korea and the U.S. would have taken other actions and pursued other options.

It was one thing to board a ship at port or in calm waters. It was quite another thing to deal with a hostile situation in waters filled with mines, midget subs, and patrol attack boats that doubled as suicide weapons. There, anything could happen.

The minesweeper had done a good job already of clearing the mouth of the Strait. The *Kang Nam* had relatively clear sailing through the opening to the Strait. It would get trickier, though, as it came closer to Bandar Abbas—within range of several of Iran's own destroyers.

As the *Kang Nam* started to approach Bandar Abbas, Bingham suddenly got nervous. He couldn't pin it down. But something wasn't quite right. Perhaps it was the manner in which several dozen fishing vessels and patrol boats were arrayed in a relatively small space. Perhaps it was the sight of Iranian destroyers waiting to receive the *Kang Nam*.

But what really concerned him was that there

had been persistent reports from his sonar operators of new movement nearby, on the *other* side of the *McCain*, in between it and the 5th Fleet command stationed outside the mouth of the Strait. Something had slipped in behind the *McCain*, for whatever insane reason.

Meanwhile, the North Korean freighter was being forced to follow a relatively set path toward the port. It was almost as if someone was forcing the *Kang Nam* to sail a certain way, in a certain direction, through the waters that led to Bandar Abbas.

Bingham phoned Truxton. "Sir, I'm concerned. We won't be able to track the *Kang Nam* much further. We're about to hand it off to the Iranian navy and then hold off on any further progress. We're at a point where we can't assure that all of the mines have been swept."

"Understood," Truxton said. "I can see from your video transmission that there are quite a few smaller boats in the area."

"That's what concerns me. There's no use for them, except to—"

Truxton grasped the implications almost immediately. "Other than to make sure the *Kang Nam* follows a preset path. They're sending the *Kang Nam* into something. Captain, do your best to warn the *Kang Nam*," he said somberly. "Have they ever acknowledged any of your attempts to communicate with them directly?"

"No, sir, they haven't."

"Try again. We have no choice," Truxton said. "I'll let Washington know what's happening."

Seconds later, their worst fears were realized. It happened quickly. Just as the sonar operators reported in that they'd detected the telltale sounds of a torpedo tube opening, Bingham and the others aboard the *McCain* watched as a single torpedo approached the *Kang Nam*. To an observer, it almost appeared as if the torpedo had been launched from the bowels of the *McCain*.

But the torpedo did not hit the *Kang Nam*. It came close, then hit a mine depot right beside it. A massive explosion erupted in all directions. It was obvious, to anyone watching, that the torpedo had hit not one but several mines, all closely clustered.

The explosions struck the *Kang Nam* broadside, immediately tearing a gigantic hole in its side. A few seconds later, as the weapons cargo aboard the freighter started to catch fire, there were additional explosions aboard the *Kang Nam*. And, shortly after that, the North Korean freighter began to sink slowly into the murky waters of the Strait.

54

PYONGYANG, NORTH KOREA

The worldwide news media reports of the sinking of the *Kang Nam* were conflicting. Those
controlled by the West quickly claimed that the
North Korean freighter ran into mines planted by
Iran. But Iran, just as quickly, cited eyewitness
accounts of a torpedo that had come from the
direction of the USS *McCain*, sinking the *Kang
Nam* from the massive mine explosions.

Based on the reports from both Truxton and
Bingham, the White House quickly issued a
statement that the United States had not been
complicit in any fashion with the sinking of the
Kang Nam. The U.S. had done everything in its
power to safely shepherd the freighter into port, it
said. The U.S. had not fired the torpedo, but it
stopped short of accusing another nation of firing
the shot that led to the sinking.

None of this mattered to the leaders of the North
Korean military establishment. They expected
the Americans to lie about their role in sinking the
freighter. It was an act of war, and North Korea
must respond. They pressed the Dear Leader, Pak
Jong Il, for an immediate, retaliatory response.

The Korean People's Army and the national defense commission were unanimous in their recommendations at the emergency meeting in Pyongyang. They'd quickly converted the Dear Leader's youngest son and successor, Pak Jong Un, to their position. The act demanded an immediate response, and Pak Jong Un had been swayed to their thinking and recommendations.

Of course, for Pak Jong Un, this was a defining moment in his young political life. He desperately needed the military leadership behind him in order to succeed his father. Without their support, he would never survive the transition to power. So he quickly and loudly proclaimed his support for their position in the small leadership meeting.

But there was a slight problem. The Dear Leader, who'd seen much in his many years as the absolute leader of the most secretive military state in the world, wasn't convinced that the Americans were responsible for the sinking of the *Kang Nam*.

He'd been in power for a very long time and understood why leaders took actions. North Korea's own initial intelligence reports made it clear that the American Navy had made it known they intended to shadow the *Kang Nam* to port—and nothing more.

Granted, it did appear as if the American ship was responsible for the action. But Pak Jong Il was demanding more proof before he would authorize the drastic response the military establishment was attempting to foist on him.

As the long meeting dragged on, it became quite clear to North Korea's military leaders that they were losing the debate. Pak Jong Il was going to decide against direct action and opt for a diplomatic effort to determine the truth of what had really happened south of Bandar Abbas.

Shortly after the meeting, several of the military leaders decided it was long past time for the transition in power within North Korea. This was a defining moment for North Korea's military establishment as well. If it showed weakness toward the U.S. now, it would never recover.

North Korea had always pledged "total war" against the U.S. if attacked, and to do nothing would place its nuclear facilities—and its place in the international arena—in permanent decline. Some sort of appropriate response was mandatory, they believed.

The leaders met privately with Pak Jong Un following the meeting. They reminded Pak that some percentage of all receipts from military-run commercial ventures went directly into his father's personal bank account. That would disappear immediately if the military cut him— and the son—off for any reason. But there would also be much more severe consequences if his father chose to go against the military establishment's wishes on this.

The young, impetuous leader listened for several

minutes, then quickly agreed to speak with his father. He would deliver their ultimatum. Either North Korea responded, forcefully, with a literal shot across the bow—or the transition to power within North Korea would begin immediately, whether Pak Jong Il was ready for it or not.

55

THE WHITE HOUSE WASHINGTON, DC

It had been a very long three days for DJ. He'd gotten almost no sleep. He was fairly certain he was starting to develop an ulcer. He was popping antacid like it was candy. He'd worn out the carpet between his office and Anshel Gould's in the West Wing. The confrontation with Iran was sapping everyone's energy and well-being.

And it was about to get worse. Satellite pictures had just confirmed that a missile launch pad erected at Musadan-ri on North Korea's northeast coastline—just south of Camp 16—had just gone live and hot. North Korea had often bluffed that they intended to launch their longest-range ICBM, the Taepodong-2, toward Hawaii.

No one in the Pentagon, or elsewhere, took the threat seriously. North Korea had tested its long-range ICBMs twice, and both had been spectacular failures. At most, the Taepodong-2 could fly four thousand miles. Hawaii was another five hundred miles beyond that range.

There was simply no credible intelligence anywhere to suggest that North Korea had the wherewithal to actually fire an ICBM with the range to reach American territories. And even if one had the range, it had never shown the ability to keep the missile together and on-target. Finally, even if it reached Hawaii, it would have a very tiny nuclear payload, or none at all.

But that still didn't mean the White House and Pentagon could ignore the North Korean threat, or the action that was now underway on their ICBM launch site at Musadan-ri. The Pentagon had already deployed anti-missile interceptors and sea-based tracking radar between Hawaii and North Korea. It was prepared to shoot a single missile out of the sky long before it ever reached Hawaii, should it come to that.

But Dr. Gould had sent a cryptic note to DJ that there was more behind the threat looming at Musadan-ri, one that had just surfaced. He asked to meet with DJ, Susan Wright, and a few others briefly to talk it through before he met with the president.

Anshel had an uncanny knack of bringing discrete groups of senior White House aides together around specific issues that, he knew, they cared about deeply. It was one of the many tricks that Anshel employed to keep people and groups distinctly loyal to him. They felt special—indebted to him—because he chose to include them in certain areas they were passionate about.

DJ made the quick walk to Dr. Gould's office. He knew every patch of carpet, every turn, by heart now. He could make the trip there in his sleep, or with a blindfold on. But he'd never seen Dr. Gould so tense when he joined Dr. Wright and the others in his office.

"I don't need to tell all of you here that we need this problem with the *Kang Nam* and North Korea like a hole in the head," Anshel said when they'd all pushed their chairs close to his desk. "To make a bad situation even worse, Ethan Lee —our ambassador in Tokyo—has learned that Japan's prime minister is about to give a major foreign policy speech that will move it away from the U.S and more closely aligned with China. That will seriously complicate any action we take against North Korea.

"With Russia's move into Georgia and Azerbaijan, Iran's actions in the Strait, and Israel's continuing paranoia that forces are coalescing around them on three or four fronts, the last thing we need is a new conflict with North Korea. But that's what we have."

"But North Korea's ICBM threat is a joke," DJ said. "Everyone knows that—"

Dr. Gould held up a hand. The room grew silent. "Yes, but that's not the problem any longer." He held up a piece of paper.

From his seat, DJ could see that it appeared to be an e-mail or text of some sort. He and the others waited for Dr. Gould to brief them.

"This is a transcript of a text sent from one of North Korea's political camps," Anshel continued. "We believe it to be from a credible source, someone most likely in a position to know what they're talking about. It says, quite bluntly, that the North Koreans have successfully built a cesium nuclear device based on old technology known in the 1960s. It appears to be a fission-fusion-fission device."

Susan Wright gasped. Unlike the others in the room, she knew what the possibilities were with such a device. And, if true, it presented a truly horrific threat to the planet itself—especially in the hands of a nation that might actually think of itself on a suicide mission. The contamination from detonating such a device could do harm to half the planet, for some time.

"But they have no ability to deliver such a weapon," Dr. Wright said. "None whatsoever. It simply isn't possible. They can barely keep their ICBMs stable at launch. It could never handle such a weapon as an actual payload."

Anshel didn't respond right away. "The intelligence says the device isn't a payload," he said finally. "It's in a fixed location, in a nuclear test facility near Camp 16 and the Russian and Chinese borders, and it's quite large. It is also now armed. Pak Jong Il recently visited the site to look at the final preparations himself."

Susan Wright closed her eyes for a moment and offered a silent prayer. The old nuclear science literature had always talked about the possibility of such a doomsday device, but the United States, Russia, China, and others had long ago abandoned efforts to create such a weapon.

There was no need. Superpowers had invested in nuclear miniaturization, targeted missiles, and payload technology. They'd moved well beyond the world of mutually assured destruction that had once framed armed conflict between superpowers.

But new superpowers were emerging in a very chaotic, dangerous world, and others were willing to take enormous risks to achieve nuclear parity. It made sense that North Korea would attempt to build such a weapon while it refined its ability to launch missiles and deliver nuclear payloads that way.

At a minimum, such a device almost assured that neither the United States nor South Korea would ever consider attacking North Korea. And, perhaps that was their rationale for building such an insane weapon in the first place.

"We're absolutely certain that the intelligence

is credible, and that this is possible?" DJ asked.

"It's credible, and the intel says the information comes from a nuclear scientist who worked on the project," Anshel said. "We have no way to verify its accuracy, but if it's possible, then we have to take it seriously."

"Which means we have to be careful not to escalate anything with North Korea in the next twenty-four hours, even as we explain the *Kang Nam* incident," Susan offered.

"I would say that's an understatement," Anshel said.

56

MUSADAN-RI, NORTH KOREA

The Taepodong-2 missile that was now fully vertical on the launch pad looked impressive. The North Korean military had a film crew capturing the event. Even if the missile flew just a short distance before disappearing into the Sea of Japan, the KPA leadership had ordered that the footage of the launch be made available immediately.

If nothing else, North Korea would show resolve in the face of the American act of war with the While those charged with the ICBM missile launch at Musadan-ri had no way of knowing it, the KPA's gambit with Pak Jong Un had been successful. He'd convinced his father to act, though it hadn't been easy.

The son, however, did not know of the cesium doomsday device. It was the most closely guarded military secret in a country of military secrets. Only a select few who'd worked on the project knew of its existence. It was there in the event that other things went horribly wrong. It was North Korea's final, dead-hand move against an aggressor that entered its territory.

Had Pak Jong Un known of the device's existence, he might not have pressed his father to do as the KPA was demanding. Had he known that North Korea possessed a weapon capable of poisoning half the planet, he might have chosen a different course. But he didn't know—which was precisely what the KPA wished. They let the son know only so much and not any more.

Pak Jong Un's father, of course, was another matter entirely. But since his stroke, he was virtually incapable of confronting the KPA leadership on any level.

When the Taepodong-2 missile finally lifted off the launch pad, the workers let loose with a loud cheer. They all watched on their video monitors as the missile headed out over the water.

None of them believed the missile would ever make it even remotely near any of the islands that made up Hawaii. Still, it was thrilling to think that it *could* make it there. That possibility changed everything.

So when, by some miracle, the missile made it through its booster phases and was still flying after three thousand miles, the workers and leadership responsible for the mission all started to collectively hold their breaths.

There was no payload on the missile, of course. But that hardly mattered. The KPA wanted to send a large, unmistakable message to Washington. Every second the Taepodong-2 remained in the air, the louder that message became.

And then, in the literal blink of an eye, it was over. Somewhere over the water—at least one thousand miles from any possible target—the American tracking and anti-missile system deployed around the islands did its job. It took the missile down without any fanfare.

But the KPA and national defense commission leaders who'd sanctioned the launch didn't care. They'd achieved everything they wanted.

Now they were prepared to take the next step with the U.S., if they had to. They gave Pak Jong Il his instructions, then sat beside him as he placed calls to the leaders of Russia, China, and Japan.

57

Foggy Bottom
Washington, DC

Kim Su Yeong stared straight ahead in her windowless cubicle. She was doing her best not to cry. But the unclassified report from the American embassy in Seoul broke her heart. She stared hard at the pictures to keep herself from growing too emotional. It helped, a little.

Su had been careful to mask her inquiry. She'd placed a dozen names in her unclassified request to a branch chief at the embassy. She knew the State Department tried to track political prisoners in the North Korean prison camps—the ones North Korea adamantly maintained did not exist —and she had hoped they had some information on the fate of Kim Grace's children.

Su had asked for a family history for each of the names in the report—where the children, fathers, mothers, grandparents, etc., were for each of the dozen names she'd submitted. Su had known that the request was a big one and would make some poor analyst's life miserable for a few days. But she didn't care. It was something that had to be done.

Su had done her best to liven her cubicle up in one of State's many warrens at Foggy Bottom. She'd plastered three walls with color pictures of mountains, rivers, and beautiful vistas—many of them photos of the Korean Peninsula from the one visit she'd managed to arrange for herself as part of a diplomatic mission to South Korea.

There weren't many perks working for the Korean desk at State, but she could at least make official requests. She'd used everything she could muster for the request around Kim Grace's children. She'd come right to the edge of classified requests. She was certain of that, but part of her didn't care. She felt obligated to the woman in Camp 16 who shared her very common last name, for some unexplained reason.

Kim Su Yeong loved her job at State. It was everything she could have hoped for as a first job in DC. She had more than enough authority for someone so young. She had plenty to keep her busy. She was able to go out for dinner with friends a couple of nights a week, and her loft apartment that she shared with three other female friends was always brimming with activity.

Su always managed a bright, cheerful smile for her coworkers. She was friendly and outgoing, more than happy to join coworkers and friends alike for activities after hours in Washington, or for congressional softball matches on the Mall.

Yet she did not date. Her friends constantly

teased her about her globe-trotting boyfriend who was never around. They were always trying to set her up. But Su was happy with her relationship to Nash. She knew that, at some point, their lives would make sense in one location, and they would be married. She was certain of this, though she never talked about it much with her friends.

Su had a deep, quiet, abiding, Christian faith. It was part of nearly every thought and action of her working and personal life, yet her friends rarely, if ever, heard her speak of it. Su was one of those Christians who believed that a human being is known by what they do and who they are—not by the pretty words they speak or the pious deeds they describe as a sign for others to observe.

Su heard the still, small voice clearly in almost everything she did. And it was that voice that always reassured her that there would be a time and a place for her marriage to Nash. They both had work to do first.

She and Nash had never really talked about it, but she knew that they both wanted to have children together. She could imagine herself as a mother some day, with young children running around her in a modest home somewhere in DC. She imagined that future together with Nash quite often, at odd moments of the day.

Su also liked to curl up with a good book—or, occasionally, with one of the 150 books she'd already downloaded to her Kindle that she never quite managed to get to—when others weren't around. It was one of her very favorite activities.

The current rage in best-selling women's fiction was a time-honored theme that always struck at the very core of women like Su—stories of young children ripped somehow from the arms of a young mother, and then the frantic, desperate search through heaven and earth to either find or locate the missing or abducted child. Sometimes the children were found. Sometimes they were not.

Su simply could not imagine what it would be like to lose a child. She could think of nothing worse than this, which is why writers always returned to the theme over and over again. A mother raising a child for the next generation was more important than anything she could possibly imagine, Su believed. Losing that child would be a devastation she hoped never to confront.

Which is what made the report in her hands right now so deeply troubling, on so many levels. It represented one of the worst fears any mother could imagine.

Kim Grace had raised three wonderful, loving children before she'd begun to question the North Korean military's fascination with a cesium dooms-day device and then its determination to build one. Su could imagine the life she'd tried to build for her children.

The report included paragraphs on Kim Grace's children and husband. For her husband, there was a brief description of his death. The analyst had pieced together a couple of items, which seemed to indicate that her husband had died at a camp and then been returned to his home for a quick, nondescript funeral service.

For her three children, there was only a headline—"Missing, Presumed Dead"—followed by a brief description of the three children.

The analyst speculated that the children had likely been sent off to prison camps somewhere in North Korea and had never been heard from again. The likelihood that they were still alive—based on history and statistical analysis—was slim, the analyst concluded.

It was at that point that Su had begun to cry softly. She'd never met Kim Grace, and most likely never would, but she could imagine this brave woman somewhere in a terrible prison camp, wondering what had happened to her children. And the only news that Su, or anyone, could muster was that they were missing and presumed dead.

After a few minutes of grieving, however, Su pulled herself together and was now prepared for whatever she needed to do next. She glanced at the tiny world clock she kept in her cubicle. She knew that if she Skyped Nash right now, she would most likely reach him. Nash always worked into the early morning hours, and she was able to reach him more often than not at this time of day.

She put her headphones on and placed the Skype video call to him. Nash answered within two rings. He had a two-day stubble going.

"Hey! I was just thinking about you!" Nash said brightly, then stopped. "Oh, I can see that something's wrong. What's up?"

Su fought back tears. "I got the report back, Nash. The one on Kim Grace."

"And?"

"And they couldn't find any record of her children. It just lists them as missing and presumed dead. Her husband died in prison camp."

Nash reached out and lightly tapped the video camera. It was one of the things she liked so much about Nash. It was his way of saying that everything would be all right, even though he wasn't physically sitting there to console her.

"That doesn't mean they aren't still alive," Nash said. "We can work, somehow, to get her out of that camp under some sort of a prisoner exchange and then use the system to try to find them. Don't give up hope, Su."

She blinked fiercely. She didn't want to give up hope. "I was sitting here, wondering what it would be like if we lost all of our children like that one day—"

"Don't do that, Su," he said quickly. "You'll just make yourself crazy that way. Stay focused on what we would need to do in order to get this woman free of that prison camp. Look into that, okay? It will give you something to pursue."

Su nodded. She loved the way Nash jumped straight to the mission at hand. He was like a relentless, positive storm. "I will," she vowed. "So what news do you have? How's your father?"

Nash didn't even know where to begin. There were some things he probably shouldn't be talking about over an open-source channel like Skype. But he filled Su in anyway on the back-channel mVillage discussions he'd been having, that very evening, with both Razavi and Ehsan in Tehran.

Whether he meant to be or not, Nash was now involved deeply with the opposition leaders' efforts to get to Shahidi and begin the process of arranging some sort of a dialogue.

Nash knew it had been almost a generation since any American leader had even set foot in Tehran and that his efforts would most likely come to nothing, but he felt compelled to see the discussions through to some sort of conclusion.

Nash was running every exchange, every nuance, past his father at every step of the discussion. His dad was encouraging him to press forward. Nash was making more progress, his father said, in a matter of weeks than entire divisions at State had managed in years of trying to open discussions.

Still, Nash told her, they were a long way from any sort of face-to-face discussion with Shahidi. And anything short of that in the very complicated world of Sharia law and Islamic politics in Tehran would mean nothing. Shahidi was the key. He alone could determine Iran's relationship with the United States and, by extension, the nation of Israel.

Nash made certain that Su was calm before he said good night to her. He wished he could somehow help her with the search for Kim Grace's missing children. But he knew that this was Su's work, and it was something she would need to wrestle with on her own.

58

MOUNT VERNON SQUARE
THE INTERSECTION OF 7TH AND
K STREET NW
WASHINGTON, DC

The suitcase was innocuous enough and didn't draw any unusual glances by the couples and workers who were beginning to gather there for the lunch hour. It was hardly out of place in the open air park in Washington—one of several within ten blocks of both the Capitol and the White House—where the homeless routinely left their belongings out in the open.

This particular part of DC was dominated by the

unusual, elongated building that housed National Public Radio. The slim building was like a finger pointing directly at the park, just across the street. Two relatively new office buildings met at the intersection. The FedEx Kinko's at one of the corners was a popular destination for hundreds of workers nearby.

The suitcase was left on the ground between two park benches about one hundred feet north of K Street. A DC recreation center was just three hundred feet farther north and east from the spot.

The location had been carefully selected. It was close enough to both the Capitol and the White House complex that the incident would have impact, yet far enough away that there were very few security cameras operated remotely at the intersection.

Because it was in an open-air park—with lots of people around—it would be impossible for anyone to remember later who'd been in and out of the park. There were no cameras aimed at the interior of the park. It was an ideal location.

Two men had driven a Honda Civic up to the park and had circled the city block twice until they were able to park about midway up the street. They'd waited inside for nearly ten minutes before exiting quickly. One man left first and walked up toward the park benches. He turned and, with a slight nod, signaled for the second man to follow behind him with the suitcase, which had been sitting carefully in the back seat.

The men had, until quite recently, been servicing several QVStops in Frederick, Maryland. They drove a contract fuel truck and visited several stops on a daily basis.

Though they didn't realize it, the two men were quite fortunate that the FBI agent who'd first made the connection between QVStops, Venezuela, and Hezbollah at a remote gas station in Savannah, Georgia, had never managed to get his superiors to take the connections seriously. If they had, their mission might have been detected or even derailed before this day.

The men were light-skinned, clean-cut, and well-mannered. It was very difficult to tell their country of origin. Had someone asked for their visa papers and passport stamps, they'd have seen that both men had trained in Venezuela before coming to the United States to work.

By all accounts, both men had come to the United States to give themselves a chance of a better life. They kept to themselves. They did not visit any local mosque—many of which were now regularly under some sort of homeland security surveillance, despite repeated protests from international human rights groups in the U.S.— and worshipped privately with a small group.

They were respectful, law-abiding, gainfully employed foreign nationals working in a country that respected and welcomed all groups of people into a melting pot society. They were here to do their jobs and make a life for themselves.

There was nothing, and no one, to lead anyone to suspect that they'd come to the United States with just one goal—to someday leave a dirty cesium-137 suitcase bomb in Mount Vernon Square, near NPR and a DC recreation center with hundreds of children, in downtown Washington.

The two men had worked, trained, and acquired the necessary ingredients over the course of three years. The hardest piece—the cesium-137—had been easier to acquire than either man could have imagined. It simply disappeared from a nuclear medicine shipment one day and arrived in their hands the next.

As they'd been taught, they carefully packed the cesium-137 inside as many sticks of dynamite as they could fit into the suitcase. They set the fuse with a remote signal relay, put the suitcase into storage, and then worked each day at their jobs, waiting for the word to reach them through channels from Tehran that it was time to deliver and set off the dirty bomb.

When the word arrived, the two men didn't say much to each other. They simply placed the suitcase in the Honda Civic, drove through rush-hour traffic toward downtown Washington, and went through the routine they'd trained for over the years.

They'd been told to set the bomb off at 11 a.m.,

East Coast time, and then leave the area quickly. Both men knew there was some risk of contamination reaching them, but it was a risk they were more than willing to take. Both men believed that Iran and the United States were actively at war with each other, and they were both committed to doing the right thing for their country.

Neither of them knew that, precisely at 11 a.m. in New York City and Boston, two nearly identical cesium-137 dirty bombs would also go off in open-air urban parts of both major cities. The combined death toll from the immediate explosions and later radioactive contamination would be in the thousands, the IRGC planners estimated.

More importantly, up to ten city blocks in all three cities would need to be evacuated until the entire area had been sanitized and reclaimed. It would take all three cities months, and perhaps years, to recover from the three interconnected acts of state-sponsored terrorism.

Meanwhile, at almost the same time, across the Atlantic Ocean, Tehran had given the signal to both the Hamas and Hezbollah leadership in southern Lebanon and Gaza to unleash the full extent of their rocket and missile arsenal. They were, they told their allies, retaliating against Israel for its strikes against Iran's nuclear facilities and its decision to use tactical nuclear weapons near Shiraz.

When all three suitcases were to be detonated in

the three largest cities on the U.S. eastern coast, tens of thousands of missiles with significant and deadly payloads would be launched at every major city in Israel. The timing would be such that the missiles would rain on Israel's three largest cities —Haifa, Tel Aviv, and Jerusalem—just as people were in their cars heading home during rush hour.

The IRGC knew the rockets, missiles, and payloads landing in all three Israeli cities would also inflict pain and suffering for Jews and Muslims alike. But it could not be avoided, the IRGC knew. There was no greater psychological pain that they could inflict on Israel—and no greater instrument of war they could bring to bear against their sworn enemy. They would accept the casualties.

The two men returned to the Honda Civic near Mount Vernon Square. They turned the radio on as they waited for 11 a.m. to arrive. They sat there listening to the end of the local broadcast of an NPR show as they waited. Neither man knew—or would have cared—that the employees working at NPR involved in bringing the broadcast to them were just a stone's throw from their car.

Precisely at 11 o'clock, one of the men triggered the remote relay. An instant later, there was a massive explosion, sending bits and pieces of both metal park benches flying in all directions. Big chunks rained onto the outdoor playground at the recreation center nearby, hitting several of the children.

More than a dozen people sitting or standing near the immediate blast were killed instantly. Another two dozen or so were wounded by the bits and pieces of shrapnel and metal. Ambulances from four DC hospitals were on the scene within minutes, along with two dozen camera crews.

No one realized, of course, that the blast had also released highly radioactive cesium into the air. It would be at least another fifteen minutes before the emergency crews detected the radioactive levels and began the chaotic evacuation process. By some estimates, hundreds of people were con-taminated from the blast and subsequent dispersal of radiation.

The blasts at the same time in Boston and New York inflicted as much damage and had likely contaminated even more people.

But as horrific as the video and pictures were in the three American cities—all of which were on CNN within thirty minutes of the bombings—the scenes of devastation from the barrage of Zelzal-2 and Fajr-5 rockets in the three Israeli cities were far worse.

Literally thousands of people were killed by the rain of rockets by the end of the first hour. The videos showed dozens of cars piled up on the sides of roads in all three cities, and any number of buildings that had collapsed under the blasts from the rocket payloads.

Iran and the IRGC had stockpiled tens of

thousands of rockets in southern Lebanon, parts of the Golan Heights controlled by Syria, and Gaza for years, waiting for this day of victory.

There was immediate speculation and panic that some of the payloads were chemical. CNN and Al Jazeera alike quickly carried video of nearly everyone who was willing to venture outside in Israel wearing mandatory gas masks.

So great were the scenes of violence and devastation in the United States and Israel that virtually no one could even bother to pay any attention to the sudden movements of troops in both Russia and China toward a mountainous, remote part of northeast North Korea.

Even as Russia and China were moving troops toward their borders with North Korea, both countries were also systematically ordering the evacuation of major cities within two hundred miles of that part of North Korea. Russia was systematically ordering the evacuation of both Vladivostok and Ussuriysk, while China was moving people from Changchun.

Neither country gave any public explanation for their actions—either the troop movements or the evacuations. But, in truth, there was too much else going on in the world at the moment for anyone to care or even ask.

There were also reports that the Japanese government was sending vague warnings to residents of cities on their western and northern coastline to stay indoors as much as possible in the next twenty-four hours. The public announcement referenced the possibility of contamination in trade winds.

The world's press also largely ignored the fierce border clashes with Russian troops in Georgia and Azerbaijan over the fate of the Baku pipeline. The clashes were dismissed as a regional war, of almost no consequence beyond continued Russian interest in the states of the former Soviet Union.

Also nearly consumed in the madness of the moment was the expected U.S. reaction to North Korea's launch of its Taepodong-2. Even though the American ABM system had worked on the single rocket and had made sure it fell harmlessly into the ocean long before it came near Hawaii, the entire world knew that the United States would react in some fashion.

The U.S. had placed every section of the DMZ on the highest possible alert. Like Russia and China, it was massing troops close to the North Korean border, but for reasons much different than those of both Russia and China. No one knew, precisely, what would happen next. But everyone wanted to be prepared.

As the sun began to set in Israel and hung high in the sky over scenes of devastation in three major cities in America, it was already a new day in North Korea. There, the sun was just beginning to rise over the mountains of northeast North

Korea, Camp 16, and the underground nuclear facilities.

Even as one day of devastation was ending in parts of the planet, a new day was dawning for the leaders in Russia, China, Japan, the United States, Iran, and Israel, who would make decisions in the next twenty-four hours that would determine the fate of the planet.

Was a third world war inevitable?

59

JERUSALEM, ISRAEL

Judah Navon gathered the members of the Knesset together for an emergency session in Jerusalem that evening, after the sun had set. Not all of the Knesset members were able to be there. Some were too far away from Jerusalem to make the trip. Two had been hurt in the missile attacks.

Navon, like the rest of Israel, was badly shaken by the coordinated missile attack from Hezbollah, Hamas, and militia operating in parts of the Golan Heights controlled by Syria. The death toll was still rising as the population in three cities dug out from the rubble. It was, by far, the most serious threat to Israel in a generation.

But Navon was under no illusions. He and

every member of the Knesset knew precisely who was to blame for the attack. Unless something else intervened, Navon knew that a counterstrike into Tehran—as well as Damascus, south of the Litani River in southern Lebanon and Gaza—would occur almost immediately.

He'd already heard several members of the Knesset talking about the use of offensive nuclear weapons in Tehran. They were entirely serious. Navon knew it would take a great deal of discussion to move some of the Knesset members away from this option, and he might not succeed.

His opening remarks to them were short and direct. "Countrymen," he said as he stood before the assembly, "I know all of us hoped and prayed that such a day would never arrive. But it has arrived.

"Thankfully, our missile defense shield saved major parts of our cities from devastation.

"But the missiles were many. They came from the north, from the east, and from the south. We are now fighting a war on many fronts. Our enemies conspired to deal a fatal blow to our nation, but they have failed. And, now, my friends, they will pay a dear price. What we must decide here, tonight, is the nature of that price. Whatever we decide, we must make it very clear to our enemies that they will never again succeed in efforts to destroy our people. Never again."

Following his address, Navon sat and listened

as leaders of the Knesset spoke their minds in succession. The session was closed to the press, so the opinions were candid. Key leaders from both the IDF and the Mossad sat near Navon, taking the Knesset's temperature. They were prepared to act quickly, in whatever fashion the political leadership chose.

The talks were angry, passionate, and defiant. But all of them turned, at the end, to one common enemy. The Knesset was now of one mind. Iran must be confronted, once and for all. And they were prepared to use first-strike nuclear weapons to settle things, if necessary. And if that, in turn, led to a much wider confrontation on a global basis, then so be it.

Israel now maintained an arsenal of nearly four hundred nuclear weapons. They could be delivered as cruise missiles from their Dolphin submarines; from their F-117s and modified F-16 fighters; from their recently completed Jericho 3 ICBM system; and even from fifty thousand feet over Tehran from the IAI Eietan, their unmanned surveillance vehicle.

The IDF left the Knesset meeting to draw up plans to deliver some of that arsenal. It would take something just short of a miracle to keep the IAF planes and missiles out of the skies over Tehran.

60

PYONGYANG, NORTH KOREA

Pak Jong Il took his time with the bowl of ramen noodles his kitchen staff had graciously prepared for him. He had much to consider, and he was glad of the chance to work through various scenarios in the privacy of his study in his presidential palace apartment.

This particular study was his favorite. It was full of pictures taken during hunting parties in the mountainous regions throughout North Korea. Many of the pictures featured endangered or threatened species killed during those trips with military advisors who'd served him well.

Pak allowed advisors to bring certain endangered species back to North Korea in order for the animals to be hunted or filmed in cage fights. In nearly all of the pictures, his advisors were grinning from ear to ear with the Dear Leader, a fresh kill in the foreground.

Pak had achieved wealth and power far beyond anything his own father had amassed. He'd ruled North Korea with an iron fist for so long that it had become second nature to give an order and expect it to be carried out immediately.

He'd survived a withering stroke, and at least two military coup attempts that the world knew nothing of. But he'd also grown wiser about the ways of the world as he'd remained in power.

In fact, Pak no longer believed the fiction that the United States and South Korea would invade North Korea some day. Pak was a realist. He was only able to spend half a billion dollars on the military each year. South Korea spent forty or fifty times that amount. And the United States spent one thousand times that. The combined might of both militaries dwarfed his.

Yet neither had ever given any sort of indication that they actually meant to move north of the Demilitarized Zone. The U.S. threat was a fantasy designed to keep the North Korean people in line, nothing more. Pak knew that but never spoke of it, even in private.

Until now. The KPA's foolish, strong-arm move to save face by firing a Taepodong-2 missile at an enemy 4,500 miles away had achieved just one thing—it had awakened a sleeping giant in the United States. Even now, reports were coming in that the United States was serious in its efforts to mass troops at the DMZ. It was preparing for some sort of a massive military action into North Korea.

Meanwhile, both Russia and China were sending serious troop levels toward his country at the northern end of North Korea. But those troops were massing to deal with the nuclear testing facility, Pak knew. Intelligence reports were screaming loudly about the cesium device they'd built and armed near Camp 16. News about the device had made it out of North Korea somehow.

Almost overnight, North Korea's "dead hand" had been forced. The combination of the Taepodong-2 launch and the news that North Korea possessed a massive doomsday nuclear device of some sort had sent not one, but three, world superpowers to North Korea's doorstep.

Pak Jong Il, though, was far from panicked. He'd always been able to deal directly with American presidents, and this time would be no different. If need be, he was prepared to give up quite a lot to force the U.S. military forces to back down—including, even, their nuclear arsenal.

And he was also fully prepared to tell both the Russians and Chinese that he would disarm the cesium device if they would agree to pull their troops back from North Korea's northern border. He would give up whatever he needed to in order to keep any of these troops from actually entering his country. This was his plan for staying in power, and he was supremely confident in his ability.

Pak knew that, once any of the armies entered, they would make short work of the North Korean military's outgunned, under-fed, and dispirited troops. The fiction of North Korea's military might was much, much greater than its fact. He was prepared to give up whatever was necessary to keep any of these troops from entering.

There were nine nations in the world with nuclear weapons. And, yes, North Korea was one of them. But their conventional military capabilities were almost laughable compared to their enemies. Pak Jong Il did not want to retreat to the mountains in the north, his hand on the cesium device trigger. He wanted to hand a legacy of power and wealth to his youngest son—not annihilate his country in a direct, suicidal confrontation with a military superpower.

If Pak had one failing, though, it was the trust he'd placed in the KPA generals who'd surrounded him for years. He'd grown close to them. They did exactly as he commanded. They'd made him rich beyond his wildest dreams as they'd deposited a percentage of all the commercial ventures they ran directly into his own personal bank account.

He'd confided his strategic diplomacy plans to two of those generals closest to him. Both men had been at his side for twenty years and more. They were his closest advisors and his most trusted confidants. They were like brothers to Pak.

The two military advisors had tried, quite forcefully, to dissuade him from appeasing the Americans by agreeing to dismantle nuclear devices and arsenals. They told Pak that North Korea's military leadership was united in its belief that North Korea must show strength at this most critical time to the enemies at their door. They could not show weakness, as Pak was proposing.

Pak Jong Il had been quite insistent, though. The generals had eventually grown quiet and compliant. They promised Pak that they would do as he commanded. They left his study to begin drawing up lists of nuclear weapons, stockpiles, and arsenals that Pak could use as bargaining chips in the coming hours.

Pak was confident that, even now, he could succeed. He'd never failed. He'd always gotten exactly what he wanted. There was nothing that had ever exceeded his grasp. Nothing.

So it was with mild surprise that Pak realized he'd been poisoned. They'd placed the drug in his bowl of ramen noodles. Pak was resigned to his fate as the tendrils of the poison spread through the neurons of his brain and caused him to slip into a coma.

The last thing he saw as he slipped away to his death was one of his favorite pictures, nicely displayed in an ornate frame on a nearby wall—a picture of a freshly killed Siberian tiger between the two military advisors who'd just left his study. The irony was lost on Pak Jong Il.

61

THE WHITE HOUSE
WASHINGTON, DC

"So I guess this would be a really good time to get those direct, bilateral talks started in Iran and North Korea, wouldn't it? The ones we haven't been able to make any progress on in, oh, say, the last twenty years?" the president said.

Only Anshel and DJ knew Adom Camara was joking. They'd been with the president on so many occasions, through so many tense situations, that they could tell when he was serious—and when he wasn't.

Camara liked to defuse extraordinarily tense situations with laughter, humor, and, occasionally, talk about how poorly his fantasy football team had done the past Sunday or the latest Redskins football coach about to be hired or fired. It took the edge off and gave people a chance to breathe and focus.

A third world war was about to begin? Two of the nine nuclear countries in the world were threatening to use first-strike nuclear weapons in the next twenty-four hours? Russia had invaded two of the former states in the old

Soviet Union? Fine. We'll get to all of them.

Camara, by design, made everything look easy. He wanted those around him during moments such as this to believe—*really* believe—that everything would be just fine. *Don't worry; it'll be all right.* Every glance, every word, every subtle change of demeanor told those around him that he could deal with the situation—and that they could too.

Nearly two dozen senior administration officials —with specialties ranging from Iran, Israel, and North Korea, to nuclear science and emergency response—had gathered in the Oval Office at the president's request at the end of a very long day of chaos. Arrayed around the room on the chairs and couches, most sat forward nervously at the edge of their seats. Most were experts in their respective fields.

The only outlier was Kim Su Yeong, the young State Department aide who wore a temporary White House badge that read *Su Kim*—the name she went by in most places in the United States. Su had been told she was there because of her father, her back-channel connection to North Korea and, through Nash, to the opposition leaders in Iran.

Su would shortly learn a final, important reason that she'd been invited, based on very recent intelligence known only to Camara, Anshel, the NSC, a small group of NSA officials, and the chairman and vice chair of the joint chiefs.

It struck Su as strange that no one, in all these years, had ever managed to move bilateral discussions between the United States and both of those rogue nations—Iran and North Korea—into reality. Why not just take Air Force One to Pyongyang, or to Tehran? But who was she to second-guess years of diplomacy? She was just a kid, after all, with no real experience in foreign affairs.

The group had been carefully selected by both the president and Dr. Gould. Camara had an uncanny knack of knowing who worked for him—even within the bowels of his administration. He knew, somehow, which assistant secretary of this or that was knowledgeable in a certain area.

He had a thorough grasp of the capabilities of nearly every senior political appointee who'd come to Washington to work for him. It was, at times, a little unnerving to those who worked for him at the White House. The guy was just *smart* —easily the smartest president ever elected.

Unlike the other aides who'd chosen seats strategically throughout the Oval Office, Anshel preferred to stand off to one side. DJ joined him and casually leaned up against the wall adjacent to the carefully concealed door that opened inwards to a private bathroom.

Other than Anshel and DJ, though, none of the

others really knew the president's frame of mind. Was he worried? Was the crisis too big for any one human being—even the commander in chief of the most powerful nation the world had yet seen—to manage? Could Camara handle a crisis with two nuclear powers, in different parts of the world, at the same time?

Anshel and DJ knew the president was up to the task. If anyone could handle situations at this level—in a place so high that the lack of oxygen caused most people to grow disoriented and dysfunctional—it was Adom Camara. Time and again, he'd shown the ability to navigate and think clearly while others were gasping for air.

One of the reasons DJ loved talking sports with the president was that there was an easy analogy, and a common language, between sports and politics at this level. Only a quarterback playing in the Super Bowl—with billions watching—could understand that sort of pressure and deliver a pinpoint pass to the back of the end zone in the final two minutes of the fourth quarter.

And only the president of the United States could understand what it was like to go before the eyes of the world and assure them that everything would be fine—not to panic, that all would be well. Camara possessed that rare ability. Few had it, and fewer still survived the brutal gauntlet that anyone had to run in order to sit at the desk in this office.

• • •

"Okay, let's get down to it," Camara continued once everyone was settled. "I was only half-joking. We need to get serious about direct talks with Tehran and Pyongyang."

Camara turned to Susan Wright, who'd also been invited—to her simultaneous delight and consternation. "Dr. Wright, perhaps you can quickly update everyone about your discussions with General Zhubin, the head of the IRGC? That's the closest we've come to any sort of direct, bilateral discussions with those in power in Iran in some time."

Susan coughed nervously, then recounted her discussion with Zhubin quickly. She emphasized that the U.S. had, in fact, met his demand to condemn Israel. They'd also met Iran halfway by not entering the Strait of Hormuz yet. But the other points—like a real plan for a free, Arab state that would satisfy Iran and Egypt alike—seemed unrealistic.

Even as Susan talked, though, it was hard not to despair. Her conversation with General Zhubin seemed like a distant memory, given the taqiyya terrorist actions Iran had clearly ordered their proxies to take in DC, Boston, and New York. The American Congress, like Israel's Knesset, was calling for blood, and quickly.

"So will General Zhubin take your call, Dr. Wright?" the president asked when she'd finished.

"Honestly, Mr. President, I have no idea," Susan answered. "I can try."

Camara nodded. "Thank you." He turned to look directly at someone sitting at the back of the room. "There's someone here—Su Kim, from State—who can tell us about discussions that have taken place off the books with Iran's opposition leaders. Su, can you tell us about Nash Lee's talks with Ehsan and Razavi in Iran?"

Anshel leaned forward. "For those who don't know the back story," he said quickly, "Nash Lee is the young CEO of Village Health Corps, which also runs mVillage. He's been engaged, privately, in back-channel discussions with a leading centrist cleric, Ahura Ehsan, and Reza Razavi, the opposition leader under house arrest."

Su was startled. She'd assumed that she'd simply sit here, listen, and answer questions in private, later. She wanted no part of a discussion where so much hung in the balance.

But she was also not afraid. She may have been young, but she and Nash were alike in their willingness to speak forthrightly when called on. That trait, in fact, was what defined their generation.

Like Susan, she told her story quickly and efficiently. Nash had communicated with Ehsan that morning, which was evening in Tehran. Su was able to report that Ehsan was set to meet privately with Shahidi first thing in the morning in Tehran.

"What is Ehsan asking Shahidi to do?" the president asked.

"To talk to the United States, mostly," Su answered.

"Good," Camara said. "So, between Ehsan and Zhubin, perhaps we can see some movement. We need a chance to meet, face to face. We'll need it quickly, before Israel acts."

"Which is imminent," Anshel added.

The president looked back at the group. "However, we may have a more immediate problem, as hard as that is to believe," he said somberly. "North Korea may, in fact, present a more difficult problem in the short term."

"Greater than an Israeli retaliation with nuclear weapons in Tehran?" asked DJ.

"Yes, I believe so—for our own American troops, in the Korean Peninsula, and for millions of people in South Korea, Japan, and even parts of India, China, and Russia," the president answered. "Some of you may have heard public reports by now of a cesium doomsday device that has been built and armed in the mountains of North Korea, south of Camp 16 and not very far from the launch site at Musadan-ri."

He cocked his head toward Su again. "We have Su, and Nash, to thank for that knowledge. They received a report from Camp 16 through mVillage.

We've since been able to verify the information. This knowledge is largely why the Chinese and Russians have begun to evacuate major population centers near that region, while sending in troops at the same time. That, combined with the need for us to respond to the Taepodong-2 launch, has forced us to push troops into the DMZ."

Camara paused, as if unsure how this group could handle the news he was about to give, or the risks he was calculating. "But what the world does not yet know," the president said, "is that the situation in North Korea has just changed dramatically. Pak Jong Il—the leader we had assumed was in control and that we would be dealing with in the next few hours—has been murdered. At this point, we simply do not know who is controlling North Korea—or what their intentions are with their nuclear arsenal."

The room was deathly silent. Camara was right—this was worse, even, than the situation between Israel and Iran. The United States had always been able to maneuver with Pak. Now, with Pak gone, all bets were off. The future was impossible to predict.

"How?" asked DJ.

"We don't know, exactly," the president said. "We believe it was poison. We have a human asset in the presidential palaces—well below the areas directly serving Pak, but in a place to hear news such as this. It happened late in the evening, in Pyongyang. We don't know yet whether there will be an announcement—"

"Most likely not," Anshel said. "It took them months to let the news out about Pak's stroke. They can go a long time without letting the world know that the leadership has changed hands."

"So who has power now?" DJ asked.

"The military," Anshel said, shrugging. "Technically, Pak's position as Dear Leader has passed to his youngest son, which has been in the works for some time. But Pak Jong Un is in no position to deal with the military leadership. They will call the shots."

"Unless," Camara said, "we can draw him out, into the light." All eyes turned toward the president to see what he meant. "If we can bring him toward us, in the open, then perhaps we can talk. Anything may happen in the darkness. But bring a discussion out into the open, into the light, and it is another matter entirely."

"But that doesn't seem possible," DJ said flatly. "We've never had any contact with the son. We have no connection there whatsoever. How would we possibly draw him out into the open?"

President Camara turned back to Su and simply watched her reaction to the question.

Now Su knew why she was here. "I can," she said softly, trying to keep her voice steady.

"How?" DJ looked confused, as if he suddenly was the only person at the table who'd somehow managed to miss important pieces of every conversation because they'd taken place at the opposite end of the room.

"I've met him," Su said. "We had coffee together, at a Starbucks during a world student conference, seven years ago. I just didn't know it at the time."

Su didn't mention that his best friend, who'd also been there, was now at Camp 16—and one of the sources of information about the cesium device. It was You Moon's phone that had sent the texts to her through mVillage. She felt certain the president knew this. But she wasn't about to volunteer that information here.

DJ sat back, stunned by this news. "You realize that you're one of only a small handful of people outside North Korea who've ever talked to him in recent years?"

"I do now," Su answered. "At the time, he was just another kid at the conference. We talked about normal things, like the NBA playoffs, mobile phones, and global warming."

"That's, well . . . that's just unbelievable," DJ said, shaking his head.

"So the question is how to get to him," Camara said. "And what do we ask him to do, presuming we can get to him?"

"I think I can get to him," Su offered quickly. "Or, at least, I can get to someone who will have the ability to communicate directly with his mobile." Whether You Moon would take the risk of sending a message to his boyhood friend—given that it was Pak Jong Un who had sent him to Camp 16—was another question entirely. But Su could make the request.

Camara stepped toward the center of the room, rubbing his hands. "Great! In the interim, I'll propose that we need to take two very large steps in the next twelve hours. As a prelude to both, I'll go live with a statement—to the networks—that's really aimed at an audience of one."

"Saying what?" DJ asked.

"That I intend to board Air Force One, tonight, to fly to Pyongyang to meet with the president of North Korea," Anshel said. "And, second, that I will leave for Tehran after that to see Rev. Shahidi."

62

LILONGWE, MALAWI

Nash exchanged messages with Su immediately after the White House meeting, and then connected by Skype when she'd gotten back to her office at State around 9 p.m. It was just before dawn for Nash. Both of them felt like they hadn't slept in weeks.

The president was scheduled to give a brief, five-minute talk on the networks in thirty minutes. DJ and others had started writing the script the moment the White House meeting broke.

Neither Nash nor Su talked about the seriousness of the news they were dealing with, and the efforts that both were undertaking. There would be time to consider that later.

As they were talking on Skype, a text came in from Ehsan. He would deliver the message to Shahidi later that morning that the president of the United States would announce his visit to Tehran within the hour. Ehsan couldn't predict Shahidi's reaction, but he promised Nash that he would do everything in his power to convince the Supreme Leader to meet the Americans halfway.

The two of them talked through the words of a text that she would send to You Moon, asking him to contact his boyhood friend. They both knew this would be an enormous risk for both You Moon and Kim Grace. It could, possibly, lead to their executions.

But Su had given her word to the president that she would try. It was too late to go back now.

Once they'd finished wording the message, Su sent it to You Moon. It was midmorning there, and she could only hope that he would see it in time. Then the two of them talked about the decision that Adom Camara had just made and would announce to the world in a matter of minutes.

For a sitting American president to fly, uninvited, to Pyongyang and then to Tehran in the midst of everything that had happened was dangerous, unprecedented, and so full of personal risk that neither of them could imagine it.

They could both imagine the herculean efforts being waged right now by the national security staff and the joint chiefs to keep Camara from going.

For all anyone knew, North Korea or Iran could try to shoot Air Force One down, surround the plane once it was on the ground, or attempt to breach his very limited security once he was outside the plane. It was one thing for special U.S. envoys to fly to either Pyongyang or Tehran—which had happened on occasion—but quite another for a sitting American president.

Only a neutral meeting place, like the United Nations, could assure the president's personal safety. Yet Pak Jong Un would never be allowed to leave North Korea. And Rev. Shahidi had never left Iran to meet with a world leader. He was not about to change that position now. Even Andrei Rowan and Li Chan, China's premier, flew to Tehran to meet with Shahidi.

Truthfully, Nash and Su couldn't envision Camara going to either Pyongyang or Tehran. It was too dangerous. Both came to the conclusion that, at some point, the U.S. national security apparatus would keep the president from actually landing in either location.

But announcing his visit to Tehran did one thing—it kept Israel from launching any nuclear first strikes, for the time being. They'd be forced to wait and see what might come of the talks. It accomplished that, at least.

They watched the president's live broadcast together. Su turned the TV toward the camera on her computer monitor so Nash could see, and they listened while the president made his statement. As usual, Camara's oratory was brilliant and mesmerizing. It was hard not to believe— and trust—that he would do everything in his power to achieve the impossible.

Just as he'd promised, the president announced to a world wondering where the next shoe would drop that he intended to fly toward Pyongyang tonight, and that he would go to Tehran after that. There was no ambiguity in the statement.

As Su signed off for the night to head back to her apartment, there was still no word back from You Moon. She could only hope that her message had gotten through.

63

<hr>

Camp 16
North Korea

The prisoners received only one break every day—a brief opportunity to eat lunch that almost always consisted of stale bread, some sort of unrecognizable vegetable, and water. The prisoners always ate quickly, then returned to hard labor.

Because it was a rare opportunity to walk and stretch his legs, You Moon always took advantage of the break to walk back to the living quarters. He ate as he walked and ignored the sentries armed with machine guns every few feet in the heavily armed compound.

Today, as usual, he took a quick peek at his mVillage account on his secret Nokia mobile hidden inside the stuffing of his mattress. Since he and Kim Grace had connected with Kim Su Yeong, he'd checked it religiously twice a day, at lunch and at the end of the day.

He had no real hope of ever hearing back from Su, but he always hoped. What his friend would do with any information she received, You Moon couldn't imagine. But, over time, Kim

Grace had begun to change You Moon, and he wanted to return her kindness.

Their constant talks had begun to change You Moon's heart. Thanks to her tireless friendship and willingness to give him her knowledge, You Moon had begun to read parts of the Bible. He'd managed to work his way through two of the gospels in the New Testament.

He always gently teased his friend that he wasn't promising anything, but that he would surely give her God a try. Nothing else had worked, he would laugh.

When he saw the icon blinking on his phone, telling him that he had a message from the girl he'd met seven years earlier, You Moon could barely keep his hands from shaking. He opened the message and fought to blink back tears.

As he read it, part of him was a little angry—and instantly crushed—that there was no news of Kim Grace's children to pass on to her. Su was silent on that.

But the message that Pak Jong Un's father, the Dear Leader, had been poisoned by the military leaders in Pyongyang nearly caused him to fall from his bed. He knew, with certainty, that no one in North Korea yet knew this. He doubted that Pak Jong Un even knew the real truth behind his father's untimely death. Most likely, they'd told him his father had suffered another stroke.

But the second part of Su's message gave You

Moon even greater pause—the request from Su to him that he contact his boyhood friend and plead with him to meet with the president of the United States, who was flying to Pyongyang even as she wrote the message.

Su had written:

I know the risk this means to you. The world is on the brink of nuclear war. Only your friend can help avert it by meeting with the president when he arrives in Pyongyang. You may be the only person who can tell Pak Jong Un the truth—about his father's death, and the cesium device hidden near Camp 16 that now threatens millions.

You Moon closed his eyes and, for perhaps the first time in his young life, asked someone greater than himself for guidance.

An instant later, convinced that a still, small voice had answered, he quickly wrote a message to his friend. In it, he told his friend the truth— that his father had been murdered by the North Korean military, and that those same leaders were prepared to trigger a device that would utterly destroy their country and those nearby.

He urged his friend—who'd sent him to prison for life over a small, meaningless dispute—to meet with the president of the United States. It was, he wrote, perhaps the last hope for his country. He then pressed the button, sending the message to the last known mVillage address for Pak Jong Un.

You Moon wondered how long it would be until the guards took him away to the wooden execution post and a firing squad in the nearby woods that surrounded the camp.

64

TEHRAN, IRAN

In the very same study that the Supreme Leader often considered the means of war, he now entertained Ahura Ehsan and several other clerics to discuss a possible framework for peace.

None of them spoke of the threat now posed by Israel, or the very real possibility that nuclear weapons could rain on Tehran at any moment in retaliation for the massive missile strike against Israel's three largest cities. That was too much for them to address in this meeting.

Shahidi had never met President Camara. He occasionally wondered if he would ever meet the man. Circumstances were such that the two might never meet. Shahidi would never travel outside of Iran, and no American president could risk coming to Tehran.

And yet Camara had, on television, promised a deeply troubled world that he would make the trip to Tehran. As Shahidi had watched the telecast, he could only wonder about any man who would do such a thing. He was either crazy, or brilliant—or, perhaps, a little of both.

Ehsan, as he'd promised, delivered the information he'd received from the White House via Nash. Shahidi said nothing—and committed nothing—as he listened to Ehsan. But, as with the telecast, Shahidi had to marvel at the man's courage.

Camara had shown an ability to intercede personally on the world stage before. He'd singlehandedly tried to forge a consensus among India, China, and others on global warming, and had almost succeeded. But this took that sort of personal intervention to another level entirely. Shahidi had to respect that.

At the close of his meeting with Ehsan and the others, they asked the Supreme Leader about his intentions. "If the Americans are serious about peace—and their president is willing to guarantee real progress, such as a meaningful Arab state and security to Iran—then I am willing to entertain the visit," Shahidi said. "You can tell the Americans we will meet."

"And we will assure the American president's safety in Tehran?" Ehsan pressed.

"Yes," Shahidi said, smiling. "We will roll out a

real red carpet and welcome him into our home with an open heart."

"Truly?" Ehsan asked.

"Yes, truly," he answered.

Shahidi, of course, very much doubted that any American president could guarantee either of these conditions. Israel was simply not willing to move toward either of them, in any meaningful fashion. Strong-armed efforts from their closest ally were not likely to change their minds, he believed.

But he would meet with the American president. He could at least do that—even as he privately wondered if they weren't just a matter of days away from the beginning of the time when the Jewish Dajjal and the 12th Imam, the Mahdi, would appear on the world stage as his empty-headed president often talked about in public.

65

PYONGYANG, NORTH KOREA

Pak Jong Un missed his friend. You Moon was the only true friend he'd ever had, and he could use a friend right now. The news of his father's death and the knowledge that the leadership mantle had now passed to him was almost too much to bear.

The truth, which he would never admit to anyone, was that he regretted the decision he'd made in haste to send his friend away after their dispute.

But Jong Un also had a great deal of pride, and he was fiercely competitive. He had been *very* angry with his friend at the time. You Moon should never have challenged him the way he did. It was a direct threat to Jong Un's authority, and his friend deserved to be punished for his mistake.

Still, over time, Jong Un had thought better of his impetuous actions. He would never bring You Moon back from Camp 16, of course. No, that would severely undermine his position and resolve as the next leader of North Korea. One did not admit any mistake, no matter how much one might think otherwise. No leader in his position could ever admit to a mistake.

Despite this, however, Jong Un had not deleted his friend's contact information or mVillage page on the personal computer he kept in his private bedroom. Sometimes, when he was feeling especially alone, he would sit and reread some of You Moon's posts that he still kept in his archive.

Today was an especially bad day. Jong Un was more depressed than usual. His father's closest military advisors had warned him that there would be no official announcement of his father's death. They said that the change in leadership would be announced later, at an appropriate time.

For now, however, the North Korean people

would be told that Jong Un's father had fallen ill, and would not be making any public appearances for a while. They also ordered Jong Un to essentially remain in hiding while they dealt with the Americans and others.

Under no circumstances, they told him, would Pak Jong Un meet with the American president if the man foolishly chose to land in Pyongyang. They would deal with it through proper channels, the military advisors assured him.

The advisors came to visit him with regular updates. But, Jong Un knew, it was mostly for show. None of them were giving him much real information.

Which is why, he knew, he would need to search mVillage forums and elsewhere for actual news of what the rest of the world thought of North Korea just now.

Bored and frustrated, Jong Un called up his mVillage account to search the forums. He realized, with a start, that a new message from You Moon had arrived in his inbox. He sat there for nearly a minute, just staring at the message that had been forwarded from the mobile he now rarely used. Jong Un simply could not imagine how his friend had sent him a message.

Jong Un blinked twice, glanced around his bedroom nervously, then opened the message. He wondered, vaguely, how long it would take the security agency to catch up to the message.

He read it quickly. Its contents shocked Jong Un as much as the fact that You Moon had been able to send him the message in the first place.

His father had been poisoned? And the KPA leadership was prepared to detonate a cesium doomsday device—one that would do untold damage to North Korea—that even he knew nothing about? It just didn't seem possible.

And yet, Jong Un knew, it might very well be true. There was no reason for You Moon to deceive him. The mere act of sending the message would likely guarantee You Moon's immediate execution, once the security apparatus tracked it down.

If Jong Un's father's closest military advisors— some of whom had been his own friends and advisors since childhood—had murdered his father, it was only a matter of time before they dealt with him as well.

Pak Jong Un knew he needed to move quickly. Without thinking through the consequences, Jong Un sent a message back to his friend:

Tell the Americans I will meet with their president when he lands in Pyongyang.

66

ABOARD AIR FORCE ONE SOMEWHERE OVER THE NORTH PACIFIC OCEAN

Even now, as they were beginning their slow descent toward Sunan International Airport north of Pyongyang, every national security advisor even remotely involved with the White House continued to urge the president to reconsider.

But Camara had made up his mind. He would land in North Korea and ask to meet with whatever North Korean president they presented to him. Only a few were aware of the message Pak Jong Un had forwarded to his boyhood friend.

Adom Camara had taken risks his entire political career. Friends and colleagues had urged him not to run for the presidency. He was too young, too inexperienced, they'd told him. Camara had ignored that advice then, and he was ignoring the national security advisors now.

This was not a time to worry about personal security, Camara said. Too much was at stake. Without some sort of leadership, the world would tip very soon toward the abyss. Someone had to act first, before it was too late.

Camara had spoken to as many leaders as he could manage on the flight across the Pacific. He'd reached Andrei Rowan, and then Li Chan in China. Rowan had encouraged him to press forward on both fronts in North Korea and then Iran. Neither man had spoken of Russia's actions in Georgia and Azerbaijan.

The Chinese premier, though, was more circumspect. He wouldn't discuss China's plans if events got out of hand in North Korea. He also refused to discuss China's views on the confrontation between Iran and Israel that was threatening to engulf the region and, perhaps, the world. Camara chose not to press the issue, for now.

When he reached Judah Navon, Anshel joined him for the call. Navon, as usual, was blunt and also insistent that Israel reserved the right to do what was necessary to protect itself. Camara did not argue the point but asked Anshel to walk Navon through the peace plan that had been circulating now for several weeks.

Navon knew of the plan and had seen early drafts. Quite frankly, he told Camara, it was far too radical to be taken seriously in the Knesset.

At the end of the call, though, Anshel and President Camara both asked Navon an equally blunt question. What price was Israel willing to pay for a permanent peace with their sworn enemies? How many more would die until both

Iran and Israel met and settled their differences?

Navon hedged. Bring back a willingness from Shahidi and the radical elements in Iran that they would recognize Israel's right to exist, stop building nuclear weapons, submit to permanent inspection of their military and nuclear facilities, and pledge to stop funding proxies at Israel's border in Lebanon, Syria, and Gaza, and Navon would make sure the Knesset took Anshel's peace plan seriously. But he doubted that Shahidi would agree to any *one* of those elements, much less all four.

Sitting in the back of Air Force One, DJ was nervous. Camara had asked him to stay close by with the White House press pool throughout the trip. Less than a dozen reporters were now traveling with the president, but the network feed to the satellite when they landed would be carried to a worldwide audience. Whatever happened, it would happen with billions of people watching at the same time.

DJ half expected to see tanks assembled on the tarmac at Sunan. But as Air Force One touched down, the airport seemed more deserted than anything else. North Korea had seemingly ordered a halt to all commercial air traffic in and out, so the place seemed calm and almost peaceful.

DJ knew that virtually every fighter and available air force asset operating in the Korean

Peninsula had scrambled and was close by, if need be. But he seriously doubted that the North Korean military would attempt anything foolish.

What seemed infinitely more likely, to DJ and the press pool, was that the president would walk off the plane, only to be met by a phalanx of KPA generals. They, in turn, would tell Camara, politely, that Pak Jong Il was indisposed and unable to meet with him. They would offer to carry whatever message Camara offered back to Pak. And that would be that.

At least, that was the conventional wisdom. The American media was already reporting that it was an extraordinary gamble by the president—though likely doomed to failure before it had even begun—and not dissimilar to personal efforts he'd made in the past on the world stage.

Nevertheless, the pool network crew went live as the plane landed. They began to broadcast video to a waiting, global audience from the moment the doors to Air Force One opened.

DJ stood by the network crew, keeping a careful eye on the small knot of military officials who'd gathered under an awning near the spot where the plane had been directed to taxi. DJ strained to see whether anyone who looked remotely like Pak Jong Un was among them. All he could see were military uniforms.

And then, clearly unplanned, a black town car pulled into view from one side of the Sunan airport. A solitary North Korean flag flew at one corner of the car, convincing DJ that it was an official government vehicle of some sort. It came to a stop fifty yards off to one side of the plane and the North Korean military group that had assembled under the awning.

DJ watched, in some fascination, as the North Korean military group that had planned to meet Camara grew highly agitated. They were clearly not prepared for this, whatever it was.

The Secret Service team surrounding Camara stopped the president, urging him to wait and see what was happening in front of them. The network pool crew kept broadcasting.

One of the rear doors on the town car opened. A lone occupant emerged. He was dressed so casually that virtually no one on the American side could imagine who it might be. DJ, though, recognized the replica Chicago Bulls jersey and tugged on the network producer's sleeve.

"I think that's Pak Jong Un," he whispered. "Tell your guy to stay on him—not the North Korean military."

The producer nodded and kept his crew tightly focused on the town car and the young man now striding purposefully across the tarmac.

The North Korean group under the awning could only watch in horror, frozen as their young charge disobeyed them. He was clearly going to meet with the American president, and none of them knew what he was going to say. Their new Dear Leader had clearly decided to color outside the lines.

In the space of a millisecond from the unblinking eye of live television—with billions of people watching as he gladly and freely strode across the tarmac in his distinctive replica Chicago Bulls jersey to meet the president of the United States— Pak Jong Un had gone from the most mysterious, least photographed young leader imaginable to one of the most recognized faces in the world.

DJ was impressed.

67

PYONGYANG, NORTH KOREA

With the world literally watching over his shoulder, Adom Camara had negotiated a tentative peace with the young, new leader of North Korea. The American president had come to the meeting prepared to take bold, new steps, provided he saw movement on the other side. He had.

Camara had offered that the United States would permanently and formally end the state of war between the United States and North Korea that had continued to exist since the truce at the end of the Korean War in the 1950s. The United States would sign a peace treaty with North Korea, and remove all American troops from South Korea and the Korean Peninsula.

In addition, Camara pledged, America would immediately provide massive amounts of food aid to the starved people of North Korea, normalized trade relations, defined security guarantees, and an immediate infusion of American-trained engineers to help with North Korea's substantial energy needs.

In return, Camara asked Pak Jong Un for his assurance that Russian, Chinese, and American inspectors could immediately work with the North Koreans to dismantle the cesium device in the northern reaches of the country, and that North Korea would agree to end its nuclear weapons program and a finite timetable to make the Korean Peninsula nuclear-free.

With his own North Korean military advisors standing by, watching helplessly—and the world watching the talks in real time—Pak Jong Un had agreed.

He, too, recognized that this was a chance— perhaps the only one he would have in his life—to make decisions to assure the safety and well-being of the North Korean people. If he let this opportunity pass by, Pak Jong Un knew, he would inevitably be crushed by the military that had so recently poisoned his father. The choice seemed obvious.

• • •

"Sometimes showing up is half the battle," the president said privately to DJ and Anshel as they left Pyongyang and Air Force One was back in the air, headed to Tehran.

"I'll say," DJ said. "That was intense. Who'd have guessed that Pak Jong Un would just appear like that?"

"Actually," Camara said, "I thought it might be a possibility. That friend of Pak's—the one who's in Camp 16—got back to Su Kim. He'd communicated with Pak, who then said that he'd meet with us. I think the knowledge that the military had poisoned his father—and that it could quite possibly be his own fate—is what pushed him over the edge."

"But you'd still think that the military would have stopped him," DJ said.

"Not if they didn't know about it in advance," Anshel said. "It looks like Pak made the decision himself, without consulting any of his advisors."

"Do you blame him?" the president said. "I'm not sure I'd trust anyone if my closest advisors had just murdered my father in a bloodless coup."

"Good thing they don't allow that sort of thing in America," DJ said, laughing.

"Yeah, good thing," the president said. "That wouldn't be much fun, would it?"

Camara had made only one minor request at the end of the meeting. It had nothing whatsoever to do with the national security agreement, but it was something that had been on Camara's mind nevertheless. He'd asked Pak to consider freeing the political prisoners at Camp 16—including both You Moon and Kim Grace.

Now that they knew about them, American intelligence sources had confirmed from satellite imagery that both You Moon and Kim Grace were still alive at Camp 16.

Whether Pak would honor the request was impossible to know. Most likely the North Korean military officials who would now have to deal with their impetuous young leader would allow the peace process to proceed for a time, free a few prisoners, and then execute both You Moon and Kim Grace once the public scrutiny had lapsed. But Camara, for his part, wasn't about to forget about them.

68

THE NATIONAL GARDEN TEHRAN, IRAN

Despite nearly two days of continuous flying, the few White House aides who'd accompanied the president on Air Force One were still going at light speed.

It reminded DJ and other veterans of the presidential campaign of the barnstorming days where they'd tackled a dozen events a day. Everything seemed possible when you were in the middle of a campaign. You made big decisions on the fly, and prayed they were right and wouldn't later explode in your face.

The difference now, of course, was that this was no presidential campaign. You could recover from mistakes on the campaign trail with quick apologies or lightning fast counterattacks. A mistake here and this would be their last look at a recognizable Tehran. Israel's entire complement of nuclear weapons was armed and ready, waiting for the outcome of today's talks.

The president had been able to catch four hours of sleep during the flight before moving head long into a series of briefings with every conceivable Iran expert they could muster. At the top of his list was a brief on perhaps the most classified program in the United States—a covert effort to deliberately sabotage the electronic and computer systems underpinning Iran's nuclear program.

But beyond what the intelligence agencies knew about Iran and its programs, Camara wanted to know everything they had on Shahidi.

He was focused like a laser beam on the mind of the man who'd risen through the ranks of the military, the Revolutionary Guards, and then the presidency before taking over as Iran's supreme ruler.

By the time they'd landed in Iran, Camara felt like he was ready. The president had been prepared to take bold, though long overdue, steps with North Korea. With Shahidi and Iran, he was prepared to go even further to preserve peace.

Unlike Pyongyang, where the world had literally watched events unfold, Shahidi and several clerics from the 12-member Guardian Council had demanded that the talks take place in private, away from the press and the public.

They'd chosen to meet in central Tehran, in the Ministry of Foreign Affairs at Bagh-e Melli. Known outside Iran as the "National Garden," much of the architecture throughout Bagh-e Melli was pre-Islamic. The main gates to the compound were built during the Qajar dynasty.

Both the privacy and the location were perfectly acceptable to Camara and the White House aides. The Ministry of Foreign Affairs was old, but it was a fairly neutral site. Members of the Guardian Council would join the meeting at some point, depending on signals given them from Shahidi. Or, at least that's what Camara and the White House aides had been led to believe.

To the Secret Service and military leaders assigned to protect America's commander in chief, though, the location could not have been more problematic. There was virtually no opportunity to call in additional military support in central Tehran, should something go wrong.

Camara, though, was not worried—at least not for his personal safety. He could not imagine that Iran would be so foolish as to attack an American president while the world watched. Iran had learned much in the years since they'd held American hostages at the embassy in Tehran.

No, what worried Camara was that he would not be able to make enough progress with Shahidi before leaving Tehran, and that Israel would begin its campaign almost from the moment Air Force One left the ground in Iran. He knew that he had this one chance to make significant inroads.

The network and press pool did their best to stay with the American president. They were broadcasting live as a small military escort led them from the airport to Bagh-e Melli and into the halls of the Ministry of Foreign Affairs. But they were forced to cool their heels in the old, ornate hallways as Camara, his aides, and his Secret Service detail disappeared into the bowels of the building.

DJ promised to shuttle back and forth, bringing updates. The American press wasn't happy about the arrangement, but there wasn't much they could do about it. This meeting was being run under rules established by Shahidi and the Guardian Council.

As Camara entered a final, inner council room set up for the visit, DJ was surprised to see that all twelve members of the Guardian Council were present.

Shahidi, for whatever reason, must have decided to have the council present for the entire discussion. Half were clerics, dressed in full religious garb. Their heads were covered. Their bodies were cloaked in flowing white robes that gathered where they sat and billowed as they walked. The other half, all lawyers or legal scholars expert in Sharia law, were dressed in suits and ties out of respect for their American visitors.

As they entered the room, Camara approached every member of the council and greeted them. Then he approached Rev. Shahidi. The two men shook hands briefly, said their polite introductions, and then took their seats. It all seemed incredibly formal to DJ.

For the next three hours, President Camara sat patiently as first one member of the Guardian Council and then another—speaking through interpreters—presented what could only be described as a very long list of grievances against the West, laced with fiery rhetoric more suited for the mosque, church, or temple.

Rev. Shahidi did nothing to stop the Guardian Council members from speaking their collective mind to the American president. Camara, for his part, remained respectful and attentive throughout.

DJ was amazed at Camara's willpower and stamina. It was like a bad Kabuki dance as far as he was concerned. They took no break during the three hours. Shahidi chose to wait until everyone had delivered their speeches to the American president, then called a break.

The press, of course, didn't believe DJ when he reported back during the break. They couldn't believe that nothing beyond rhetoric had been offered in three hours. DJ just shrugged and made his way back to the council room.

After the break, though, it was apparent even to DJ that the preamble was over. The Guardian Council was gone, replaced now at the table by General Zhubin, Hussein Bahadur, and other IRGC leaders. The entire tone of the meeting shifted immediately.

DJ wondered, vaguely, where Iran's president was hiding. It didn't matter. They were now meeting with the only leaders who mattered in Iran, those who truly controlled the theocracy. Still, it was curious.

Camara wasted no time once he'd been given a chance to speak. In a somber, measured tone, the American president told Shahidi and the IRGC leadership that they had badly miscalculated by attacking the United States and Israel. The IRGC leaders said nothing.

The United States was not prepared to retaliate

immediately—either for the bombs in the three American cities or the recent actions against the 5th Fleet in the Persian Gulf, Camara said.

"We are at war," General Zhubin interjected. "You have no basis for retaliations. You initiated the conflict when Israel attacked our facilities unprovoked. War knows no rules."

Fair enough, Camara agreed. Israel, though, was another matter entirely. Without something tangible in hand, he told them, Iran could expect to see a first-strike against Tehran and other population centers in Iran almost immediately. Shahidi and his IRGC advisors were unmoved by this as well.

"And is that what you traveled all this way to tell us?" Shahidi asked finally. "That your puppet, Israel, is about to attack us with their illegal nuclear weapons?"

"No, Reverend Shahidi," Camara responded as firmly as the circumstance allowed. "I am here to propose something we should have done a generation ago, after the Second World War. I am here to give you my word that Israel will consider giving up their southern district—including a real capital—so that a free, Arab state can be established there.

"I am here to tell you that the United States will build the infrastructure for that new Palestinian homeland, and that we will guarantee its security," he said. "We will make sure that every refugee, in every camp in the region, is given an opportunity to come home at last from exile.

"I am here to tell you that I now believe that Jerusalem can be partitioned fairly, in such a way that Jews and Muslims alike can worship.

"I am here to tell you that, in return for your vow to end your nuclear weapons program, the United States and Russia will build whatever you ask to fulfill your energy needs—including whatever you need to operate a civilian nuclear program.

"And, finally, I am here to tell you that the United States will personally assure your own national security—and your economic prosperity. We will lift all sanctions immediately."

"And in return?" Shahidi asked.

Camara had considered raising the issue of releasing both Razavi and student and opposition leaders like Majid Sanjani, who'd been so instrumental in getting both parties to this table. But that would have to wait for another time and place as the peace talks between the U.S. and Iran progressed.

"You must publicly and permanently recognize Israel's right to exist," Camara said. "Beyond the end of your nuclear weapons program, you must agree to submit to regular inspection of your civilian nuclear facilities. But—and this is more important than all the others—you must permanently end your support of all proxies at

Israel's borders. That includes Hezbollah, Hamas, and Syria."

"So, is that all?" Shahidi asked, his face still an impassive mask.

"Yes, that's all," Camara said, smiling for the first time since he'd arrived in Iran.

"Then I will take your proposed terms of a peace agreement under advisement and consult with the Guardian Council," Shahidi said, nodding once toward the American president. Iran's Supreme Leader rose to leave the negotiating table.

DJ marveled that Shahidi had never once presented his own opinions. And, yet, he'd achieved what he'd hoped for—simply by waiting patiently. For the second time, in as many days, DJ was suitably impressed.

Epilogue

BAQA'A REFUGEE CAMP
JORDAN

One person can do the impossible.

The phrase had been repeated so often in the past twenty-four hours, the television commentators and journalists—still struggling to grasp the meaning of the tense, historic meetings in both

Pyongyang and Tehran—had begun to state it simply as a fact.

The young American president had, in fact, done the impossible, with half the planet watching. He'd formally ended a Korean War that should have ended in 1953 but hadn't. A peace treaty between North Korea and the United States was, even now, being drafted and circulated to both nations and the U.N. Security Council.

It was long overdue, the world press had concluded. The outlines of a peace between North Korea and the United States had been in place for a generation. Several past American presidents had come close to a nearly identical peace agreement but had fallen just short.

It was curious. The press had moved to the nearly unanimous belief that peace on the Korean Peninsula was something that had been largely inevitable. All it had taken, they'd concluded, was a willingness to communicate.

History remembered those who crossed the finish line, the commentators said—not those who came close.

The United States had already begun to draw up plans to withdraw its troops from the Korean Peninsula, as promised. Russia and China were making plans to visit the nuclear test facility in the mountains of North Korea.

The KPA leadership was, grudgingly, making plans to begin the process of dismantling its nuclear arsenal. It had refused, however, to even acknowledge the presence of its prison camps, or consider any inspection of facilities beyond its civilian and military nuclear sites. North Korea's conventional national security measures were its own business—not the world's.

The outlines of a second peace treaty—infinitely more difficult to imagine—was also beginning to circulate at the UN and elsewhere. Like the Korean peace, this plan was based on the outlines of an agreement that had first been proposed more than a generation ago.

The White House had framed the proposed peace accord between Iran and Israel—based loosely on key parts of the original Palestinian homeland plan before the United Nations in 1947 at the close of the Second World War, like the inclusion of Beersheba in a new Arab state—as a plan that could unite both Shi'a and Sunni factions that controlled various nations.

It would not appease stateless terror groups such as Al Qaeda. But, for nations and leaders who needed to operate under the rule of law, it was a very good place to begin.

The United States had already opened discussions with leaders in both Jordan and Egypt. Reactions in both were muted but favorable. Because both nations would surround, and largely enforce, a new Palestinian homeland in what was now southern Israel, their support was critical.

It was, they'd acknowledged, a radical plan—but the only sort of plan that could ever succeed.

That 1947 plan would have created a real Palestinian homeland alongside the new state of Israel. What was needed now was a place that could attract Palestinian refugees spread across a handful of nations surrounding Israel, the United States argued.

As part of the proposed peace between Iran and Israel, the White House had also included a new plan to permanently partition Jerusalem that would grant both Jews and Muslims the opportunity to worship at sites that included the Dome of the Rock and the true location of the First and Second Jewish Temples.

It was based on the conclusive scientific evidence —now beginning to circulate widely outside Israel—that the First and Second Temples of Israel had never been located on what was now the holy Dome of the Rock. That had come as quite a shock to many.

What was worse—for Jews—was the news that the Western Wall was most likely a wall remaining from the Roman temple of Jupiter built by Hadrian, not from the original Jewish Temple, as many believed.

Israel and Iran had both agreed to a temporary ceasefire while the proposed peace agreement began to circulate. No one, of course, could predict how long the ceasefire would last, or whether something new might cause hostilities to start again. But it was a beginning. There was much work to be done. The Eilat-Ashkelon oil pipeline —once a fifty-fifty joint venture between Iran and Israel—was now back on the table for discussion. While the peace talks were underway, Israel had shelved plans to retaliate against Tehran with nuclear weapons.

Oil prices had begun to fall on the news that hostilities had ended in the Persian Gulf. The world economy had begun to stabilize. Russia was still engaged north of Iran, near the Baku pipeline, but most chose to focus on the end of the immediate conflict in the Strait of Hormuz as oil traffic was set to begin again.

Elizabeth Thompson had to smile. There was no real TV in Baqa'a—just an Internet connection to YouTube that served as the refugee camp's television station—but the outdoor café she stopped at every morning for her first cup of coffee had become the center of the camp.

Because it was one of the few establishments in the camp with an Internet connection—which the proprietor had paid for in order to get access to international soccer matches—the people of the camp had descended on his café in the past two days to watch the worldwide broadcasts that had been available via both Internet and regular TV.

Every chair and table in the café had been

overflowing for the past two days. No one wanted to return to their homes, for fear of missing some new development. Elizabeth, too, had remained close to the café to keep track of the world events. It was compelling stuff—and had a direct bearing on her life's work at the Palestinian refugee camps.

Now, with the news that perhaps there might be a new Palestinian homeland just across the Jordanian border in southern Israel, Elizabeth had seen real joy on people's faces for the first time in all the years World Without Borders had been ministering in the refugee camps at Baqa'a and elsewhere.

A friend at a nearby table in the café—a young man she'd grown to know over the years who was always on the edge of the knife, torn between radicalism and the hope for a better life for his new family—turned to her.

"Is it real, Dr. Thompson?" he asked. "Will there be a real homeland for my people soon?"

"I hope so," she answered truthfully.

"So Israel will let us live in peace and create a home?" he asked.

"For you, for your family, I will believe," she answered. "With God, all things are possible. All conflicts end, one way or another."

"So let us hope that ours has ended, and that we will soon see our homeland," the man said, smiling. "For my family and for my people."

"Yes," Elizabeth said. "We can always hope."

Q & A with Jeff Nesbit

Q1—Is Camp 16 real?

A. While North Korea denies its existence, it is quite real. By all public accounts, Camp 16 is the secret, heavily fortified prison compound in the northern mountains of North Korea where the military sends exiled government officials, their family members, and others it considers to be "enemies of the state." Camp 16 is located near two nuclear testing sites and facilities, and there have been reports that prisoners at Camp 16 have been forced to take part against their will in nuclear tests. Publicly available satellite images clearly show the outlines of Camp 16, including structures that serve as barracks. *The Washington Post* even published an interactive map showing the location of North Korea's secret prison camps, based on satellite pictures and unclassified intelligence reports.

Q2—Is a fission-fusion-fission doomsday bomb—like the one in the novel built by North Korea—really possible?

A. Unfortunately, it is possible. Physicist Leo Szilard once described the possibility of a cobalt-laced nuclear bomb that could send highly radioactive cobalt-60 airborne particles to earth as a "doomsday device," because it was theoretically capable of wiping out life on earth. A fission-fusion bomb containing cobalt would release a large amount of cobalt-60 into the environment—creating long-lasting radio-active fallout that would have a devastating impact on life on the planet. Such a device could theoretically be devised as the ultimate bluff, or threat, in a last-stand political standoff. The United States and the former Soviet Union abandoned research on such a nuclear doomsday device in the 1950s, because such a weapon served no useful military purpose.

Q3—Is Iran, in fact, building secret uranium-enrichment facilities inside Revolutionary Guards' compounds throughout Iran?

A. Yes, in at least one instance—and, perhaps, in several other locations. As I was developing *PEACE*, I wrote about an unmanned U.S. drone equipped with a quantum cascade laser array system that detected uranium hexa-fluoride levels in the atmosphere above a previously unidentified Revolutionary Guards' weapons compound, triggering Israel's decision to attack Iran's nuclear facilities. Two months after I'd written these chapters—

which were based on reports in the open literature of decisions by the IRGC to consolidate all nuclear weapons testing and research at their closely guarded complexes—world leaders announced that, in fact, Iran had secretly built uranium-enrichment facilities inside an IRGC compound at Qom. The speculation is that Iran has built—and hidden—similar uranium-enrichment facilities in other IRGC locations.

Q4—Is it true that the First and Second Temples in Jerusalem were not, in fact, ever built above the rock formation that's in the Dome of the Rock?

A. Despite nearly two thousand years of tradition, it now does appear as if the First and Second Temples in Jerusalem were never built on or around the Dome of the Rock—one of the most holy shrines in Islam. Both ancient Jewish Temples were almost certainly built south of the Dome of the Rock, in an area that is much closer to the original city of David in antiquity and is located in a section without any current structures. What's more, it's also likely that the Western Wall (previously known as the Wailing Wall), revered by Jews worldwide as the last remnant of the old Jewish Temples, was never part of the ancient Temples but was more likely part of the replica of the Roman temple of Jupiter built on the Temple Mount after the destruction of the Second Jewish Temple. A prominent Israeli architect, Tuvia Sagiv, has conducted his own private research over the years and has built a highly credible scientific case behind the premise that the First and Second Jewish Temples were not built in the area under the Dome of the Rock. A fourth-century commentary by Jerome would also seem to indicate that a statue of Hadrian within the temple of Jupiter complex in Jerusalem may have been built precisely over the Holy of Holies. "So when you see standing in the holy place the abomination that causes desolation: or the statue of the mounted Hadrian, which stands to this very day on the site of the Holy of Holies" (Jerome, *Commentaries on Isaiah 2.8; Matthew 24.15*). Based on this commentary and another temple of Jupiter found in Lebanon that has similar dimensions, it is highly plausible that the Holy of Holies was directly below the Roman emperor's equestrian statue—in an area that is now the El Kas fountain.

Q5—Would the F-117 Stealth fighter, in fact, be a "silver bullet" for Israel if it chose to attack Iran in an effort to disable its nuclear weapons capabilities?

A. The F-117—the world's first Stealth attack fighter—was unceremoniously retired to the Tonopah airfield in Nevada in 2009. The Bandits who fly the aircraft have said publicly that the aircraft is still more than capable of carrying out Stealth missions. The newer F-22 Raptors, which also use Stealth technology, have largely replaced the F-117's mission capabilities, rendering the F-117s obsolete. But the F-117 Stealth attack fighters have successfully patrolled skies in Iraq and elsewhere in the Middle East for the past quarter of a century—and could, conceivably, do so again. Retired U.S. military officials have said publicly that they're glad the F-117s have been mothballed in a place where they could be brought back, if needed. The F-117 —a single-seat aircraft with a black, angular shape and radar-evading technology—was designed to fly into heavily defended areas and drop payloads with surgical precision. Not a single F-117 Stealth fighter was hit during Desert Storm in Iraq in 1991. The U.S. has permanently pledged to maintain Israel's air superiority in the Middle East, and Israeli defense analysts have begun to argue that the F-117 would be an adequate temporary solution for that pledge until export versions of the F-22 and F-35 are made available to Israel, Japan, and other U.S. allies. Israel currently does not have the

Stealth attack technology to defeat Iran's air-defense systems in one continuous mission. The F-117 (and successors) could, possibly, change that equation.

Q6—Does Iran possess an attack fighter comparable to the modified F-15s and F-16s in the Israeli Air Force, and what does this mean for Iran's ability as a regional military power?

A. There have been recent, published reports that China has offered to sell export versions of its powerful, new J-10 aircraft to Iran. Military analysts believe the J-10 is comparable to the American-built F-15s and F-16s, which make up the bulk of the IAF arsenal. If the reports are true, it means that Iran would have the ability to strike, or retaliate against, Israel with this aircraft. In short, it would remove the qualitative edge that Israel has always possessed related to air power in the region. The irony, of course, is that China likely developed the J-10 with considerable technology assistance from the defunct Israeli Lavi project, which itself was based on the American-built F-16 fighter.

Q7—Would Israel really consider the use of tactical nuclear weapons to destroy Iran's nuclear weapons plants bunkered inside Iran's Revolutionary Guards' compounds?

A. According to published reports in *The Times of London* and elsewhere, Israel has drawn up plans to use tactical nuclear weapons to destroy Iran's uranium-enrichment facilities. While Israel has never commented on the extent of its nuclear weapons capabilities, it is widely known to possess multiple platforms to deliver nuclear weapons—including precision, targeted, tactical nuclear weapons from attack aircraft. Citing Israeli military sources, for instance, *The Times* reported that IAF squadrons have developed the ability to deliver low-yield nuclear "bunker-busting" payloads. Conventional, laser-guided bombs would create a path, and tactical nuclear bombs would follow in behind and explode deep underground, minimizing the radioactive fallout. The question is whether IAF aircraft carrying such payloads could successfully navigate through Iran's air-defense system. According to *The Times*, Israel has drawn up such secret plans only in the event that it decided to act unilaterally—without U.S. assistance—and after ruling out a conventional attack as insufficient to complete the mission. U.S. authorities have told the Israeli government on several occasions that it would never sanction the use of tactical nuclear weapons against IRGC nuclear facilities, according to published reports.

Q8—Has the U.S. military, in fact, developed a weapon that can knock out the guidance systems on anti-ship cruise missiles like the Sunburn?

A. While there is nothing in the open literature to confirm that such a capability exists, the Department of Energy's nuclear weapons laboratories began research 20 years ago on an aerial bomb that could generate high-power microwaves over a wide area, according to reports of congressional testimony in American newspapers. At the time, the research was focused on the ability to destroy electronic guidance equipment controlling ground-based intercontinental ballistic missiles in the former Soviet Union. So, the possibility exists that research has advanced to the point where such technology can be used to counter anti-ship cruise missiles in flight.

Q9—Is the type of terrorist attack with dirty cesium-137 bombs in urban cities in the United States possible?

A. In short, yes, it is possible. Security experts have been concerned for years that terrorist organizations might consider the use of such dirty bombs in urban settings in the United States and elsewhere. In fact, some published reports have quoted Hezbollah leaders openly declaring their intention to carry out such attacks. A Hezbollah leader in Iran once said that they have thousands of volunteers in place and that they were prepared to launch "Judgment Day" scale attacks around the globe if provoked. In addition, according to published newspaper reports, Venezuelan President Hugo Chavez has visited Iran more than a half-dozen times in the past decade to meet with Iran's leadership, and Iran's president has likewise visited Caracas on several occasions. Economic ties between Venezuela and Iran are deep, and extensive. In 2008 Turkey stopped an Iranian shipment on its way to Venezuela with nearly two dozen containers labeled as "tractor parts"—but which, in fact, contained equipment designed to set up an explosives lab, according to published wire service reports.

Q10—Is the third, and youngest, son of North Korea's "Dear Leader" in line to take over from his father? Is he really a fan of the NBA in America? Did he once see Michael Jordan play in Paris?

A. While it is nearly impossible to know the extent of the leadership succession planning in North Korea's highly secretive and closed military society, infrequent reports do seem to indicate that Kim Jong Il is, in fact, making plans to hand over the reins to his youngest son, Kim Jong Un. And, according to at least one published report, the Dear Leader's youngest son is a fan of the NBA. Michael Jordan and the Chicago Bulls once played exhibition games in Paris in the fall of 1997—at the same time that the Dear Leader's son was secretly attending a private boarding school in Switzerland near the North Korean embassy. There is only one published picture of the youngest son—and possible successor—in North Korea that has ever been published or circulated anywhere in the world.

Q11—Is Japan, in fact, moving away from its position as the United States' most trusted ally in Asia, vastly complicating strategic U.S. military interests in the region?

A. There are clearly concerns in the U.S. that the new government in Japan has decided it may be in its self-interest to distance itself from the U.S. on certain strategic matters. This possibility presents extraordinary difficulties for the U.S. in Asia and has led to a series of increasingly confrontational discussions and meetings between U.S. and Japanese officials —including a reported ten-minute showdown in Washington between the leaders of both countries that was so direct and confrontational that the Japanese diplomatic corps chose not to publish a transcript of the meeting. U.S. and Asian officials have speculated that Japan may be considering a significant policy shift away from the United States and toward a more independent foreign policy.

Q12—Is a lasting peace with North Korea a realistic possibility, or simply wishful thinking?

A. The Korean War resulted in a truce—but not peace—between the United States and North Korea. The truth is that the outline of a meaningful peace accord between the two countries has been in place for some time. What has been missing is the political will of leaders in both countries to finally reach an accord that would formally end the conflict and allow the United States to remove its military forces from the DMZ and the region. At various times, North Korea has offered to make the Korean Peninsula nuclear-free through dialogue and negotiations, in return for an infusion of capital and economic help and a permanent end to the U.S. military presence in the region. It is nearly impossible to assess whether North Korea's stated intention of wanting to ease tensions with Washington is real, however, due to North Korea's paranoid leadership and closed military society.

Q13—Could North Korea's Taepodong-2 intercontinental ballistic missile actually reach Hawaii or other U.S. territories?

A. No, it can't. Most military analysts dismiss the possibility that the Taepodong-2 could ever make the four-thousand-mile journey to Hawaii and remain intact. And it is simply inconceivable to think that any ICBM from North Korea could ever make it to a major American city, much less deliver a nuclear warhead there on impact. North Korea regularly threatens "all-out war" against the U.S., but there is almost no possibility that such an ICBM could ever do any significant damage to any U.S. territory. Still, the remote possibility does exist that North Korea could someday launch an ICBM in the general direction of Hawaii as a "shot across the bow," which has prompted the U.S. military to put defensive anti-missile systems in place in the Pacific.

Q14—Are the *Kang Nam* North Korean cargo vessels real? Are they delivering nuclear parts and materials to Iran and rogue nations in the world?

A. Yes, the *Kang Nam* cargo ships are real. And, yes, they are likely smuggling illicit nuclear materials through international waters to rogue nations—an effort that is now clearly banned by a new United Nations anti-proliferation resolution. American ships have tracked *Kang Nam* cargo vessels on several occasions, but none has ever triggered the U.N. resolution and requested to board and inspect the cargo. If the American Navy ever did make such a request, the North Korean government has said it would consider such a request an act of war.

Q15—Has Hamas actually acquired and tested a rocket capable of launching from Gaza and reaching major cities in Israel?

A. Yes, Hamas probably acquired and test-fired such a rocket. Israel's military intelligence chief said publicly in late 2009 that Hamas test-fired a rocket that flew 37 miles into the sea. A rocket with that range could launch from Gaza and reach Tel Aviv, according to published reports. A spokesman for Hamas denied the test, claiming that it was nothing more than a pretense for Israeli military operations in Gaza. But it seems clear from naval interdictions—some of which have been reported to the United Nations—and smuggling activities that Hamas has acquired the ability to deploy these types of rockets in Gaza. With greater cooperation between Hamas in Gaza and Hezbollah in southern Lebanon, it seems likely that rockets with this range are now deployed both north and southwest of Israel.

Q16—Has Hezbollah deployed as many as forty thousand rockets in southern Lebanon capable of reaching major population centers in Israel?

A. Yes, almost certainly. In late 2009, for instance, the Israeli navy captured a ship bound for Hezbollah through Syria. Israel told the United Nations that this was the fifth time in 2009 alone that it had captured ships containing weapons originated in Iran and bound either for Hezbollah or other Iranian proxies. Journalists were invited to view the contents of the captured ship once it was towed to a port in Israel. Its contents were spread out and displayed on shore. Journalists who viewed the ship's contents on shore reported that, in this one ship alone, Israel discovered three thousand rockets bound for Hezbollah and southern Lebanon. Credible, published reports indicate that Hezbollah may have stockpiled as many as forty thousand rockets in various parts of Lebanon and the mountains overlooking northern Israel, waiting for a day and a time to launch them at population centers in Israel. Without a doubt, it is one of the most serious threats confronting Israel's national security in a generation.

Q17—Is the sleepy fishing village of Jask really a naval outpost for Iran in the Strait of Hormuz?

A. Not yet. But as I was writing *PEACE* and speculating about the possibility that Iran's military leaders would station covert naval operations at Jask—and stage asymmetrical attacks against the 5th Fleet from there—the *New York Times* reported that American military authorities were, in fact, worried that Iran might position some of its naval assets at Jask. And Iran has likely concealed some of its anti-ship cruise missiles at various locations in the mountains that overlook Jask.

Q18—Is "asymmetrical warfare" a real threat to the American 5th Fleet in the Strait of Hormuz? Has Iran acquired enough submarines and fast speedboats to take part in such an attack? Is the USS *Abraham Lincoln* vulnerable?

A. While the 5th Fleet—with the Nimitz-class supercarrier, the USS *Abraham Lincoln*—is the most formidable naval presence in the world, war games have, in fact, revealed that a swarming, asymmetrical attack could do significant damage. the *New York Times* reported in 2009 that a war-game scenario in 2002 showed that a swarming, asymmetrical attack in the Persian Gulf could actually defeat the U.S. Navy. Whether Iran could mount such an asymmetrical attack is difficult to assess, but the threat is real and credible. The American Navy has plenty of assets in place to counter such an asymmetrical attack, but a concerted effort on Iran's part to build or acquire dozens of small, attacking craft could form a credible threat, most analysts believe.

Q19—Is the anti-ship cruise missile, the Sunburn, real and part of Iran's arsenal?

A. It is real and most likely now part of Iran's arsenal. Some have speculated that it is the one single weapon that could defeat American forces in the Gulf and the Strait of Hormuz. According to published reports, the American Navy was struggling to develop defenses against the Russian-made SS-N-22 Sunburn as recently as a few years ago. Some have called the Sunburn the most lethal missile in the world. It can, in fact, deliver a two-hundred-kiloton nuclear payload, hit speeds of Mach 3, remain close to the ground (or sea), and throw in extreme maneuvers to elude defense systems. U.S. ship defenses can track and shoot down Sunburns, but only if they see them in time. Some military analysts have speculated that, with enough Sunburns in the arsenal fired in a coordinated fashion, they could overwhelm even the most sophisticated anti-missile systems. What is not known is the extent of anti-missile systems developed and deployed in recent years to combat the Sunburn. I wrote in *PEACE* that it is possible to knock out the guidance systems in Sunburns while in flight, but this is just an educated guess on my part. *PEACE*, after all, is just fiction.

Q20—Has Israel's navy, in fact, sailed through the Suez Canal to prepare for a possible attack on Iran?

A. Yes, it has. According to published reports, at least two Israeli missile-class warships have sailed through the Suez Canal. Israeli Dolphin submarines have also sailed through the Suez and deployed to the Red Sea, clearly showing that it has the ability to put a naval strike force within range of Iran on short notice. Israel has clearly strengthened military and diplomatic ties with Egypt in recent years, largely as a response to Iran's nuclear ambitions.

Q21—Is there really a 1540 Committee at the United Nations?

A. Yes, there is. It's based on UN Security Council Resolution 1540 adopted in 2004. It is designed to support efforts to keep "non-state actors" (terrorist groups) from acquiring nuclear, chemical, or biological weapons. The 1540 Committee regularly meets to help establish domestic controls to prevent proliferation of materials and technology.

Q22—Is it really possible to develop a worldwide text-message network with databases, media, and messaging that works even in repressive, totalitarian countries?

A. Yes, absolutely. While totalitarian governments and dictators have been able to successfully block Internet, satellite, television, and radio communications, the advent of ubiquitous cell phone use worldwide has forever changed the global media landscape. One-to-many text message capability has created the opportun-ity for media to emerge even from paranoid, repressive countries like North Korea. The concept of the mVillage, which has such a dramatic impact in *PEACE*, is based on this very technology.

Q23—Could Iran's Shahab-3 missile reach Israel with a nuclear payload?

A. It's possible, though not very likely right now. The Shahab-3 technically has a range of two thousand kilometers, putting it within range of Israel. But whether it could reach Israel is debatable. And the likelihood of its reaching Israel with a nuclear payload, right now, is nil. Tests of the Shahab-3 in Iran clearly show that it can be fired from a mobile launch pad. But whether it could make the trip, intact, to Israel is questionable. Expert opinions on the capability of the Shahab-3 vary wildly.

Some call it a glorified Scud missile, which is notoriously erratic and crude. Others maintain that North Korean military planners have helped Iran stabilize the missile. But most agree that Iran is probably years away from the ability to attach a nuclear weapon to a stable Shahab-3 missile capable of reaching Israel.

Q24—Are there, in fact, clerics in Iran who would like to see peace with the U.S. and Israel?

A. Yes, there are such clerics. Ayatollah Emami-Kashani, for instance, delivered a sermon in 2008 in which he clearly said that Iran was not a threat to either Israel or the United States, and that it was willing to hold talks. "We do not wish to go to war with Israel," he was reported to have said. Others have echoed this sentiment—that Iran has no wish to directly attack Israel but will respond if provoked.

Q25—Is "from Dan to Beersheba" a realistic peace option in Israel?

A. The phrase "from Dan to Beersheba" appears numerous times in the Bible. It represents the area traditionally settled by Jews in ancient Palestine. Some would argue that this represents the most logical homeland for Israel and could create an opportunity for a free Arab state to the south of Beersheba. The radical peace plan proposed by the White House in the novel is based on this concept and the outlines of the original 1947 partition plan at the United Nations after the Second World War.

About the Author

Jeff Nesbit has been a national journalist, the communications director to the vice president at the White House, and the director of public affairs for two prominent federal science agencies. He has also written seventeen commercially successful novels for adults and teens with Thomas Nelson, Zondervan, Tyndale, Hodder & Stoughton, Harold Shaw (now part of Random House), Victor Books (now David C. Cook), and others.

He wrote *PEACE* after extensive research into the truth about the conflict between Israel and Iran, which is threatening to destabilize the Middle East. One of the underlying principles of *PEACE* is that the "salt of the earth"—great and small—must act now. Decisions surrounding the Israel-Iran conflict made by world leaders and nations—the earthly principalities and powers that govern us—will determine the fate of the planet. Events are moving quickly.

Possible scenarios and events in *PEACE*—like a secret prison camp in North Korea, hidden taqiyya terrorist cells in the United States, the threat of a cesium doomsday bomb that can irradiate half the planet, the possibility that the U.S. will sell Stealth planes to Israel, the premise that the First and Second Jewish Temples were never built above the rock under the Dome of the Rock, the radical peace plan for Israel based on the biblical phrase "from Dan to Beersheba" and the outline from the original 1947 UN resolution on a Palestinian homeland, or Russia's military interest in oil fields to the south and in Israel—are all quite plausible and based on science and research. The second and third novels in the Principalities & Powers series—*OIL* and *TEMPLE*—will also be based on extensive research and background into the real, truthful nature of the global conflict surrounding Israel.

Nesbit also managed a successful strategic communications business for nearly fifteen years. His clients and projects included dozens of national nonprofit, trade associations, media companies, Fortune 500 companies, major health foundations, public relations agencies, and advocacy organizations such as Discovery Communications, the American Heart Association, the Robert Wood Johnson Foundation, Yale Medical School, Harvard Business School, the American Red Cross, Porter-Novelli, CTIA, the Kaiser Family Foundation, Burson-Marsteller, the Chandler-Chicco Agency, and others.

Nesbit was also a national journalist with media organizations such as Knight-Ridder Newspapers (now The McClatchy Company), ABC News' Satellite News Channels (acquired by CNN), States News Service (when it was managed by the *New York Times*), nationally syndicated columnist Jack Anderson, and Ralph Nader's *Public Citizen* magazine.

www.summersidepress.com

Center Point Large Print
600 Brooks Road / PO Box 1
Thorndike ME 04986-0001 USA

(207) 568-3717

US & Canada:
1 800 929-9108
www.centerpointlargeprint.com